KAYLA MAURAIS

Also by Kayla Maurais

Violet Moon

SOUL SUCKER

Originally published in 2023

Second Print Edition April 2024.

ISBN: 9781088023310 (Paperback)

ISBN: 9798992966541 (Hardcover)

ASIN: B0BNFCC125 (Ebook)

Edited by Jennifer Lindsay

Cover Art by Jasmina Belarbi @ArtofMina

Map Art by Rachel @LuffStudios

Previous Editors: Caroline Fowler Davis, Cassandra, and Paige Lawson

For my beautiful, divine inner child.
You are the true dreamer.
These words are for you.

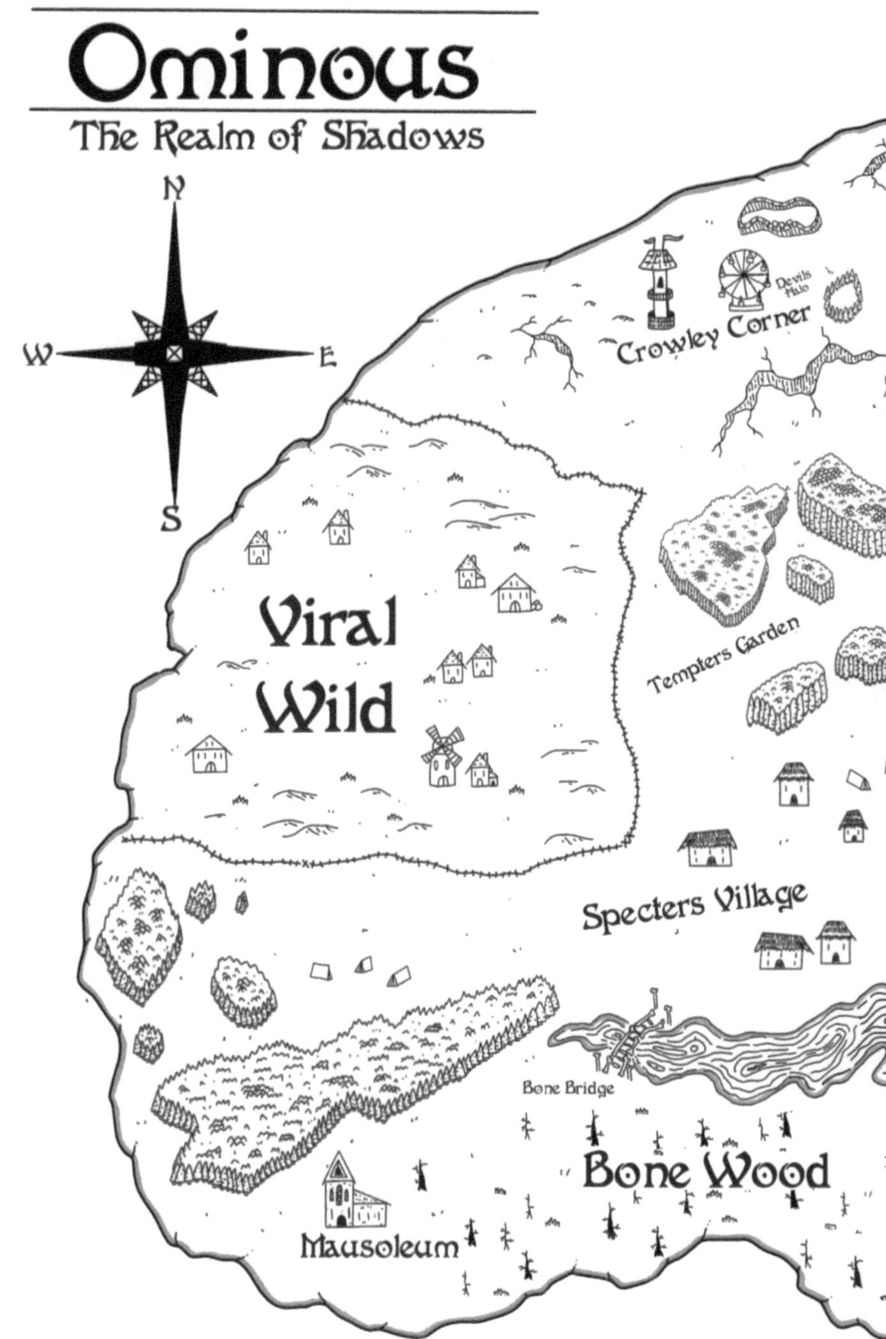
Ominous
The Realm of Shadows
N
W
E
S
Crowley Corner
Devils Halo
Viral Wild
Tempters Garden
Specters Village
Bone Bridge
Bone Wood
Mausoleum

Hexes Pass
Ruins Of Ore
Lake Ichor

Dear Reader

Thank you so much for taking interest in *Soul Sucker*. I started writing this book pre-pandemic, and it has evolved over the years into a passion project. These characters are special to me. My hope is that they become special to you, too. With that said, I feel it is my duty as an author to give readers a heads-up on some of the content they'll be reading in this book.

While content warnings are not officially required in the publishing space, readers pick up books for a variety of reasons and, if they aim to escape the stresses of day-to-day life, I wouldn't want to add to those stresses by inviting them to read something they might not be comfortable with.

Soul Sucker was written with teens in mind, but some of the content might not be suitable for those under the age of 15. *It contains depictions of body horror, blood, gore, explicit language, violence, unhealthy parent/child relationships, panic attacks, anxiety, and the loss of a parent. It also references sex, substance use, and emotional trauma.*

Please consider this information before moving forward. If after reading this you still choose to turn the page, buckle up, pack your glow beams and spice zingers, and hold onto your travel journal. You're about to go on quite the adventure.

KAYLA MAURAIS

1

Shea

If Dash screws this up, we're dead.

A gust of wind billows around me. I lean back against a jagged rock tall enough to block the chill. My tight-fitting breather mask constricts my face, but it's necessary. Like all planets in the Realm of Souls, air quality on Lark is thin. Without my breather, it'd be like sucking noxious oxygen through a straw. My lung tissue would rupture. My chest cavity would expand.

I'd black out before the air bubbles infiltrated my bloodstream.

I'd be completely brain-dead in three minutes flat.

The thought makes me chuckle. As if I'd ever get myself in such a predicament to begin with. I'd have to be negligent enough to forget to secure my straps.

Which would never happen.

My little brother, on the other hand, attracts life-threatening situations like stale cronuts attract baby crumb lizards in the heat of summer. The digiband clamped around my wrist beeps. I check the notification. User offline. *Shit.* He's turned off his tracker. Again.

I press comms. "Dash, report."

My gaze narrows in on the notification bar, empty save for a check-in message I'd sent to Headquarters earlier. Dad expects us home in an hour, and I've never missed a deadline in my entire life. I certainly don't plan on it now.

I ping Dash again. "Status. Location. Anything?"

Nothing. Notification: *Undelivered.*

I'm going to kill him.

Wait here, Shea. I'll steal the spirit-creature thingy alone, Shea. It'll draw less attention. I'll be in and out in ten minutes tops.

Yeah. Right. We never should've split up.

I pull back my hood and peer around the rocks at a cluster of canvas dwellings in the distance. They stretch for miles in the shadow-laden desertscape, floating inches above the ground like the Star Spirits which inhabit them. The transparent, faceless beings loiter around their dwellings. Their long, silver cloaks glisten in the starlight. They don't speak, rather they communicate via telepathic thought. Or that was what the Universal Database said when I looked them up.

I bet the Board of Galactic Studies would revel in a sight like this. If the authorities knew the things I've seen or the places I've been in the past eighteen years, their skin would crawl. If I were to submit even a smidge of the classified research I've gathered, an Intergalactic Space Relations agent would come knocking on our door, launching a full-on investigation into my family's operation.

Regardless, I'll write a study worthy of publication in the Universal Database. I will make sure the name Shea-Lynn James is known across the galaxies, like the revolutionaries before me.

Unfortunately, today is not that day.

I abandon my hiding spot. Darting between rock clusters, I stick to the shadows and keep a close eye on the Star Spirits nearby. Mom used to tell us stories about them. Born from the fallen stars of Lark, they have the power to rise and walk among us in human form. Some venture off and integrate with other populations until they become middle-aged. When it's time, they return home to Lark so they don't risk losing their spark or die out completely.

We're not supposed to be here without an invitation. If those Star Spirits catch my brother or me, they could alter our existence with one bolt of raw celestial power, marking our souls for eternity. Forever branded an Enforcer and a Thief.

Sweat pools on the base of my neck. I take off toward the outer edge of dwellings in search of my brother. Damp sand cakes in the grooves of my water-resistant boots. I quicken my strides, tear my way through a canvas tent, and clamber over bronze carts of medicinal herbs. Then I'm back into the open air once again.

It's been about eight years since I joined James Co. On my tenth birthday, Mom showed up with a homemade citrus cake, as any loving mother would. Dad, however, tossed a couple of beat-up weapons we call glowbeams on the table and told me I was old enough to join the family business. We steal and sell for profit. It isn't an honest living, but it becomes second nature when you've been doing it for as long as we have.

At least, to me. This is the fourth time Dash has been late on the retrieval this month.

I wait for a Star Spirit to pass before I burst into another dwelling, this one home to a devotional altar piled high with crystals. As I turn, my arm knocks over an amethyst cluster. My chest constricts, and though I manage to tip the cluster upright, the irritation pressing against my diaphragm doesn't lessen. I mean, how hard is it to locate a tutelary, lure it in, and return to our meeting spot anyway? They're soul-protecting constructs created by Star Spirits. This place is crawling with them. Yes, one can only view them with interdimensional goggles.

But Dash is currently in possession of our only pair.

The howling wind picks up. Another empty dwelling. And another. In the next, I let out a yell, kick over a suspended cot draped in silk. He always does this to me—takes his sweet ole time as if we haven't got other places to be. Must be nice to dance through life without a care in the world.

We're going to be late. I'm out of breath, at the end of the line. The final tent presents itself, a flickering glow radiating between the gaps. I swear, if he isn't in here—

I burst inside.

Dash lifts his head. "Aye, Shea, I knew you'd come."

For someone tied to a center post, he's stupidly cheerful. Glowbeam up, I square my shoulders and scan the tent, ready to face any Star Spirits that might get in my way. "How many are there? What did they do to you?"

"Whoa, you need to—"

I throw a sharp glare.

A lock of shaggy, dark brown hair slips from the band of wide-lens goggles slapped on Dash's head. "I'm cool. My soul is cool. And like, uh... two Star Spirits?"

"You better have it." I step over a basket of moon worm silk, knitting itself into a ceremonial cloth near the hearth. Tipping the barrel of my glowbeam into an armoire, I make sure we haven't got any company. The ancient symbols adorning the door catch my eye. I fight the urge to take out my travel journal and trace them for further research. *They're stunning.*

"Now, now," Dash says. "I'm hurt you'd question my capabilities."

I kneel next to my brother and whip out my blade.

Once his wrists are free, he pulls back the right side of his vest and pats his hidden pocket. His hazel eyes glint in the floating candlelight. Whatever he's got tucked away purrs.

Touché. "How'd you get it?"

"Plucked it off a Star Spirit when they escorted me in. James Co.'s infamous interdimensional goggles worked like a charm."

I roll my eyes. "At least tell me you put up a fight this time."

Dash purses his lips and looks at the floor. He fiddles with the industrial piercing in his left ear. "Yeah. About that... "

I close my eyes. "Dashiel. Tell me you did not get caught on purpose." He tries to walk away. I grab him by his goggle strap and let it snap against his skull. He yelps. "You told me you wouldn't do this anymore. We're partners. How am I supposed to rely on you if I can't trust you?"

"It's easier if I get caught. They don't suspect a thing!"

"That's bullshit. You're better than that, and you know it." His excuses for laziness are growing old. "You realize every time you do this, we take twice as long to finish a job."

He crosses his arms. "This reprimanding is taking just as long."

With another eye roll, I reach into my vest and pull out a brass portal key. I've worn it since Dash pickpocketed it off a mage during a gig on planet Verve years ago. "I'm done letting your negligence interfere with jobs. We'll finish this conversation later."

"Ohhhkay. If you say so."

Biting back a retort takes every bit of willpower I have. It's impossible to make a point when he never understands. At seventeen, Dash has already been captured, kidnapped, taken—you name it—more times than I can count. Yet, he forgets I'm the one who must come to his rescue. *I'm* the one that must explain to Dad why we're late. Every. Single. Time.

He massages the red marks on his wrist. They've calloused. "I did my part, okay? Who cares how I do it?"

"*I* care. And stop switching off your tracker."

He snorts. "I will when you stop trying to micromanage me."

"We don't have time for this, Dash!"

"I don't appreciate you raising your voice."

"I'm *not*."

I keep my stance firm. He blinks wildly. The wavering expression on his face is priceless. He'll cave first. Always does. That'll be the Thief in him. Enforcers are trained to stick it out.

That includes meaningless quarrels.

After a few more moments of tense silence, my brother sighs. "Fine. Let's go home."

That's what I thought. I relax my shoulders, hold back a smirk, and grip my portal key. Summoning a Door takes concentration. The first time I tried, I called forth half an entryway with no clear view of the other side, and Dash nearly lost an arm. Dad was less than pleased because Dash had mastered the art of theft, stealth, and hacking in a few days. For months, I studied and practiced skills expected of an Enforcer. Meanwhile, my brother kicked back, drank Fizzies milkshakes, and played Holoblocks on the console. When I questioned the balance of responsibility, Dad reminded me that someday this business will be mine.

A flash of light glimmers outside our tent, catching my peripheral as I ready to summon our Door out of here.

Dash takes two steps away and peers through a window flap. His shoulders tense, and I immediately shiver. I already know we won't be taking the easy way out before he says, "Star Spirits headed this way."

Moments later, we slip out the back. Our little quarrel is now a blip in the past. My brother and I are partners again. I'm at his heels. Boots pummeling the sand, battering slick patches of desert rock. Dash is faster than I am. Always has been. When it comes to speed, my heavier set frame is no match for his athletic build, but I know he'd never leave me behind.

Pinpricks of electric light shatter the dark. Hot wind bites my cheeks. Another gust of oxygen filters through my breather, stinging the back of my throat. I glance over my shoulder. My eyes grow wide. A dozen Star Spirits glide across the sand at great speed. They gain on us, wielding lightning in their translucent hands.

Dash cuts right. "Head for the canyons!"

I skid in the sand, falling into pace with my brother. Our path brings us near the Celestial Canyons, where an array of metallic, open-top spheres sit idly on a pulley system meant to suspend them across the gorge. *This is where the Star Spirits come to catch the stars.* Images from books in our home library fill my head. I shove Dash into the nearest sphere, eager to press all the buttons.

Star Spirits zing blades of light at us in retort.

Dash ducks. "Tell me you know what you're doing!"

Ignoring him, I try the many dials, gears, and levers.

"Shea-Lynn, tell me—"

"I know what I'm doing!"

As if I'm staring at one of the labeled diagrams in my research books, I skim the control panel in search of the lever that will release our sphere.

Dash hovers by my ear. "Hurry up."

"Don't rush me."

Focus, Shea. It's your job to get us home.

Another luster explodes overhead. Our sphere jolts, sending us to our knees. I flip the switch. We zip out into the canyon. The suspension cables tug taut. Disregarding the airiness in my stomach, I close my eyes and begin the summons. *This is it.*

Our sphere sways. Dash keeps me steady.

"They're trying to pull us back in," he says.

"I need a second."

Light blazes through the dark. My eyes spring open.

What now? I pop up. Before, the Star Spirits were waiting at the edge of the canyon like a pack of angelic wolves. Now, they're gone. The only Star Spirit in sight sits stationed in a sphere suspended a few yards from us.

An eerie silence claims the sky. A sky on fire.

The first meteor plummets. The remaining Star Spirit catches hold and throws it back, allowing the fallen star to gather momentum. It accelerates and gets sucked back up into the atmosphere. Dash hangs out the side of the sphere to get a better look.

I turn to my portal key. *"Imagine you are standing at a Door. This Door is oval with wood panels and wrought iron locks. This Door leads to planet—"*

Another jolt sends our pod careening wildly from side to side.

My knees bounce off the floor.

Dash knocks into me.

Bullets of light continue to plunge in the space around the pod. They collide with the void like rain, detonating upon impact. One spark catches our control board. Another zips up the wiring. Those sparks meet and short-circuit the release lever keeping us midair. One of our four suspension cables snaps, tilting us off-center. I gasp, bracing my feet against the sphere's edge before we slide along the incline to our untimely deaths. My brother slams into me from behind. I hold my ground. My portal key dangles before me, flitting among the meteor ash.

Adapt. Think fast. Remember what Dad taught you.

The pounding silence in my head breaks, and noise floods back in like a rogue Skyway train running off its tracks. Dash screaming my name. Plummeting stars zinging around us. Our sphere groans in protest, clinging to its remaining support cables. I dig my fingers into the metal bindings and curl my toes into the soles of my boots, slipping another inch.

"Stop moving," I hiss at my brother. Our way out is hanging around my neck, right in front of my face, but both my hands are occupied. "Do something! I'm holding us both up!"

"We're going to dieee! We're going to—"

Not today. We're not dying today.

Our second suspension cord snaps.

I squint. The sweat from my forehead burns my eyes. The heaviness in my gut sinks deeper, and our sphere tips back, sending us sailing across the canyon like a pendulum.

As the canyon wall nears, the remaining two cords detach. Brisk air whips my hair and tattered bits of my vest. My portal key necklace slips between my fingers. The force of free fall tears Dash's breather off his face like it's nothing, and it disappears into the abyss. *Fantastic.* Now, I've got less than a minute before he blacks out. Less than forty seconds before the canyon floor claims us. Thirty seconds before we're absolute toast.

My little brother falls silent, his head hanging forward. *There's still time. I can still do this.* I wrap my body around his. The fiery stars blur. We spiral through the air, destined to become sibling splats. I reach above my head, wedging my fingers beneath the taut chain. Tug it down. Grip it tight. Palms sweaty. Key secured.

If I don't get us out of here in time, we're both dead, and then Dad will really think I'm unfit to take over the family business.

"Imagine you are standing at a Door. This Door is oval with wood panels and wrought iron locks. This Door leads to planet Diggs."

Bits of the Door I summoned materialize into thin air. Splintered wood, rounded at the corners. A wrought iron lock. The familiar glow pours in from its cracks. I fumble for the frame. Before we crash into the canyon, I pull us through, and the Door slams shut behind us.

Somewhere nearby, Dash groans, telling me he's still alive. Good because I'm going to kill him. Thanks to his refusal to follow protocol, I've got murk water in places I'd rather not discuss. Leaves soak my unruly locks of brown hair, and my ass is bruised, but at least we're not stains on the canyon floor.

As I trudge toward the bank, I adjust the levels of my breather to check the air. Planet Diggs is in the First Realm, like our home planet, Sarasing. Air quality is thick. Breathable. I remove my breather. Take a few breaths to acclimate. Scanning the surrounding area for Dash, I spot him in a sludge puddle, coughing and clutching his head.

I hover over him. "Are you alright?"

He untangles a spiked toad, desperately trying to escape from his goggle straps. It croaks, and he croaks back, "I think I just saw my whole life flash before my eyes."

"You blacked out from lack of oxygen." I tap my digiband to check the clock. Nearly falling to our deaths put us behind schedule, but we can still make it back to Headquarters in time. "Luckily, I got us out before your lungs collapsed. Take it easy until you get used to the atmosphere. I'm going to scope it out, see if I can find the buyer's location."

I step over my brother's outstretched legs and follow the road. His coughs echo around me, allowing me to keep track of him.

We're in the middle of nowhere. Which is exactly where we want to be. A crescent moon hangs in the sky, its rays streaming through the wrought iron streetlamps. At the end of a dirt path is a small, rundown cottage puffing wood smoke, just as the brief said there would be.

Dash appears at my side with the toad cradled in his arm. "Is that the client's house? Also, do you think Dad would be mad if I took this home and kept it as a pet? I named him Arnold."

"No. Get that out of here—" I knock the toad out of his hands. It flops onto the path and hops away into the shadowy thicket. "Seriously? We're on a *job*. We have five minutes."

"Well, sorry. But that reminds me." Dash puts on his interdimensional goggles, which stayed firmly on his head despite his useless breather. "Gotta make sure the other little guy survived the trip."

A flutter of excitement takes over me. I keep my composure, though. My brother unzips the compartment in his vest, cups his hand, and allows the unseen being to crawl into his palm. On my end, he's holding air. On his end, I know he's holding something extraordinary.

Tutelaries usually are. However, I've only ever read about them.

"Dearest sister, I can feel you hovering over my shoulder." Dash glances back, and I pretend to fiddle with my digiband. "Admit you're dying to see it."

I purse my lips. "I don't know what you're talking about."

"Take a peek." He offers me his goggles. "Come on. For research?"

My gaze narrows on his empty, cupped palm. I *am* dying to see it.

"A quick peek for research." I put the goggles on.

The rose-colored lenses shift, bringing me into the ethereal realm of view. Dash urges me to hold out my hand. I do, and a white wisp of a creature appears. A lizard with glimmering geometric markings wriggles up my arm. I've never seen anything like it. A toothy smile spreads on its tiny, oblong head. It glares at me with bold emerald eyes. As it rolls onto its back, I notice the spiral on its fleshy underside. An engraved spiritual mark all tutelaries have.

Dash nudges me. "Smile any wider, and your face might freeze like that."

"Oh, shut up." I nudge him back.

"I believe that beloved creature belongs to me," a drab voice says behind us.

Okay. Play times over. Dash and I whip around back-to-back. Goggles off. Our glowbeams up and ready. As the hooded figure emerges, the pungent smell of metal and myrrh carries in the wind.

"Mathias Burgess," I say as the newcomer lowers his hood.

Archaic First Realm lore gets things wrong. Folk stories aren't facts. The majority of vampires aren't bloodthirsty, violent heathens. Those I've encountered are, at most, humble cowards with an iridescent light allergy. And Mathias fits the profile. Sullen eyes, one missing an iris altogether. Dirt caked under his brittle fingernails. A sickliness hangs about him in the wrinkle of his pale, leathery skin.

He holds out a skeletal hand. "Miss James."

I refuse to shake it. "Cut the small talk. You owe us hefty coin."

"I—I already paid your father." Mathias stumbles, slowing his movement each time he nears the warmth radiating off a nearby streetlamp.

And here we go. "You're lying."

"I'm—I'm not. I swear."

I aim my glowbeam at the vampire. He raises both hands and blinks, stunned by the warning flash. "You have two seconds to deliver your end of the bargain, or we take this tutelary back where it came from."

Mathias cringes. "NO—I mean, *okay*, I don't have it. I don't have the coin."

"Knew it." I prod Dash and give him a wink. "Let's go. I'm sure Dad can sell this elsewhere for double the price."

Dash grins. "Triple even."

This usually works in situations like this. Buyer thinks we're going to leave. Buyer panics and begs. Buyer makes up for their own negligence.

Because let's face it. People suck. Creatures suck. Trusting anyone to hold to their own promises SUCKS. My mother would give the clothes off her back to any stranger. No skepticism or questions asked. She'd trust them. And I wish I could be like her. I really do. But I've seen the cost too many times to be that foolish.

Dash pretends to stuff the tutelary back in his vest as we walk away. We're halfway down the road, getting ready to summon a Door home, when I hear a wavering, "Please. I'll—I'll do anything."

There it is. I put my hand up and side-glance my brother. We backtrack, meeting Mathias at the outer edge of his streetlamp safety-net.

I cross my arms. "What do you have to offer me?"

"I'll give you a vial of my blood." He wrings his trembling hands. "Or a fang from my adolescence. They're all in a jar tucked beneath my sleeping crate."

Dash chortles. "You keep all your baby teeth in a jar?"

"They sell," Mathias insists. "I've seen it."

"Not for enough," I reply.

Dash leans in. "Aye, offer her something better!"

The old vampire alternates his gaze between us. A bead of sweat forms on his brow. I know the look. Hell, I know it. And it kills me every time. This is going to get messy.

"Well?" I say again, handing my glowbeam off to Dash so I can grip the knife hanging on my belt with both hands.

"I—I don't—"

I leave my brother's side, grab a fistful of Mathias's cloak, and yank him into the light. A cry escapes the vampire, his pale skin sizzling in the artificial heat.

He falls to his knees, shaking. "I need this tutelary."

"You buyers are always the same." Pulling him closer, I whisper in his ear, "Lucky for you, I'm feeling generous. I'll finish this deal with you, but not without taking a payment of some sort in return."

I glance back at Dash. He nods without hesitation. A Thief will stand by their Enforcer because we make the rules. Even if it's gruesome. Even if it doesn't go as planned. This outcome is on me and me alone. I'm the one who must face our father if we don't deliver the product and collect some kind of payment in return. Dash did his part back on planet Lark. Now it's time to do mine.

"What—what will you take?" the powerless vampire cries.

I roll up the sleeve of his cloak and wipe my blade. In the tiniest moment, the Board of Galactic Studies comes to mind. If they could see me now. I can only imagine what they'd think. "A finger or two," I say. "A finger or two will do."

2

Dash

I'm in a love-hate relationship with stealing.

A deep-rooted sense of control settles inside me when I take something that isn't mine. I'll admit it. I know what I do is wrong. It doesn't mean I wanna stop. The stealing, that is. I could, however, live without all the near-death situations. The phantom trapped in the washroom mirror at the Hover Rink is tiring of hearing my resignation speech. Yet, I still haven't worked up the courage to tell my sister or Dad that I want nothing more to do with James Co.

I'd tell all the phantoms trapped in ALL the mirrors on Sarasing before telling them.

I let my hands wander in search of something to fill my pockets as Shea and I walk along the array of vendor carts crowding Spinners Pier. The ocean waves rage beneath the worn boardwalk at our feet. Bursts of briny air dissipate in the sweaty rush of intergalactic citizens. I pocket a bag of custard chips off one cart, juice-filled pods off another, and a roll of spice zingers from the last. By the end of the line, my pockets sag with plenty of snacks for later. I can't remember which rom-com is playing on the late-night channel tonight, but they're all binge-worthy.

I unwrap two sizzling cinnamon candies and shove them into my mouth.

Shea checks her digiband. "I'll never understand why you like those things."

"Because they make my mouth feel numb," I say, licking sugar off my fingers.

She scrunches her nose, falling deeper into her usual obsession with the tech strapped to her wrist. A giant velociraptor from Old Earth could plunge from the sky and wipe out the entire Vacationeer District, yet she'd still make it home on time.

I pop the last spice zinger into my mouth, savoring the after-kick. Shea crosses the boardwalk toward the storefronts. Does she ever stop and enjoy the moment? I keep at her heels, occasionally pocketing last-minute items like game tokens and holo-point cards. As we cross into the west side, relief spreads through me. We're finally home.

Spinners Pier is the 11th stop on the Skyway Silver Line. As a glorified tourist attraction, the Vacationeer District is one heck of a cover-up for our family business.

The line outside Palms is a mile long today. Eager out-of-realmers wait to pay hundreds for the latest novelty psychic scams. I run my hands along the new spools of sheer fabric on the loading dock at Grimm's Garbs. Retro beats fill my ears, ping-ponging between neighboring nightclubs lit up in neon, and as we stroll past Bay's Baubles, my belly flutters. The life-size Holoblocks capsule simulator is now on sale.

Our motion triggers the digital advertisement posted over the shop.

"Play Holoblocks: Holocity—the game of strategy and strength—from the comfort of your home," I say along with the chipper AI. "Collect those multi-colored holographic blocks like a gaming ninja and defeat as many levels as possible before the clock runs out!"

I moonwalk around Shea in the same synchronized manner as the entertainment AIs do on the screen.

She side-eyes me. "Stop it."

"Youuu love it. Don't lie."

"Love is a strong word," she says.

I stumble into a trash bot picking up stale fries, brush myself off, and catch up with her in the crowd. "I put the console on my birthday list. It's too big to steal on my own. They've got tons of theft droids."

"Uh-huh."

I catch a whiff of fryer grease from Tee Tee's Tentacle Shack, and my entire body thrums. The digital sign on the teal-blue shack says the wait time is less than ten minutes. This never happens. I step up to its order kiosk and scan my eyeball.

Shea reaches over my shoulder and deletes the entry. "No. I've got two rotting bloodsucker thumbs in my vest pocket. We need to get them on ice and to Dad."

Tee Tee, the massive, mucus-green space slug roasting a batch of steaming tentacles over an open flame beckons to me. My mouth waters in anticipation of those warm, herbed hopper-flour tortillas they always come in. The sweet and tangy sauce drizzled on top... It doesn't matter that I forgot my Universal Comms earpiece at home, Tee Tee knows my order by heart.

Shea's still glaring at me, boot tapping the walkway and body tensed up like it's all she can do to keep herself from grabbing me by the wrist and dragging me home like she did when we were kids.

"Look, Shea, you made me get rid of Arnold—which was a devastating loss I can't even talk about right now—so I'm getting my Tee Tee's taco if it's the last thing I do." I re-scan my eyeball, blinking past the retinal burn. "You can go home, though. I'll bring you back a side of squid nachos with that savory honey sauce you like."

My beautiful sister sighs. "Ugh. I'll wait for you. It's fine."

I hold back a smirk. Fine. What a word. We didn't make bank on planet Diggs, which is why she doesn't want to go home alone. She did everything she could have done. It wasn't her fault that bloodsucking vamp didn't have the coin he'd promised Dad.

A pair of thumbs will sell. We'll find some eager potions master, space witch, or other being that prowls the Underweb to buy them off us. For the same amount we were bilked, even. But Shea didn't do exactly what Dad asked. We both know what that means. Better if I'm there to soften the Henry James guilt trip blow.

Sticking annoying close to me, Shea continues to fiddle with her digiband while we wait for my turn to order. A couple of giant mosquito creatures with lacey-pink wings and telsons squeeze by. They sip cherry heart slushies from Pup's Slush Shack through extra-long straws. One knocks an arm with Shea, and I hold my breath for a second, fearing she might pluck off their wings. Instead, she ogles, a familiar glint in her eye—the one she gets when she discovers something she hasn't seen or heard of before.

Something worth logging in her travel journal.

I watch her contemplate the thought, a hand hitched at the pocket in which I know she keeps her journal. When she catches me staring, she clears her throat and returns to her tech. My sister's a curious lil' bean. One that refuses to overindulge in her guilty pleasures, unlike us regular teenagers. Lucky for her, guilty and pleasure are two of my favorite words.

I use my shoulder to break through the rush. "Hold my spot. If you must order for me, don't you dare let Tee Tee add dehydrated meal worms to the spread."

"Wha—Dashiel. *No.* Get back here."

Too late. I'm gone.

I follow the winged creatures to a boutique cart and wait while they try on Spinners Pier swag. As they browse hats, I slip behind them and dip my fingers into the taller one's satchel. Shea will appreciate this. Doing a bit of research for her will make her feel better. I pull up a passport card, wedge myself between the mannequins, and glance at the profile. Looks like we got a couple of Mees on holiday from planet Monsoon. And they're staying in the Fancy Schmancy District. Very fancy indeed.

One Mee slips the vendor three coins for a holographic visor. Before they walk off, I return the passport card and keep the cherry heart slushie they left behind on the counter. Shea said she needed to keep the bloodsucker thumbs fresh, right? Nothing cooler than a slushie.

"Did you just steal that?"

I turn, almost dropping the cup. Two familiar faces have me cornered between a mannequin and the sun googles display. Zena's glacier-blue gaze freezes me to the spot as heat creeps up my chest. Behind her, Chip fishes a pack of herbal smokes from the pocket of his green Sarasing Academy Holoblocks team jacket.

"Zena! Hey! What are you two doing here on Spinners Pier this fine afternoon?" I tuck the slushie under one arm, wiping a streak of syrup on my pants so I can lean in and kiss her. Chip's husky frame blocks me. So close, his sweat and pinewood cologne overpowers the fryer grease aroma in my nose. "Whoa, Chip. I can't quite get around ya if you stand—"

"Are you going to answer her question?" he asks.

I glance from the slushie to Zena, the heat in my palms making it slippery. "I didn't steal anything from this cart. At least not today. The Mee left it behind, and my sister needs it for something, so I figured I'd recycle because you know how important rec—"

"Okay. Um, Dash. We should talk." Zena brushes a blonde curl behind her ear. The globe light off a nearby club glints pink on her cheeks. I've never seen someone so beautiful. I should write her a poem about that later. "For a moment, maybe... uh, privately?"

Chip takes a drag of his herbal smoke. "Make it quick, Z. Dinner's at seven."

Dinner? Why would Zena go to dinner with Chip? She doesn't even like Chip. She told me he was the rudest guy on the Holoblocks team.

"You at least got the flowers I sent you the other night, right?" I ask her.

"Did a Mee leave those behind too?" Chip mutters.

I glare at him. "No. They were from Pinkie's Floral."

"That high-end place off the Purple Line?" He scoffs. "Yeah, okay."

The sudden urge to pickpocket Chip's zonecard so he can't pay for his dinner later crosses my mind. Zena grabs my arm and drags me off to the side before I can get close enough.

"Yes. I got the flowers. They were lovely." She hugs herself. "I—I don't think we're going to work out, Dash. Chip and I are kind of a thing now. I'm sorry."

My heart gives a wretched tug. "I thought we worked well together. I really like you."

"I know. We did. And I like you too." Zena sucks her teeth. "You're always so busy with work." She glances at Chip for a moment, and my tender heart splits. Dinner, huh. "I want someone who can go to Academy events with me. Someone who isn't afraid to be intimate. You understand what I'm saying, right?"

"Zena, I'm not afraid to be intimate. I told you I wanted to get to know you better. What are your hopes and dreams? What makes you happy? In an ideal world, we'd read poetry together and star in Academy plays. You know that kind of bonding before we—"

Chip steps between us. "I'm hungry. Let's go, Z."

"I'm sorry, Dash," she says, and they take off into the crowd.

I hang my head. Single again. Without even a love letter farewell, or a kiss to remember her by.

Behind me, Shea-Lynn clears her throat. I don't move. Of course, my big sister would show up now.

"That's why I don't date." She holds out my steaming tentacle taco. "Zena was definitely cheating on you this whole time. You can't trust anyone these days."

"Some of us want to date." I'm still watching Chip and Zena. He grabs her hand. Soon they become specks in a trail of herbal haze. "Chip didn't believe I got her flowers from Pinkie's Floral."

"He thinks we're poor," Shea says. "Here. Take your food."

"Why would he think we're poor? We aren't poor." As we walk, I chow down on my tray of tacos. Through a large mouthful, I add, "Besides, why would that matter? Love is about the person and who they are on the inside. Not riches. Not looks. Not anything else."

"How optimistic of you. If only it were that simple." Shea checks her digiband again and quickens her pace. "Look, we don't have time for this. I'm sure that someday you'll make someone very happy. Sadly, that someone will not be Zena O'Hair. You just have to deal with it."

That's her answer to everything. You just have to deal with it.

"For your information, Zena doesn't even like Chip. He talks badly about all the girls. Including her and the rest of the Holoblocks cheerleading team." I reach into Shea's pocket and take the vamp thumbs and her travel journal without her noticing. "Which I wanted to try out for, but you wouldn't—"

"I didn't realize you were interested in cheerleading. You need to forget about Chip and focus."

"No, no. I don't think I need to focus on the job—and not the cheerleading team, though that would be cool, the actual team!"

I plop the thumbs in the cherry heart slushie and make a messy note in her journal about Mees with the ink stick stuck between the pages. Shea's so preoccupied with her brief, she doesn't notice when I slip the journal back. "There's another tryout next week. They're looking for a new captain for the varsity squad. The old one graduated and went on to play for the major leagues. I gave Dad the sign-up brochure."

"You don't have time for sports, relationships, or friends. We have an overflow of runs coming up. Hours of prepping to do."

Heinous Hades. She needs to give it a rest. We almost died this morning, and she's already worried about the next gig.

I imagine myself saying something confident like—dearest sister, I'm quitting the family biz so I can lead a normal teenage life—but all that comes out is a monotonous, "Yeah, yeah."

Shea guides us across the busy streetway towards Fizzies, the confection shop whose basement we also call our humble abode. Its pastel blue and purple sign is a welcome home that never gets old. Mom always says it makes our home smell sweet. I pocket her favorite Fizz-tarts as we pass through the shop on the way to the back whenever I can.

Upon entering Fizzies, Shea nudges me, bringing my attention to the three broad-shouldered men sitting at the fountain counter. Intergalactic Space Relation agents, otherwise known as ISR dipsticks. They're hard to miss in their sleek, slate-gray government-issued uniforms. Brand-spanking new glowbeams hang on their belts. I make eye contact with the one making love to a frosted cookie and wink at him before we duck under a curtained archway toward the lift.

"Second time this week they've come hanging around here." My sister presses the call button on the far concrete wall. "I saw in the Daily Report they busted an underground market ring in the Remedial District a few weeks ago."

"Welp. Can't trust the Sicky Place."

"The ring was selling stolen spacecraft parts. I bet you anything ISR is making their rounds looking for similar illegal trades."

"Guess it's a good thing we aren't part of an illegal trade," I say, and she throws me a look that would win a prize for the least impressed sister in the galaxy.

The lift doors split open and deliver us into the front hall of our living quarters. We stop and kick off our boots at the mat. Shea hangs up her vest, then flips her long brown hair over her shoulder and searches her pockets.

I hold up the slushie. "Looking for these?"

"No, I'm looking for the thumbs." She pulls her pockets inside out and double-checks the hidden compartments. "Maybe they fell out when we were walking? I can't find them."

"Yeah, because they're in the slush."

My sister's eyes gloss over.

"What did you just say?"

"I put them in the slush to keep them cold." She swipes the drink cup out of my hand, and a dribble sloshes onto the hardwood. "Whoa, take it easy. I thought you'd be happy."

She groans. "Dash, you didn't. Tell me you didn't."

She marches down the hall of our windowless basement accommodations. Past our closet-sized bathroom and into our drab kitchenette. She pushes aside an overflowing heap of Spinners Pier takeout containers in the sink and tries to wash the thumbs under the automated tap. The icy chunks rinse off. The cherry-pink hue doesn't. She bites back a wince.

I throw my hands out. "I don't see what the big deal is!"

I keep at her heels all the way around the maze of hallways, past Mom's hospice library, to the double doors leading to Headquarters.

Shea triggers the motion sensor. The biometric scanner light blinks green, confirming her identity before allowing us entry. Hints of cigar smoke lingers. As the air thins, Dad's many half-human-half-AI hirelings take form, hustling about the multitude of inventory in organized chaos.

Between stock swaps and off-planet runs, Headquarters is ever-changing. The space is wide, like a warehouse, making it nearly impossible to see through to the other side. Someone stuffed the metal shelves, from the floor-to-ceiling, with every bell, whistle, odd, and end you can think of. Siren scales and squiggles. Season globes and trinket gears. Items take up every inch of free space—technical, supernatural, antique, or plain extraordinary.

Shea and I enter the whirl of commotion, ducking and weaving to avoid knocking into hirelings. Some rise up and down the wrought iron spiral staircases leading to the lower levels. Others slide along ladders that run the length of the shelves, passing items back and forth to be sent out through our collection of Gallivants. These tricky devices ship products to the outer galaxies, realms, and to any of our space cargo crafts.

We craft Gallivants out of anything.

Great-grandfather Alden invented them in the year 2955. He'd created one out of an old Easy Bake Oven. He had a thing for vintage Earth mementos. You simply put an object inside to transport it and wait for the spark. A glittering sulfur smoke means it went through.

We pass my favorite Gallivant in Headquarters to date—a corroded treasure trunk Shea and I scavenged from the depths of an outer realm ocean.

My sister fiddles with her portal key. "Let *me* break the news about the thumbs."

Tucked away on a wooden platform awaits Dad's workstation. We climb the steps. A hireling catches a cylindrical container from a chute directly above our heads. They set it on Dad's massive desk. It slides open to reveal two cheeseburgers and a side of curly potatoes.

"Mouthwatering," I comment as Dad takes a bite. "Is that Lippy's or Grand Sam's?"

Dad chokes through a mouthful. "Oh, good. You're back." He sets down his cheeseburger, adjusts his glasses that are way too hipster for his middle age, and wipes ketchup off his bristly chin. "Neither. I ordered out of galaxy."

Shea clears her throat. "Sorry it took us so long, Dad. Dashiel got taken by a Star Spirit, and by the time we got to planet—"

"Taken is one word for it." Dad opens the thick leather-bound ledger on his desk and raises his salt-and-pepper brows. I roll my eyes. We get it, Henry. You think I'm a shameful excuse for a son. "Let's get to the coin. Our liaison in the Residential District is demanding the advances we took in extraterrestrial stock last month."

My sister's line of sight falls to the dried-up, syrup-stained vamp thumbs in her hands.

This won't be good. Maybe I really did screw this up.

Dad clears his throat. "Well? Let's have it. I haven't got all day." I put a hand on Shea's shoulder. She shrugs me off and sets the thumbs on Dad's desk. He narrows his stone-cold gaze at them. He picks one up and rotates it under his lamp. "What is this?"

To her credit, Shea doesn't flinch. "Mathias didn't have the coin. You taught us to always finish deals. Vampire fingers will sell to make enough profit."

Dad alternates his gawking stare between us. "Is this some kind of joke?"

Shea shakes her head. "We put the appendages in slush to keep them... fresh."

Dad snatches the other crusty thumb from his desk and chucks them across the platform like nobody's business. They narrowly miss a hireling's head.

"What can I do with appendages soaked in sugar and artificial dye?" Dad tousles his short curls of graying-brown hair. "This is beyond irresponsible. Do you have any idea what this does to our profit base?" Dad's gaze flicks to me for a second. He rounds his desk to face Shea head-on. "I expect better from you two. Especially you, Shea."

Back in the day, I used to get into yelling fights with Dad. I'd call him out on his ruthless moves and demeaning words. Every single time it resulted in him being harder on her than me. Shea's the real reason I've stayed this long. I stopped taking Dad's distaste for me to heart a long time ago. He knows as well as I do, she'll carry the burden of his reprimanding to her grave. I don't care if he's our father, our boss, or the criminal living beneath Fizzies—Dad's a bully. One that pathetically feeds on the fear of others.

It's better if I keep my mouth shut. Sometimes I can't help it. I'd rather he yelled at me right now. This isn't even her fault. None of this is in her control. Not the thumbs or the coin.

"The slushie was my idea, Dad," I say. "Also, I got dumped today, if you care."

Shea slaps her forehead. "I told you to stay out of it."

"No. I will not stay out of it."

My sister elbows me in the side so hard I think I might shut up, but my refusal to let Dad belittle her takes over. I match him stare for stare.

"Maybe you should start vetting buyers or taking a deposit before you send us out."

Dad doesn't answer me. He just sits there, a smug look on his face. It's killing him, I know it. I know he's itching to knock me in the teeth whenever I mouth off.

"Did you hear me?" I approach his desk.

Shea grits her teeth. "Dashiel."

I don't care anymore. I'm gonna say what I wanna say. I was going to tell my sister on her own. Now it feels pointless. "Your clients are all sketch balls. I'm leaving this—"

"ENOUGH!" Dad smashes a fist on the desk so hard it sends a heap of folders flying. I swallow the sudden lump in my throat. Even the hirelings startle. He points at me. "You watch your mouth. And you—" He motions to Shea, a vein bulging in his forehead. "This should never have happened. You're the leader of this team. You prep for the job, handle the heckling, and ensure the job gets done right, no matter what. Understood?"

Now my sister's voice is small. "Understood."

"Wonderful." He slams down in his desk chair and brushes aside his now lukewarm cheeseburger. One of his file folders splits open. He catches me staring and slaps it shut. "Now, let's talk about your next assignment."

The contents of my gut swirl, making me queasy. The Hover Rink phantom would've been so proud—I was *this* close to quitting. But at what cost? Would it have been the right time to leave when Dad's on a power trip? On second thought, when isn't he on a power trip?

A hireling raises a hand from the other side of the warehouse. "Incoming!"

Stepping back in line with my sister, we catch the tubes that drop above us in sync. Compliant Shea opens hers immediately and starts reading. I wait, staring at the bobbing head of our dear father, the supposed ringleader in this sadistic operation.

He's going to brush this one aside, isn't he? Nice.

"A medicine run for Mom?" Shea reads out, looking up from the digital scroll in her hands. "I don't understand. This isn't an assignment. It's an errand."

Uh, what now? I unscrew the capsule in my own hands and tap the glowing scroll inside. It unravels holographically, summarizing a job on Ominous, a planet in the Realm of Shadows.

"Mine must be a misprint." Shea reaches over my shoulder for a better look at my scrolling brief. "Okay. So, it looks like we're going to drop off a classified—"

"It is not"—Dad's eyes don't lift from his ledger—"a misprint."

"You're sending us on separate assignments?" I ask.

"That isn't standard protocol." The slight waver in Shea's voice has returned. "A Thief and an Enforcer always work together."

Dad snaps his fingers, and two hirelings appear at his side. He hands them an envelope. "Put out this message in the comms Gallivant to trading post 188 in Galaxy LDV17."

Once the hirelings are off, Shea says, "I think we should stick together. After we go to planet Ominous, we can double back to the Ornate District to pick up the medicine."

I nod. "I agree. Together is better."

I sometimes seem like a space case, but I'm grounded, I swear. I will always stand by the ones I love. Besides, the Realm of Shadows sounds like a tricky place. I've never been to planet Ominous before. I don't want to be left alone with all things that go bump in the night. I sleep with a nightlight for Goddess' sake. This is too much.

"My word is final." Dad focuses on the ink scrawl before him. "Oh, and Shea—Dash will need the portal key for his travels. Hand it over to him before you go."

My sister hesitates, tugs at her key all the same, and a shudder courses through me. That key is her nightlight. As she hands it to me, I try making eye contact. She avoids my gaze.

"You're dismissed now," Dad says without glancing up from his work. "I need to talk with your brother alone regarding his assignment."

Wow. I don't even know what to say.

Shea saunters out of Headquarters a little pink-faced. As the door shuts, a noise escapes her that could almost pass for a sniffle. I want to run after her and hug her.

Dad shuts his ledger. "I'm sure you're wondering why it's you."

I keep my fists curled at my side. "I'm sure you're going to tell me."

"The client requested a one-person transport." He plucks a leather-bound box with a tiny gold lock off his desk. That's when I notice the Sarasing Academy Holoblocks sign-up brochure crumpled among the other clutter on his desk. Stained with watermarks, it's become a well-loved coaster. I bet he hasn't even looked at it. "Unfortunately, Shea is not a Thief."

"What, the client requested a Thief?"

"Not exactly." Dad looks at me for the first time today. "*I* need a Thief."

I swallow hard. "According to the brief, it's a delivery."

"This is the item you'll be dropping off to the client." He slides the leather-bound box toward me. I catch it with ease, a simple flick of my wrist and palm. "You meet with him, give him the box, and then I need you to take something for me without him knowing."

"What's in it?" I shake the box against my ear. Like I do every year around the holidays with the gifts Shea wraps a month early and sets beneath our decorated Yule log stack.

Dad leans back, kicks his feet up. "Doesn't matter what it is."

I shove the box into my pocket. "I think I deserve to know."

"The client is working on a creation of sorts." Dad messes with the tip of his quill. His fingers stain, and he wipes them clean on my Holoblocks brochure. "I can't disclose further details, but it's small, probably in a vial or a tube—I need you to steal one of them."

This monster is up to something. He shuffled those folders extra quick earlier.

"You're to be discreet," Dad continues, sitting up. "It's a simple job, and they've already paid, so all you have to do is deliver and pull. It's important that you get this item for me."

My throat goes dry. I stare at my feet, wishing I could tell him I refuse to help him.

"I'm not daft, Dashiel. You want to leave this business.

I lift my gaze to his. "How did you—"

"I've known for a while now," he says. "You and I know I can't run this business without you. An Enforcer is nothing without her Thief."

Well, I wasn't expecting this. "If I do this for you, you'll let me out?"

"Oh, no." He chuckles. "You're doing this for me because it's your duty. I know it hurts you when Shea takes the brunt of the blame between the two of you. So, if you pull what you tried to pull earlier, try to leave, or disrupt this operation, I will make both your lives, but mostly hers, a living hell."

"You mon—"

"That'll be all, Dashiel."

Dad rises. He stalks off across the warehouse, leaving me with a mysterious box in my pocket, a mission that makes zero sense, and a rising heat inside my chest.

What kind of father blackmails his children? Shea wouldn't even believe me if I told her. As much as I hate it, I'm stuck. But I won't give up. Henry James will not decide my life for me. While an Enforcer is nothing without her Thief, a monster is nothing without his lackeys.

I'm going to have to convince my sister he's up to no good, more no good than James Co. usually entails. How? I don't know. Shea's whole life revolves around this business. She eats, breathes, and sleeps the job. There's no way I can leave now.

Not unless she quits with me.

3

Shea

The moment Dash exits Headquarters, he tosses me my portal key.

"Here," he says, voice gruff. "Take it back. I don't want it."

I peel away from the wall and catch it. "Wait, what?"

He crosses the hall into his bedroom and slams the door behind him. *Unreal.* Dash has a job to prepare for, a serious one. Now isn't the time for one of his defiant fits.

With one fist clenched around my key, I throw open his bedroom door with the other. A fuzzy vest with flashing lights glued to the zipper launches at me. I dodge it, and it hits the wall behind me, knocking a shelf of Starships and Spacespirits game accessories askew.

Dash rifles through his dresser. "Don't step on my new dice."

I glance down at the array of game dice sprawled out on the carpet, an inch away from my boots. *Goddess.* His bottomless pit of a living space has gotten worse. A heap of unwashed bedding has piled up on his worn mattress. Takeout containers, wrappers, and a hodgepodge of all the other items he's stolen over the past year are strewn about. His *treasures*, he calls them.

More like my next offering to the robotic dumpsters that patrol the pier.

"Okay. Dashiel—" He zings a pair of pants. I catch them and fling them over my shoulder. Really, when was the last time he had a trash bot in here? "We need to talk about this."

"About Dad? My thoughts exactly." He abandons his dresser, kicks aside an empty bag that once held enchanted flytrap seeds, and picks up a deck of tarot cards, smoothing them over in his palms. “He’s an actual piece of work. I was wondering how long it would take you to notice.”

I straighten a leaning tower of Planet Pizza boxes. “Uh, no. I’m talking about the gig. What did he say about the assignment?”

“Nothing.” Dash focuses on the 9 of Swords card in his hand. “All he did was reprimand me for talking back to him... ”

A wave of relief settles on my shoulders. I should’ve known better than to assume the worst. “You know he doesn’t like when you challenge him. He’s the head of James Co.”

“He’s also our father. Sometimes you forget that.” Dash sets the cards down on his gaming desk, perhaps the cleanest surface in this dumpster-fire of a bedroom. His three high-tech monitors are set up and angled just right, pristinely kept along with his keyboard and consoles. Not a speck of dust on any of it. I often daydream about a life where he takes our work as seriously as he does Holoblocks or other Academy extracurriculars.

“I haven’t forgotten.” I join him near his desk. “Did Dad say anything else about the client, the terrain, or the authority figures that might apprehend you if you’re caught? I’m sure there’s a blurb in the database somewhere we can study.”

He checks his play-by-play board and unsticks a post-it that’s lost its grip. “Nah, I don’t think I’ll be studying.”

If a sigh had claws, it’d rip my throat to shreds. And despite the other monster, the green monster, inside me reminding me *I* should be the one going, that I’ll miss countless bits of prime material for my research journal in any hopes of someday impressing the Board of Galactic Studies—I want my little brother to succeed.

In fact, it’s part of my job to make sure he’s ready for this.

I offer him my portal key once more. “Here. Take this. Everything is going to be okay. Let’s print you a rundown. I’ll help you call a Door to Ominous.”

A groan escapes him. He moves into his closet, kneels, and begins digging through a pile of dirty clothes. The stench makes my eyes water but I do my best to ignore it.

"Don't you ever want to take the afternoon off and play Whack a Ghoul at the Bay Baubles arcade?" he asks.

What is he talking about?

A jean vest with fringe flies at me. I dodge it. He's having a hard time, I get it, but he needs to grow up. "You can play games when you get back. Right now, we both have to go. Dad gave us orders. Now we obey them. That's what we do."

"Quit talking to me like I'm five." He unhooks a spare backpack from a metal shelf teeming with plushies and oversized sweatshirts. "And no, that's what *you* do, Shea-Lynn."

I swear he does this on purpose. Dash goes through phases of loving and hating this life, but we were both born into it, and Dad needs us to be on top of our game.

"Don't think of it as working for Dad." I nearly slip on a half-deflated water floaty shaped like a Tee Tee's tentacle taco but find my balance. "Do it for Mom."

"Don't use Mom to guilt trip me. That's not fair." Dash brushes past me, nudging me a bit more than he needs to. "I *always* do what I do for Mom. And for you."

I frown. Mom, I get. Without us and the business, her health suffers. The price of her herbal remedies skyrockets each month. But me? That doesn't even make sense.

"Are you going to do the research or not?"

"Shea, I will pull up a tab on my digiband before I meet the client. *Okay*?"

No. That's not good enough for me. I cross my arms. A tab? A tab about what?

"I still feel you're going to forget, so let me pull up a quick little rundown before you go, and that way, you'll be all set to—"

"Noooo," Dash whines. "Focus on *your* mission. I'll take care of my own."

I'm pulling up the rundown anyway. He'll thank me later.

I watch him rearrange an old donut box where baby crumb lizards have gathered paper debris and wads of food for a nest.

"Forget a mini trash bot," I half joke. "Maybe we can get you an organizing AI when you get back... or a full-on excavating service."

He collapses in the cleared space on his bed. "I get it. I'm a hot mess. You don't have to keep telling me."

I log onto one of his computers and wait for it to load. As it does, I glance over my shoulder at my brother, now thumbing through a heaping nail polish bin. He picks a bottle of plum purple and settles in to apply a coat. *He's about to leave for a job, and he's painting his nails.* Great. Just great. *Bite your tongue, Shea. Let it go.*

Instead, I stare at the play-by-play board above his desk. He's fully planned out his next Holoblocks game with his Academy buddies. Detailed plays, strategies, moves—all typed out with care. He's even delegated roles to specific teammates. *Unbelievable.*

"Why can you lead an entire Holoblocks tournament, plan out plays, and use intense levels of organization, but in real life, you're a mess?" His computer home screen fades into view. I grab the controller and skim for the database. "Tell me the difference."

"It's a different world in Holocity, Shea," he says. "You wouldn't understand."

If my eyes roll back in my head again, I might lose them. "You're right. I don't—holy hell, Dashiel. How many folders is... Why do you have so many links open? And where is our Universal Database icon?"

His eyebrows soften as he paints his thumbs. "Those folders are my written plays and poems, and those links are my inspiration boards. If you delete any of them, I will scream. Also, I deleted the Universal Database ages ago. It was clogging up the feed."

"Dash—"

"I *told* you. I don't need a rundown. I'll figure it out."

And here I thought using a computer would be easier than reading the small screen on my digiband. I set down the control and rub my temples. *Good grief.* I'd do anything for my little brother. He's my best friend, my partner in this business, but this is impossible. I retreat from his desk and join him at the edge of his bed, breathing in the astringent, nose-biting smell that wafts off the fresh coat of polish he's slathered on his nails.

"I don't want to hear it," he starts.

"I don't think you realize how much I prepare for our assignments beforehand. We're talking rundowns, research, and packing. Going without a plan is—"

"Foolish. Yep, I get it."

"Stop saying you get it."

"When you stop letting Dad boss you around, I'll stop saying it." He screws the top back on the polish and tosses it into the bin. "If we're gonna talk about anything, it should be that."

My cheeks warm despite my fight for composure. Typical Dash. Changing the subject on purpose to avoid responsibility. "I don't let him boss me around. Doing what he asks is our—"

"Job, yeah, *you* keep saying that." Dash blows on his nails. "You aren't one of his hirelings. You're his daughter. He's a monster, and he doesn't treat us right."

I can't believe he's saying this right now. My brother is this free spirit who flits around without a care. He never has to worry about anything. Not preparing or packing, studying or researching. Having a backup plan isn't even something he's familiar with.

I fight the burning sensation in the back of my throat. It's a rare occurrence. Today it's overstaying its welcome. "If I didn't carry the extra weight of this team, listen to Dad, or worry about Mom, we'd get nothing done. Okay? Without me, we'd be lost. And if I ever spoke to Dad the way you do, he wouldn't just *talk* to me. There'd be actual consequences."

Dash scoffs. "You think I don't have consequences? Wow. Okay."

"Name one," I say. "Prove me wrong. Prove to me that nothing ever falls on you when we screw up. Prove to me you don't get a free pass on everything you do."

My brother's eyes gloss over. He purses his lips and rises to put on his boots. Another typical Dash move. Silent treatment followed by the bail-out. Running when it gets too real or too hard or too much to handle. Instead of facing the issue head-on, he runs like a coward.

I could waste my breath to further prove my point, but it's useless. He's never going to see things my way. He will never understand how I feel or how his actions directly affect me. Dad treats me differently than he treats Dash, and for once, I wish my brother could empathize with me on that.

Dash puts on his pack. "Can you just call me a Door, please?"

Sometimes I wish he wouldn't run. Sometimes I wish he'd fight back, argue with me, and hash it out until we're both satisfied with mutual understanding. I want to understand him. I do. I can't do that if he doesn't meet me halfway. And the other part of me, the stubborn-Enforcer part of me, enjoys being right too much—even if it means we have to maneuver around whatever this is.

Dash holds out my key, now hanging around his neck, and I take it between my fingers. I still haven't figured out how the key does it, but the right words always find me.

"Imagine you are standing at a Door. This Door is square, made of rotting wood, and has a brass handle. This Door leads to planet Ominous."

Beside us, the Door I summoned appears among the disheveled piles of debris. It unhinges, allowing gray light in through the gaps. Without looking back at me, Dash throws it open all the way, hesitates as an eerie howl fills the room, and enters the Realm of Shadows.

A pit forms in my gut. *I should say something.* He shouldn't go without a plan. On the contrary, perhaps taking a risk will help him understand my efforts. As right as I want to be, and as much as I want that realization to be proven true, he's still my little brother and my partner, and I love him.

"Dash, I—"

He slams the Door behind him. As I reach for the handle, it fades. The last of it disintegrates, and I'm alone once again. Should I wait for him to return? Knowing my mother is out of medicine means she can't wait for Dash to take his sweet time. And he *will* take his sweet time. The pit hasn't left my gut. As I cross back to Dash's desk, it swells.

I open the tracking application I installed on his computer months ago. It connects directly to his digiband. He'd turned it off on planet Lark. I turn it back on, lock the command, and a small portion of the anxiety wreaking havoc in my chest releases, his blinking location now a steady blip.

He'll be fine, Shea.

Before I leave for Dad's errand, I stop by the hospice library off the main hallway of our home. I haven't seen Mom yet today, and there isn't enough time to sit with her or to read the book about stars that Dash and I often take turns reading to her. I check on her all the same.

A circle of shelves filled with antique books invites me into the small space. I pull back the sheer curtains drawn around her four-poster bed. She's sleeping in a covered and curled heap, the mobile hanging above playing a soothing instrumental tune as it spins. Mom made it herself when we were younger, out of reclaimed wood and hand-blown glass. I've always been fond of it, particularly the two acrylic figures that oscillate in the middle.

One is a brown bear. The other is a stunning, hand-crafted bird with coral plumes.

Mom turns in her sleep, and I tuck her blanket up to keep her warm.

I allow myself a moment to admire her. The soft purse of her lips, the creases in her forehead, and the freckles along her nose. Dash and I have her freckles. We've been told we have her smile, too. It's been so long since I've seen Mom smile. Not the forced bit of enthusiasm she uses to try to hide her pain, but her deep laughs, the vitality in her brown eyes, the way she runs her hands through our hair while we lay with her—I miss it all.

Mom always had this sparkling energy about her. It fills all my childhood memories. Then one day, that energy around her went out. Dad sent for healers from every planet and realm he could think of. Eventually, we found an Enchantress in the Ornate District—or the Fancy Schmancy District as Dash calls it—willing to brew an herbal remedy to keep her going. It wasn't a cure. It was temporary. I was eleven the last time a healer set foot in the James household. Seven years have passed, and nothing's changed except the rising price of her medicine and Dad's tolerance for *everything*.

Mom tells us stories about a version of my father I vaguely remember. She goes on about a tender man with a warmth in his heart. A warmth that turned cold after he took over the business from our grandfather. Someday, that business will be mine.

Does that mean I'll change too?

I wince at the thought as I exit the hospice library and grab my pack at the entrance of our home. I slip into my boots and vest, call the lift, and exit through Fizzies onto Spinners Pier.

The Skyway station is a block away. As I walk, a breeze hits my bare neck, reminding me how often I reach for my portal key without even realizing it. It'd be much easier to call a Door to the Ornate District.

The sidewalk traffic grows thicker. I near the station, its rising platform towering overhead. A smile surprises me as a memory floats to the surface of my bubbling thoughts. When we were little, Dash and I would ride the Skyway for fun. He'd squish his face against the glass as we whizzed through the sky at high speed. I'd pry him off the window and clean the smudges left behind before the next group of passengers embarked. Just like Mom would have.

He'll be fine. He isn't little anymore. He can handle one run without you.

I check my digimap to be safe, prodding it to load his tracker blip. It remains where it was the last time I checked, meaning he hasn't moved. His vitals are steady. He probably doesn't know where he's going. *Great.* Or maybe the service isn't as good as I thought it'd be. How good *can* service in the Realm of Shadows be anyway?

The platform quakes beneath my feet with the rattling of the invisible tracks, and the Silver Line Skyway pulls up in all its stellar glory. A bullet train fashioned for sky travel; it's built like most subways save for the whirling thrusters jetting out the back. Several compartments slide open. I enter one, finding a seat near the rear.

Other humans and creatures of all backgrounds and classifications fill in around me until there's little breathing room. A speckled Slog, dripping blue exoslime, blocks me in against the metallic paneled wall. They're of the highest intelligence but sticky upon contact. I cringe and wipe the goop off my shoulder, jerking sideways as we take off.

The Slog's tenor is static through my Universal Comms earpiece. "Sorry."

In return, my words squelch out in Slog-speak through my device, "No worries."

We rock back and forth, slowing at each stop. I stare at Dash's tracker most of the way, incessantly refreshing my map to mark any changes. As the Skyway compartments continue to thin and fill up, including the Slog, the tracker location doesn't change.

"Why isn't he moving?" I mutter under my breath.

I switch into my Universal Database application and pull up a page on the Realm of Shadows, specifically Ominous. At most, I find a statement made on a Falsi.com page by a Second Realm traveler claiming to have survived the fall-out of a spellcasters war; 'This planet is void. Doomed are the souls that walk here.'

Bullshit. Anybody can edit a Falsi.com page. Sounds like an invalid source to me. I bet there hasn't been a submission to the Board of Galactic Studies. Another missed opportunity, I suppose. Sometimes the shops in the Ornate District have books on rare outer-realm planets. I could check while I'm there. Though given my previous search, it's doubtful.

The overhead announcement calls the end of the Silver Line. I switch to the Green Line and, finally, to the Purple Line. Dash's tracker blip remains exactly where it is. Must be a service issue. *Yeah, that's it.* He's okay, he's fine... but what if he's not? No, he's FINE. Dad taught me to remain calm. To deny the thoughts that trigger anxiety inside me. They are weak and unnecessary.

My brother is going to be okay.

A warbled voice over the speaker filters into my earpiece. "Purple Line: Verdure Way."

The compartment doors split, filling the interior with notes of lavender and rose. Blooming season in the Ornate District at Verdure Way is always my favorite time of year. Vines come to life around me, as I step out on the platform, twisting and folding onto the wooden guardrail that leads down into Central. A light citrus mist coats the air. Unlike my home district, there is room to walk here without bumping into anyone else. I take a deep breath, the tension leaving my shoulders.

Living near Spinners Pier is tiring. Dash adores it. He loves the food. He enjoys the freedom the hectic rush lends in stretching his stealthy fingers. I've never cared much for tourist season, which isn't a season because it goes all year round.

I prefer the stillness of places.

Cobblestones lead me into a sprinkle of boutiques operating out of old brownstones. Tasteful operations like florists and bakeries, galleries, and tea-tasting venues. Mom used to say that a place like this must exist by magic. It has that grounded aura that draws people in. The inhabitants are primarily Enchantresses from the forgotten planet Ravish, so there may be a bit of truth to Mom's theory.

I wait for a break in the light traffic before crossing the streetway and heading toward one of their apothecaries, Belladonna, where an Enchantress dressed in a soft baby-pink cloak tries to haggle one of the young cafe workers into taking giant skull-flowers. Instead of blossoms, skulls decorated with yellow petals stem from their thick, green stalks. I decide they are oddly beautiful, despite being morbid.

The Enchantress flashes her dazzling smile. The cafe worker, whose name tag reads Frank, blushes. *Gods, he can't be much older than Dash.*

Frank takes the skull-flower, laughing in a trance-like way.

I reach behind him and pluck it out of his hand. "Why don't you ask the pretty shape-shifter what the catch is before you walk away with this skull-flower."

Frank is about as clueless as Dash, too. "Uh, wha—what do you mean?"

"Are you new here?" I ask, handing the skull-flower back to the Enchantress.

She glares at me, her words floating, yet subtly hissing, off her tongue. "He started at the cafe yesterday. You leave us be. Your business is with Nadine, not me."

"*Tell* him what the catch is," I say again and cross my arms. I can be persuasive when I want to be, and the Enchantress knows it too.

She scoffs. "The heart of the first person he falls in love with. Is that such a hefty price when our skull-flowers are one-of-a-kind? I think not."

Frank turns a delicate shade of green. "The heart of the first—Oh, Goddess."

I grab his shoulders and prompt him in the café's direction. "Yeah, exactly."

He stumbles back the way he came, smoothing out his apron. I glare at the Enchantress. She turns a cheek at me, nose up in protest. I won't apologize for costing her business. Making any kind of deal with an Enchantress is dangerous territory. Most of the time, it isn't worth it. They leave a mark, too. Like tutelaries, Enchantresses are each born with a specific sigil somewhere on their body. When you make a deal, that mark appears on you, and they own you until you pay up.

Part of me appreciates what they do. Because it's not so different from what I do. Only, I don't steal souls or hearts. I just chop off bloodsucker thumbs.

Strings of rustic chimes jingle above the apothecary door. I'm hit with the aroma of spice and herbs. Two Enchantresses work in the shop today. One cuts and weighs crystals at the back counter where stone runes float above apothecary jars. The one I'm looking for, Nadine, is watering the orchids that grow in the soil crevices along the planked walls. I can tell it's her by the tiny, triangular sigil on her upper cheek.

All Enchantresses are shifters, and it's hard to imagine that their true form is utterly hideous—sagging gray skin, thin, wiry hair, razor teeth, and soulless eyes. No matter what form Nadine takes, her sigil remains.

Last month, when Dash and I visited, Nadine was much older. Today she is middle-aged, wearing a long, flowing dress made of rose gold silk. Her plunging neckline glimmers. A crown of tulips sits atop her head, and her curly blonde hair runs the length of her back.

Nadine turns, and the sweeping train of her dress tugs. Our gazes lock. She gestures for me to meet her at the front. I wait at a counter that's been fashioned into a terrarium. It blooms with succulents and thorny roses. Their petals flutter in my presence, shifting as Nadine joins me. Her long, glittery fingernails tap the glass surface between us.

A sweet serenade of a voice comes out of her mouth. "Shea-Lynn James."

"Nadine." I nod. "I'm here to pick up our monthly order."

The Enchantress's umber irises gleam. She scans my face with pursed lips and breaks into a sly smile. She reveals a glass bottle with a cork of clear, shimmery liquid wrapped in a flowering vine from her sleeve. I don't know what's in the medicine. It's an herbal brew conjured by magic. While I've never seen Nadine's mark on Dad, I know he must've promised something in return for this. Something you can't come back from. If skull-flowers are traded for lover's hearts, I can't imagine what remedies to keep your partner alive cost.

Nadine slides the bottle toward me. "Where's that thieving brother of yours?"

It's difficult to steal when the Enchantresses have literal eyes in the back of their heads. This is the one place Dash can't pull.

"He's on a pickup run," I say, and Nadine immediately shifts. Same dress and hair. Identical face. This time younger, around my age.

"What do you say we make a deal? A lover for you; a life for me?" Nadine croons, reaching to tuck a loose wave of hair behind my ear. "Unless you don't like what you see."

She's depicting a gorgeous girl my age. Of course, I like what I see, but looks aren't everything. Enchantresses know how to draw you in. They flaunt some variation of your greatest desires in front of you, hoping you'll crack.

Nadine should know better than to try with me.

I pluck the bottle of medicine and grip it tightly. "As gratifying as your flirtatious manner is, I'm afraid your energy is malicious no matter how beautiful you appear to be." Backing away from the counter, I tuck the bottle into my vest pocket. "It's going to be a *no* from me."

"Fine." Nadine hisses, returning to her middle-aged form. She blows her soft, glossy bangs out of her face and rests on her elbows. "Tell your father he owes me double next month."

"Another rise in price? Is that the deal he made with you? Eternal debt?" I linger by the bookshelf next to the door, thumbing through ancient texts that make the Universal Database seem minuscule. "What would an Enchantress need with bags of coin?"

Nadine examines my every move. "You'd be surprised."

My finger lands on a book bound in sagging leather. *No.* Not leather. But a familiar feeling. This can't be... skin?

I pull the book off the shelf. It has no title.

Nadine draws closer. "Interested in the Realm of Shadows, I see."

I glance at her, finding she's changed forms yet again. Now she is a small, charming, freckle-faced child in a pointy witch's hat and a short-sleeved black dress.

"Yes," I say. "Planet Ominous."

The peachy hue drains from Nadine's young cheeks. Her now emerald eyes grow grim. My sinking pit returns. That's never a good sign.

I open the book. To my dismay, the parchment pages are blank.

"Are the chapters charmed?" I ask.

Nadine reaches around me with a smirk and taps the middle of the splayed book. At her touch, symbols bleed onto the page. And I mean literally bleed. Black and red blood soaks into the parchment, smudging into thousands of illegible words. They speak, chanting in a chorus, and their shrieks fill the shop. The glass bulb overhead shatters. I drop the book.

It falls open on the floor, crimson liquid pooling beneath it. Still in her child form, Nadine kicks it closed with a shiny mary-jane shoe. The red stains fade away. She picks up the book and files it onto its shelf.

"What in the deepest corner of hell was that?" I ask.

"The cry of a million souls lost in a spellcaster's Great War, the same war that drove us off our home planet, Ravish, back in the day."

Nadine shifts back to her middle-aged form so she's tall enough to wipe a drop of blood off my neck. A shiver courses through me. "Anything that touches those unhallowed grounds becomes a part of its withered past."

"No—no—" I stammer, pushing away from Nadine.

I tap my digiband, bring up my digimap. Dash's blinking tracker blip is now frozen and off the radar altogether. *It's a fluke. He could be anywhere by now.*

He could be in danger, too.

"I have to call my brother. He's *on* Ominous now." I hit the comms application and press the call button so hard the screen scuffs. "Pick up, you precarious fool... "

"Your First Realm tech won't work there. Ominous is a magnetic field," Nadine says, and I meet her gaze, the chill of it boring into me deep enough to leave a mark of its own. "Your father should've known better than sending him to a place like that. My condolences."

Condolences? That's preemptive.

Nadine must be wrong. I search her face for anything that'll give her lies away. Like I do with the clients I prod and pick at when they don't have the coin they owe us, but Nadine is as calm as they come.

My heart hammers in my chest. "Tell me you're lying."

"You and I both know I wouldn't lie about this."

She returns to her flowers. As I watch the spout of her watering pail flood the roots of thorny roses and the bell-shaped belladonna, a sinking heaviness clings to my ribs.

If Ominous is truly that dangerous, why would Dad have sent Dash there?

And I let Dash go without a plan. I let him go without proper supplies or defense mechanisms. I let my little brother venture off into the unknown when it's my responsibility to take care of him. *Gods.* I need to get home. I need to get home *now.*

4

Dash

I knew the second putrid bog water squelched into my boot, I'd made a major mistake. I never should've caved to Dad. Now I'm stuck in the middle of nowhere. Flanked on every side by carnage trees.

Instead of sap, they seep blood from calloused bone trunks and branches. Stringy bits hang loose from their twisted boughs. The bits glisten in the bright moonlight as they sway in the frigid breeze, triggering a bit of acid reflux in me.

Is that muscle matter? Gods.

A cloud gathers at my lips as my body instinctively curls inward. I should've worn my insulated vest. On any other mission, that's a detail Shea would've taken care of for me, and if she hadn't triggered me so much before I left Headquarters, maybe I would've let her take care of me this time too.

I take a cautious step forward, testing my footing. It seems to hold my weight. For now. I take a second step trying to think of anything but what the fluid mucking up my boots is.

Something creaks nearby. I pause to listen. Nothing but the whistle of the wind in the bone trees.

A quiet snort escapes me as I carry on. How can Shea think I don't understand the consequences? This business is the *greatest* consequence. Dad basically blackmailed me into staying, and Shea thinks I get a free pass. Yes, I would be lost without her. I'd also be free if I weren't so worried about her. If I didn't feel obligated to stay because of what Dad would do to her.

The singing gale rattles the wood. I shiver, ogling at the massive skeleton-like tree overhead. Its outer coating slips from its lanky frame with a squelch, and I cringe. A fleshy heap plops to my left. My stomach churns. I'll be having nightmares for the rest of my life.

Head up, Dash. It's a quick gig. Find the buyer, deliver to the buyer, steal *from* the buyer, and get out of this ghastly place.

I notice instantly the moment the ground begins to shift up and my footing becomes stable. Moments later, a gathering of clouds swallows Ominous's moon whole, masking the wood in a gray haze. Thick fog fills in at my feet. I search for any sign of life or the dwelling that's supposed to be out here. According to Shea, Doors always spit us out near our target location. Here's hoping I'm in the general area. If I'm expected to wander off the trail, I'm gonna have a much bigger problem on my hands than my impending frostbite.

Steal one of the guys' creations. Wonder what it is. Knowing Dad, it's something wicked that'll sell for serious coin on the market. My boots crunch damp roots that snake the ground. I hug myself to keep warm, stopping at a slight rustle. A ping of anxiety plays tug of war in my chest, a knotty battleship of fight or flight. *I should go back.* I could call a Door and tell Dad it was a flop. Better yet, tell him this planet doesn't actually exist. That his client was lying this whole time, and the deal's off. Coin is never worth the price of our lives.

When is Dad gonna get that?

Shea is counting on you. You might be at the tail end of an argument, but she's counting on you.

Another brittle branch snaps. On second thought, maybe she'll understand. There's *gotta* be some way I can convince Dad to go easy on her.

The faintest glow flickers on the horizon, the acrid smell of charcoal and burning flesh filling the air. A silent skeleton skulks ahead in a thicket of carnage trees. I grasp Shea's portal key, still hanging around my neck, and breathe through my heart palpitations.

Is *this* the guy I'm supposed to meet?

"A bit nippy to wander around without your birthday suit, isn't it?" I squint in the black. The skeleton stops, its jaw falling slack. "I'm with James Co. Dashiel James, here."

Even if it could speak, I doubt it would. Ran into one of these suckers at Spinners Pier once. However, it'd been dismembered and shoved into a sack to sell on the ancient Brood holiday, Ossein. I chew my bottom lip. The skeleton clinks closer, and the glow of my digiband illuminates its hollowed-out eyeholes.

Heinous Hades, that's gruesome. How do I manage this one? Do skeletons have pockets? Do I leave the box on the ground? And what about the guy's creation? I should check the brief. That might tell me more.

I tap my digiband. It crackles. The churning in my belly returns. No service. The tech is completely fried. *That can't be good.*

"Uh... well... " I glance at the skeleton, still waiting for me like the ghost of Yuletide's past. "I think I'm out of range. Lemme"—I dig into my pocket and pull out the leather-bound box with the tiny gold lock Dad gave me before I left—"give you this."

The skeleton springs to life. Was it waiting for the box all along? So... this *is* the guy? Huh. Interesting. Two more skeletons round the tree and join the first, making it three against one. Number one's rib unhinges. *Gah. No. I'm done.*

I inch back, the arches of my feet aching in my boots. I might not have tech, but I've got Shea's portal key, and I'm faster than a Skyway train.

The bonemen chatter at me as they move in on my position. The grand exit I planned earlier? Yeah. This is my cue. "You know, I think I'm supposed to meet *another* group ofskeletons."

A high-pitched whistle comes from somewhere ahead. Before I can respond, I'm in the skeletons' clutches, one on either side, the third keeping behind. Their skinless appendages poke holes in my shirt. A pelvis nudges my hip. It'll be bruised tomorrow. For being muscleless dudes, they're surprisingly strong. They force my shivering body up a slope of dirt, and an outline of a structure emerges in the fog. The mist thins, and the ruins of an old mausoleum take form.

NOPE. I for sure didn't sign up for this.

"Look. Maybe we can work it out. I give you the box and you set me free? Come on. It's a great deal. I'm a horrible hostage! I promise you. I'll bore you to tears. Well, if you *could* cry."

They pay no attention to me. Which is a first because I'm an attention hog. My heels skid, begging to halt. They jerk me toward the base of a marble staircase covered in writhing black moss. Next to it, a stone statue of a dark king wearing a crown and bearing a rusted sword has become home to hundreds of prickly spider-like creatures.

The wrought iron door at the landing creaks open. Spiders scatter, leaving a purple goo that reeks of soured milk, behind.

"I have coin! My family has lots of coin. We're rich. It's all yours. All of it!"

They ignore me again, forcing me up the stairs where a fourth skeleton waits with a blazing torch. Its entire form chitters, including the centipede using its left eye socket as a racetrack.

This keeps getting better and better.

I'm pushed into the entry chamber, the darkness disappearing behind me as the gate swings back into place. Oozing wax candles cast light upon the collapsed graves of the forgotten. Thick cobwebs blanket the stone walls. Leaning against the altar in the center is some skull prince wannabe with crossed arms. His outfit is stellar. The fancy, long black cloak and the eclectic bone rings on his fingers are working for him. He's got your standard dark hair, killer jawline, and stunning, lust-worthy silver eyes. Eyes that seem vaguely familiar, but I can't place them. *Weird.* I can, however, confirm he's another one of Dad's somewhat sexy, yet terrifying as heck, sketch-ball clients.

Behind him and his altar is a fifty-gallon fish tank with—well, I can't tell if they're leeches, eels, or worms this far away—writhing in murky water. And to top it all off, some random guy is passed out in the corner. A wicked web of veins and bruises encompass his frail body. Every orifice seeps black sludge.

Yeah. This is the one party I'm okay missing out on.

I make eye contact with the skull-prince wannabe. "You must be the client. The real one. It seems I've stumbled into a personal moment for you, so I'm going to hand you this box and be on my way."

"You'll be on your way soon enough." He raises a brow, takes the box from my outstretched hand, and snaps his fingers at his skeletons. A skeleton pulls over an old wicker chair. Another forces me to sit. "Unfortunately, I can't let you leave until I test the quality of the product. I'm sure you can understand. I've been cheated by your father in the past."

I curse my father silently before replying, "I mean, yeah, I totally understand."

The client rounds his altar, which looks surprisingly like Mrs. Crumbly's science lab after I blew up an energy elixir in chemistry class Ninth Year. He prods his mess of test tubes, petri dishes, and apothecary jars teeming with herbs, pulling a glass slide from the mix. He reaches for his microscope of all tools, then unravels the twine on the box I gave him.

Opening the latch, he takes out two small vials of colored liquid, one purple and the other red. With a pipette, he sucks up a drop of each and releases them onto the glass slide before donning his goggles and examining the liquid beneath the microscope.

This is the first time I've been kept in an evil lair without being physically tied down or shackled to a wall. It's kinda nice. Not as threatening as I first thought, what with a horde of skeleton lackeys and a guy bleeding out in the corner. Maybe this place isn't so bad after all. And maybe his creation, whatever it is, won't be so hard to steal either.

"So, you're an evil scientist, I see." I teeter back and forth in my chair, scooting myself closer to the altar. "That's fun. How long have you been doing that? Also, I hope this isn't a weird thing to say, but you could totally model for the Occultist Fashion magazine."

"I am not an evil scientist," he mutters. "And your forced flattery is incredibly irritating. Once I test the product, you'll be free to go unharmed."

"Oh, no, I know. I was just saying." The skeletons tip me upright as I teeter backward. I steady my feet and run my fingers through my hair. "Well, if you aren't an evil scientist, what are you?"

"I am an alchemist. However, if I succeed today, I might as well be Death."

A smirk spreads across my lips. "Nah. I've met Death. She's lovely."

"Oh, you have, have you?" the client claiming to be Death asks.

"Actually, I did meet her. She was signing autographs at Grimm's Garbs a few years back. Nothing like you'd expect. No scythe or anything like—"

"Go wait on the other side of the mausoleum, and for the love of the Underrealm, be quiet, or I'll sew your mouth shut with a dull needle."

"Welllll, then. If you're going to act like that, I take back what I said about you being a model."

I stand, grip my chair, and drag it behind me in an ear-piercing scrape. Fake Death glares as if I'm a bug under his boot. As a skeleton tries to move me along faster, I wave a hand. "Yeah, yeah. Silence or dull needle. I heard him."

Once I'm settled in my corner, Fake Death produces an empty glass dual-vial, joined in the center with a twisted cork, from his cloak. After mixing one drop of purple liquid and one drop of red liquid in a separate glass jar on the altar, he fills each end of the dual-vial accordingly.

I cross my arms. For someone who isn't an evil scientist, he's doing evil-scientist-like things. He takes off his goggles and calls forth a blue spark between his fingers. Okay, evil-scientist-like things mixed with spellcaster-like things. *My bad*. Aiming his spark at the vial, he warms the tube until it bubbles to his liking.

As Fake Death snuffs his spark, he turns to his skeleton lackeys. "Bring me the host."

The host? There's more? Wait. Am I the host? I sincerely hope not.

I straighten, the tension in my shoulders deflating as they fetch the unconscious man from the floor instead. They drag him before Fake Death, positioning him on his back, and I look closer at the sullen man's top half.

It's faint, yet there in the gentle rising and falling of his chest. My throat goes dry. *Gods, he's still alive.* Thankfully unconscious, but still. The skeletons clear the area and give their master the room he needs to hover over the host. Fake Death prods the bulge on the sullen man's neck, a bullseye amid the web of darkening veins that have taken over his body.

"Note this is a trial host," Fake Death says to the skeleton now taking notes with a scroll of parchment and an ink stick for him at the altar. This isn't the oddest job I've worked. But it ranks in the top three. "If the creation perishes, we'll try soul extraction another way."

Soul extraction? Did he say creation? I've been waiting for this moment. My fingers tingle. I'm going to leave here unharmed and with a souvenir. Uncorking the purple half of the dual-vial, Fake Death steadies it between his fingers. He jerks the host's head forward and tips the purple liquid into his mouth. The bulge on the host's neck pulses, his body literally snaps in half, and the host wakes in agony.

His screams send memories of pain ripping through me, any pain I've ever felt, brought back up to the surface in one hollow howl. Any inkling of security left inside me is gone. If Fake Death's capable of this, imagine what he'd do to me if he caught me stealing from him—if I couldn't pull it off.

Where is this doubt coming from? You always pull.

The host's shrieks grow louder, and the bulge on his neck bursts open. My Tee Tee's tentacle taco threatens to come back up. Black blood splatters so far that it slicks my forehead. I widen my eyes, dry heave, and wipe the blood from my face on my sleeve. There's a reason Shea's the Enforcer and not me. Just this morning, she literally chopped off a bloodsucker's thumbs, and I swirled them in cherry slushie juice, which I have yet to process fully.

That was humane compared to this.

From the open wound on the host's neck, a slimy, black creature like the ones swimming in Fake Death's tank emerges. It curls toward the opening of the wound, resting at the lip of the host's charred and bloodied flesh. Up close, the worm is plump and pointed, glimmering scales running the length of its back. Around it, the host becomes thinner and smaller until he is nothing but dust.

I should say a prayer for the guy.

How the heck am I going to wrangle one of those leech monsters and get it home to Dad?

Fake Death plucks the creature between his fingers. He uncorks the red side of his dual-vial with his teeth and spits it out. The cork lands on his altar, between two jars holding individual worms, and a bitterness coats my tongue. If I wanted to steal one of those soul-sucking creatures, those in the jars would be my chance.

There's no way in Hades I'm dipping my hand into that tank.

With one gulp, Fake Death tosses back the red liquid. He turns up his wrist, letting the soul sucker rest. The creature opens its tiny mouth, revealing a row of razor-sharp teeth. It sinks its points into Fake Death with delight and deflates, releasing every bit of what I assume is the dead man's soul into Fake Death's body.

I'm running out of time. As soon as he finishes this trial, I lose my chance to pull. Yet my body is heavy like sand. I can't move. I'm torn between running out of here and snapping into Thief mode long enough to appease Dad.

For Shea. For Mom. For my own sanity.

After this horrendous display, I've never been more sure of leaving than I am right now. I'm going to march home and tell Dad off, and then I'm going to convince Shea that she needs to leave, too.

Also, I will need lots and lots of therapy after this.

Fake Death closes his eyes, his breath evening out. He takes in the high from the sullen man's soul and reaches out to steady himself against the wall. I crack a finger knuckle.

As I stand, my legs shake. *You're going to pull. You're the best Thief you know. Forget you just saw a man get his soul devoured by Fake Death.* This does not differ from any other gig. I force myself to breathe, keeping my gaze on the skeletons and Fake Death, whose physical appearance is shifting, renewing, if you will. His hair regains its sheen, his skin becomes smooth like porcelain, and the glint in his silver eyes glows brighter.

A smile spreads across his lips. He summons his power, testing a ball of emerald light in his palms. As he turns away from me, aided by his skeletons, I move toward the altar with quick feet. I slip the smaller of the two jars holding a soul sucker into the pocket inside my vest and slam back down into my wicker chair before Fake Death and the skellies turn back to face me. All without being seen. All without screwing anything up.

I'm total aces at theft. Heck yeah.

I gotta tell the phantom at the Hover Rink that again.

"Make note that the host didn't survive. I suspect it's because the worm completed the full transfer of the soul," Fake Death tells the note-taking skeleton. He glances over his shoulder at me. "Shows over. You can tell your father we're square. You're free to go."

I've never left a mausoleum so fast in my life. And I've left a lot of mausoleums in my life. A chill settles in me. Wind rattles the carnage trees. When I get home, I'm going to put in my letter of resignation, make amends with Shea, take a hot bath with soaks, crawl into bed, and eat an entire box of Fizzies double-glazed donuts solo-style.

First things first—a Door. I fetch Shea's key and widen my stance. This isn't my forte. I'm giving it my all here. I don't care what Door appears as long as I get the heck outta here. I clear my throat, ready to recite the summons, and a burst of cerulean light explodes behind me.

The jar in my vest pocket hisses.

I freeze. *Crap.* He knows.

Without looking back, I break into a sprint for the thickest part of the wood.

"Go to planet Ominous, they said. It'll be fun, they said!" I cry out, dodging sagging limbs and leaping over upturned trunks of bone. "It's in the freaking name, for Goddess' sake."

I slam my back against a thicker trunk out of sight, clinging to my sweat-soaked vest. *You can do this. Call a Door.* I don't know how Shea works under pressure the way she does. I can barely summon the courage to keep the key steady between my fingers, let alone a Door right now. A thread of cerulean light reels back and forth across the starless expanse. The sound of bone clinking fills the air. I shudder. The skeletons near, searching for me.

Once they move on, I'll say the summons.

They'll move on. They won't find you.

The jar in my vest pocket quakes. I cover it with my hand. *No way. You're not giving me away. Nuh-uh.* After a moment of silence, the clanking of bone subsides. I peer around the trunk into the daunting black. No spellcaster's light in the sky. No lackey skeletons lingering nearby. The slightest whistle in the trees is my company now.

I grip the portal key, swallowing hard. "*Imagine you are waiting, no, standing at a Door. This Door is—*"

A hand yanks the key's cord from behind, racking the back of my head against the trunk. *Gah. No. Please no.* Stars fleck behind my lids. Fake Death tightens his grip.

His breath huffs hot on my neck. "Did you really think I wouldn't notice one of my creations missing? They are *bound* to me."

I gag. "Let *go* of me. You're gonna—"

He pulls and twists, and I force my fingers in the loop of the cord to stop it from cutting into my neck. The knot finally breaks, sending the portal key whirling through the air. Fake Death tosses an orb of magic burning hot between his palms to catch it. *That was my way home.*

I'm screwed. Beyond screwed.

Fake Death wields his line of light against my ankles, keeping me down. Waves of heat ripple the surface of my skin. My pulse quickens. He hits me again, whirling my body through the air, tossing me like a sack of yams. My body breaks the ground, and a shard of splintered bone slices into my arm. I cry out, the rippling remnants of pain taking over me once more. Blood pools at the wound.

As I roll over to feel my side, the jar in my vest shatters.

NO. NO. NO. Fake Death drags me toward him. I scream through the pain, fighting with the zipper of my vest. I tear it off and leave it behind, curling my body to ride out the motion of being hauled across the bone and cartilage-covered ground.

Tears well in my eyes. My entire body throbs. I can't tell what hurts more—my wounds or my heart, ready to explode in my chest.

Fake Death appears over me. "Get up. Now."

"I literally can't. I can't move," I say back.

He grabs me by the shirt, using a burst of light to keep me standing. I cower in his presence as he draws me closer, nose to nose. That familiar feeling washes over me. *I know this guy. Where do I know this guy from?*

Every inch of me burns. My digiband is out of service. My sister's portal key is now hanging around Fake Death's neck. Shea herself isn't coming for me this time.

I'm truly on my own. I'm truly going to die.

I swallow hard, tears streaming down my cheeks. Fake Death holds up the soul sucker that must have come from the shattered jar.

He lets it dangle in front of my face. "Doesn't matter how many times we play this game, you and I, you always get in the way."

Whaaaat is he talking about?

Fake Death slaps the soul sucker on my arm, and it hisses, finding its entry point.

As it slithers inside, a rippling sting disperses in my veins. It sinks deeper inside me and nestles snugly beneath my skin. Fire courses through my body. Like poison, it filters into my blood, and with a neurotic tug, the soul sucker latches onto my inner being.

5

Shea

Nothing is going to happen to Dash.

I burst into Fizzies full force and collide with the attendant refilling the massive tubes of candy that line the back wall. She drops her bin of exo-slime flavored jellybeans, spilling them across the reflective floor and beneath the scurrying feet of customers.

"I'm sooo sorry," I shout.

In the back room, I enter the lift and slam the button with my palm. If Ominous is a magnetic field, comms won't work. Without a tracker, I won't be able to find Dash.

Maybe he's home now. Maybe he's sitting with Mom, telling her all about his travels. Maybe he's set up in his bed, prepping for his next Holoblocks tournament, stuffing his face with Fizzies double-glazed donuts. *Yeah, that's where he is. He's home. He's safe. He's okay.*

The flutter in my gut tells me I'm wrong.

The lift slides open. I slip into the entryway of our home, keeping my boots and pack on in case I need to leave for planet Ominous at a moment's notice. Mom's medicine sinks heavily in my vest pocket. She'd be devastated if anything happened to Dash.

All I know is if my little brother isn't back yet, safe and sound, lounging in his dumpster storm of a bedroom, I will cause a major—

I halt in the sitting room archway. Dad sits around the hearth with four ISR agents and a bearded man, non-government, who wears an olive-green tweed suit and a matching bow tie. A hireling serves them tea in our finest porcelain—the set we pull out of storage once a year on Tasting Day, a Sarasing holiday dedicated to inventing mixed drinks. Instead of her typical gray jumpsuit and protective goggles, the hireling is dressed in a polka-dotted house apron and a bowler hat with rainbow-colored feathers sticking out the top.

What in the galaxies is going on here?

Dad sits forward in his armchair. "Shea-Lynn, darling, welcome home. Tell us how your volunteer session went at the Creature Cage."

A middle-aged woman with a straight silver bob and sharp cheekbones clears her throat. I haven't seen Commander Derry in years, but I know she and my father have history.

She sets down her untouched teacup and takes out a tube of mauve lipstick from her pocket. "Your father tells us you've been tending the flying pigs."

Creature Cage, flying pigs, eccentric tea parties—this is code. One of many fronts to dupe ISR into thinking we're your average family. The one where I'm just another eighteen-year-old Creature Cage tender who spends her free time wrangling flying pigs and dodging airborne waste pellets. Have to say, it's my least favorite front.

"The piglets are hard to manage." I observe the way Dad watches Commander Derry apply her lipstick. Almost... lustfully... dare I say. But he wouldn't. Not while Mom is lying in the other room on her deathbed. "One piglet never returned from sky-grazing today. We couldn't track him back to the pen because our tracking system is down. Did you hear anything?"

"I have not. Given it's your job to keep the piglets in line, I would think you ought to be the one to find the piglet and bring him back." Dad sips his tea. There's grit to his words. "That's your responsibility. Right?"

I hold my father's stare a moment longer. "Right."

"Are they decent pets?" The ISR agent to Commander Derry's left asks. "My son has been asking for a companion. We've already said no to fire lizards and hellhounds."

Seriously? "Oh, yeah. I'm sure flying pigs make great pets."

"The Academy is tracking your volunteer hours, *I'm* sure." Commander Derry crosses one leg over the other. "Given that you and your brother are part of our homeschool cohort, documentation of your extracurriculars is highly important."

Her blue dagger eyes don't intimidate me. I'm used to staring down ghouls and humans with sinister intentions. My father trained me for scrutiny like this. I won't crack.

"My brother and I are model students." I clasp my hands behind my back, my chin held high. "Our grades are superb. Up to academic standards if you'd like to check, Ma'am."

Truthfully, Dash and I stopped homeschooling a couple of years ago. Classwork began interfering with our business assignments. To keep up the facade, Dad sends Dash to Sarasing Academy every month to update our attendance files. When he isn't ogling over the Holoblocks team, my brother sweet-talks the office AI and hacks into our records.

The reports sent to the ISR Homebase, *Ophelia*, are always up to par.

Commander Derry smiles. "I can assure you we've noted how scholarly you are, Miss James. That's why Mr. Beachum insisted on joining us today."

She motions to the man in the tweed suit. I really don't have time for this.

"Mr. Beachum is a member of the Board of Galactic Studies," Commander Derry continues with ease, a phrase I didn't think could lure me in so well. "He's here to speak with you personally if you have a moment to spare."

I rub my bare neck, wishing I could fiddle with my portal key to calm my nerves. *Keep composure. Dash is just taking his sweet time like he always does.* "I apologize. I need to touch base with the Creature Cage about that missing piglet—"

"Again, I assure you," the commander says, smiling at me, "this won't take long."

The tightness in my chest heaves. Dash's life could be at stake. Every second counts. Dad expects me to handle this. But this... this is a member of the Board. Not just a representative. A *member*. And he wants to speak with me.

Gods, Dashiel. This could not be happening at a worse time.

"I didn't realize the Board of Galactic Studies did home visits," I say through an uneasy laugh, trying to maintain composure and sound intelligent all at once.

Mr. Beachum rises from his sunken armchair and shakes my hand. "We don't, but we made an exception in your case. We tour the schools on surrounding planets every year to scout out potential applicants for our fellowship program. When we visited Sarasing Academy, your name came up more than once from several former teachers."

"Wow, that's—I don't know what to say."

"They told me you were part of the homeschool cohort. I didn't think I'd get to speak with you." Mr. Beachum chuckles. "Luckily, I ran into Commander Derry on the Skyway train. She was on her way for a routine visit, and I thought I'd tag along."

I lock eyes with Dad. "How... lucky."

Commander Derry raises a brow. "Fated like the stars."

"If you're willing," Mr. Beachum says, "I'd love to sit down with you and discuss the fellowship application further. Maybe discuss your plans for after graduation?"

Realization hits me like an electric pulse. He wants to sit down... now?

"Shea will work for me following her graduation," Dad says, and the ISR agent nearest to me stirs. "Someday, she'll take over the family business."

Commander Derry uncrosses her legs. "And what is it you do again, Henry?"

"I sell stocks and bonds." Dad snaps his fingers at his hireling. She brings him more tea. "There's nothing wrong with stocks and bonds. It's a loaded market. As you know."

"Depends on what you're selling," Commander Derry says.

Mr. Beachum clears his throat. "Well, Shea, I'd still love to sit down with you."

The throbbing in my temples deepens. I chew the inside of my cheek. Even if I wanted to, I don't have time to sit down.

I have to make a choice. Goddess damn it all to hell.

"I would love to, Mr. Beachum." When his face lights up, it pains me even more to say what I'm about to say next. "But I can't right now. I'm so sorry. I'm—"

I can't even finish my half-assed apology. What a poor excuse for turning down the opportunity of a lifetime. Without looking back, and with my brother in mind, I take off down the hall and slip inside Mom's hospice library.

The door shuts behind me. I press an ear against it.

Commander Derry's voice rings out loud and clear. "Agents, search the place. You know the drill. Block off the front door. Nobody leaves until we're done. Confiscate any contraband."

The burning in the back of my throat is rare but not unfamiliar. I close my eyes and swallow until it all goes away. *What are you doing, Shea?* I'm doing the right thing. That's what.

But is it the right thing?

What I want doesn't matter right now. Family matters. Dash. Mom too. I could never leave home and venture off on some fellowship program. Forget learning from the greatest scientists and voyagers of all time. Forget honing my skills and researching to my heart's content. I couldn't do that. Not without neglecting the commitments I made long before today.

The curtains to Mom's four-poster bed are drawn back. She sits up with a handheld starglobe, watching constellations swirl around the inky smoke it contains. Her soft, pink nightgown smells of fresh linen. Whether it's bringing her sweets from Fizzies or helping her cast star projections in the ceiling, we give her as much normalcy as we can. She's bed bound, but her mind is still sharp. I chew the inside of my cheek again, this time tasting blood. Her thinning hair is coming loose from the braid Dash wove it into yesterday. I'm no good at braiding hair.

My throat burns again. What will we do if I can't bring him back?

Mom's dry lips turn up as I pull up a chair and take out her medicine. "Don't worry about ISR. Your father has everything under control. They'll have their fun and be on their way."

I'm not worried about Dad. Knowing him, he's got a cloaking token hidden inside Headquarters somewhere. Commander Derry will walk through the double doors, and an empty closet will appear. They're the least of my worries right now.

"I think Dash is in trouble, Mom." I uncap the bottle of shimmering remedy and fetch the pewter spoon that floats on the shelf above her bed. "What do you know about planet Ominous?"

Mom's fingers go rigid. "Your father promised me he wouldn't send your brother there." She takes the spoonful of medicine and swallows it. "Tell me he didn't, Shea."

I wish I could lie to her. I really do.

I glance at my digiband as if a message will appear by some miracle. "The brief Dad gave Dash was vague. What do you know about the client?"

Tears form in my mother's eyes. "He's a young spellcaster. He claimed he had a cure for my condition. I thought it seemed too good to be true, and we knew very little about the planet, but your father insisted on making the deal anyway."

Dad makes a lot of deals. That doesn't tell me anything.

I need her to focus. "I know this is hard, but what about the object he sent Dash to deliver to the spellcaster? Dad didn't mention what it was, did he?"

"No, he didn't," she says, and a shudder courses through my entire being. "The spellcaster requested a one-contact meet up. Your father was adamant that Dash go over you."

I need to talk with your brother alone regarding his assignment.

Logically, sending me to deliver a classified object to a client would have made the most sense given my skill set. I would have been in and out. A foolproof delivery with zero setbacks. There would only be one reason to send Dash instead. Not to prove a point or punish me for screwing up bloodsucker thumbs. But because my brother is an exceptional Thief.

The run wasn't just a delivery. It was a pickup job.

"Nadine's remedies aren't working like they used to." Mom's hand finds mine. I know she's trying to comfort me, but something about this doesn't feel right. "My time is coming, and your father won't admit it, but he's scared. He was willing to do anything."

Mom's remedies were never meant to be a cure. I figured we'd have more time.

In training, Dad warned me not to let my emotions cloud my judgment. It's a weakness, he'd tell me. *They'll use what you love against you.* He wouldn't go against his own teachings. He wouldn't make a reckless call like sending Dash to Ominous unless it was intentional. Would he? Knowing the potential risks? His love for Mom, I can understand.

Sending his son into potential danger without backup doesn't even make sense.

I push away from the bed. "I'm going to find Dash."

Mom clings to me. "Shea, think about this—"

"Dash is my responsibility. Bringing him back is *my* job."

If I keep saying it aloud, I'll believe it too.

"I promise I'll be careful." I run my hand through Mom's hair.

She buries her face in her palms. The image burns a hole in my heart, so I focus on my pack instead. I won't be able to stop at Headquarters to gather supplies or prep thoroughly for Ominous. I'll have to work with what I've got and whatever else I can find here in the library.

In the closet near the door, I rifle through boxes that have been collecting dust for over ten years. This used to be Dad's office. He'd meet with clients here instead of inviting them into Headquarters. Deals were drawn on parchment back then, some signed in blood. Now, most of them are digital. Done over comms Gallivants or video appointments.

Planet Lark was a simple run. I'd packed my usual provisions—healing kit, rations, metal melts, glowbeam charger, recant box. Dash depleted the aqua orbs and devoured the protein bars while we were waiting for Star Spirits. But snack replacements aren't what I'm looking for. If Ominous is a magnetic field, my digiband won't work as a means of communication. Neither will a tablet or a handheld radio. What will I use? *Think.*

"I need a charmed conch shell, a transporter cube, anything that operates by magic, Mom. Something small and compact. If it uses electromagnetic waves, it won't work." I tear open bins, rummage through layers of weapon mock-ups and blueprints, and toss aside gears with missing parts. "That way, I can contact Headquarters or Dad if I need backup."

Mom lifts her head and rubs her eyes. "I'm sorry. I don't think I have those."

"It's okay. I'll figure it out... " I pull out a burlap bag from far back in the closet, past Mom's jackets that haven't seen the light since they were packed away along with Dad's things. The initials on the bag read A.J. *Alden James.* This belonged to Great-grandpa. Might be promising. Might not.

I tug at the drawstrings and view the three items nestled at the bottom. One is a pair of scuffed-up digiglasses with no charge. The second is a keycard for the shop he used to own on planet Nevarnost, Trinket Gears. That was, of course, before it got obliterated by a geographical storm. And the third object is a small, naked troll doll with a tuft of neon-pink hair and a plastic jewel glued to its belly. I've never seen anything like it before. It fits into my palm. As I run my thumb along its metal neck seam, my stomach flutters.

It's a Gallivant. Which might work. They use magic when an electrical signal isn't available. More than likely, it's a prototype, so it might not work as smoothly as our updated devices, but it's all I've got. I unscrew the troll's head and examine the hollow, metal-lined cavity inside. Leave it to Great-grandpa Alden to craft one out of such an obscure item.

"It'll do." I shove the troll into the side pocket of my pack and zip it up tight. "Now, I need to figure out how I'm getting out of here. ISR's blocked off the exit."

"The dumbwaiter across the hall?" Mom suggests.

"Good thinking." It'll take me up a level. I can exit through Fizzies. I skirt across the room, kiss Mom's head, and tuck her in. "I'll bring Dashiel back safe and sound."

"You be careful, fierce girl," she whispers. "Ask for help if you need it."

With a nod, I place another kiss at the corner of her mouth and make for the door. The commotion with ISR sounds far enough away. I should be able to slip out and into the dumbwaiter without being caught.

Hospice library secured. Bag packed. Eyes front. *Ignore everything else.*

My fingers fumble with the call for the dumbwaiter. As the gears churn inside the wall, I clench my jaw. Once it arrives, I clamber inside and press the closing mechanism.

A hand jets out and blocks the latch.

If I must, I will break an ISR agent's hand and claim ignorance later.

As I grab the door, about to slam it shut, Mr. Beachum, of all flipping people, pokes his head into the dumbwaiter. "Shea, wait! I just wanted to—"

"I realize this is incredibly rude of me, and I might be throwing away a very generous offer, but now isn't really a good time, sir."

Mr. Beachum yanks up the door. *Gods, if this guy messes up my escape.*

"Yes, there seems to be some kind of search going on, and I'm not sure where you fit into all of it, but I couldn't let you leave without telling you to—"

"Sir, I know. Again, I'm so—

"Apply for the fellowship anyway," he blurts out. The dumbwaiter is now rising. Door closed or not, I can't stop it. Neither of us can. He leans his upper body into the narrow shaft, calling after me in echoes before I'm taken away. "You'll need to complete a research project and submit it before graduation to qualify. Some of our applicants have received positions on one of our various expedition teams... " And then, fainter, in the hollow of the concrete walls below me, "... we'd love to have someone like you."

Someone like me. Before Dash and I left the Academy, I studied my ass off. I fine-tuned my craft. I made connections, knowing this might be a potential career path. Mr. Beachum's offer is everything I've ever wanted. Scientists proved the existence of multiple realities decades ago. Somewhere in the multiverse, transcending time and space, another version of me goes back to Mr. Beachum, sits down with him, and discusses a future that current me can only dream of.

I tumble onto the floor of the Fizzies taffy lab. Unstick my foot from a waste bin of wrappers and old sugar boxes and press ahead. Another version of Shea gets accepted into the Board's fellowship. She goes on, travels the galaxies, and makes history. Much like I believe the theory of right person, wrong time is something people tell themselves to soothe the pain of heartbreak—right opportunity, wrong moment is one of those sentiments too.

This version of Shea is supposed to go to Ominous to save her brother. This version of me now must figure out how she's getting there without a portal key. Or how I'm supposed to locate my brother without proper tracking. Dad is dealing with ISR. He's a cloaking token away from being apprehended. Mom couldn't help me even if she wanted to. I don't have light years to spend in cryosleep to get to the Realm of Shadows on my own.

Dash needs me now. Urgency rattles my bones.

Only one person can get me to planet Ominous without a portal key. A James as nearly clever as I am. Someone who knows Dad's twisted ways.

Dad hasn't spoken to his older sister in years since she quit her role as Thief in their siblingship, abandoning him to work the business on his own. I haven't seen her since I was ten years old, but if I want to get my brother back, Mom's right. I'm going to need to ask for Aunt Merik's help.

6

Dash

My holding cell spins faster than Whitney Pearson's bedroom did the night we downed a bottle of imported nebula whiskey from planet Lye and gave each other our virginities. It was the beginning of Tenth Year, a month before Shea and I joined the homeschool cohort.

It's just sex, she kept saying. Which was fine because, for some people, it is. But for others, it isn't, and I am unapologetically one of those people.

Despite my obvious drunkenness at the time, I remember every moment in her twin trundle bed with the yellow marigold sheets. I knew it had meant nothing to her when she'd refused to cuddle me afterward, handing me my clothes, and waiting until I was dressed, before escorting my tipsy butt to the nearest Skyway station.

Yellow marigolds twinkle in my unfocused eyes like stars. I half expect Whitney herself to hover over my curled-up body on the frigid concrete. *"So, can you like... go now?"*

I sit up, clutching the splitting temples on either side of my head. Part of my right arm burns where the black leech slithered inside, the entry point now bruised and oozing pus. The other part of my right arm, the nasty gash from where I'd fallen in the woods, leaks blood. Bits of cartilage and bone have embedded in my skin.

It's raw, and *I need a healer from the Sicky Place STAT*.

Shaking, I tear the bottom of my shirt and do my best to tie a makeshift bandage. I run my fingers over the bulging lump beneath my skin. The writhing swell twitches like the sullen dead man.

He snapped in half. My stomach lurches. Now *I'm* a dead man.

"Oh, Goddess. It's *inside* me," I croak, curling back into a ball. I try to distract myself from the sickening sensation by making note of my cell.

I'm in your standard diabolical holding cell. Judging by the darkness beyond, Fake Death's left me somewhere in the lower level of the mausoleum. It's made of stone. Iron bars on one side. Padlocked door on the other. One pitiful torchlight, a single barred window, and my empty pack to keep me company. The shackles on the wall are not attached to me—thank the Goddess. Those are always a pain.

The last holding cell I was in at least had water, moldy snacks, and a cot to lounge on while I waited for—oh, that's right. My sister isn't coming to save me.

"This can't be the end for me." I position myself beneath the torchlight to savor every scrap of warmth it offers. My fingers are useless hunks of ice meat. I've lost too much blood to pump the heat back in. "My sweet Shea-Lynn, please...*please* come find me."

"You're acting quite dramatic," a soft voice says from the shadow-laden corner. A figment of my imagination, perhaps.

I wipe my nose on my sleeve. "Well, I was the star of my Ninth-Year theater production, a space opera rendition of *Romeo and Ghouliet*."

After a pause, the shadow-laden corner speaks again. "Were you Romeo or Ghouliet?"

"Neither." I sit up and tuck my knees against my chest. "I played the obsidian dagger. It was a metaphorical role. I performed a one-liner in the final act. Many tears were shed."

"I'm sure it had nothing to do with Ghouliet's sacrificial demise."

"Thank you for saying that. I take pride in my acting work." I place a hand over my heart. "Who are you, is the question. Have I died and gone to penance for a life of thievery and crime?"

"Why are you talking like that?"

"I'm speaking with dramatic effect."

Another flutter of movement comes from that dark corner, followed by a half-hearted chuckle. A girl about a year older than Shea crawls forward. A real girl. Not an apparition. Her long, raven hair hangs in waves around her face. She brushes it back, revealing the golden tint in her eyes. As she sits cross-legged in front of me, her plum, high-waisted skirt bunches, as does the stained, off-white button-up with long puffy sleeves she wears. Given the crystals and charms dangling around her neck, I'd guess she's a spellcaster like Fake Death.

Again, like Fake Death, she's familiar, but I can't place her. *What is up with that?*

"I see he's dragged you into this," she says.

"I don't know what you mean."

With a sigh, the girl gestures to the inflamed patch on my arm. As she does, her blouse tugs, revealing the charred and crusted bruise peeking above her collar. *She's got one too.* Flashbacks of the sullen man getting twisted like a pretzel infiltrate my mind. I banish them.

"How far did you get before Valerian caught up with you?" She motions me forward to examine my other wound. It's already soaked through my makeshift bandage. "I'm going to assume Roger didn't make it. It didn't sound like it."

She prods my bandage. I wince. "Uh, Valerian? Roger?"

"The spellcaster with a wicked magic curveball and the guy he ruthlessly murdered."

"A wicked cur—oh, you mean the skull prince. I've been calling him Fake Death."

She unravels my soaked bandage, tosses it aside, and picks at the splinters of bone lodged in my inflamed skin. I hold back a gasp. Tears well in my eyes.

"Fake Death." She smiles coyly, removing a piece of cartilage. She tosses it over her shoulder, and it lands in the shadow-laden corner with a plink. "Yes. That suits him better."

I force a smile back. "Glad you think so. Shame about Roger, though."

"Roger was one of Valerian's lackeys. He's the one that brought me in." She yanks up my sleeve further and wipes her bloody fingers on her skirt. Then she removes a shard of stuck bone. It stings. I gasp.

She looks up at me. "He didn't deserve it; nobody ever does, but karma came for him anyway, didn't it? He trusted Valerian and thought offering me up for death would save him."

"I almost got away." I ruffle my hair with my free hand, casually wiping the sweat pooling on my forehead. *How is none of this fazing her?* She pulls at my skin. I grit my teeth.

"I ran—I was hiding in the woods. Fake Death showed up and was like, hey, you're a host now, and... Are you sure using your fingers like that is sanitary? My sister goes on and on about infections all the—AHHH!"

"Sorry. That one was deep." She holds up a sliver of bone coated in my blood and tosses it over her shoulder to join the growing collection piled in the corner.

More of my blood stains her fingers. This time, she wipes it on my sleeve. "I wouldn't be so hard on yourself. Fake Death is a powerful spellcaster."

"His soul suckers were powerful, that's for sure."

She snorts. "Soul sucker? Do you have a nickname for everything?"

"Well, I—GAH, that really stings."

She raises a brow, flicks another bit of bone, and grabs my free hand to press it firmly against my wound. "Put pressure there while I tear some fresh cloth strips."

As the heat finds my ears, I'm extra thankful for the shadow covering us. I'm not usually this off my game either, but she's pretty, and she's got a heavy grip on my cursed arm and well, you know... I'm feeling things... "Where, uh, where did you learn to pick and clean wounds?"

"Mainly my father. He was a healer." She tears her dress. The rip prickles the goosebumps along my arm. "I'm Euphoria, by the way. Euphoria Delevingne. Spellcaster. What nickname would you give me?"

Gods. Even her name sounds alluring. *Euphoria Delevingne.*

I can't get sidetracked with flirting right now, but maybe a little won't—

"No. Dashiel. No," Shea's voice mutters in my head. *"I'm not coming to get you. You're going to bleed out. You're going to die. You have no portal key. No way to call home. You're doomed. Think with your head, not your heart. Find a way out of that frigid cell."*

"You okay?" Euphoria asks, beginning her wrap.

Her fingers brush against mine. I shift my gaze into hers, batting my eyelashes a bit. I can't help it. It's who I am. And we're sitting so close together while she mends me so well.

"As far as nicknames go, I'd say Effy—no, Effs. Let's go with Effs." I hold out my bloody hand for her to shake. "I'm Dash. Dashiel James, human from planet Sarasing. I'm a Thief, theater nerd, fried food connoisseur, and an aspiring Holoblocks captain."

"Wow. You really do like nicknames." She shakes my hand and continues her work, tying the knots on her cloth strips so tight the soul sucker inhabiting me squirms.

I chew the inside of my cheek. "I do indeed. I appreciate how a good nickname feels, like a song. Sicky Place, ISR Dipsticks, Carnage Trees, Fake Death, Soul Suckers—"

"Shhhh!" Effs presses a finger to my lips. "Do you hear that?"

I shake my head.

She springs up, taking all the warmth we'd generated together with her, climbing up on the cell's single window ledge, and peers into the night. She motions for me to join her, and I find the strength to pull myself up.

My good hand steadies me against the rough wall as I stare out into the wood beyond the bars. In the distance, Fake Death and his skeletons convene in a thicket of carnage trees.

A Door fashioned of cracked glass appears next to them. I clench my fist. Fake Death's got Shea's portal key, our only way out of here alive, and he's about to walk away with it.

Cold dread nips at my stomach. How does he even know how to use it? Unless he's had proper training?

A skeleton opens the Door and steps through. It slams shut behind them all. My heart sinks.

"Where is he going?" I whisper, admiring Effs's delicate profile in the dark.

"Oh, he's probably headed home to Crowley Corner," she whispers back.

"Crowley Corner? What's that?"

Effs hops off the sill. "It's the abandoned amusement park where we live."

"Wait." I step down and join her by the cell door. "You *live* with this guy?"

She smooths the pleats in her skirt. "I used to, yes. We were lovers."

Effs rubs her golden eyes, a smear of my blood on her cheek. I'm itching to lean over and wipe it away for her. *Settle yourself, Dash.* "Okay. Do tell. I love a good romance story."

"I wouldn't call it all romantic," she says. "I sought him out, opened my heart to him, and then when he realized I would not give him what he wanted, he used me and ran off with another spellcaster instead."

"The *same* thing happened to me with Zena O'Hair!"

She smiles. "Then you understand."

"I *do*. I really do."

Her smile fades. She crosses beneath the torchlight to sit, offering me another look at the streaky veins spider-webbing the edge of her neck. How long before that happens to me?

"It is a bit more complicated with Valerian, I'm afraid," she says.

I sit next to her on the floor. "Why is that?"

"I refuse to open the portal to the Higher Realm. Until I agree to do so, his plan is to consume my soul and find a way in himself. He's quite determined. I'll give him that."

"How would consuming *your* soul help him get into another realm?" I ask.

"Because we're the same soul. He thinks consuming my portion will give him the missing knowledge he doesn't have on his own—specifically the codes to open the portal."

I tuck my knees into my chest. "Now you've lost me."

"If you believe we are all simply souls inhabiting physical forms, you might also believe in reincarnation or past lives. That with each lifetime, a soul gains knowledge."

Mom mentioned something about this once. Though I vaguely remember because while Shea took notes in her journal and asked follow-up questions, I fell asleep.

Effs continues, "And if you believe that with each lifetime, souls learn lessons, then you might also believe that when a soul reaches its capacity, it becomes so expansive that it cannot be energetically contained in one physical form. Therefore, that soul splits into two. The same soul, but in two bodies. Neither is incomplete. Both are whole on their own. They mirror one another. When they incarnate together, they are each born with a set of codes—think pieces of a puzzle—and when they've mastered duality, they are given the opportunity to move into sustained physical union with one another in the Higher Realm."

It's a bit over my head, but I understand what Effs is saying. "So, Fake Death is your twin soul. Only you've been romantically involved. But you're the same person... "

Hmm. Maybe I don't understand.

She chuckles. "Valerian and I have spent many lifetimes together. Sometimes, we are lovers. Sometimes, we are family. Sometimes, we are friends. It doesn't matter what we are or who we are. It only matters that we are each meant to heal our inner wounds, face our differences, and achieve balance within ourselves by unlocking one another's codes. The combination of our codes allows us to strengthen and expand our soul knowledge."

I scrunch my nose. "And what does this have to do with a... portal?"

"The opportunity to open the portal to the Higher Realm presents itself once in every lifetime we incarnate together. We've never been able to open it. We've never been aware or evolved enough to even begin to understand how to open it. This lifetime is different, both Valerian and I have a general understanding of what's going on, but he's still missing codes. He doesn't understand the depth of our soul connection like I do or what the portal really is."

"Can't you just tell him?"

"I've tried. Many times."

"But you *won't* tell him how to get into the Higher Realm?"

Effs scoffs. "Absolutely not. He isn't ready. The Higher Realm operates at a certain level of awareness, a state of consciousness he has yet to master. If I give him the codes to the Higher Realm now, he'll attempt to cross the threshold too soon, and he will destroy himself. No. I won't do it. I refuse."

I wince. "Instead, he gets to destroy *you* by sucking out your soul... "

"Yes." Effs crosses her arms. "That is exactly what will happen."

"Okay, but if your soul split because it can't be contained in one body, won't Fake Death destroy himself by consuming your soul anyway?"

"Possibly. Probably."

I'm so confused. "Why not tell him how to get to the Higher Realm, then? If he's going to implode either way, why not save yourself and let him destroy himself on his own terms?"

She furrows her brows. "In order for him to go to the Higher Realm, I must go to the Higher Realm first, and I'm not ready to go either. Is *none* of this making sense to you?"

"No, it is." I scratch my head. *Kinda.* "You're okay with dying?"

"I've made peace with it." She rests her head back and closes her eyes. "Maybe in the next life, we'll figure it out—"

"Uh, *whoa.* Hold on." I pull myself up again. "Maybe you have another life after this, but what about me?"

Effs fluffs her skirt. "It is very unfortunate that Valerian dragged you into this, but he will not budge. Kellie's Comet will arrive in three days during Crowley Corner's annual Festival. According to Valerian, the comet is the portal. He won't stop until it passes."

I pick at my makeshift bandage. "Look, I don't want to die, Effs. There are a lot of things I haven't done yet, and I don't think I'd go to a happy place. I've taken a lot of things that aren't mine. Like a lot of things. That, and I always thought I'd die peacefully at home in my bed with my partner and our children by my side. Our home has bay windows overlooking the ocean and my vegetable garden. *Bay* windows!"

She sighs. "I hear you, Dash. I do."

"Isn't there like a third option? One where we get out of here, convince Fake Death to give us the cure, and then you forget all about him and the Higher Realm . . ?"

"In three days?" she asks.

I blink at her. Is this how Shea feels when I act like this? Because if she were here right now, she'd hear three days and find some way to figure it out in one. *Gods, I miss her.* I can't... work with this. *I'm* usually the one that gets to contemplate our impending doom. While Shea figures everything out. I can't self-destruct *and* pick up the extra slack here.

An unsteady pulse throbs in my neck. This dynamic will not do. If I rely on this girl, I'm actually going to die.

"I'm not judging, because my sister usually gets me out of predicaments like this, but don't you want to at least try to break the cycle on your own?"

Effs's golden eyes brighten. "Your sister. Is she coming to get you?"

"Shea... doesn't know where I am," I say, and the hopeful light in Effs's eyes dies. *Tell me about it.*

Then, she seems to come to a decision and pulls herself up. "Okay. I do want to break the cycle. I want out."

Okay. Now we're getting somewhere. Wanting out is something I can understand.

Figuring out a way out will be harder, but hey... baby steps. "Do you think Fake Death will come back soon?"

"More than likely, he won't return until right before Festival."

I scratch my head. Glance around. Now a crumpled heap in a blood puddle, my pack piques my interest. Did I stash any anything that could help us escape? I don't think I brought anything truly useful at all. I've always had Shea for that.

If this is the Gods trying to prove a point, congratulations—they've made it.

As Effs notices me fetching my crumpled pack, she says, "You have something?"

"Uhhh. Well... " I grope the bottom. "I'm checking. I didn't, uh, plan for this."

She hovers over my shoulder. "Anything?"

"I'm looking. It's just—" I paw through my empty backpack as if by some magic a plethora of life-saving supplies will appear.

I check the last pocket, but all I find are Fizzies wrappers and arcade tokens.

Effs presses her lips together. "You don't have anything in that pack, do you?"

"Well, uh—" I scratch the back of my head and double-check the back pockets. "Shea usually handles all the preparations for our assignments, if I'm being brutally honest."

She scoffs. "What good are you, then? Other than comic relief in these dark times."

I pace behind her. "I'm sorry. I'm a Thief, okay? I've never had to think about anything else other than taking what isn't mine." She stops short, and I'm quick on the counter. "What about you? He's *your* twin soul. *You're* a spellcaster. Use your magic to get us out of here."

"Use your magic." Effs mimics me, raising her voice. "My magic is the only thing keeping me alive. What do you think this sucker is feeding off of? When my magic is spent, it'll go after my soul, and despite time running out, I'd like to keep it for as long as I can!"

Ohhhhkay then. If magic is feeding her sucker, what does that mean for me? I don't have much time left. Fighting with her is not going to help me.

"I'm sorry," I say flatly. "I don't know what I was thinking."

She releases the tension in her shoulders. "Thank you. I, too, am sorry for losing my temper and thinking of you as another self-important and useless teenage boy."

Well. I'm going to assume we weren't flirting earlier, then.

I clasp my hands together. "Look. My sister may or may not be coming for me, and while I still hold on to a glimmer of that hope, there might be another way out of here."

Effs crosses her arms. "I'm listening."

Oh, Gods. She wants an actual plan.

I didn't think we'd get this far.

What was the preachy-pep talk Shea gave me before I left? I can map out and plan a Holoblocks tournament like a boss, but I can't do crap in the real world?

Yeah, that was the one. Does this count, though? I mean, I'm not wearing my goggles or my biometric gloves. And with no holographic drop-down menu displaying my inventory, all we've got is a cold cell, an empty pack, and a few bloody bones Effs plucked out of me.

I focus on one bone in particular, in a puddle mixed with my blood. A small, sharp bone with a pointed end. One that might be big enough to pick a lock with.

"You've zoned out, Dash," Effs says.

"Yeah, I do that a lot."

I retrieve the bone, cross the cell, and align it in the padlock's keyhole.

"My brain is an odd place. Shea tells me I need to stop drinking fizzy drinks, and Aunt Merik keeps giving me the name of a therapist she really likes... "

I move the bone just right. *Click.* As I swing the cell door open, it creaks, and Effs's eyes widen.

"I think maybe I just need some decent friends in my life. You know? Or maybe a better sleep schedule. Those crumb lizards living in my closet have been keeping me up late at—whoa whoa, what are you—"

Effs bolts for the cell door and knocks against me. She takes off into the dark.

I put my hands on my hips and let out a huff. "I believe I was just used again."

Why does this keep happening to me? I sling my backpack over my shoulder and unhook the torch from the wall. Letting its light guide me, I make my way for the corridor. This escape seemed easy. Shea would say too easy.

I follow the curve of the wall. It leads into another hallway.

A snarl echoes ahead. My grip on the torch tightens. The sucker in my arm pulses.

My legs shake like gelatin, the kind our grandmother used to make for our birthdays because she couldn't bake for the life of her. Man, what I wouldn't give for some dome-shaped grape gelatin with little star sprinkles and an accompanying cake-cutting fairy to slice it into bite-sized pieces right about now.

A squelch perks up my ears. I freeze.

I swallow the lump in my throat. Is that teeth gnawing... flesh?

Two small glowing orbs near, bobbing amid the black. The wobble in my legs intensifies. I fight to keep my torch steady. Impossible to do with shaking hands.

As the creature takes form ahead of me, my breath hitches in my throat.

I extend my torch, illuminating two glowing antennae sticking out of its oblong head. Oily fur. Two iris-less eyes. A freakishly enormous jaw filled with rows of translucent teeth.

It scrapes its claws, which are the size of my head, against the stone, and lets out a roar that shakes me to the core.

7

Shea

Aunt Merik's cul-de-sac is the last stop on the Green Line in the Residential District.

Asteroid Ave.

Three blocks away from the Skyway station.

I try to breathe past the tightness in my chest. All the units look the same—cutesy townhouses and bungalows painted a prism of colors. My next inhale carries with it the smell of steak being flipped on a grilling block. A young Vega, whose second set of tentacles haven't come in yet, waits by said grill, holding a platter heaped with brine melon. Another group of children, various species, plays a community game of virtual kickball in the center quad. Their guardians keep close eyes on them from the comfort of their yards. They look up at me through their sunspecs, as I pass through, then go back to their gardening and sunbathing.

Their lives will always be ordinary.

My hand grazes the railing of Unit 121. The calico morph cat on the porch swing licks its eight paws, offering me a soft meow. I press the call bell and step away from the door.

Will my aunt even help me? A Thief and an Enforcer are supposed to be bonded for life. They're supposed to stick it out till the end. She left Dad at the height of his career, right after he'd inherited the business from Grandpa Luke. She made it clear she wanted nothing to do with us. Not a single phone call or card on our birthdays, no visits on holidays—*nothing*.

Merik James abandoned this family. Now she's all I've got.

Moments later, the door opens. A girl of about eight with bright James family freckles and curled pigtails stares back at me. No idea who she is. Probably a cousin.

Another part of my aunt's life we weren't allowed to be involved in.

I put my hands on my hips. "Uh, hello there. I need to talk to your... mother."

Suddenly Merik appears behind her, gently nudging the girl back inside. "It's okay, Novalee. Why don't you go on and play Starships and Spacespirits upstairs with Finley?"

Once my cousin is gone, my aunt sizes me up. Her brown eyes glisten in the late-afternoon sun. She hasn't changed much. The same straight row of bangs and short, wavy brown hair styled to accentuate her features. Dimples on the apples of her full cheeks. Her bohemian style is in full swing, too, with the flowy shawl and crystals she wears draped across her shoulders. The only difference is my aunt is pregnant. *Very* pregnant.

"Shea-Lynn, this is a surprise."

She opens the door all the way. Another little cousin, this time the spitting image of her free-spirited mother, attempts to escape. My aunt scoops her up quickly.

Hell. How many cousins do I have?

I accept her gesture and walk inside.

As the door shuts behind us, I wipe my boots on the doormat. "Look, I'm sorry to come unannounced, but I didn't know who else to—"

"Hold on a sec." Aunt Merik wrangles her squirming toddler, and I notice the modest diamond on her finger. She calls up the carpeted staircase to her left, "Charles! Can you come down and take the kiddos? My niece is here. We need girl time."

My little cousin runs free, steps on her mother's bare feet, and warrants my aunt's sigh. "*Alone*, if possible. It's been a while!"

Merik's apparent partner, Charles, calls down, "Kids!" and three more between the ages of four and seven pelt around the corner from the living room, wielding cardboard swords and makeshift crowns they've cut and pasted out of parchment.

Once they've all gone upstairs, I'm led into the kitchen, where rows of baking sheets lined with homemade granola bars sit cooling on the counter.

"You want one?" Aunt Merik takes one for herself, acting like this is just another hangout session and she hasn't been MIA for the last eight years. "I make them for Dash when he comes by." She licks her thumb and laughs. "He tells me they aren't sweet enough."

Her words are like a punch in the gut. Dash and Aunt Merik.

"Wait, did you just say Dash came by—here? As in, recently?"

Aunt Merik wipes crumbs from the corner of her mouth. "As in the last few days. He came and played Holoblocks with Charles on Wednesday. I made a boiled dinner."

Last Wednesday. Dash told me he was going to the arcade with his Academy friends.

Merik rounds the center island and places a hand on my shoulder. "What's going on, Shea? Is he okay? You're scaring me."

No, he isn't okay, I want to scream. My brother tells me everything. Even personal things I don't need to know like how kissing boys with tongue is better than without tongue and how spicy Tee Tee's tacos wreak havoc on his bowels. He never mentioned he comes here, that he's seen our aunt in the last decade, let alone a week. What else has he been keeping from me?

Merik frees up a barstool heaped with baby clothes. "Here, please sit, and we can talk about—"

"I don't have time to talk. Dash is on planet Ominous. Dad sent him there to pick up something ghastly." I pace. I don't know what else to do. "If I had my portal key, I could call a Door and go to him, but I don't have it. I gave it to him before he left."

I pause and turn to her. "Help me."

She grabs another granola bar. "I understand you're worried, but we need to think about this logically. How do you know he's in trouble?"

Why is she acting like this? Calm? Collected? "Didn't you hear me? He's not responding. His tracking is offline. I *know* he's in trouble. I know my brother. My gut says something is wrong." A wave of heat washes over my body. *We're wasting time.* "Dad's being profiled by ISR. You're all I've got right now. Get me to Ominous so I can bring Dash back. It's the least you can do for abandoning this family and my father."

My aunt leaves my side. She places the granola bar in the sink, picks up builder blocks at the foot of the stove, and tosses them in a toy box. Then she straightens a fingerpainting of a Slog riding a unicorn on the fridge.

Seriously? What the hell is she doing? Why isn't she listening to me?

I step forward. "Merik, are you going to help me, or are you going to be as useless to me as everyone else I rely on to get things done?"

She opens a drawer, takes out baking parchment, and begins rolling granola bars. "You know, it's been a while since someone spoke to me like that."

My entire stomach twists into a knot.

"Excuse me?" Maybe calling her useless was a bit too much, but I stand by what I said. "You're the one that left us. I'm not sure how you expect me to act."

She lets out a half-hearted laugh. "That's what Henry told you happened?"

I pick at the corners of my fingernails until they bleed. "Yes. His exact words."

Aunt Merik holds my stare. "Your father forced me to quit after I stood up to him. He didn't like that. I wasn't allowed to come back. Even though I wanted to."

Her breathing is steady, voice steady. She keeps her hands at her side, relaxed. She's not lying. It means someone else was lying. It means *Dad* was lying.

Why would he do that? Why would he keep our aunt from us?

"I'm sorry. I didn't realize—"

"It's okay. I'm not surprised that's the story Henry told you."

Aunt Merik looks around her home at the fruits of a life she and her partner built for themselves. A furnished space with cozy comforts. They probably have a real backyard for their children to play in. It's clear my aunt has found her peace away from my father and the business, and it pains me I've upset her by accusing her, but the clock is ticking, and I don't know how much time Dash has left.

"I realize this warrants a bigger conversation," I say. "But Dash could be in danger. Can you help me find him? Please, Merik. He's my little brother, and I'm worried about him."

I recognize the look in her eyes. The same look stares back at me in my bedroom mirror as I get ready for an assignment. The look that overtakes me while I study up on the lore. Aunt Merik knows what it's like to love a brother as much as I do. Our family roots run deep.

Maybe she took Charles's last name when they committed to one another, maybe she didn't, but she's still a James deep down.

Otherwise, she would have sent me away five minutes ago.

"Let's save Dash," Aunt Merik says. "But afterward, you and I are having a chat."

She yells up the back stairwell, "Charles, I'll be right back. I'm headed out to the storage unit.

The tightness in my body untangles. I don't know what my aunt means or what she could possibly have in a storage unit that could help me, but she's *helping* me.

"What's with the cheddar?" I ask, referring to the three broken chunks of cheese on the dash of Merik's hover-jeep.

"It's common courtesy to leave a tip," is all Aunt Merik says.

She parks in the lot behind a yellow building whose concrete walls have rounded divots like Swiss cheese. A blinking board displays the name Pippa's Storage, and as I get out of the jeep, I spot another advertisement pushing a specialty price for renters looking to secure a unit while traveling via cryosleep.

From there, we pick up a transportation cart manned by tiny, brown mice. One works the pedal. Another the operating panel. The one perched on the mirror turns on his miniature Universal Comms headpiece and nods to my aunt.

"Unit 111, please," she says.

"Certainly." The mouse relays the request, and we begin to move.

Our cart carries us through a labyrinth of identical gray halls, stopping at Unit 111.

Aunt Merik hands the mice the hunks of cheddar. I follow her off the cart and across the line of metal-plated storage units with digitized lock screens. She places her hand on a scanner, which beeps when it recognizes her biometrics, and the lock switches to green.

Aunt Merik beckons me inside with a smile I haven't earned, and I have difficulty returning the favor. I shouldn't have snapped at her earlier. She was trying to help me. I didn't know my father treated her that way. He gets angry when people go against him, but to shut her out of our life completely? That seems unnecessary. I'd be upset if Dash refused to listen to me, but I wouldn't snub him off forever. Would I?

No, I wouldn't. I couldn't.

Besides, Dash would never refuse to follow my lead. He's my Thief. I'm his Enforcer. We made a promise to one another to work in this business as a team for life.

I enter the dark storage space behind Aunt Merik, an array of overhead lighting picking up our motion on the sensors. The vast unit illuminates. My aunt walks on. I stay where I am.

Her storage unit is filled with objects I haven't seen before, and I've seen just about everything. It's like Headquarters on a smaller scale. Only the inventory is encased in glass cubes, jars, and tanks. All set up on floating shelves that wrap the unit in a perfect square.

I pull up the camera application on my digiband. *Stop. No. Damn the nerd brain.* I don't have time now, but I can always come back and archive the shit out of this place later.

Dash would have a field day in here. I shove away thoughts of him tied up somewhere or possibly held against his will. *Okay. Maybe a couple peeks at my aunt's Thief horde wouldn't hurt...* I tap a display, home to a fleshy ball floating in a muddy substance. By the second nudge, the squishy round uncurls, showcasing its spikes and razor-sharp teeth.

"The electric urchin," Aunt Merik says across the unit. "Picked that one up from a crystal mine on planet Echo. Venomous. Deadly upon contact. You touch it, you die. Literally."

Ooo. Another quick peek. That's it, though. *Remember your missing brother?*

Aunt Merik uncovers a flat, rectangular object wrapped in a canvas tarp, releasing a cloud of dust. She coughs and waves her hands around. I check on the electric urchin, and the bulbous sea creature has finally settled back into its deceptively harmless form.

"Why do you have all this here?" I join her and help her pull what now feels like a wooden board out into the open.

"Funny thing happens when you have kids." She brushes herself off and kicks over a metal stand. "Can't leave treasures from your thieving days lying around anymore. Charles and I decided it was best. Plus, Pippa's Storage gave us a killer deal on the monthly renting fee."

"Hence the cheese," I say, and we hoist the covered board upright together. Nearby, a glass tube holding a glimmering puff of gray smoke catches my eye. I pick it up.

"Hey, this is a contained acid cloud. Dad was looking for this at Headquarters last week. Someone had ordered it off the online catalog, but he realized the bounty on the felon's head was worth more than the deal, and he turned the guy into Commander Derry instead. Why do you have it?"

"I took as much as I could before Henry kicked me out. Call it an act of rebellion or my compulsive stealing problem. I've since gotten help."

The gas inside the tube sizzles, and my aunt prods me to set it back down. "He still talks to Derry? Can't say I'm surprised by that either."

"Yeah, why? She's the head of ISR."

Aunt Merik stands on her tiptoes and brushes away cobwebs gathered at the top of the canvas tarp. "Honestly, it's none of my business."

"Derry's an old flame. I know enough."

Merik clutches the tarp. "As I said, it's not my place to talk about it."

Hmmm. Dad's eyes *were* wandering in that meeting. A look is a look. It could mean anything. But maybe I don't know as much about my father as I thought I did.

"I'm sure Dad has his reasons for everything he's done."

"Families are complicated, Shea. I didn't realize it at the time, but leaving the business was the best thing that ever happened to me. Your relationship with Dash is sacred. If you aren't careful, you could lose it—break it beyond repair. When you find him, you both should think long and hard about your future. My advice is to get out while you can. *Live* your life."

"Someday, the business will be mine. Dad's relying on me."

"Is that what you really want, or is it what you think will make your father happy?"

Rarely does a question take me off guard. Answers pop into my head intuitively all the time. Solid answers, true-to-me answers. Why doesn't the answer to her question come as easily?

Why, when I tell myself it *is* what I want, does my stomach pinch?

Aunt Merik doesn't know what she's talking about. Our father makes mistakes, everyone does, but he cares about Mom. And sure, I could have researched to prepare Dash for Ominous to avoid complications, but there was a reason Dad didn't tell me about it. A good one. A logical one.

But maybe that's why Dad *didn't* tell me.

Because he knew it wouldn't be... safe.

In my silence, Aunt Merik yanks the canvas tarp from the board. Underneath is an old antique Door covered in dead tendrils and wilted petals. The symbols outlining the frame remind me of the Star Spirits on planet Lark. I raise my brows. A small thrill courses through me. I think I'd be fangirling if I wasn't overanalyzing Dad's intentions right now.

Did he know Ominous would be unsafe, or was he so determined to cure Mom that he didn't care?

"This Door won't lead you straight to Ominous, but it will guide you into the Hallway of Doors, which is what your portal key connects to."

I suck in a breath. "As in the Hallway of Doors in the Realm of Souls?"

"Yes. Do you have a breather?"

"Always." I reach around my backpack, take my breathing device out of its storage pocket, secure it to my face, and tweak the settings so the oxygen levels adjust.

"Great. Let the Hallway guide you. Remember, this isn't like having your portal key. All the navigation falls on you. You must trust the Hallway and your instincts. Once you open a Door and enter it, you won't be able to return, so choose wisely."

"I will. Thank you, Aunt Merik, for doing this."

"No problem," she says. "And keep my guidance in mind, will you?"

Staring into her eyes is like gazing into my own. I feel for her, but whatever happened between she and my father won't happen between Dash and me. I won't let it.

"Imagine a Door. A Door that connects to all other Doors," my aunt says.

The Door rattles and thrums. Around the frame, it glows. I clutch the doorknob and twist, ready to enter the ethereal beyond. Holding the base of her belly, Aunt Merik waves me onward. I adjust my backpack straps, cross the threshold, and take in the rush of cool air.

It sucks me in. Then the Door swings shut behind me.

A surge of adrenaline soars through my being. I'm back in the Realm of Souls. A place that not even the Board has explored in full. This would make a killer research project to submit for the fellowship... if it weren't an illegal means of travel, and I were actually going to apply.

A stark, white wall stands where the Door was, my tether to planet Sarasing, Pippa's Storage, and Aunt Merik completely gone. I'm standing in a hallway, one I'd only read about before today. Filled with Doors, a myriad of them, against a backdrop of marble floors and high vaulted ceilings. Open archways draped in beading and silk. Some are dressed in trim. There's stone, brick, metal, and every variation of wood.

Every book I've ever read on ethereal study in the past says the Hallway of Doors is not just the bridge between realms and planets and worlds. Within it are the soul records of every being in existence. All the lives I've ever lived are housed here somewhere behind a Door—in a Record Room of their own. Knowledge only meant to be seen by those beyond the veil, Dash jokingly refers to them as the Cosmic Classifieds.

A flutter in my chest brings back my focus. One could get lost for days reading all the sacred knowledge here. To understand why we are the way we are. Why everything happens. Like why

Mom had to get sick or why Dad and Aunt Merik can't overcome their differences.

But this is the present, and my little brother is still out there.

I position myself in the center of the Hallway of Doors, noting how far it goes, an endless stretch on either side. Once I get to Ominous, Dash and I can use my portal key to get home. Finding my way to planet Ominous seems impossible, but my aunt said I must trust that I'll be shown the way, so that's what I'll do.

I close my eyes. "Guide me there. Show me Ominous."

Take me to Dash, I think over and over. *Take me to my little brother.*

As I open my eyes, a ripple of movement rides the center of the hall. Could it really be this easy? Simply ask and receive?

Show me planet Ominous. Bring me the right Door.

A rumble vibrates beneath my feet. Ringing fills my ears. The Hallway of Doors grows, and the massive wave of energy rattles. It whips through me, nearly knocking me off my feet. A series of clicks, and the walls move. Like a Skyway train taking off at full speed, the Doors fly by so fast that a hint of nausea plagues my gut.

Air flits my stray hair. I keep my balance the best I can. Smudges of color, the many Doors against a grand marble canvas whirl together like a masterpiece. Then, as if I've fallen down a chute, I am plunged into a frigid darkness lit by torchlight.

My heart rakes against my ribs. *This is it. The Realm of Shadows.*

I straighten, riding the last pull of movement. The comforting angelic Hallway is no more. Like a roulette wheel from a Spinners Pier gambling center, the surrounding Doors slow to a crawl. They sink into the stone walls. As they settle into place, I relax my shoulders.

Now we're getting somewhere.

The Door to planet Ominous is square. I remember it vividly from when I summoned it for Dash. Only, all these Doors look too similar. Rundown. Blood-spattered. Made of rotting wood. The passage to my brother could be any of them.

Once I enter a Door, I can't return. I decide it's between two of them, identical save for their knobs. One is wrought iron, and the other is a brass handle.

Ugh. What handle did the Door I called for Dash have?

I close my eyes and try to picture it. A draft prickles the back of my neck. When I'm holding my portal key, images of Doors and what they look like pop into my head. Something to do with the magic of the key. But without it... I rub my eyes until stars fleck behind my lids.

It had to be the wrought iron knob. Maybe there's something on the database.

As I tap my digiband, the tiniest motion whizzes past my peripherals. I pull my glowbeam off my belt and scan the hall. I might not know much about Ominous, but I know enough about the Realm of Shadows. I could run into anything here.

I guide my laser scanner up the curve of the wall. The grated ceiling leaks a warm, stale mist. *You're alone. Get a grip.* Letting out a huff, I sheath my glowbeam and return to my digiband. No service. *Dammit.* Is the entire realm a magnetic field too?

I put my hands on my hips, alternating my gaze between the two Doors. Experiments were my least favorite part of science class. Too many hypotheses to prove right.

To avoid wasting any more time, I throw open the Door with the wrought iron knocker. My expression falls. Humid air wafts, clinging to my skin. A murky swamp stretches on for miles before me. A rancid puke-green sun setting on the horizon. No land masses in sight.

Dead end. As I try to shut the Door, water splashes over the lip. I jump back, eager to keep my boots dry. Once the wave settles, I grab the handle again.

"Come on. Latch shut." This time, the Door catches.

It thuds. *What the hell?* I kneel and examine the threshold.

A disembodied gray hand jets out of the swamp. It clasps my wrist, its nailless fingers curling around my digiband. Gritting my teeth, I pry it off and fling it away.

Damn hands. Getting handsy with me. Screw this place.

As I attempt to get up, a second hand latches onto my right thigh. A third leaps into the air. It grabs the strap on my chest. I gasp. *Hell no.* Growling, I rip the curling hand off and toss it back. The other two are next. I zing them as far as I can, and as I turn to get up for real this time, I'm yanked off my knees. My chin slams the metal bar across the Door's threshold.

I scream.

The sound of my voice echoes, beckoning more hands to rise. *Quick. Get up. Get up, Shea*. A gush of swamp water drenches me. Twenty hands maul me at once. They pick and pry. They cling and stretch. I'm halfway through the Door, halfway in the swamp now.

One hand gets ahold of my belt. Another wraps itself in my hair. A third finds my wrist again, a direct draw to my digiband. *Get rid of it. It's useless on Ominous. It's you or them.*

With another yell, I unclip my digiband. Then my belt. They sink out of sight. I focus on my hair, wrangling the hand in my soaked locks.

I flop in the water, now up to my waist. *You can do this.*

Dash and I have been in predicaments before. There isn't anything we can't get ourselves out of. Rather *I* can't get us out of. Hands anchor their twisted fingers in my pack. As I thrash, they work together and pull me further into their world.

Thick, warm liquid rises to my armpits. *You cannot let them drag you under.*

I'm in their world now. I eye the Door, still open a crack. Forget getting pulled under. If that Door closes, I'm stuck here. *Get your glowbeam. Get it now.*

Hands crawl up my torso. I claw at them. They yank off my mask in retort. My lungs tighten. Air is breathable here, but what about Ominous?

Fingers pull at my cheeks, their skin crunchy and calloused. Whiffs of spoiled flesh fill my nose. They seize every bit of me they can. Even my pudge, which I've grown to love about myself, but it's just the right amount of solidity to drag a girl beneath the bubbling sediment.

I'm in over my head. Too dark to see underwater. *Gods.* I continue to thrash. My lungs beg me for air. I grope for my glowbeam again. It's—why isn't it here?

A hand clamps over my mouth. Another finds the strap of my breather hanging around my neck. Infinite fingers leave slimy, cold trails on my limbs.

I sweat. I shiver. WHERE IS MY FUCKING GLOWBEAM?

My chest rises and falls in uncontrollable waves. The hand around my neck squeezes. I have to remember my training. Remember any of what Dad drilled into my head: *if you're going to die, you better die fighting for every last breath.*

My fingers curl around a familiar handle and trigger.

I blast the hands off my legs. Kick to the surface. As I break air, I suck in and blast another. It flies through the air, shrieks, and splashes into its swamp. The remaining hands swarm my glowbeam all at once and drag it under with a burble of swamp goop.

There are too many of them. I bite one near my mouth and spit out the taste of death souring my lips. It doesn't flinch. None of them flinch. It's like they don't feel pain.

I flip over in the water, finding it shallow enough to stand. They're heavy. So heavy. Weighing me down. I'm alone. My glowbeam is gone. My digiband is toast.

Think, Shea-Lynn. Think. What else can you do?

With every bit of strength, I heave my body back toward the Doorway. It's barely ajar, the whistling wind threatening to slam it shut.

Multiple fingers pulling at my eyes. Nose bobbing above the surface. Foot slipping. Hands mauling me. *Think. Adapt. Overcome. FIGHT.*

But I don't know if I can this time. *Goddess, somebody, anybody—help me.*

A pair of bright peach-pink eyes stare back at me from above. A rush of adrenaline surges through me, a warmth that takes me by surprise. My entire body slackens as the clamping fingers and far-reaching grips release, some of them scattering to attack the peach-eyed creature too. Whatever it is, these armless hands want it bad.

The reduction of weight gives me time to counter. I bite the hand clamped around my mouth again as hard as I can. With a satisfying squelch, it slithers away into the murk along with the others I kick and fling away. I sputter, hack up phlegm, and flounder for the edge.

A gush of swamp water carries with me, washing over the floor of the Hallway. The Door to swamp land slams shut behind me. I steady my breathing. Clutching my chest, I catch the peach-pink eyes staring at me with a familiarity that I can't place. Into focus comes a giant, graceless bird with feathers of soft coral and red undertones in its defined plumes. Its glittering eyes grow wide. It spreads out wall to wall, a spiral etched under its gentle wings.

"You're a tutelary." I keel over and cough up more swamp water.

I clear my throat. Keeping my eyes on the bird, I sit up and adjust my sopping-wet backpack. *A tutelary saved me?*

I think of the vampire Dash and I paid a visit to not long ago. Tutelaries protect the souls they are bound to. But I am bound to nothing. Not that I know of. This tutelary can't be mine, yet it helped me.

The great bird squawks and disappears in a puff of glittering dust. I sit there on the ground until its echoing purrs also fade away.

My pack is soaked, but I'm happy to still have it. Given that my digiband, glowbeam, and breather are long gone. I stand. An ache resonates in my knees. Shivers run the length of my spine. *Holy hell,* I almost died. But I'm okay. I'm alive.

I put my hands on my hips and allow myself a couple of deeper breaths in and out. It was definitely a brass handle. *You're an idiot for second-guessing yourself.*

The Door with the brass handle reveals a wasteland lit by a bright waxing gibbous moon. The soft glow of an old mausoleum flickers on the horizon, giving me the feeling of validation that this is where I need to be to track Dash down. Clusters of osseous arboreous lead the way, which are trees that take on the appearance of skeletons after they molt in the Shedding—a phenomenon that happens on multiple planets, in multiple realms.

They rid their skin and pump vitamin-rich blood into the ground to nourish the frozen soil, so when it thaws in spring, it's fruitful. By the looks of it, the osseous arboreous are in the middle of the Shedding. Which means it's late autumn.

Looks like I'll be facing the chill after all.

8

Dash

I'm a dead man. No. I'm deader than a dead man.

The massive, bulbous-eyed creature lets out another shrieking roar that burrows deep inside me, deeper than my soul sucker. Sticky saliva splatters my cheeks. My torchlight goes out, wafting smoke up my nose.

Heinous Hades. What am I still doing here?

I ditch the useless torch, spin on my heels, and bolt in the other direction. Huffing stale air, a pit in my chest. Past the cell block where Effs and I had our meet-cute, full speed toward whatever else is down here—I really don't know where I'm going, but anywhere is better than into the belly of a beast with two bobblehead eyes.

The creature's massive paws pummel the textured stone beneath me, and the entire corridor shakes. I let out a scream, praying I see the light. Anything that'll let me know I'm in the clear.

Around the next corner, I pick up my pace, the stinging air in my throat turning into a raw burn. *Please don't be a dead end. Please don't be a dead end. Please don't be a dead end.* Is that a glow? Up ahead? Maybe it's a way out.

Behind me, the creature continues to shriek, spit slicking the back of my neck. I burst into another corridor, this time bigger, a torch fixed in all its darkest corners.

No, wait—*it's a crypt room.*

The creature bulls its way behind me, sure to catch up in seconds.

I scan the space, my eyeballs catching the dry burn too. A wall of tomb compartments. Dried bouquets of bone flowers with frayed black ribbon. Broken stone slabs. Stacks of rotting wood. Rusted shackles bolted to the wall. No exit.

Giant sarcophagus center stage it is.

I fumble for the edge. Pry my fingers against the seal. It jiggles but doesn't budge. The creature's howls grow near. My pulse races. I've never felt my heart beat so fast before. I throw my body forward to push aside the sarcophagus's outer cover.

It's not enough. I won't fit.

Hot air grazes my back, followed by a snarl.

It's right behind me. Gods, it's right behind me.

My fingers curl, rigid and frozen. I can't turn around. I'd rather it eats me alive from behind. Preferably in one bite. An uncontrollable shake takes over my body as the creature's snout prods my back, sniffing its next meal—*me.*

I blink wildly. A single tear streaks down my face, and I brace myself for the sensation of being ripped limb from limb. I mean, hey, maybe it'll be a painless death. After watching Roger and seeing my intended future, this may be a blessing in disguise.

A glass flask hits the wall to my right and shatters. Slivers shower me, cutting into my clothes. I shield my eyes. A bit grazes my cheek, and I gasp. The creature howls, retreating from where I stand, and I turn as an entire set of glass test tubes whirls through the air.

It bursts at my feet. *Effs.* She hurls another beaker, juggling the remaining heap in her hands. As it explodes above the creature, the beast cowers and backs into the corner. Its hair spikes the length of its back. Foam seeps from its jaw. With each loud shatter, it covers its head with its paws.

"You came back!" I cry out, sprinting to her.

She hands me a beaker. "Forgive me, Dash. I saw an opportunity to escape and took it. But when I heard the viscus inside the mausoleum behind me, I couldn't leave without at least warning you!"

She hurls another rounded flask, littering the stone floor with more glass. "They have sensitive eardrums. They don't like sharp noises!"

"Gotcha!" I toss the flask. The sound makes the viscus roar.

The tension in my body deflates. Thank the Gods for strong and capable women. This is what Shea would have done if she were here.

Effs zings a petri dish above the viscus's head like a saucer. The viscus flops on its belly. After another yell, it claws at the floor, filling the air with its scratching and whimpers.

Then its body stiffens, a low-gutted snarl replacing its cries.

I hold out a hand to Effs. "Another beaker. I'll give us a head start outta here."

With wide eyes, she backs against the wall, feeling for the opening into the neighboring corridor. "I've run out of things to throw, I'm afraid."

Well, shoot.

The roar that envelops the viscus's body next beats any Skyway warning siren I've ever heard. Before I know it, Effs and I are racing the way we came, the endless dark labyrinth of corridors sucking us in. She tugs me to the left. We clamor into a stairwell. Behind us, the viscus claws at the walls, eager to swallow us whole for what we've done to it.

Up the stairs. Through the door, into Fake Death's makeshift lab. Effs swings the door shut, and together we put our backs against it, doing our best to keep it closed. But the latch is busted, and there's no outrunning this thing. Not even with my natural-born agility. And that's saying something.

The first slam almost sends us forward, but we hold our ground. Dig our heels into stone. Backs and heads pressed against each other and the wooden frame, which threatens to snap at any moment under the viscus's weight.

I grit my teeth, riding out another push. "There's gotta be something."

"It must have devoured the soul suckers," she says, glancing at the tank behind the altar, now shattered and empty. "Otherwise, I'd say we could distract it that way, lure it in with bait, maybe lock it in a cell downstairs."

"You mean kill it."

"We cannot kill it." She closes her eyes and rests her head back against the bobbing door, which is slowly wearing away from the scratching behind it. "Life is sacred on Ominous. Not to mention, souls are sacred. We kill it, and we waste it. It is a *last* resort."

I blink at her. "I think this IS a last resort, Effs!"

She shakes her head. "We can make a run for it."

"It'll find us in the woods in no time!"

The viscus rams the door. I groan, shifting my shoulder against the strongest bit of the frame. I don't know how much longer we've got here. If Shea were here, she'd have a plan. She'd figure out a way to—who am I kidding? She'd chop its head off and call it a day. I don't want to seem like a useless scaredy-cat right now, but...

"Can't we make the soul count?" I brace my feet against the floor. "Something—please, Effs. Please!"

"Ominous is still recovering from the Great War." She looks around the lab as if an army of ISR agents will infiltrate the mausoleum, glowbeams blazing, and save our skins. *If only.* "Life must be preserved. Taking its life is NOT an option."

She isn't making any sense. "And us suffering an indescribable death is?"

The viscus hisses. It heaves with every ounce of its being. I feel myself slipping. Before I know it, I'm on the ground. The door splinters around us. The viscus shakes its coat, ridding itself of the fallout. As it arches its back and opens its jaw to tear us apart, I grab Effs and shield her, hugging her as close as possible.

She buries her face into my shoulder. My eyes go wide.

Then a straight-up sword catapults through the viscus's chest.

Effs's hold on me tightens. The whole-body-shaking sensation finds me again. As the viscus staggers, the sword unsticks. It collapses in a heap, revealing my big sister, Shea-Lynn, standing behind it. A now bloodied sword dangles in her left hand. She lets out a heavy breath, her cheeks deepening their flush. Water drips from her clothes, creating a small circle around her. Dirt residue makes a matted mess of her hair.

I can't tell if I'm dead or if this is real. Either way, my sister continues to surprise me.

Shea opens her mouth to speak, but as the viscus stirs, she stops. It opens its jaw and allows a white wisp of energy to exit its body. Effs untangles herself from me, crawls over the stone-littered floor, and falls to her knees before the beast.

She reaches out, feeling the last bits of the soul before it disintegrates into thin air. The golden hue in her eyes deepens as if acknowledging a higher power's presence, but soon after, they settle a lackluster gold once again.

"You—you just—" Effs stammers.

"Saved your damn life," Shea snaps, letting the sword fall.

It clinks the ground. I spring up off the floor.

"Shea-Lynn!" I cry, throwing myself in her arms. "I thought I'd never see you again!"

Normally, when I try to show Shea any physical affection, she pries me off her like the sand leeches that stick to our legs when we swim in the ocean at Spinners Pier, but to my surprise, she accepts my embrace. Her arms go slack. She *hugs* me back.

"I was worried about you," she says near my ear, muffled by my neck. "We didn't leave on the greatest of terms—"

"I know, I know. I agree."

"What did it ever do to you?" Effs asks.

Shea untethers herself from me, her eyebrows quirked high. "Excuse me?"

I've only known Effs a short while, but her current expression is new. More hardened. "The viscus. The creature you just ruthlessly slaughtered. Whose soul you so carelessly wasted."

Shea looks at me, then back to her. "I'm sorry—who are you exactly? And why are you not thanking me for saving your ass? It was going to devour you both. I had no choice."

Effs purses her lips. "You always have a choice."

My sister scoffs and lets out a laugh. Gives me a look as if to say, *is she for real right now?*

I shudder. The last time she gave me that look, she cut off a pair of bloodsucker thumbs and shoved them into her vest pocket like a couple of Fizzies' infamous jelly-belly beans.

And if Shea wasn't already annoyed enough, Effs turns and re-joins the dead viscus on the floor, not before muttering, "It was unnecessarily barbaric. As if we didn't have enough collective karma to deal with already," under her breath.

Shea picks up the sword. *Oh my Gods.*

"Sheaaa!" I pull her back, tug the sword away, and toss it across Fake Death's lab. It lands next to what's left of Roger, and I cringe, remembering that not only do I have to break the news to Shea that I've lost her key, but I'm a ticking time bomb too.

"What Effs means to say is... we're happy you saved our lives, but unfortunately, on her planet, lives and souls are sacred. That's it, really. You've only offended her a bit. She's thankful, though, right?"

Effs turns a cheek. "No, I am not thankful."

"I've had enough of this." Shea glares at Effs. "I don't need to know why she's here, or why you're here, or what the beast was doing here. Since I left Sarasing, I have been through hell and back. All I want is to call a Door and get us home. So, Dash. Key. Now."

She holds out her hand. I wring my hands.

Oh, this is NOT good.

"Dashiel," Shea repeats, cupping her palm. "Give me my key."

"Well... so ... we can't leave..." I run a hand through my hair and sneak a peek at Effs, but she's hunched over the viscus.

"What?"

"Dad sent me here to steal a soul-sucking worm, and as I was leaving," the words come out in a rush, "it latchedontomeand-nowI'mgoingtodielikeRoger!"

Shea drops her hand. "I was right then. It *was* a pickup."

She knew? "How'd you—"

"I figured it out." She places her hands on her hips. "Did you really think I wouldn't? You should have told me. I deserved to know."

"I couldn't tell you! Dad told me if I told you, he'd make our lives a *living hell*."

Shea rolls her eyes. "As if. He would never say that."

"Yes! Yes, he did. He said it to me before I left."

I can't believe I'm telling her this, but it beats telling her I lost her portal key. That, and she seems to be taking it oddly well. Almost *too* well. Also, did she miss the part of my confession where I mentioned that there's a soul-sucking WORM devouring my soul right now?

She stares off for a moment and shakes her head. "Honestly, Dash, I don't even know what to believe anymore when it comes to you. You want to know how I got here? I had to ask Aunt Merik for help. Apparently, you've been visiting her. You didn't tell me that either."

"You never asked!"

"All those times you told me you were going to the arcade, you were sneaking off to the Residential District to play Holoblocks and eat homemade granola bars."

Oh, for Goddess' sake. Now is not the time for this.

Effs clears her throat. "Excuse me."

We both look at her. A viscus leg under each arm, she waits patiently for us to let her by. I gawk. Shea jerks me aside to let her through. We watch her drag the beast's body across the floor, a smear of a blood trail behind her. She kicks open the double doors of the mausoleum, letting in the sunrise. Soft, pink light streams in and settles dust particles in the air.

As the last bits of the viscus and Effs disappear out the door, I realize I'm not ready to say goodbye. Not yet. We've only just met. "Whoa. Wait up. Effs!"

"No. Stay here!" Shea tries grabbing hold of me, but I shake her loose and bolt out the door. "You've got to be kidding me... Dashiel!"

In the promise of daylight, the mausoleum is much bigger than I'd originally thought. Set smack dab in the middle of a garden that I imagine might have once been in full bloom with plush flesh flowers and an abundance of other plants.

I follow the blood smear trail through the thickest part of the wood, around the backside of the mausoleum, and down a small hill, where a cemetery sits cozily within the boundary of an antiqued wrought-iron fence. Beneath a fully shed carnage tree rests the viscus's body. Kneeling before it, Effs.

The gate pushes open with a creak. I enter with gentle steps, careful not to step on any crumbled graves and other nameless stones that line the path to the center tree, and follow a path that splits around a listing stone fountain that sits empty in the center of the garden. I reach Effs in time to hear her hum a song under her breath. Eyes closed, she holds a firm grip on the creature's blood-matted fur. Around them, a bed of skeleton flowers with twisted petals and delicate bone stems rattle in the wind.

A swell of emotion climbs the back of my throat. "Is it bad that a scene that should be absolutely horrific is oddly beautiful?"

At first, Effs doesn't answer. She leans forward and kisses the beast, shuts its eyes with the simple flutter of her fingers, and rises.

She glances back at me. "Perhaps it is as bad as me thinking your sister is a goddess-like force to be reckoned with, but she has yet to understand the difference between standing in her power and asserting her dominance to instill fear in those she wishes to control."

I've never heard anyone speak about Shea like that. I'm not even sure I understand what it means. I'm realizing I don't understand a lot of what Effs says. Or does. Or believes, even. And how do I win over a girl who I'm not sure I agree with?

My sister saved us. If she hadn't stepped in and speared that viscus like a Tee Tee's Squid Kebab, we'd be frothing inside its gut right now. Would Effs truly have chosen death instead? Then again, she was willing to give up completely not too long ago. I don't understand that either. But I can tell this creature—life in general—matters to Effs.

I don't want her to think I *don't* care, but I also don't want Shea to think I care too much.

I can't win. "I'm sorry, Effs."

"You have nothing to apologize for," she says, hiking up her dress to avoid catching on the jagged tombstones in her path. "Besides, what's done is done. We can't go back. We can't change the past. All we can do now is part ways before Valerian—Fake Death—returns."

"Who said anything about parting ways? We still have to convince Fake Death to give us the cure and Shea's key. And what about the... Higher Realm... twin soul drama... "

"I will figure it out, but *our* story ends here. You need to go with your sister back to your home planet so you don't become further involved in this. Trust me. It's for the best. If Valerian's cure came from your planet, then surely there's more of it there."

What? *No*. Come on.

"There's one problem in your plan to send us away," I say as I follow her to the uprooted fountain. She fluffs out her skirt and catches me staring at her, but I don't look away. "We have to go with you to Crowley Corner. Fake Death has my sister's portal key. We can't go home without it. Looks like you're stuck with us after all. Looks like our story's just begun."

As she closes the gap between us, my heart thumps in my chest. "Oh, Dashiel James. You are a hopeless romantic, aren't you? That is something I admire about you. I hope you hold onto that as long as you can. I was the same many lifetimes ago, but after enduring endless cycles, I've learned that not every story has a happy ending. Not the way you think it does."

"I like being a hopeless romantic."

I reach up and tuck a loose tress of her hair behind her ear. She slaps my hand away away. At first, I laugh, then my expression falls. The darkening spider veins on her neck have gotten thicker since the last time I saw them. "You're getting worse."

We're so close, her nose nearly brushes mine. "We will both continue to get worse."

Ahead, Shea enters the garden out of breath. Effs distances herself once again, and I feel the pull of her warmth go with her. It takes everything in me not to tug her back.

It's funny. I meet some people, and I usually feel like I'm trying endlessly to make them see or understand me. It doesn't feel that way with Effs. With her, it's like knowing an old friend. I can be myself. She doesn't know me, but at the same time, it's like she does.

Shea huffs. "Stop running away from me when we're talking. This is serious. I'm done playing games. We can finish discussing all this at home. Give me my key right now."

Maybe we *should* have let the viscus tear us limb from limb.

I force myself to look at my sister. "I don't have it. Fake Death took your key and made me one of his hosts for his soul-sucking worms—I'm sorry, made *us* his hosts." I wave my hand between me and Effs. "He's the only one that can fix us, and finding him is the only way we'll be able to get home."

Shea closes her eyes. I can tell she's fighting the urge to knock my lights out. Which would be counterproductive to what she said earlier, which was that she saved my life. And because Shea is a woman of logic and tact, I can at least bank on the fact that she won't excessively lose her cool. Then again, I've lied to her repeatedly. I'm one of the reasons she's here on this horror planet. I say one because Dad is truly the epicenter of this fiasco.

Look at where he's gotten us. Look at what he's done to her, to ME. This isn't *my* fault. This is Dad's fault. Why aren't we talking about that? Why haven't we both hung up our glowbeams and exited stage left by now?

"I think she's broken," Effs says, referring to Shea's deadpan.

I kick some loose bone out of the path. "Nah, she's thinking."

Shea blinks. "That key was our only way out of here."

"At least we know where it is, right?" I say.

"We certainly don't know where it is," Shea snaps back. "Do you have any idea what you've done? Are you—could you really be that moronic?"

Whoa. "That's a little harsh. I've been dealing with a lot here too."

"There's a whole fleet of ISR agents and a member of the Board of Galactic Studies waiting for us back at Headquarters. We can't *do* this right now. We can't be stuck here."

A member of the Board? ISR? What in the galaxies is she talking about?

"We won't be stuck here forever, sis. We can get it back."

I move to hug her, but she immediately resists.

"Don't touch me," she bites.

I step back. "I was trying to help!"

"I think you've done enough."

Heat rushes into my face. "All you care about is the key. What about the worm currently feasting on my soul? Huh? The key we can get back. My soul? Probably not."

Shea lets out a half-hearted laugh. "Oh, I didn't forget about the worm." She bends down and unsheathes her blade from the damp inside cuff of her boot. "Show me where it is. I'll cut it out of you, and we'll get that taken care of, no problem. See? I do care about your soul."

"NO!" Effs throws herself between us. "You cannot kill the worm."

Shea scoffs. "What is it with you and preserving the deadliest of creatures?"

"What is it with *you* and so quickly judging them as deadly before truly understanding them and their purpose here on this planet?" Effs's retort seemed to shut Shea up, which is rare.

Then again, there is nothing common about Effs.

And I've never seen my sister lose her cool like this. Lash out at others, sure thing. But this is about more than just a portal key. It has to be. Something is wrong. Something happened back at Headquarters. I'm not *that* oblivious. I know my sister better than she thinks.

Shea crosses her arms. "Fine. Enlighten me. Why can't I kill the worm?"

"My worm. Dash's worm. They're a part of us now."

"Oh, give me a break," Shea says. "I don't have time for this pacifist bullshit."

I clear my throat, which is now hoarse. "Will you just hear her out? She knows more about this planet and Fake Death than we do."

My sister rolls her eyes at me but keeps her mouth shut.

Effs relaxes her shoulders. "The worms embed themselves into the host's nervous system. They feed on the host's inner being. You kill the worm; you kill the host."

"A parasite. Fantastic." Shea tears off her pack, kneels, and rifles through its contents. "I'll just have to adapt. Evaluate. Form a hypothesis. Figure it out."

Don't say anything, Dash. Let her be self-righteous. Forget that she still hasn't asked you if you're okay or that moments ago, she was itching to gut you like a pucker fish.

"Is the parasite a magical construct or something that lives here on Ominous?" Shea flips through her journal, struggling to find a blank page. "I need to know how long we have."

Not how long we have. How long I have. I'm the one in danger here.

Effs acts like I don't see her hiding the fact that she wipes a bit of black blood from her nose on her sleeve, but I do. "Valerian created them. They must be magical constructs. We have as long as it takes for the suckers to finish feeding on our souls. Judging by Roger's untimely death earlier this morning, it takes less than a day. Though, Dash doesn't fit that timeframe. My magic delays my progress. I'm not sure what's keeping him alive."

"Don't know who Roger is. Don't care who Roger is. This Valerian guy, though." Shea stops, having come to the page in her journal where I wrote all those fun facts about Mees from planet Monsoon. She glares at me, at my scribbles, and the apples of her cheeks grow pink. "Are you kidding me, Dashiel? How many times have I told you to STAY out of my journal?"

"I... I thought you'd like it," I mutter.

"You've wasted a *whole* page." She tears the page, crumples it, and stuffs it into her pack. Eventually, she does find a blank one and smooths it out. "Alright. If the parasites are a magical construct, they won't operate entirely like other organisms. Though, we can make an educated guess. If embedded in your nervous system, it'll head for the brain first. From there, it'll work its way down your spine, and then it'll radiate out to the rest of your body. All while feeding on your soul."

Ugh. I don't wanna think about that.

"Any muscle spasms or headaches?" Shea asks.

"A minor headache. Occasional nose bleeds," Effs says.

Shea looks up. "I wasn't asking you. Dash? Headaches?"

I glance at Effs. "Uh, no. Not yet."

Shea jots the note in her journal. "What about convulsions?"

"No. None of those either."

"Great. Let me know if you start losing control of your motor functions, feeling an overwhelming sense of fear, or if your heart starts beating fast. The last thing I need is for you to go into cardiac arrest."

She tears away the edge of the page, folds the piece up, and slaps her journal shut. "In the meantime, I'm going to try to send a message to Headquarters."

My sister has this uncanny ability to make everything seem ten times scarier when she explains it in 'smart talk.' Convulsions? Vital function failure? Cardiac arrest?

I scratch the inflammation around my sucker wound, eyeing the veins that have begun to wrap around my arm beneath my skin. Where do webbed veins fit in? And black blood? Are those symptoms of living with a parasite too? Or are those just symptoms of being one with a soul sucker?

Maybe Effs is right. Maybe our story ends here.

"Hey, uh, Shea, you got to planet Ominous. Aunt Merik helped you, right? Can't we just go back the way you came? Save some time. Maybe head over to the Sicky Place on our way home?"

"Impossible." My sister pulls out a pink-haired troll doll from her pack next. As she unscrews its head, I realize it's a Gallivant—a tiny one. She shoves her rolled message inside the troll's head and seals the mechanism. "Now that we're here, Dad is our best contact."

"Sure he is." I shove my hands in my pockets. "We're *definitely* his priority."

"He is." Shea presses the pink jewel on the troll's belly and throws me a glare. "And he'll be pissed he had to take time out of his busy day to save our asses over a careless mistake."

The briskness comes too easy. "You mean he'll be pissed at you."

Shea's shoulders go rigid, as does her hold around the troll Gallivant. "Don't worry, Dashiel. I'm used to taking the blame for your messes."

My messes? As if it was my fault I got sent here. As if it was my fault some twin soul spellcaster and his soul-sucking worms got the best of me. "I did what I was told to do. You're just mad Dad sent me instead of you."

Effs leans forward between us. "I believe your strange little doll is smoking."

Shea tips the Gallivant upside down, a spark spurting from its neon-pink tuft of hair. The smell of burnt plastic hits my nostrils. I scrunch my nose. Shea unscrews the head and lets it fall at her feet while she examines the inside, which is charred. She removes the message meant for Dad, now blackened, and it crumbles to dust in her palm.

"It's waterlogged," she mutters. "Lousy first-generation prototype. I'll have to dry it out. It should work after that."

"Great," I say. "Guess that'll be my fault too."

Shea shoots me another glare. Then she stuffs the troll Gallivant into her pocket and slings her pack over her shoulder. "Until the Gallivant is dry, we can't contact anyone. Our best bet is to find Valerian Bale. If he's got my key and the cure for the suckers, he's our ticket out of here. Where would he have gone? Where can I find him?"

I realize now she's talking to Effs, a subtle yearning in her voice because Shea actually knows, like I do, just how valuable Effs is here.

We don't deserve the kindness she's shown us, especially Shea, but she steps up to appease my sister anyway. "Like I told Dash, he's headed back to Crowley Corner to get ready for Festival, which takes place in three days—"

"Three days? I don't have that kind of time. We're leaving Ominous tonight." Shea starts walking. Where, I don't know. Unless she's got a map of Ominous plastered to the inside of her eyeballs, she's as clueless as the rest of us.

To my surprise, Effs keeps at her heels. "Even if you were to go to Crowley Corner, it would still take you two days on foot."

"Better than three."

"How will you get there?"

I catch up with them both at the garden's edge. They've stopped at the gate. Shea stares at Effs, giving her a solid look-over, maybe even a couple of look-overs. I can't tell if she's sizing her up, reading her, or potentially plotting her death.

"What's in it for you?" Shea finally speaks.

Effs raises a brow. "What do you mean?"

"You want to come with us, right? You know your knowledge of this planet and possibly the way to Crowley Corner is valuable. Which means I'm compelled to accept your guidance. Which also means you want something. And as kind and peace-loving as you may appear, there's got to be something in this for you."

"There is. Like Dash, I need a cure." Effs pulls at her collar, revealing a blackened web of veins that looks even worse in the growing daylight. I cringe. My sister doesn't even flinch. "I have unfinished business with Valerian. I want the same things as you do."

Shea holds her stance. "Unfinished business?"

Effs holds hers too. "Yes. I'm more than happy to fill you in on the way. The closest village is a day's walk from here. It's due North, through the thickest part of the wood. Not a straightforward route, given most of the osseous arboreous have begun to shed, but I can get us there."

Oh, Effs is good.

"You're either too excellent of a liar for me to pick up on, or you're telling the truth." Shea pushes through the garden gate. "Either way, I'll be keeping my eyes on you."

Effs nods. "I'd expect nothing less."

I clasp my palms together. Finally. Some rationality.

Shea lets out a long sigh before stepping aside, allowing Effs to take the lead. It's gotta be killing her to know she won't be heading up the front on this one, but part of me knows it's the best thing for us all.

As Effs walks on, Shea lingers back with me. "Congratulations. Another mess for me to clean up."

Heinous Hades. Really? We're *still* on this?

"I've refrained from asking you what your problem is." I keep in line with her. My fists feel like they weigh a ton at my side. "But there's no way we can make this trek if we're biting each other's heads off the whole time. Can we call a truce until we get back?"

"I'm done calling truces. All I do is pick up the slack, and I'm sick of it."

I cut her off, bringing us to a halt. "Nobody is asking you to save my soul. You're taking on that responsibility all on your own. I think you're overreacting about this whole thing. I told you I was sorry, but this wasn't my fault. Dad's the one that sent me here. Have a little empathy."

My sister, the grudge queen, hardens her gaze. "Get out of my way, or I'll make you."

I force a laugh. "You'll make me?"

"Does it look like I'm kidding?"

This isn't Shea. This isn't even quick-to-anger but cool off in a millisecond, Shea. Something happened to her. Something's wrong with her. And I hate that I care this much.

"I know your portal key was important, okay? I get I messed up, but did something else happen? Like with Dad or Mom? With ISR? Or what's this about the Board of Galactic Studies? I feel like there's something you're not telling me."

A deeper shade of pink fills Shea's cheeks. She holds back a bated breath. For a moment, it looks like she might actually tell me. Right here. Right now. We might actually get somewhere and express ourselves together. But she doesn't.

Instead, she says, "This isn't about one thing. You're missing the point. Now move."

It's not worth it, Dash. Let her cool off. She'll get over it soon enough and be her usual, level-headed self once again.

That's what we need right now. Not this. Not fighting. Not when I could keel over like Roger, snap in half, and become bone dust any minute.

"Fine, Shea. Okay. Whatever."

As Shea passes, she knocks into me. I glance ahead, where Effs is waiting for us between two carnage trees. She's given us space, but part of me wants to tell her to run from us while she can. If she thinks she and Fake Death have issues, she hasn't met *us* yet.

Effs makes a motion to me, but Shea waves her onward as if saying, *hell with him—let's go*. I grind my teeth so hard my skull aches. I hate that I always cave. *I hate it. I hate it. I hate it.*

Mouth off to Dad all day? No problem. But there's something about my sister, something inside her I can't match. Never have been able to. Maybe it's her training. Maybe it's Dad's influence—I dunno. Maybe I'm just not as okay with throwing away years of friendship and siblingship over one stupid argument.

Maybe, just maybe, I'm realizing how much it says about her that she is.

9

SHEA

I'm still steaming as we push ahead. Euphoria and Dash walk near enough but talk quietly. Red dust lingers in the air, like bits of floating pollen and smelling faintly of rotting flesh. I barely notice. I'm not sure who I'm angrier with. My brother or myself.

The osseous arboreous trees sway around us. Half of them are draped in thick, sagging gray skin. Others stand taught and bare-boned. As the crimson sun rises, those with skin ooze a pigmented oil that slicks the ground beneath our feet. Occasionally a tree will spurt blood, and I avoid it like I avoid the laundry bot that cleans Dash's dirty socks on Laundering Day.

Euphoria's taken us into the heart of the slough as promised. And after hearing of her twin-soul tales and whatever else she and Dash gabbed on about after we left the mausoleum, there's no way in hell I trust her. I've studied past lives and reincarnation. That isn't the problem. The problem is that we're traveling with the former lover of the spellcaster who birthed a creation that now feeds on my brother's soul. Who's to say Euphoria isn't part of Valerian's master plan?

If he only wanted *her* soul, why would he go after my brother's soul too? For the sake of annoyance? Right place, wrong time?

There's more to this story. I'm not buying her 'wanting to remind Valerian of who he is so he can understand the Higher Realm' bit either. Valerian Bale knows who he is. He knows who she is. He knows what he wants.

You can't soul-shake a villain into submission.

Besides, I don't care about Euphoria's troubles. I agreed to let her tag along because said ex-lover has my key and the cure for my brother's condition. Everything else is irrelevant.

"I think you're in denial," Euphoria says, and I cast my gaze to the left, where she and Dash plod side by side along the viscera-strewn path. "I've never once received a love letter from a boy, and I don't know that I would find it that romantic."

Dash shakes his head. "Nah, see, it *is* romantic. It is very romantic."

"And do these people write you letters back?"

No, they don't. Not once. Never, I want to scream.

"Well... not really."

My brother runs a hand through his hair. I peek at the faint, black spider vein now showing beneath his skin. I'm not going to panic, that's the last thing I'm going to do, but it doesn't seem to be getting any better. At the mausoleum, I made it clear I was done with Dash's nonsense. Chiming in on this conversation would only disprove my state of annoyance. If that even makes any sense.

"But that doesn't mean someone won't someday," Dash continues. "Don't you think, Effs?"

Euphoria quirks a brow. "Actually, I think it's all a bit strange."

"*I* think we need to focus on the task at hand," I mutter.

It's taken every ounce of my inner being not to stop, journal, and study the flow of runoff or the osseous arboreous themselves since we set off a few hours ago. I'm missing prime research, my brother is a love-sick puppy dog, as per usual, and the spellcaster won't stop sneaking glances at me. Her eyes aren't daggers, she's too soft for that, but they are that streak of sunlight that threatens to blind you when a bit of glass catches the reflection just right. It's uncomfortable enough that her gaze makes my stomach twist every so often, but I'll be damned if I apologize for saving her life. I don't care what she says about the beast or this planet. There isn't anything she can do to make me feel bad.

Euphoria's eyes find me again, and I think of something else to say, so the pit in my stomach will stop gnawing at me. "How much longer to the village you mentioned? It's getting dark, and I want to ensure we get there before nightfall."

I've been keeping track of the sun since we left the mausoleum too. It rose as a reddish-brown blip above the horizon, giving the forever illusion of dawn, and now that we've been walking awhile, I don't think it'll rise any higher. It seems to do the opposite. Still light enough to see the tip of my boots but not bright enough to warm the chill out of my skin.

"Days are short on Ominous, but it'll stay light for a while," Euphoria says. "And we're about twelve miles from the village if I had to guess."

Dash groans. "Twelve miles? That's so far!"

"We've been in worse predicaments. You'll be fine," I say, without taking my eyes off the horizon, which seems to be a never-ending void of bleeding trees.

"Fine? Are you kidding?" My brother blinks at me, nearly knocking into a low-hanging skeletal branch. A chunk of skin flaps onto his shoulder. He quickly flicks it away. "We've never been in a situation like this before. This *is* the worst."

"Planet O'Brian. You lost your breather, swore to me you could hold your breath—you couldn't—and I had to swim your dead weight back to the Door with twenty Beta's on our tail, all of which were extremely pissed we'd stolen their ruler's crown. *That* was worse than this."

"I don't remember that at all."

"My point exactly."

I wait for him to counter, but he doesn't. *Smart move, little brother.* I have an entire journal section worth of experiences where I've risked my life for him. Twenty-five percent of which he wouldn't remember anyway. Seventy-five percent of which he'd claim were terrifying regardless of the circumstance.

I've always been in control of my brother's safety. I've always been able to save him with my smarts and strength. I've always had the weapons to cut him loose or the gadgets to set him free, but this is a soul-sucking worm. This won't be as simple. There is an infinitesimal chance I might not be able to save him this time, but I don't want to think about that yet. I don't want to limit myself or doubt my capabilities. I was trained for much worse, and I will figure this out too.

I *will* save my brother.

I tug at my vest, still damp and heavy on my shoulders. Another harsh truth—I'll need to find a change of clothes if I'm going to survive. We all will. Without my glowbeam, I'm unarmed. Without my digiband and with a waterlogged Gallivant, I can't contact Headquarters.

We're vulnerable out here. Not a situation I want to be in.

"Did you at least bring snacks?" Dash asks.

Of course he'd ask something like this at a time like this. "But of course. Because your stomach was the first thing I thought about as I left home to find you."

Euphoria tries to hide her smirk, but I catch it anyway. I roll my eyes. One minute I'm a viscus-slaying brute. The next I'm a late-night comedy show. Dash, however, maintains a scowl and refrains from making any more comments about his stomach.

But I can't stand wasting time, so I pull out my travel journal and an ink stick from the side pocket of my pack. If I can't document the geographical details, I can at least gather more intel on why Dad might've thought Valerian's creations could cure Mom. Or why he was intentionally willing to sacrifice his son to get one.

No, Shea. Dad wouldn't do something like that.

I click my ink stick. "So, Euphoria, is there anything else Valerian might use the soul sucker's for besides attempting to consume your soul?"

"Here we go with the journal interrogations," Dash says with mock annoyance.

Ignore him, Shea-Lynn. "Maybe he wants to consume *all* the souls."

Euphoria chuckles grimly as she steps over a half-shed trunk leaking pus. “No, I’m afraid not. Valerian might be stubborn, but he isn’t diabolical. He has been working on these creatures for years. I suspect a few innocent lives were lost in his trials. This really is about the two of us.”

All this because the guy wants to get into the Higher Realm? Really?

I’ve never heard of that realm before, and I’ve studied almost all of them. They taught us about the five major realms at the Academy. Though, humans have only ever fully explored the first three. Dash even came up with a song to help him remember.

First Realm. Second Realm. Third Realm. Realm of Souls. Realm of Time.

The Realm of Shadows is in the secondary tier along with thousands of others.

“Are we even sure the Higher Realm exists?” I ask. "I would have read about it."

Dash scoffs. “I’m surprised your internal hard drive hasn’t surpassed its max capacity. Since you know sooo much more than the rest of us.”

“Says the boy whose tablet hard drive is clogged up with unfinished scripts and literary poems that might never see the light of day.”

“You have no idea how hard I work on those scripts.” Now Dash’s voice is a clatter of noise that blurs into the back of my brain. “At least I’ll submit them someday. You’ve got loads of written work that’ll never go anywhere.”

“Oh, you write too?” Euphoria asks.

I slam my journal shut. “He writes gushy plays.”

“Not Dash, you.” Her gaze finds mine unexpectedly. *Gods, her eyes are familiar.* Almost uncomfortably so. They search me a moment more like Nadine’s do every time I come to pick up Mom’s medicine. It warrants the familiar twist in my chest that

I loathe. "Though I'd be happy to hear a poem or read one of Dash's plays sometime."

"I write... research. That's it. I'm not sure what it has to do with anything."

"Actually, I find it really interesting. Valerian's mother was a liaison and scribe for inter-realm communications. She had one of those stickers too."

Euphoria motions to the faded Board of Galactic Studies sticker adorned with a parchment map and a golden compass stuck to the cover of my journal. I picked it up at an occupation fair when I was six. Now half-peeling and nearly colorless, it's seen better days, but I refuse to get rid of it.

"You mentioned the Board of Galactic Studies back at the mausoleum. Do you work for them too?"

Dash clears his throat. "Shea *wishes* she was a member of the Board."

"Enough," I say to him without making eye contact.

He mutters something crude under his breath about my job.

I let it roll off my back. "I have a hard time believing Valerian's mother was a scribe for inter-realm communications. There's barely anything written about Ominous anywhere, aside from a book I found in an Enchantress shop."

Euphoria hops over the cracks in the path. "Sadly, most of what his mother intended on submitting was lost in the Great War. A war Valerian and I started over three lifetimes ago. We'd incarnated as sisters. Grew up ruling opposing covens. We fought endlessly over land. Neither of us won, and both of us perished in battle. The war may be over in this lifetime, but Ominous is still recovering. I fear it won't fully recover until Valerian and I master this life lesson."

Dash lifts his head. "Wow. You must be sick of this planet by now."

Euphoria smiles. "Not really. Bits of past lives come to me in visions and dreams as I get older. I remember parts of myself. Each life is different enough that it's still an adventure. Sometimes I even run into other versions of myself, which helps fill in the gaps too."

"Other versions of yourself?" Dash asks.

Maybe it's because I've refused to participate in this conversation, but Euphoria's eyes wander toward me as she replies, "Yes. On more than one occasion, I've run into another version of myself from another lifetime. Time isn't linear. Everything is happening all at once."

I could verify her claims by bringing up a multitude of research I've done on the multiverse, but I choose to keep my mouth shut. I'm not here to make friends. I'm here to save my brother, and I don't care to learn a lick about Euphoria. I want nothing to do with her. I just want my portal key and the cure for the parasite.

"I think we should stick to the task at hand," I say again, and Euphoria grabs my arm without warning.

We halt. My body tenses. Dash knocks into me but quickly finds his balance too.

He finds a stump of bone to sit on. "Finally. A break. My feet are numb."

"Not quite." Euphoria points one step in front of my boots, where a sizzling liquid runs along the hill. I watch it hit a heap of bone and eat away at it until there's nothing left. "Acid stream. Depending on the tree type, it drains from the core of some osseous arboreous once they've shed. Another inch and you'd have lost your foot."

I lift my gaze, finding hers. Her grip on me softens. Again, the feathered gold of her irises search my face for a response, glinting in the small ray of red sun that peaks through the graying clouds. I don't give her one. My heartbeat, however, skyrockets. *Nerves.* Not sure why. Nothing is intimidating about her.

Euphoria is alluring. I'll give her that. Interesting. Cunning, for sure. Maybe even... beautiful. But the darkest of beings can appear beautiful.

"I know I'm supposed to keep my mouth shut... " I cling to Dash's words and let them lure me back to reality. "But are we going to go right or left here at the fork in the path?"

I glance over my shoulder, then follow his outstretched hand to an off-centered wooden sign stuck in the ground. Beyond it is a path that splits in opposite directions.

"Uh, well... " I wipe my sweaty hands on my pants and distance myself from Euphoria. There's something off about her. And I've decided I don't like it. Still, she knows the way, and therefore I'm obligated to put some trust in her. Emphasis on *some*. "Which way is best?"

"The Bone Bridge is to the right. If it hasn't shed, it'll cut hours off our trek. The path leads into Specters Village. Left will take us the long way toward Lake Ichor. We'd have to go through the heaviest bit of the Shedding."

Dash cringes. "Neither way sounds promising."

"The shorter route does." I veer onto the path that curves right, straight up a slope. "It's the smartest option. We shouldn't waste unnecessary time."

Euphoria falls into pace with me again. "As long as the bridge is safe."

Dash springs up from his bone stump and jogs to catch up with us, maintaining a steady tread at my other side. "Why wouldn't it be safe?"

I roll my eyes. "It'll be safe."

"Not necessarily," Euphoria says. "If the bridge has already shed, then it's nothing but bone. If it's nothing but bone, nothing is tethering it to the ravine."

I press my lips in a line. "I'm sure it'll be fine."

"Gods, not another ravine," Dash says. "And does *everything* shed here? Geeze."

Euphoria chuckles. "Everything in the Bone Wood, yes. Even the inhabitants."

She hikes up her skirt to avoid a puddle of bubbling goop. A bit sizzles the leather of her boots, and she wipes her soles on a clean patch of dirt. I go around the goop, hobbling to avoid an uneven stretch of ground and a faceplant. Dash's long legs give him the advantage neither of us has, and he steps over it completely.

Ugh. I can't help it. I have to know... "What do you mean by even the inhabitants?"

Dash throws me that look he always gives me when my nerdy side gets the best of me, and I avoid his gaze altogether. The last thing I need is for him to use my weaknesses against me.

And yes, the uncanny knack for constant knowledge *can* be a weakness sometimes. Especially when it means admitting intrigue or indulging in someone like Euphoria to feed me bits of information I don't already know.

"It's quite simple, really." She lets her dress fall at her side once more. As she smooths out the ruffles, she adds, "Like the osseous arboreous, the inhabitants grow a new inner and outer body layer come spring. There's a rebirth ceremony, a tradition as old as Ominous itself. It's a magnificent celebration, a chance to start over and become someone new."

A bitter taste coats the back of my throat. It's in the air. There's no escaping it.

"It sounds poetic," Dash says.

Euphoria nods. "It kind of is, I guess. For them, every cycle is a new beginning. That's what makes these woods so sacred."

"Everything is sacred, apparently," I mutter.

Euphoria murmurs back, "Indeed it is."

My cheeks warm. She skids in a stream of entrails flowing down the path's slope. They squelch beneath her wedged heels, and I swallow a mix of stomach acid and saliva. I think of the viscus back at the mausoleum. How Euphoria fell to her knees before the creature, savoring the silvery wisps of life that rose from its body.

If life is really that sacred, how can she talk about her past lives, riddled with violence and death, with such vigor? If life is so sacred, how can Valerian justify his creations or wanting to consume her soul? Surely, it's an act. Life isn't actually sacred to her. Or to him.

"I think I see the bridge," Dash announces, walking ahead.

Euphoria slows, lingering with me. I stare at her side profile. She can tell me more. Much more. Everything I need to know. In that, I can piece together how it all relates to Dad and Mom. Because I don't have enough information yet. I need more. I crave it.

A tiny flutter races through me at the thought. I know I'm not applying to the Board's fellowship, but I'll admit I indulge in the idea of this entire planet being a spectacular entry. Of Euphoria and her many lifetimes being a spectacular entry. Again, if this were any other circumstance and my brother's life wasn't on the line, of course.

Ahead, Dash's voice carries. "Hey, you two! You're gonna wanna see this!"

"Famous last words," I say.

"Never a good sign," Euphoria says back.

I glance at her again. She walks on. She's done that a few times now. I think I'm talking to myself or commenting for the sake of it, but she's listening. She's always listening.

I slide my journal into my inner vest pocket. A stale fog coats the air. It tickles my throat, making me cough. My lungs tighten as I join Dash and Euphoria at the drop-off's edge.

"Another canyon," Dash says. "As if I wasn't traumatized by the last one."

The canyon isn't even a thought compared to what lies between it. A massive spine sits splayed across the gorge. Twists of porous vertebrae connected by thick cartilage discs. Anchored by fibrous bands, ligaments ride each side like a rail. The entire structure rattles in a gust of wind, and the few strings of muscle stretch, further bowing the center.

Euphoria lets out a sigh. "It's a shame it's already begun to shed. It would've knocked about an hour off our walk. We could've made it to Specters Village before dark."

Dash leans over the edge, grimacing at the long distance from here to the ground. I try not to stare at the spider veins decorating the curve of his neck, but it's hard not to. "Agreed. I vote to go back and take the long way around."

And waste *more* time? He might not even have that amount of time.

"It'll be stable enough to cross," I say.

Dash groans. "This is *not* safe. It's not worth an hour's walk!"

This time, Euphoria glances over the edge, then across the gorge where the ligaments strain and pull. "I have to agree with Dash on this one."

No. They might not think an hour or two is worth it, but I do. An hour could mean the difference between us getting to Crowley Corner in time to convince Valerian to cure my brother and prevent Dash from losing his soul or going into cardiac arrest before I even have the chance to help him.

I approach the bridge and run a hand along the smooth ligament secured to the end bone that anchors it to the ravine. The thick, intertwined chords and elastic fibers have dried out, but they'll hold. They have to. "If we stagger our positions, it should handle our weight."

Euphoria stares off, possibly mulling things over in her mind, but I don't need her permission or mutual agreement. We're crossing here. I've decided. It's final.

Dash swallows hard. "Let me guess. I have to go first?"

"No. Euphoria can go first," I say.

If this were any other situation, I'd never risk this. In Biology, we learned that the average ligament can endure between 12 to 15% maximum strain in the human body. It would take time to calculate the capacity of an entire spine bridge or the capacity of ligaments that are a day away from deteriorating altogether. Time we don't have. Time my brother doesn't have. And he might be the ultimate piss-off right now, but I won't risk his life when I can risk hers instead.

He's still my priority. In case this *is* a mistake.

"You don't have to go first," Dash tells Euphoria.

Her eyebrows knit together. "It's okay. I get it."

My brother shakes his head. "Shea, why don't you go first? Huh? If you think it's soooo safe, you walk across the bridge and lead us to the other side."

I cross my arms. "Euphoria will go. She doesn't mind."

"How can you even—"

Euphoria cuts him off with the touch of her hand to his arm. "It's alright, Dash. I'll go."

I ignore my brother's death glare and maintain a firm stance. Euphoria approaches the first vertebrae plank. She dangles a foot, tests the sturdiness of the plank, and inches her way forward. The bridge groans beneath her weight. It sags, stretching the ligaments on either side, but it seems sturdy enough to hold.

A smile spreads across my face. Thank the Gods and Goddesses above.

"You're being a jerk," Dash says once Euphoria is three more planks in, and out of earshot. "She hasn't done anything to you. You didn't have to speak to her like that."

I keep my eyes on Euphoria, observing how she gracefully tests a plank closer to the sagging middle before fully committing to her step. She's slow but efficient, and I'll send Dash on his way once she passes the middle. His weight will balance hers and ease up ligament strain.

My brother waves a hand in my face. "Did you hear me? You're out of control."

"I'm doing my job," I say flatly. "Someone has to do it."

"Doing your—*Gods.* Can you just—I like her, okay?"

"How typical of you to fall for every person you meet."

"You know, you're really getting on my nerves."

"You've been getting on my nerves since you were born."

"Wow, Shea-Lynn. Just—WOW."

"Be thankful I didn't send you out there first," I say.

He scoffs. "Please. You wouldn't care if anything happened to me anyway."

I grit my teeth, the heat climbing my neck now ten times hotter than before. I don't mean to be cruel, but I can't help it sometimes. Dash pushes and pushes, and I can't let him win.

No way he gets the last word. "Watch it, Dashiel. That's all I'm going to say."

"Just because you threaten me doesn't mean I'm going to shut up." I glare at him this time, and to my surprise, he adds, "It's true, right? Because this isn't about me. This is about looking good for Dad. Heaven forbid you screw up for once in your life."

"YOU are the fucking screw-up, Dashiel! YOU will never be anything else!"

He's either going to shout something equally cruel back at me or he's going to walk away. There's really no in-between when it comes to my brother. And he might lie from time to time, but I know him better than he knows himself. I can almost guarantee it.

Silence tells me it's the latter, the easier option. *That's right, Dash. Walk away.* I hug tighter to myself, locking my stare on one particular hanging of skin that won't seem to drop off a nearby tree no matter how much the wind rattles it.

Dash is becoming braver. I'll give him that. For someone who doesn't love confrontation, he was dangerously close to taking part in an explosive one.

Another gust of wind washes over me. I force myself to look at the bridge, where Dash is probably waiting, slumped shoulders, for his turn to walk across. But my eyes immediately find Euphoria, still crossing the sagging middle.

Wait. Why is she waving her arms like that?

I redirect my gaze. Dash. Already on the bridge. Before he's supposed to be. Navigating vertebrae with thinning connective tissue. Every step puts more pressure on the bridge. The strings of fibers moments away from snapping in half.

I'd gotten so caught up in our bickering that I didn't even think to tell him. It's not going to hold them both. It can't.

Shit. Shit. Shit. "Dashiel! Stop moving! Wait for Eup—"

He cranes his neck, a scowl plastered on his flushed face.

The first ligament snaps. My stomach flips.

A larger strand on Euphoria's end is the next to go.

Her side of the bridge tilts. She's tossed aside but catches a bone plank before rolling over the edge. I rush forward. No idea why. An instant reflex, maybe? I know I'm not strong enough to hold the bridge on my own.

You've got to do better.

Euphoria tightens her hold. The last ligaments on her end split into two, sending the entire bridge swinging across the gap toward me. The structure slams against the canyon wall, dangling there like a flap of dead skin.

Everything happens at once. Dash screaming out my name. Euphoria telling him not to move.

My heart might explode, but panicking won't help me now.

I have to think. I have to plan. I have to—

You have to act fast.

I throw off my pack.

Ignore Dash's screams.

Focus on the task.

My hooks and recant box, a small aluminum cube containing a reinforced line system, solar-powered and at half charge, are in my hand in a matter of seconds. *It'll be enough.* I tear away my outer vest. One locking carabiner on my belt loop. Another wrapped and secured around the thickest osseous arboreous within reach.

My heels are at the edge of the canyon.

My thumb scans into the box's digipanel.

It lights up. I brace myself. Knees bent. Arms tense.

"I'm coming to get you," I yell to Dash.

The ligament directly to my right splits. It sinks, and Euphoria and my brother let out screams that wrack my brain and turn it into mush.

I'm not going to be able to save them both.

Dash is your priority.

He will always be your priority.

Switch to belay function. Brake-assist on. Friction boost turned up. Rappelling requires a controlled descent. And of the countless times I've done this in the virtual climbing gym at the Academy growing up, none of my training sessions prepared me for this.

Then again, most kids were only in there to fulfill a physical education credit.

Dominant hand operates the brake.

One foot off the ledge.

Back straight.

I take a deep breath.

Bounding down. Faster than I'm supposed to. But there's no time. The last ligament twists, tugging against the vertebrae. Beneath me, the bridge oscillates with a wicked groan, each rotation wearing at the ligament, testing its strength.

Even the strongest points can only bear so much.

Dash waves his hand. "Another foot and you're here! I can almost reach you!"

Sweat streaks my temples. I huff deep breaths, fire in my lungs. My line snags, and I shudder, fumbling for my recant box. Ease up on friction. Press the untangle mechanism.

You've got this.

I zip upwards. The gap between us goes from a foot to three.

"What's going on? What are you waiting for!"

Ease *up* on friction. *Press* the untangle mechanism.

The coil won't budge.

"My—my recant box is stuck!" Above, the ligament heaves, and the spine bridge sinks further. *There isn't time.* "Dash, climb up to me! Use the vertebrae. Like a ladder!"

He obeys. "It's because you descended like a freaking hopper bug!"

"It's *because* I didn't have time to grab proper equipment!"

Euphoria doesn't wait to be told. She's at Dash's behind, scaling the vertebrae as fast as she can. My brother reaches me first, and I hook him onto the secondary carabiner.

He looks up. Eyes wide. "Oh, fu—"

The ligament finally snaps.

Dash sweeps Euphoria into his arms.

I lock my recant box. *We're not going anywhere.*

The Bone Bridge crashes hundreds of feet beneath us, splintering into a dust cloud. The blood-red river sweeps it away with the current. Relief spreads through me. Our cables sway with our movement. Euphoria buries her face in my brother's chest.

He adjusts his hold. "What? Not having any fun?"

She lifts her head. "I'm... I'm not a fan of heights."

Same. I shake my recant box and trigger the restart. I manage the settings. Not enough sunlight. No solar charge. Charging panels defective. Fucking useless.

Euphoria winces. "The line isn't going to break, is it?"

"It'll hold," I call down. "It's built to withstand meteorite harvesting in open space."

My brother smiles at her. "Maybe we can take you some time if you—"

"Dashiel," I snap. "I need you to focus."

"I *am* focused. We're dangling here like that ball thingy in the back of my throat."

"You mean your uvula?" Euphoria asks.

"Yeah!" Dash chuckles. "Get it? Because we're surrounded by body parts."

I slam my recant box against a rock. "What is wrong with this thing?"

"Not that I don't love hanging around, but—"

"Hush. I'm working on it."

"She's working on it." Dash changes his hold on Euphoria, and she wraps her arms around his upper torso. "Though this is cozy, aye? Like... in a friendly way."

Euphoria scrunches up her nose. "It's incredibly uncomfortable."

Oh, for Goddess' sake. "You useless piece of—" I pummel the recant box against my palm. It fizzles in and out, revealing one option. And it isn't favorable.

I glance down at my brother and Euphoria.

"You don't seem pleased," Dash says.

"It's out of charge. The retraction function won't work."

"But that means—"

"The canyon wall is too smooth to climb, and we don't have the equipment. The only way we're getting out of this is by descending manually." I try not to think about everything I'm leaving behind by not returning for my pack. At least I have my journal.

And I'm pretty sure that's the troll Gallivant poking me from my side pocket. Everything else—*I'll figure it out.*

I take a deep breath in and out. "Euphoria, where does the canyon lead? Can we get to the village if we travel the river below us?"

"Uh—" She closes her eyes, speaking into Dash's arm. "It'll guide us back around the long way. Though, I'd very much like to discuss this on the ground if that's okay."

"Yes, Shea, take us to the ground," Dash says.

I roll my eyes. I press the emergency release button, which will lower us slowly on a manual gear and pulley system, and I let out the longest exasperated sigh.

10

Shea

Dash hasn't said a word to me in miles, but it's probably for the best.

I messed up back there. Big time. I know it. Dash knows it. Hell, even Euphoria knows it. That makes twice now that I've acted impulsively in her presence.

Not that I care what she thinks.

My journal keeps me busy. As we walk, I flip through the pages. Sketching the landscape and the riverbed, crusted over with layers of viscera and foaming acid rapids traveling North.

In the next mile, Euphoria hums an eerie song. One I recognize but can't place. I resist the urge to ask her about it and try my best to keep my mind occupied. Time seems to pass slower than death. It only reminds me I'm not on the best terms with my brother. Usually, he fills the silence with nonsensical rants and jokes.

Like when we trekked across planet Kincaid in the middle of a snowstorm. We'd been sent to fetch a time-traveling device called a Transporter from an abandoned ISR lab tucked away in a middle-of-nowhere mountain range. Dash recited one act of a romance play aloud on the train ride up and another on the ride down. I chuckle to myself, thinking about it.

"What's funny?" Euphoria asks.

My smirk fades. "Nothing."

Dash raises a brow, and I can picture him standing up on the train, waving his hands and belting out sonnets about love. "Something must be funny because she never smiles."

"That isn't true," I say.

"Is *too*."

"Is *not*."

Euphoria sighs. "Let's play a game, shall we?"

A game is the last thing we should play. "How about you tell me more about your past lives on Ominous."

"Tell you what." She kicks a heap of gunky intestines. They hit a rock, wrap it like garland, and my stomach writhes. "I'll tell you whatever you want to know if you play."

A bribe? Really? Does she actually think I'm going to fall for that?

Dash smirks. *He* thinks I'm going to fall for that.

I cross my arms. "No. Nice try, though."

"Oh, come on," Dash says. "Would it kill you to have a little fun?"

"It's alright. She doesn't have to play," Euphoria says.

My brother shoves his hands in his pockets. "I'll play. What's the game, Effs?"

"Two Truths and a Lie."

I scoff. "What are we, in Kinder Year?"

Euphoria steers us clear of another acid puddle, rippling beneath a jumble of soggy bark. "Does it matter? Since you're not playing?"

"Guess not," I mutter.

"I'll go first," Dash says.

Euphoria nods. "Alright."

"Hmmm." He chews his lip as he thinks. "Okay. I had my first kiss when I was fourteen, and it was behind the bleachers at a Holoblocks tournament with a boy named Micah Sanders—"

"For Goddess' sake, we don't need an entire story for each one," I snap.

Euphoria raises a brow. "I thought you weren't playing."

I stop myself from slipping on a slick slab of bone, half-buried at the edge of the riverbed, and catch up again. "I'm not playing. I'm just saying."

Dash glares at me. "*Anyway.* I had my first kiss when I was fourteen. I scored the highest on my survival study assessment in Ninth Year and—"

"Well, that one is obviously a lie," I mutter.

This time my brother stops and throws his hands out. "Are you playing, or are you not playing? You can't just interrupt the game."

Euphoria's eyes are on me. Again. What's new.

I lift my chin. "Fine. I'm playing."

"Well, clearly—"

"But it won't be a very fair game."

"Why is that?" Euphoria asks.

"He's my brother. I know him."

"You don't know everything about me," Dash says.

"I know enough about you."

"Whatever." He runs a hand through his hair. "Uh, my last one is that I hate working for James Co., and I'm quitting after this gig on planet Ominous."

I let out a laugh. "Funny. Number two is obviously a lie. Number three is also a lie. You can't have two lies, Dash. The game is called Two *Truths* and a Lie. Play it right, or don't play at all."

A string of muscle matter drops onto Euphoria's shoulder as we pass beneath a cluster of trees. She brushes it off without flinching. "I think number one is the lie."

"No. I remember him telling me about Micah Sanders. That's the truth." The same tree sheds another layer of muscle, and I sidestep to avoid the fallout. "My brother obviously doesn't know how to play this game."

We both glance at Dash.

He shakes muscle off his boots, a frown plastered across his face. "Yeah, Shea-Lynn. You're right. I don't know how to play. I'm that daft. You win. It's your turn. Go on."

"Fine. I will."

The last time I played Two Truths and a Lie, I was a Third Year at the Academy, still playing virtual hopscotch during recreational hour. I try to think of something good to say. Something Dash won't figure out. But who am I kidding? Dash barely pays attention. I could say anything, and I'd stump him. This is going to be easy.

"Before we left the Academy, I was the top student in my graduating class. I listen to classical music every night before bed, and the family business will be mine someday."

There. Let's see how long it takes them to—

"You don't listen to classical music before bed." Dash keeps his gaze forward as he walks. "You listen to really sad folk songs and cinematic instrumentals."

I blink at him. "How did you know that? And they aren't... sad."

"Every night, after I finish a game in the Holoverse with some of my old buddies from the Academy, I get up and check on you and Mom."

"You do?"

"Yep. Dad's usually up really late in Headquarters, so I turn off all the lights in the house. I visit Mom if she can't sleep, and then I stop by your room. Sometimes you forget to turn off your music. I turn it off, place your earbuds on your bedside table, pick up your journal if you've fallen asleep doing research, and then I turn on your star lamp so you can see if you need to get up in the middle of the night."

Wait. He does that? I always thought Dad did that.

"Yeah, so you lose," Dash says. "Effs, you're next."

She nods. "Alright. Give me a moment to think."

I stare at my brother. His glower deepens. In the dying red sunlight, there's a warmness to him now. A softness that I knew was there but hadn't really acknowledged. I always knew he cared about me, but I didn't know he did any of that. If he can take the time to routinely check on me at night and remember to tuck Mom in, why doesn't he pull his weight more?

Is it because he can't? Or is it because he doesn't want to?

Euphoria's skirt drags in a stream of acid, sizzling the hem, and she hoists it up higher. Dash helps her with the thickest bulk of fabric. I wait for them until we're able to continue on.

She finally smooths her skirt. "My two truths and a lie are as follows: I'm actively aware of almost every life my soul has lived. Not specific details, but at least the gist of who I've been. Growing up, my favorite ride at Crowley Corner was the Haunted Teacups, and deep down, I'm scared to break this cycle with Valerian because it means stepping out of trauma patterns and into a higher version of myself, maybe even a version of myself I don't feel quite worthy of yet."

Dash guesses, "You don't know every life?"

"I know a little about every life I've ever lived."

"The Haunted Teacups bit is a lie," I say.

Euphoria smiles. "Indeed. It was the House of Glass."

I hold her stare, focusing on the alternating patterns in her golden irises. It seems to be an ongoing sentiment between us now. *These looks.* I'm growing to despise it more than anything.

"How about we play Twenty-Questions next," Dash suggests.

Euphoria quirks a brow. "I guess we could."

"Okay. What's your ideal first date?"

"Oh, I'm not sure. That's a hard one."

If my eyes could roll any further, they'd pop out of my head. I wonder if anyone would notice them floating along the river, mixed up with all the other organs. Probably not. As if to prove the point, something plops onto my arm.

"*Ugh.*" I flick the blob of chunky sap off my sleeve. Another globule splatters onto my back, and I dodge a third clump of skin that plops off a tree to my left. *Double ugh.*

A colossal dam comes into view ahead. Its curve of moss-covered concrete with a series of outlets and mesh seems to be the epicenter of the Shedding. The runoff is thicker now, overflowing the riverbed, opening at the mouth of what appears to be a reservoir reeking of cadaverine and methanethiol—all naturally occurring odors that typically accompany human decomposition.

Dash gags and covers his nose with his sleeve. "It's like spoiled fish or cabbage... " A green hue rushes into his cheeks. "I... I think I'm going to be sick."

I wrinkle my nose. "Please don't. You know it makes me squeamish."

"Me too," Euphoria echoes.

"Are you two serious right now?" Dash's shouts are muffled through his shirt. "We're surrounded by literal gut juice, blood, and Gods knows what else, and you're worried about me throwing up? Something is wrong with the both of you."

"You *know* what I mean," I say.

"I really don't." He stumbles in a twist of muscle still attached to a rib cage and dry heaves. The sudden pressure in my chest deepens. He gathers his bearings. Wipes sweat off his brow. "We have to go another way. We can't go through this."

"I'm sorry. I warned you we'd have to go through the thickest part of the Shedding." Euphoria motions towards the dam. "The village is just beyond the dam there."

Great. Because I really couldn't handle another round of games and small talk.

"Is there another way around?" I scan the horizon, searching for a path in this coagulating mess, but the organ-scape is heavy. "Maybe another trail? An easier path through?"

Euphoria unbuttons her blouse. "Unfortunately, we'll have to go through it."

All the color drains from my little brother's face. "What? NO."

I shudder. She cannot be serious. As Euphoria unhooks the fullest part of her skirt, Dash's jaw drops, and I question my own judgment. She tosses her skirt behind her. It lands in an acidic wave. The next gush of frothy runoff swallows it whole. Oh, fuck. She is serious.

"No. No. No," Dash says.

What. Is. Happening.

Euphoria removes her blouse completely, and this time my little brother deepens a pretty shade of red. He averts his gaze, likely out of respect. I can't stop staring. Euphoria removes her knee-high boots, lace by lace, knot by knot. Her stockings become another stitch of fabric swallowed by the runoff goop too. After she removes her underskirt, she's left with only her necklace charms, a thick-strapped, white bralette, and a pair of matching, high-waisted underwear.

Who the hell is this girl? And I can't get over how willing she is to do this.

Suddenly, Dash is at my side, clinging to my arm. "I want to go back to the mausoleum. Fake Death and his soul suckers can have me. I'll make peace with my fate. It'll all be okay. Tell Mom and Dad and Tee Tee that I love them. Don't touch anything in my room and—"

"Stop it right now," I hiss.

"But I—

"You're doing it."

At the lake's edge, Euphoria ties up her long locks of hair with the elastic band around her wrist. "Well, are you two coming? It's best to strip down so nothing pulls you under."

"*Shea-Lynn*," Dash gripes.

"*Dashiel*." I shake my brother loose.

Euphoria clears her throat. "As everything flows into Lake Ichor, the acid isn't as potent, of course, but it'll still burn a bit, so brace yourselves."

I don't think anyone can brace themselves for something like this. Nothing in my mission-prep teachings could save me now, even if I tried. Except maybe one of Dad's golden Enforcer rules: Sometimes you have to do the unthinkable to survive.

I guess I always thought that meant to kill a man in a death match before he kills you.

Alright. I've procrastinated long enough.

I bite my tongue. I grit my teeth. All while reminding myself that I've chopped off thumbs more grotesque than this.

Dash's feet remain planted where they are. He keeps running his hands through his hair, wide-eyed and tense. It's his pre-panic attack face, and I sincerely hope he can hold it together.

Though he hasn't had one of those in years, I'm worried this might be the trigger that sends him over the edge. He isn't okay with this, I get it. *I'm* not okay with this.

I calm my voice and make my words smooth as if he is already in the middle of one of his episodes. "Try not to think about it. We're all going together. It'll be okay. I promise."

He takes off his vest and unbuttons his sweater. "You're just saying that so I'll shut up and do what you want me to do."

He's not wrong. And I know I should say something else, but he turns away. I'm already down to my tank top and undershorts by the time he strips down to his boxers. Euphoria waits patiently for us at the edge of the lake. I search for a place to secure my journal and the troll Gallivant, so they won't get swept away in the gush. Inside my undershorts might be the only option. On second thought, carrying them above my head might be best.

Dash flings his socks. "You might have to leave your journal behind."

I do my best to ignore him. At my nod, Euphoria wades into the lake. Zero hesitation. My toes curl in the mush. I gaze into the pool of skin and tissue swirling with clumps of fat and glinting liquids that resemble gasoline on the asphalt after a rainy day in the Residential District.

Yeah, that's it. Pretend you're home. Back on planet Sarasing.

"Believe it or not, Lake Ichor is beautiful in the warm season. Think of it like that if you can't fathom it any other way!" Euphoria calls back to us, about nine yards out now.

Yeah, Euphoria. I'll get right on that.

Dash steps up beside me. "She's such a badass. Isn't she?"

I allow the thought to cross my mind for a split second. A twinge of gratitude seeps in, thankful she's here to guide us through this, but then I tell myself it's situational.

"No." I push past him and take my first step into the depths. If I agree with him that she's badass then he might think I agree with other things about her too.

A burning sensation rings my ankles as I take another step into the slough. It rises up my calves. My tongue swells, tasting of sandpaper, and a slimy film coats my skin. I let my left hand sink into the surface and keep my other hand high so my journal and the troll Gallivant won't get wet. Stringy matter tangles in my fingers. I recoil. *Think of home. Think of Mom. Think of books.*

Two seconds later, Dash turns and heaves the contents of his stomach into the current.

"I'm so sorry." He chokes back. "I tried to keep it in." My knees sway. Anchoring my toes doesn't help. The squish only makes it worse. "Shea?—"

Don't think about it. Just do it. You can do this.

"You look so pale." Dash's voice sounds far away.

I swallow hard. "I'm fine."

"I know you hate getting sick or thinking about it, but it made me feel much better." My brother positions himself behind me. "I'll even hold your hair back if you—"

"Get off me!" I bark, gulping putrid air. "I need space. Go catch up with Euphoria and tell her to slow down so we don't get split up."

"Okay, okay."

He splashes onward. My eyelids flutter shut. I swallow what feels like a thousand times. Bite back the warmth in my cheeks, the sweat dripping down my brow. *You can do this.* This isn't even the worst of it. I fought off a swarm of hands. I saved our asses back at the Bone Bridge. Not to mention, I speared a beast through the heart.

You can travel through a slop swamp.

I'm going to need a serious vacation after this.

After three deep breaths in and out, I open my eyes.

Euphoria stands in front of me, a line of organ juice dripping down the indent of her collarbone. A glint in her golden eyes.

Another off the crystal stud in her nose. Why didn't I notice that before?

She offers a slippery hand. "Mind over matter, Shea-Lynn."

"Yeah, I know." I trudge around her, avoiding her offer. Then I slip on something. No idea what. Don't want to know what.

Again, Euphoria is there to steady me with a hand. She flicks half an earlobe off my shoulder. "It's going to be okay."

"I'm—" I bite my tongue. What she did *was* kind. "Thanks."

Euphoria stares at me like she's trying to figure out all the secrets I've ever had and will have for the rest of my life. Maybe it's a spellcaster thing. Maybe it's a her thing. All I know is that the idea makes my heart thud in my chest.

She leads me onward toward Dash. In those few moments, the lake drops off. Nothing left to crunch over. Nothing pulpy or squelchy to sink my toes in. We'll have to swim the rest of the way. Despite what Euphoria told us, I can't imagine taking a refreshing dip in the heat of an Ominous summer. Nothing like that could ever exist here.

The currents pick up. I'm a bobbing head on the surface. We all are now. I kick my feet, fighting to tread. Swimming with one hand makes it harder, and my other hand threatens to dip beneath the surface each time I lose my rhythm.

Dash jounces an arm's length away. "Ditch the journal and the Gallivant! You'll drown!"

I shake my head, straining my neck to keep my head up. I need this Gallivant to stay dry if we have any chance of contacting Headquarters. And there's no way in hell I'm giving up my research. We've floated toward the base of the dam, where the Shedding runoff has gathered at its thickest.

I've seen nothing like it. Not in books. Not on the Universal Database.

Oversized organs cling to us. Dash fights a twist of bone branches. Though Euphoria tied up her hair, body matter tangles in her thick locks. As I lose momentum, my journal and the Gallivant graze the foaming surface, but I force myself to kick and raise my arm higher. An unidentifiable spongy bit wraps around my ankle. Goosebumps prickle my spine.

You can do this. You're so close. You've got this.

A loud crunch shakes me to the core. I crane my neck but can't see anything through the choppy waves of skin, organs, and bone.

"Over there!" Dash exclaims. "What the heck are those?"

"They filter the river!" Euphoria shouts. "Be careful. If you get too close, they'll swallow you whole."

Buildups of skin float on the water's surface, separating the three of us. I dodge one clump that a small horde of skeleton rats with curved horns are using as a life raft. At first, I think these must be what my brother and Euphoria were referring to. They're ugly, chittering little things. Nothing to write home about. The gutter beavers on planet Sarasing are much worse.

But they aren't talking about rats.

With the rough pull of the current, our bodies are carried in the dam's direction, which now towers fifty feet over us. Treading outside the structure, among the acrid sludge, are plump creatures I can't name at first glance.

"They look like Hungry Hungry Hippos!" Dash shouts.

Leave it to my brother to name anything and everything we encounter. And they *are* like the ball-gobbling beasts from the vintage board game our Great-grandpa Alden gifted us one Yuletide. But these creatures are three sizes larger than the average hippopotamus. With spikes sticking out of their greasy-gray heads. A set of six bulging eyes each. Bulbous warts cover their entire form. When they snort, their snouts shoot mucus. It splatters up into the air like snot rain. Their jaws move with an unhinged, robotic motion as they gobble up every bit of skin, organ, and bone that circulates in their wake.

And we're headed right for them.

"Please, don't let me be Chomper food!" Dash yells.

Not this shit again. It can never be easy, can it?

Euphoria splashes at my side, fighting the pull of the current. But it's too strong. It's sucking us in. My heartbeat hammers against my ribs. *Think, Shea. Think.*

There *is* a way out of this. There must be.

Euphoria and Dash grab one another, kicking back out of the undertow. I scan the surrounding area, and I see mesh grates covering tunnels at the dam's base.

The sound of gnashing teeth nearly drowns me out. "Head for the grates!"

Dash and Euphoria pick up on my hand motions. I wave them on, my legs cramping from treading against the pull. *You need both your arms. Dash is right; you'll drown.* But I've come this far, and I can't give up now.

Euphoria and Dash break the current and wait, treading on the other side by the dam. I get sucked in further. Faster and faster, the harder the creatures gnaw, the more the raging waters sweep me in. I kick as hard as I can, keeping my eyes on my brother's mop of brown hair, bobbing amid the fat and skin coating the lake.

"Let GO of the FREAKING journal!" Dash screams.

"NO!" I scream back.

The current quickens, pulling me toward a Chomper. Unlike the viscus in the mausoleum, these creatures aren't vicious beasts. They're so doped up on entrails that they don't know what's waste and what isn't. If only I had the sword. *Or two hands*. I eye my journal and the troll Gallivant, a strain above my head. My arm wavers. Warm viscera coats my chin. *Is it really worth your life, Shea? Is your journal and a viable way to contact home REALLY worth your life?*

"SHEA!" Dash shouts.

Screw it. It isn't. As my arm falls, my journal and the troll Gallivant dips below the water. A wave of sludge pours over me, pushing me beneath the current. I stuff my journal and the troll Gallivant into my undershorts. *Better soaked than lost.* The Chomper in front of me opens its massive jaw. A fleshy pink cavity with chunky teeth and saliva oozing from its center begs to swallow me whole. My eyes widen. As it clamps down, I'm jerked out of harm's way. It misses me by an inch.

I look over, breathless, my heart pounding in my chest. Dash and Euphoria are there. Dash's hand at my waist. Euphoria's on my shoulder, pushing me along, guiding me toward the dam's edge to the nearest grate.

We fumble for the mesh covering ahead of us, the one that stands between us and the tunnel beyond. The tunnel that will deliver us to safety, to the village in the valley, away from all this. Euphoria and Dash anchor themselves to the grooves in the wall. I dig at the immovable screws, then the latch itself, but it doesn't budge.

Behind us, the Chomper that nearly took my life roars.

"It thinks we stole its meal," Euphoria yells.

Dash coughs. "Hurry up, Shea! Open the grate!"

Shaking, I flip open the lock panel. I ogle at a series of square stones. I run my wrinkled, slimy fingers over the different rune symbols. As I press the first one, it locks into place. I push the next, and it resets.

It's a lock puzzle.

"Dashiel!" I pull him over, force his hand over the panel, and shout in his ear, "They have to be pressed in the correct order, but if you mess up, the panel clears and makes you start over!"

My brother nods. "Got it."

His nimble fingers move.

An entirely new persona washes over him.

This is Thief mode.

Without looking up from the panel, he shouts, "Effs, the rune that looks like a lightning bolt, what does it stand for?"

"Wheel of Power. Letter S!"

"And the slanted F?"

"Ancestors. Odin!" she cries.

"Perfect. I think I almost got—"

In an explosive wave, another Chomper rises.

Euphoria and I dart in opposite directions to avoid the fallout. A gush of liquid smothers my head. It rushes into my throat, filling my mouth with sludge. I sputter, losing sight of my surroundings. The Chomper's teeth grind in my ears.

Its suction pulls me under the surface once more.

My eyes spring open. Burning raw in the murky water.

Help me. Please. Somebody help me.

A coral-colored light appears. The flutter of wings, like an apparition around me.

My chest tightens. Everything is spinning. *You're dying, Shea. This is it. You're drowning.*

Thrashing is useless. I can't move. I can't kick. I close my eyes. A pounding in my temples. Flashes of color behind my lids. Sinking with the weight of my body. Deeper.

Images swirl in my mind. *Dash and me as children. His brown curls flopping on his head. His smile as he laughs. The rich brown of his eyes. We're with Mom in a greenhouse choosing the flowers she'll hang in the sitting room under the artificial lamp. Her long hair flows behind her, a warmth in her cheeks. She takes my hand and points to the lilies woven in the vines overhead.* The beginning of a smile graces my lips as I drift further into the darkness below.

Then the scene morphs into another, this time a memory I don't recall...

Hands interlocking. Gentle laughter. A cabin somewhere in the mountains. Tall grass blowing in the wind, a bright blue sky overhead. And trees, lots of trees. Oaks that tower up into the heavens. Draping willows that flit in the breeze. Their trunks thick, their roots woven into the ground. Flowers, a prism of colors, uncurling in morning dew. Bare toes squishing in the fresh dirt.

It's me, but it isn't me. I remember it, but I don't. And Euphoria is there, only a glimpse of her.

Euphoria is there. Dash is there. Euphoria is *here.* Dash is *here.*

I open my eyes, holding a firm gaze into my brother's. He hitches his arms under mine and hoists me up. We kick. My body intertwines with his. We ascend. Break the surface.

My little brother saved my life. Maybe he doesn't need me as much as I thought he did.

I choke on another mouthful of sludge. The grate swings and slams behind me.

"I've got you," Euphoria says in my ear.

It takes me a moment to realize—I'm slumped against *her.*

She saved my life? Impossible. Dash is the one I saw down there.

As I lift my head, I spot my brother leading Euphoria and me out of the tunnel into fresher water, toward a stone platform adjacent to the dam. *Nowhere near me.*

What is going on?

I'm guided to a rusted metal ladder up the side of the concrete. Somehow my shaking hands find the rungs. As I climb, the valley comes into view over the peak. A small village, as promised to us, with cobblestone roads and timbered dwellings.

Maybe it *was* Euphoria down there.

But no. It wasn't.

I know what I saw. I saw my brother. I felt his hands around me. Looked right into his eyes.

You lost consciousness, Shea.

But how much of it was me losing consciousness, and how much of it was her digging around in my brain?

My focus shifts to Euphoria, slicking layers of blood and entrails off her legs and hips. I peer over the edge at the Chompers, noshing away.

I was done for back there. I could have only survived by way of magic. So, it had to be Euphoria.

Her golden eyes bore into mine. "Are you okay, Shea?"

I don't know. "What were you doing inside my head?"

"I'm not sure what you mean."

"You know exactly what I mean."

I'm inches from her now, my finger pointed at her spider-vein-covered neck. All these intrusive thoughts I've been having about her since we met, these hit-and-miss feelings I've been experiencing, did she have something to do with those as well? Dash certainly took to her. She gained his trust almost instantaneously. Is *this* how she did it?

"Tell me what you did to me down there, or we're ditching you right here, right now."

You're spiraling, Shea. You're losing control.

Dash forces himself between us, but it doesn't take much. "What is wrong with you? She just saved your life. You owe her a thank you." I ogle at my brother, a numbness taking over my body. It sends tingles across my fingers and toes. "Gods. You're so delusional sometimes."

"I'm not delusional. She—"

"I've had enough for today. It's getting dark, I'm freezing, and I'm sticky in uncomfortable places. Let's get outta here."

My brother motions Euphoria onward. She offers me one more look before she goes, and I stare after them with fire in my cheeks and fists I don't think will ever unclench. I don't know what she did or what I saw, but I do know this—Euphoria isn't who she says she is.

There's something she isn't telling us.

11

Dash

Nobody packs coin in the padding of her bra quite like Effs.

From a zipper up the side of her underwire, she tosses enough moolah down to cover a night's stay for us at Wraith's Fate Tavern, the only accommodations available in the quaint little town of Specters Village. According to Effs, the town was a station that got wiped out by the Great War. It's a ghost town now—populated by your standard apparitions.

The spirit clerk behind the circulation desk points to the transaction bar, where a faded set of numbers displays our charge. "You are three silvers short."

As Effs searches for more coins in her other bra cup, I stare at the tatters of his military uniform. He must think we're ridiculous for showing up in our underwear.

I dare to sneak a glance at my sister. Chin up, eyebrows quirked, Shea taps her bare foot against a floorboard. Wipes a smear of bile off her neck. Anything to avoid looking at me.

I should be the angry one right now. Not her. She nearly cost us our lives back at the Bone Bridge. Again, with the Chompers. I haven't forgotten what she said about me being a screw-up either. Trying to sneak my truth into a Kinder Year game was a long shot too.

I did actually score the highest on my survival exam. I didn't study. Instead, I thought about the questions as if I were in a Holoblocks game. Applied the strategies. Acted as if I were in game-play mode. But who am I kidding? Holoblocks is a game, not survival.

It was sheer luck I scored the highest. Still made a killer truth.

My soul sucker writhes beneath my skin, triggering a pulsing pain in my head. I swallow hard and rub my arm, where the veins have deepened. I think I'm supposed to tell my sister if I get worse, but would she care right now? *Could* she care right now?

I can't for the life of me figure out what her outburst was about back at the dam. It's good we're stopping. We've been traveling all day, we're half-naked, and we're covered in gut-juice. A night's rest will give us time to recuperate and scrub our scalps—because let's be honest, we REEK—and it gives *me* time to let off some steam and stretch my eager fingers.

Since we walked in, I've had my eye on the scrying mirror hanging on the wall.

Effs tosses an extra bronze coin onto the dusty front desk. "Here's a tip."

The spirit attendant whisks her payment into the register tray, pockets the coin, and plucks an old antique skeleton key fixed to a wooden Wraith's Fate Tavern tag off the row of rusted hooks behind him. "Room 212 is down the hall. Between rooms 202 and 333."

Shea takes the key. "Got it. Makes total numerical sense. Thanks."

"You know, you really shouldn't swim in the lake this time of year," the attendant adds in a dull tone, almost a moan. "You'll certainly catch your death that way."

"You would know, aye, buddy?" I say.

Shea elbows me in the side. *Gah, that hurt.*

I'm ushered down a hall lined with rustic wooden doors displaying a mismatch of numbers. Effs heads up the back, her hands clasped gently behind her. The dusty chandelier overhead flickers. A gritty substance in the rug squishes between my toes.

I run a thumb along the embroidered graveyard tapestry nailed to the paneling, and Shea slaps my hand. "Keep your hands to yourself. Now is not the time to be thieving."

"I didn't realize thievery had a time and place."

"It does when you're half-naked and dripping entrails." She clears her throat and glances at Effs. "We'll pay you back once we find a coin converter."

"Don't worry about it," Effs says.

"I'd rather not owe you anything."

A square button on the tapestry comes loose, and I take it with me, flipping it up and down. "You seriously need to learn to accept freebies."

Shea snatches the button midair. Zings it behind her.

I scoff. "That was incredibly rude."

Effs points ahead. "There. Room 212."

My sister moves to align the antique key in the lock. The heavy door swings open.

Finally. A place to rest.

Our boarding room is your standard tavern resting place. Shea and I have stayed in dozens like it. Though this one takes the cake. One rustic hearth. A greenish-brown shag rug. The faded quilt covering the lumpy, queen-sized bed looks like it died along with its housekeepers. And the highlight of the space? The lounge corner. Where a stained sofa busting with stuffing sits lopsided next to a water-ringed table, home to a hotplate and a porcelain teapot.

"The upkeep isn't the best, I'm afraid." Effs straightens an abstract painting of a shadow figure wielding silver light. "I've only stayed one other time, in another life altogether."

"What are you talking about? It's perfect!" I poke my head into the washroom off the door. The light flickers on, revealing pale-pink tile, a drain for open-style showering, and a ceramic toilet overgrown with black mold. "I'm going to sleep like a baby. It's cleaner than my room back home. No crumb lizards or dirty clothes. Ample floor space. A complete vibe."

Effs blinks at me. "Some of the things that come out of your mouth are concerning."

"Welcome to my world." Shea sorts the towels set up on the crooked shelf by the door. She finds one small, circular-shaped bar of soap in its folds. "Alright. Who wants to shower first? If nobody has a preference, then I'd like to—"

"Me!" I snatch a towel and the bar of soap.

Shea rolls her eyes. "Okay, but don't you dare use all the soap. Dashiel, I mean it. We have to ration. This is a very serious matter."

"Yeah, yeah. I will not use all the soap. I *promise*."

So... I used all the soap.

I didn't mean to. It smelled like the peppermint razz cakes I always steal from the Fizzies discount counter. Plus, the soap was sudsy. *Too* sudsy. One moment I was pulling strings of muscle from my hair, and the next, it was gone.

Shea wasn't impressed. Obviously. Effs wandered out to the supply closet to nab a couple more bars. When she returned, she claimed the washroom as her own. Looks like the spellcaster and I have more in common than I thought. I'd say she's got real thieving potential. Might have to explore that venture a little more. *Or a lot more.* It keeps my mind off trivial things. I can see it now, our first date, scouring all the finest boutiques.

"I'm not sure why *I'm* the one washing your boxers," Shea comments from the lounge corner where she's hung her soaked journal pages and the troll Gallivant's body cavity from a string across the hearth. Its head sits propped up on the table, its tuft of pink hair a smelly knot.

While I sit at the edge of the bed in my towel, Shea finishes dabbing the last layers of mucus and grime from every pleat and fold of my underwear.

"Nobody told you to wash anything," I say. "You took it upon yourself, as per usual. Leave them. I'll wash them later."

"You can't let them sit that long."

"I'll just throw them away then."

"That would be a waste."

"I'll steal a new pair."

She grits her teeth and wrings my boxers like they are the last pair of underwear left in the galaxies. The stillness is worse than her nagging. I wish we'd just call a truce.

But does she deserve that at this point? Should I let it go and wait for her to get over herself so we can continue as if nothing happened? I don't think that would work this time. I don't think she's getting over it. I don't think I'm getting over it either.

Still, I'm a lover, not a fighter.

"Look, I'm sorry, okay? I'm sorry for whatever I need to be sorry for at this point. I don't know what you want from me," I say.

I roll onto my stomach and set my chin in my hands. Shea continues to ignore me, the silence around us suffocating until Effs' soft singing in the shower wafts through the bathroom door. My sister's attempt at cleaning my underwear becomes more intense. I focus on her fingers, the way they work the fibers of my boxers. Wringing and wringing and wringing. She's probably imagining it's my face. I bet she'd like to pummel me to a pulp.

And what about me? Where's my apology? Where's my, *"I was wrong, Dash. You matter too. Who knows how long you have to live with that soul sucker inside you. You're my brother. I love you. I care about you. I believe in you. I'm so freaking sorry for how I've treated you."*

"Effs saved your life back at the dam, and you didn't even say thank you," I add.

Again, Shea continues to scrub my underwear. Her shoulders tense. As she scours the fabric, it gives and tears. A rush of color fills her cheeks. She crumples my boxers and tosses them in the dented metal waste bin next to the table.

Ohhkay. I sit up. "Can you please tell me what's going on with you?"

"Nothing is going on with me," she says, back still turned.

I slap my hands at my sides. "Come on, Shea. You *always* do this."

"I'm not doing anything. I'm cleaning. I'm thinking of our next move."

"Sit and relax! That's *all* you have to do right now."

"Easy for you to say. You don't have to worry about what's next."

"Oh, for—Are we really on this again? Give it a break. Let. It. Go."

She checks the hanging journal pages, smoothing out a folded crease. "I'm sorry, but if I don't prepare, we're out of luck tomorrow morning when we set off again."

"Nobody is asking you to prep."

"Nobody else is going to," she says.

"Tomorrow is a travel day. There's nothing *to* prep."

When she bends over to gather another heap of journal pages, I notice the fresh red stain on the back of her underwear. "You're bleeding."

"Yeah, it's a cut lip. I'll deal with it when I shower."

I spring up off the bed. "Nooo, the moon cycle kind."

Effs emerges from the steaming washroom in one of the tavern robes and grabs another towel to scrunch her hair. "Oh, you've started your cycle. Do you have anything for it?"

Shea's cheeks deepen a shade of red. "Uh... yeah... in my pack that is now... wasting away atop a canyon in the Bone Wood."

My sister's eyes water. *Oh, man.*

"You know what?" I say, "You go shower and relax. Effs and I will go on a supply run."

This is perfect for me, too, because I've been dying to get to know my cellmate more.

"I'll uh—" I glance around the room and grab a pillow off the bed, shake away its case. "I'll fill up a pillowcase with stuff from around the room, and when we're out in town, I'll switch the contents out. Nobody will know it's full of stolen goods. We get our supplies. Best trick there is."

Effs hands me a cracked vase off the mantle. "That's actually quite clever. If the run includes a fresh change of clothing, I'd be happy to join you."

"Oh, it does." I dart around the room and fill the sack up to the brim with an array of items. A shabby, hideous bed runner to add bulk. One of the smaller art pieces on the wall. Some contorted miniature free-form sculptures from the center of the side table. "Is there anything similar to cotton squares here or something else for Shea's... "

Effs smirks. "We can get her some lunar root."

I look at Shea. "See, lunar root. Don't worry about a thing."

My sister raises a brow. "But I—"

"We've got this." I motion Effs toward the door. "Be zen, Shea. Let the shower wash your troubles away. Deep breaths. We'll chat about everything when we're back."

"Okay, but Dash—"

"Rest!" I grab Effs's hand and twirl her around, out the door in a gust of peppermint razz wind.

"Okay, but you really should change out of that towel before you—"

The door slams shut behind me. I straighten my towel.

"That was smooth." Effs strolls ahead with her hands behind her back like a young child wandering the shelves of Fizzies for the first time.

Cool evening air washes over us as we exit Wraith's Fate Tavern, and a chill settles in my bones. Clouds form on my chapped lips with each heavy breath. We cross the cobblestone street toward a mismatch of no-name shops with boarded-up windows and streaks of broken glass.

My teeth chatter. "This place really is a ghost town. It's bitterly cold out here."

Effs chuckles and locks her arm in mine, nestling closer to me as we walk. "You're wearing nothing but a towel. That's why."

I chuckle. "I mean... yeah... "

"Any of the herbal shops around here will have lunar root. I'd also like to pick up some tea. I think you'll both like a sweet vanilla sleep tea my mother used to make."

"For sure! We could do that. That'd—that'd be nice."

She glances at me, her warm smile overtaking her. "Good."

The thought of Effs and I curling up on the couch next to the fire, sipping tea, and talking about deep things like the galaxies, becomes too comfortable. I run a hand through my damp hair, admiring the way the streetlamps overhead cast her in a glow.

Girls are beautiful. Boys are beautiful. All people are. But Effs isn't like the Academy peers I know. She isn't mean like Micah Sanders was when he made out with me behind the bleachers and told me I was a bad kisser. She isn't emotionless like Whitney Pearson was when I gave her my virginity. And she isn't confusing like Zena was when she showed up at Spinners Pier and told me we were over, that she and Chip were a 'thing now.'

Effs is just—it's her soul, I've decided, that sets her apart. There's something inherently beautiful about her soul. It understands me. Makes me feel at home in a way *I* don't understand. It radiates from the greatest depths of her core and envelopes her like moonlight. Even the spider veins spreading across her soft skin are gorgeous because they're part of her.

She tugs on my arm. "Threads has clothes."

"Great choice. Punny name too." My fingers tingle to life as I lead us into the building with a giant wooden spool displayed in the frosted window.

I hold open the door. Effs untangles herself from me.

She crosses under my outstretched arm. "I'm worried about your sister."

Kind of a mood killer, Effs. "I really don't want to talk about Shea right now."

"Oh?"

"Yeah. If that's okay."

The swinging door latches behind us. We enter the shop, and I'm immediately hit with the artificial perfume wafting in the air. Effs wanders toward a stack of hemmed pants. I follow her, keeping my eyes on the shopkeeper. Another ghost blast from the past, this one in a tattered flannel and overalls. He keeps his one intact eye on us. I give him my signature smile-wave combo and turn, making my full pillowcase extra obvious, so he knows I came in with it.

Effs runs her hand along a rack of satiny slips. Most of them look like they were made hundreds of years ago, but they're timeless.

"Again, it's not that I've been eavesdropping, but it's been chaotic between you two," she says.

Seriously. I close my eyes and tilt my head back for a moment. This is the last thing I thought we'd talk about.

I pick up a glass perfume bottle from a display center store. "Do you have a favorite scent? I'm happy to steal a bottle or two for you while we're here. Just say the word. I mean it."

"Now, Dash," Effs says. "Don't change the subject."

"I'm not changing anything," I say, and she tilts her head at me. "Look, I apologize to Shea all the time. I try to talk to her. It's not my fault she's stubborn and hot-headed."

"I have to disagree." Effs picks up a pair of pants for herself and for me, then sets hers down when she spots some dresses. "You may be open-minded and thoughtful. I'd even say amusing, but you can be extremely full of yourself."

"You think I'm amusing?"

Effs plucks a velvety black dress off its hanger and holds it up over her robe. As she admires herself, she adds, "Humor only gets you so far. Communication and compassion go a long way in relationships too."

Relationships on the mind, I see. Perhaps this is a first date, after all.

"Let me guess. You think I owe Shea another apology?" When the storekeeper turns his head away, I pick up a bracelet and tuck it into my pillowcase. "And there's nothing wrong with being a little full of yourself. Aren't we supposed to love ourselves?"

Effs switches out the black dress and tries a green one but quickly flips back to the black. "I think you both owe each other apologies, and I think you both need to be open to talking without judgment or bickering or walking away from each other."

"But you've seen how she acts! And besides, I *am* open!"

"I'm not excusing her by any means, but there's an ongoing push-and-pull kind of confrontation between you two that never seems to resolve itself. Nobody is honest."

She hands me the pants she chose for me earlier. My gaze lifts to the shopkeeper, now dusting behind the counter. As he bends down to get a lower shelf, I stuff my new clothes into my pillowcase and leave the shabby bed runner in their place. "You're talking about your game, right? Two Truths and a Lie?"

Effs moves on to the sweater display. "You want out of your family business. She thinks you'll never leave. You don't want to leave because of her. She can't stay without you."

"Okay. Say you're... right... " I scour the rack for something that screams—this is my last mission ever. "How would I go about fixing things, hypothetically, if I wanted to?"

"Stop acting so helpless," she says. "You clearly aren't. You're smarter than you let on."

"I don't know what you mean." I pull a long sleeve shirt patterned with geometric shapes from the rack. Effs gives it, and me, a thumbs down. "Oh, really? I kind of like this one."

"You'll thank me later." She swipes it and hangs it back up. "And you know what I mean. I might sound harsh, but I've been where you are. These are things I wish someone would have told me. You're capable. Very capable. You can lead, and you choose not to."

"Meh, leading isn't my job. That's why I'm the Thief."

"Does being a Thief make you void of responsibility?"

Ugh. No offense, but Effs is really turning me off right now. This was supposed to be fun and romantic. I don't need a pep talk or a nagging session. I already get that from Shea.

"I guess I could ask the same thing about you," I say.

Effs untangles a bronze clip from her hair and sets it back. "Oh?"

"Well, yeah." I snag one of the cologne testers. After a complimentary spritz of cedar, I switch out the bottle for the freeform sculpture. "Back at the mausoleum, you were ready to let Fake Death have your soul because you didn't think you were ready to go to the Higher Realm. In the Bone Wood, you said you don't feel worthy of stepping into your Higher Self. Maybe a part of you *is* ready to cross into the Higher Realm, but it means you'd have to leave Fake Death behind—I think *that* scares you."

Effs runs a hand along a string of costume jewelry. "You make a valid point."

"Does it scare you? To leave him behind?" I ask.

She sets a necklace back on its hook, looks at me. "There may be a small part of me that is terrified to let go of trying to control the outcome of our situation in this lifetime. Knowing that I could possibly go to the Higher Realm in three days without him does scare me. He won't be ready for a while, and sometimes I wonder if he'll ever be ready or if it'll take lifetimes more."

I put on a pair of sunspecs. "Ascend into the Higher Realm if you want to, then. Keep living your life. Fall in love. Chase your dreams. Go on adventures. Become everything you're supposed to be. Don't ever wait around for a man. Especially one that's not ready for you."

"I care about him. I don't want him to suffer."

"I really don't see how you choosing yourself means he suffers."

She puts on a pair of sunspecs as well. "Valerian is being coddled by the Divine. His scope of view is limited. A veil exists between his Divine Truth and what he knows about his human existence. Think of the dam at Lake Ichor. It filters and acts as a barrier, sort of what Valerian experiences. Right now, he's acting mainly from his ego. To align with the Higher Realm, one must act from a place of the ego *and* the Higher Self—a full integration. Duality. Balance."

"You think he's living a lie?" I ask, setting my sunspecs back.

She removes hers, too. "He thinks we made a deal with an Enchantress all those years ago. His scope is purely logical, with no ability to see beyond the palatable aspects of our connection. We volunteered to pave the way for others—a Divine, collective ripple. If I go to the Higher Realm, Valerian's veil will dissolve. Every bit of Truth he's been avoiding spiritually, mentally, and physically will come rushing into his awareness like a smack in the face. Codes he thought he understood will be corrected. Codes he wasn't meant to have in this lifetime will become known. The foundation of the life he's been living will crumble because it wasn't built to sustain his Truth."

"And what is that Truth?" I ask. "It sounds like you'd be doing him a favor."

"Everyone's Truth is different. To live in your Truth is to live an authentic life that feeds your soul, no matter what anyone else says or thinks of you. It is to be confident in yourself and your abilities, to know you are worthy of the greatest things in life.

"Valerian's Truth is that he's a Divine being, like we all are, but he's a Kingdom Builder, a Creator of Realms, a King of the Galaxies, and a Keeper of the Codes. If a soul splits like ours has, it means we've mastered lessons beyond human comprehension. We are influences, beacons of unconditional love, renegades of the stars—I could go on and on. Subjecting him to an overwhelming amount of information like this, that will essentially change his entire life *now*, and the circle of people he surrounds himself with *now*, is not a favor. It is cruel to realize you've been living a lie, that you haven't been living in your authentic Truth."

I take her sunspecs and put them away for her. "Isn't that what you'd be doing if you *didn't* go to the Higher Realm, though? I don't mean to call you out, but if you know all this, aren't you living a lie right now... " She avoids my gaze. "I'm not trying to trigger you, but you told me I should mend things with my sister. I think you should also face your own fears."

Effs bites her lip. "Again, you make a valid point."

"It's not like Shea makes an effort to see my side of things, either, you know." I poke through a barrel of silk scarves. Nothing pleases me. "I've stayed in the business as long as I have *for* my sister. She has no idea what I've sacrificed by staying. I'm not happy. In fact, I'm miserable."

"Tell her that."

"I can't—"

"You must." Effs pulls me in front of a mirror. She holds up a dark gray suede jacket with black sherpa fleece lining and a navy-blue long sleeve. "If it isn't my job to wait around for Fake Death to be ready to ascend, perhaps, it isn't your job to stay in a role that makes you unhappy."

I admire the reflection—both of us. I like what I see.

"I don't think Fake Death can be ready to ascend until he wants to be ready. Like Shea isn't going to open up until she's ready to open up. Whenever I try to force her, she gets mad, and then I regret starting the conversation altogether."

"We must understand that we can't control Shea and Valerian's reactions to *our* Truths. Much like they can't control our reaction to theirs. That's the beauty of difference." She places my outfit in my arms and then adjusts my industrial piercing so it glints in the faded light. "And you also have to acknowledge that Shea's hurt. Her emotions are valid."

"I do, Effs! But what about mine? Mine are valid too."

"They are, yes, but while *you* keep giving her a chance to acknowledge your emotions, she keeps thinking you won't acknowledge hers." Effs presses into me from behind, tilting her head to approve my reflection. "Your sister doesn't know it yet, but one of the reasons she gets so angry with you is because you aren't afraid of being vulnerable. She wants that. She just doesn't know how."

My mouth goes dry. I can barely process all this.

"She needs to let some things go first," I mutter.

"There's a difference between letting things go and brushing our problems under the rug," Effs says and retreats to a shoe display packed with hiking boots and galoshes.

Wow. Okay. What just happened? I'm not going to ignore that some of what Effs said makes sense. I haven't been as communicative toward my sister as I should have. I've lied about a lot of things. Mostly out of fear of her reaction, but lies all the same. And I want Shea to support my desire to leave this business. I don't want us to end up like Aunt Merik and Dad. *Heck.* I don't want us to end up in a cycle of lifetimes we can't break free from, like Fake Death and Effs.

Effs doubles back to the mirror and sets a pair of boots at my feet.

"I appreciate you having this conversation with me," I say.

She chuckles. "I appreciate you listening."

I close the gap between us and reach up to tuck a lock of matted hair behind her ear, which smells of peppermint and remnants of brain matter and whatever else the Chompers devoured with delight. It's kind of a turn-on. Is that weird?

"Is this okay? What I'm doing?"

Her brows knit together. "I'm not sure *what* you're doing, to be honest."

My reflection turns red. "I'm—I'm flirting. At least, I thought I was."

Effs scrunches her nose in an uber-adorable way. "You're darling, Dash, and I adore you more than you'll ever know, but I'm afraid I don't feel that way about you."

My stomach goes topsy-turvy, and suddenly, I feel dumber than the rocks scattered at Spinners Pier. "Ohhh, okay. Gotcha. I will officially stop trying to seduce you now."

"Happy to further explore our friendship, though." Effs settles for the black fitted dress with bell sleeves, very witchy indeed, before wandering to another rack.

"Now, to find something for Shea-Lynn. I'm thinking purples or a nice long sweater and knee-high boots."

Shea-Lynn. Huh. Wonder what Effs thinks about her. Is she another friendship waiting to be explored? Or is there something more there? Is that why she just spent our fake date giving me a pep talk on our siblingship? Girl alliance aside, I don't think I've seen them speak much because I'm pretty sure Shea hates Effs's guts.

Or maybe Effs is still in love with Fake Death. It's the only other logical explanation I can think of. Because I'm a great catch. *I'd* date me. I almost think of asking Effs straight up because I'm dying to know, but then I spot the two skeletons outside the shop window.

"Heinous Hades," I whisper to Effs.

She tries on a black-brimmed hat. "I'm still not sure what that means."

"It means Fake Death's minions are outside." I duck behind a wooden barrel teeming with lacey delicates. "Do you think they're looking for us?"

"We'll have to get rid of them." Effs crams a bralette into her robe pocket. Boy, she catches on quickly. "I'll distract the cashier. You stow the rest of the clothes."

"That I can do. I—"

Effs is already off. She ruffles her half-dried hair and adjusts her robe like it's something off a high-end shelf at Grimm's Garbs, then positions herself in front of the storekeeper, blocking his view. As soon as she leans over the counter and starts chatting him up, I go to work.

I'm a bit disappointed we won't be soulmates in this lifetime, but the spellcaster is sly. I'll give her that. Maybe even too sly.

Gods. Now I'm starting to sound like Shea.

I stuff the rest of our clothes into my pillowcase, including a strange viewing device with adjustment dials and lens for each eye—Looky Specs, I'll call them—and then I empty out the miscellaneous boarding room contents around the store. This might end up being the easiest thrift ever. Minus the skeletons lurking on the street corner.

"Are you excited for Festival?" the shopkeeper asks Effs. "I can't believe it's already that time of year again. I rarely attend the battle reenactment, but I might go this year. What about you?"

Effs clears her throat. "When you've been once, you've been to them all."

The shopkeeper's voice drolls on, "I think I'll wear my finest hat."

Time to put on a show. "Darling? Let's go home." I round a carousel of costume jewelry, sneakily tucking a necklace into the knot of my towel. "Nothing here fancies me, and I won't spend another dime on these hideous threads."

"Oh, happy day," Effs croons in a performance that outshines mine. "This kind shopkeeper and I were just talking about the festivities at Crowley Corner."

"Crowley Corner? No way," I echo.

The shopkeeper blinks at us. Effs wraps an arm around me. I hug her close. We keep up the charade long enough to make our escape. My saving grace is the door chimes jangling behind us as the shop door swings shut. Another successful thrift. *And* a mini skit? What a rush.

Back on the street, we hunker down behind a headless horseman statue in the center of the square. I keep my eyes pinned on the skeletons, now loitering outside Wraith's Fate Tavern.

"Were you an actress in another life, too?" I whisper to Effs, enjoying the adrenaline left over from our mini-theatrical production. "I can't wait for you to read some of my plays."

She tucks a lock of hair behind her ear. "If we get out of this alive, I'll read them all."

I let a massive smirk overtake me. Effs gasps, and that smile fades.

She clutches the bulging sucker at her neck. "Mines burning."

"Are you okay? Gah!" I slam a hand over my pulsing sucker too.

It squirms, sending a sharp pain through my arm. I clench my fist to fight the numbing sensation and swallow hard. The ache continues, tingling like I've pinched a nerve.

A drop of black blood drips onto my hand from my nose. I quickly wipe it on my towel. *That's new.* Maybe I will end up like Roger after all. Shudders course through me.

Shakily, Effs widens her fingers. "The sucker knows. It knows they're here."

Ahead, the skeletons clink. They look directly at us.

I back away. "I think *they* know."

"Run," Effs says.

"As if you needed to tell me!"

We take off into the dark, barreling beneath the rows of flickering streetlamps illuminating Specters Village. My bare feet burn beneath the chilled cobblestone. I clutch my slipping towel at the knot against my midriff, keeping it upright, and as my soul sucker continues to twist my nerves, I grit my teeth and focus on my breathing.

Effs huffs at my right. "Let's hide in the alleyway!"

Ahead, the shadows welcome us. Our bodies slam side by side, out of sight.

I rest my head back and swallow the phlegm in my throat. "We still need to get supplies. We could lure them into a shop. Use something in there to smash them to pieces."

"If we smash them to pieces, they'll put themselves back together again." Effs peeks around the corner. I follow suit, peering above her with my chin resting atop her head. "We must take their skulls. If they can't navigate, they can't find us."

"What would we do with their heads?" I ask.

Effs tightens the waist of her robe. "Burn them. Bury them. Hang them on the mantle. It doesn't matter if they're kept separate from the rest of them."

"Gotcha. I'm on it."

I glance down the opposite end of the alleyway at the array of closed shops. Wedged between a tailor shop and a gutted-out bakery is one that reminds me of our local market, Phantom Pharms, back on Spinners Pier. Dad used to take us every week after Mom got sick. She'd write the weekly supply list. We'd return with the goods.

I slink through the shadows and cross to the shop. *Always try the handle first before breaking a window or busting a lock.* That much I learned from our dear father. Rather, from the series of holographic notecards he'd downloaded for me when we first began.

They were tips from Aunt Merik. Aside from the few practice thrifts on the pier, he stuck with Shea most of our training. Kept her up late until she aced everything he set in front of her. I was the dud in the corner with the noise-canceling headphones and an AI bot feeding me instruction videos on mastering puzzles, brain teasers, and lock systems.

It's whatever. I'm not bitter about it or anything.

I try the handle of the shop and give it a good jiggle.

People leave doors unlocked all the time. Apparently, not apparitions. Using my palm, I put pressure on a windowpane and wedge my hand through the open gap. Once I'm inside, Effs checks to see if the coast is clear and joins me. I close the door behind us as quietly as possible.

As I set down my pillowcase, my eyes immediately draw to the back corner. An entire cooler of flavored milk and fizzing juice offers a steady motor buzz and a bluish glow. My mouth waters.

Effs unsticks a broom from the wall behind the apothecary counter and hands me the dirtiest mop I've ever seen. We take our places at the door. She kicks it open. On her nod, I shove two fingers in my mouth and huff the loudest beckoning whistle I can manage.

"You ready?" I ask my new friend—not lover—for life.

She wields her weapon of choice. "Oh, I'm ready."

"Excellent. Let's knock some skulls."

12

SHEA

An unsteady stream of lukewarm water washes over me.

Whether it was ever hot to begin with is a mystery. I press my forehead against the scum-crusted tile. Sudsy clumps of muscle matter clog the drain. It catches on my toes.

I grimace and shake it loose. There's nothing more I could have done today. According to Dash, taking the night off is acceptable. Doing absolutely nothing for a little bit is too.

So, why does it feel like we're giving up?

Why does it still feel like we're wasting time?

I flip the faucet, and the trickle of water lessens to a steady drip. I draw back the curtain and fumble for the towel to dry myself off. It's stiff and scratchy, and it barely does the job. In the mirror, I wipe a clean streak. My reflection comes into focus. My hair, which usually sits past my shoulders, is now a tangled mess. The dark circles under my eyes have deepened.

I prod the small gash in my lower lip. I'm not sure when it happened. Maybe I sliced it at the Bone Bridge, or maybe it happened in Lake Ichor. Either way, the cold compresses and ointment from my healing kit are long gone.

I settle for a bit of toilet paper and dab it dry the best I can. As I toss the crumpled paper, I notice a heap of other paper in the can. A whole mess of it, soaked in black blood.

Question is—Dash's or Euphoria's? My stomach churns. *Not Dash. He still has time. He's okay.* But for how long? He and Euphoria mentioned a cure, and I can hypothesize based on what I know about parasites all I want, but without doing more research, I know nothing about the damage it could pose to my little brother.

If the troll Gallivant hadn't gotten soaked, I could have contacted Dad, Mom, or even Aunt Merik for help by now. An extraction, further instructions—anything.

But we have nothing. No one. That scares me. Leaves me desperate. *Vulnerable.*

Mom and Dash like that word. Dad despises it with his entire being. I know why. Gods, I know why. Because being vulnerable SUCKS. Not even in the manner of being a perfectly polished leader or an Enforcer. Vulnerability causes you pain. It makes you weak and emotional. It lowers your guard. It clouds your judgment and makes you impulsive.

I can't afford to be any of that right now.

A pile of items has been left for me by the door. Dash hasn't been able to stretch his fingers recreationally since we arrived, and I bet the urge to pull was pressing, but this is more than I expected. A new set of clothes, including a long plum cardigan and knee-high boots, sturdy enough to make a getaway in pressing situations. Atop the clothes is a pouch of lunar root capsules that I'm assuming will stop my bleeding because there isn't anything else. Next to the pouch is an amethyst crystal necklace on a leather cord, two bars of chocolate, a new hairbrush with elastic ties, and a roller bottle of lavender essential oil perfume.

There's no way Dash thought of all this by himself.

As I dress, I imagine Euphoria helping him pick everything out. I picture her choosing each piece carefully, her lips with the defined cupid's bow pursing as she decides. The way the light catches the crystal stud in her nose and the assortment of charms hanging around her neck.

These are foolish thoughts, Shea. She's hiding something. She was inside your mind.

The human brain is unreliable when it's under stress or in survival mode. Maybe I'm fixating on something that never happened, and I only think she was inside my mind.

But I didn't imagine it. I saw Dash underwater. Then *she* was there.

Not to mention the visions in my head. We can talk about past lives and reincarnation all we want, but those weren't my memories. I won't let Euphoria try to convince me they were.

I won't let her cloud my judgment or trust her enough to let my guard down. All this time, Dash and I have followed her, assuming Valerian will hand over the cure and let us go peacefully. But if Euphoria is at war with this guy, whether in this life or the past—I don't need to know their drama, nor do I care—how cooperative could he really be? Where would we even start if we had to steal the cure and my key?

These are all the questions I need answers to. Dash doesn't understand. He says tomorrow is a travel day, and we don't need to prepare, but we should be spending *all* our time prepping for what we're going to do when we reach this Crowley Corner place.

All the fun and games, they're over now. We need an actual plan. A good one. For all we know, Euphoria could be lying or leading us to Valerian right now.

Dad wanted one of those soul suckers for a reason. This isn't the romance-drama turned twin-soul illusion Dash thinks it is.

Dad also says smaller lies stem from bigger lies. Which begs me to question how often Dad's lied to my face. He left important details about Ominous out of the brief. He kept me out of the loop. He sent Dash to steal something dangerous, even though he knew the risks.

For a moment, my world seems to tilt. I don't know what to believe anymore. I don't know who to trust.

I grab the rest of my new belongings and exit the bathroom. I really should find a moment to thank my brother. Because of him, I'm dry. I'm warm. I have lunar root. The perks of knowing a good Thief, one who now lounges fully clothed beneath the covers of our only bed, sipping tea from a cracked teacup, munching on bags of pork crisps, all while two very real human skulls bask in lamplight on the other pillow.

Don't even want to know. "Nope. This bed is mine." I toss my hairbrush and chocolate into the dusty folds of the quilt. "You can sleep on the rug."

"Shhhh. Would you—" Dash sets down his tea and points to Effs, asleep on the warped sofa next to the now blazing hearth. "Effs is trying to catch some z's."

"Okay."

"And just because I'm the guy doesn't mean I should have to sleep on the floor like a dog." He rolls up his snack bags and gathers his skulls. "I reserve the right to curl up at the foot of the bed like a dog instead."

"Fine, but if you start tossing and turning or sleep fighting like you did the time we had to share a hammock in that jungle on planet Plex, I will kick you onto the floor without remorse."

"I had a heat rash, and the mosquitoes were eating me alive!"

"Well, you shouldn't have worn that sweet cologne."

"It was in *season*—" Across the room, Effs stirs, and Dash sighs. "Look, I don't want to fight right now, okay? I'm tired of fighting."

He drags himself toward the edge of the mattress and fluffs a discolored throw with mangled tassels. After a few moments, he wipes his hands on his new jeans and lays back. "You're welcome for everything, by the way."

Sitting cross-legged in bed, I begin the treacherous process of brushing out my hair's knots. It doesn't matter how much I scrubbed in the shower. It'll take weeks to rid myself of the lake residue.

"I was going to say that I appreciate everything you took for me."

There's a pause. He stares at me. I avoid his stare. Neither of us knows where to go from here. I'll admit, I haven't been easy on him. Part of me wants to keep bickering if it means we can reach a mutual understanding. The other part of me knows he won't listen long enough to.

He watches me work through my hair's matted knots. Then he mutters, "Effs and I had to fight off a couple of skeletons that found their way into the village, but we managed to get away. We're getting closer to Fake Death."

My fingers get tangled. "And?"

"I just couldn't part with the skulls. I had to keep 'em."

"*No*—I mean, did you learn anything else about this guy?"

His eyes light up. "Not really, but Effs thinks she can talk some sense into him."

"Look, I know she's told you this over-romanticized story about how they've been trying to master duality over lifetimes or whatever, but I think we should be a little more realistic."

"A little more realistic? You don't believe it? You said you've researched past lives and reincarnation. That her story made complete sense."

"I've researched St. Nicholas too, but that doesn't mean Father Christmas is real," I say.

"Hey, now. Great-grandpa Alden believed in Father Christmas."

"We need to focus less on Euphoria's relationship issues and more on getting the cure and my portal key so we can get home. We need a *real* plan. Helping them 'master duality' to achieve union in the Higher Realm and 'convincing a man of who he really is' isn't a plan."

"What if getting the cure and your portal key is a direct by-product of that plan?"

I let out a long sigh. My brother is a romantic, a storyteller, and a performer. If a situation even comes close to being cinematic, he'll throw logic out the window, call himself the main character, and play his part until the metaphorical credits roll.

He'll never understand. Our brains aren't compatible. We're just too different.

"I'm too tired to think about it anymore. We'll figure it out in the morning." I struggle through the tougher gnarls of hair and curse under my breath. "Goddess, I swear—"

Dash crawls over. "Here, let me?"

"Your hands are all—"

"I wiped them off. No chip grease. I promise." He shows me his clean palms. I allow him to take the brush. He adjusts and sits behind me. "I'm used to doing it for Mom."

I'm sure he misses it. And her. I do too.

Closing my eyes, I take in the soft pull of my little brother brushing out my hair. His movements are swift and practiced. When he's done, he parts my roots and braids like he does with Mom's hair. A chill rides up my back.

Habit or not, I welcome it. "I'm still mad at you, you know."

"I know you are." His placid words don't sound like him. Not the campy and witty, unapologetic Dash I know. Maybe he *is* finally starting to get it. Or maybe he's numb like I am about all this, and he craves the release of surrender too. "I wish you'd tell me why you're upset."

"I... I tried telling you." I lean into his movements as he tightens his form and finishes off the first braid. "You don't get it, Dash. Everything falls back on me. What I do. What you do. I'm responsible for so much, and you don't have to worry about anything."

"That isn't necessarily true." His motions slow, becoming more delicate. "I always assumed you wanted the responsibility because every time I try to help you or take some of the burdens, you tell me I won't do it right or you can't trust me with it."

He's not wrong. I don't trust him with pressing matters. I'd rather do it myself because I've been the only one I can truly count on for the majority of my life. I know that unless I do it myself, it doesn't get done.

"We don't have to talk about it." He uses his teeth to open the second elastic. "I just want you to know that I'm sorry, and I want to work on understanding your feelings more. Effs told me it's better to hash things out than brush them under the rug, and I agree with her."

I force a chuckle. "You've been talking to Euphoria about me? Great."

"Yeah, and I think you should give her a chance, Shea."

I allow my gaze to fall to where she sleeps soundly, at the array of herbs and an empty teacup on the floor beside her. "Dash, we don't *know* her."

"Maybe *get* to know her. Give her the benefit of the doubt." He smooths his work, tucking in any flyaway hairs. "She brought us here and paid for us to stay. She saved you. She's shown us nothing but kindness."

He pauses, then adds, "I know you think I'm naïve and irresponsible, and I am to an extent, but I wish you would let go sometimes. Let go of the need to control everything or predict every outcome. Let go of the need to assume before you know. I'm a space case, but the best experiences have been because I go with the flow. I let situations unfold, and I remain open to everything and anything."

"It's very easy for you to live like that because you don't have pressure on you."

"Yes and no," he says. "I think the difference is that I don't let people put pressure on me. I'm not perfect, and there's a lot I need to learn, but why let someone else tell me how to live, what to do with my life, or how to be? I want to live a life that I love and that makes me happy. I'd hate for you to miss out on a good thing, that's all."

Dash's words sit heavy in my chest. Would he say the same about the Board fellowship too? I know he would. That seems like a fantastic thing. Letting people in isn't so certain.

"Well, you and Effs seem like you've become great friends so far," I say. "I'm happy for you."

Dash smirks. "I think that's the first time I've heard you call her Effs." He tightens the ends of my second braid. "And you could be friends with her, too, if you wanted."

"It isn't that I don't want to get to know her. It's that—"

"You can't. I know. I know it's hard for you." My brother finishes my hair and collapses next to me in our heap of blankets. "But trust me, Effs *is* one of the good ones."

I'll never understand how Dash so willingly gives everyone he knows the benefit of the doubt. Even after his ex, Zena, broke his heart on the pier, he was up and ready to let the next person in. *How?* How is he not jaded by that? How can he not be hurt by someone stringing him along and then getting rid of him when they're bored?

The idea I could have another friend in my circle, someone else to share my thoughts with besides Dash or Mom, appeals to me. But I won't do it. I can't do it.

My brother rests his head on my shoulder. "If I tell you something else, can you promise not to get upset? Can I be honest with you?"

"Yes, Dash."

"I'm sorry I didn't say anything about visiting Auntie. I first went to see her last year after our run on Violet Moon, after Dad pitched a fit about the moon worms we nicked not being the right ones... even though they sold like popping candy on the market. Mom wasn't doing well, and you were busy and... I needed someone to talk to who understood what I was going through." He pauses and buries his face in his hands. "I... I don't know if I can do this anymore, Shea. You know, the business. Working for Dad. Going on runs. Being a Thief."

My heart sinks. The words he spoke when we played Two Truths and a Lie back in the Bone Wood echo in my mind—*I hate working for James Co., and I'm quitting after this gig on planet Ominous.* Was he serious about that? Had I been wrong? His kiss story could've been a lie. I vaguely remember him telling me about Micah Sanders. What if him scoring the highest on his survival exam was the truth?

"You heard me, right?" my brother says.

"I... did. You always say that, though. You don't mean it."

"We're having a heart-to-heart. I'm being serious. I... don't... want to do this anymore. I'm not happy."

His body warmth fades as he scoots forward and rubs his eyes. "I really want to go back and spend my twelfth year at the Academy. I'm seventeen, and I've never been on the official Holoblocks team. I'm dying to get back into theater. I wanna spin artsy pottery that nobody understands in the Maker's Studio, and I want to eat week-old squid burgers and crinkle fries in the cafeteria. I wanna be normal for once. I want... I want planet Ominous to be my last run."

I hate working for James Co., and I'm quitting after this gig on planet Ominous.

So, it was true. He does want to quit. He hates this life, the life and bond we built together. I'm not sure what to say. It's not completely random, but it's hard to digest. I've never thought about working with anyone else but Dash. I can't imagine working with anyone else. Now *I* wish I'd known sooner. Why did he wait this long to tell me?

And how do I respond respectfully without feeling betrayed?

"I'm glad Aunt Merik was there for you when you needed someone." I pick at my nail beds and keep my eyes down. "I'm sorry I was too busy for you..."

He puts his hand on mine to stop me from pulling an old hangnail. "We don't have to talk about this anymore, okay? I just wanted you to know. I needed you to know."

I lift my head. "How are you so sure that being... normal is what you want?"

"It's not about being normal, really." He chuckles. "It's about making my own path and doing what I love. Right now, that's Holoblocks, but maybe down the line, I'll do something else. Like driving cargo crafts and traveling the galaxy or working at Tee Tees. I just like knowing that I have options. That's the whole point of life. Going with the *flow*."

The burning in my throat makes it hard to swallow. I tell myself I don't know how Dash feels, that I can't understand where he's coming from, but I do. Mr. Beachum showed up at my door and offered me the chance to follow my path too. And I didn't take it. I didn't officially turn it down either, but I didn't take it. Now Dash wants out? *He* does? Who will take care of Mom if we don't go on runs? Who will deal with Dad and take over the family business? Who would hold this family together if I... hypothetically... wanted out too?

"Hey, hey—" My brother lifts my chin and forces me to look at him. I wipe the beginnings of a tear from under my eyes. "What's wrong, Shea? What's going on? You can tell me. You know you can tell me."

And for a moment, I almost tell him about the fellowship and Mr. Beachum, but instead, I focus on his arm where his soul sucker resides. Before it was swollen, maybe a little bruised, and the black spider veins hadn't spread too far. Now, they've reached his neck, and his lips are blue.

I grip the squirming bulge under his skin, and he winces. "You're getting worse, Dash. How are you feeling? Headaches? Muscle spasms?"

Dash shrugs. "A little headachy, I guess."

"The bloody tissues in the bathroom trash, were they yours?"

"I'm okay, Shea. I look worse than I feel. I promise." He glances at Effs. "And no, they weren't mine. They're probably hers."

"We need to figure this out."

I run my fingers along his wound. The soul sucker inside rides the motion of my thumb and curls into itself. Dash tenses. Maybe it isn't entirely like a parasite. Maybe it numbs its victims like steely blood worms from planet Rion. Or maybe it embeds into its host's muscles like the pygmy scroungers that live in the gutters at Spinners Pier. I wish I knew more. Not knowing is killing me.

What if I can't fix him?

What if Valerian Bale doesn't have the cure? Dash wanting to leave the business is one thing, but I can't let him die.

I drop his arm and shift to the head of the bed. Morning can't come soon enough.

I wriggle under the covers. "We need rest. Tomorrow, I'll ask Effs more about Fake Death. Maybe she knows something we can use."

I lean over and tug at the pull switch on the bedside lamp. Dash remains by my side. Through the darkness, I can tell he's smiling. For what reason, who knows.

"You called him Fake Death," he whispers.

"*Yes.* Now lay down and go to sleep."

Dash shuffles to the end of the bed, tugging another spare pillow with him. As he settles in, his breathing evens out, and faintly, he says, "I'm glad we're making progress, Shea."

Me too, little brother. My heavy eyes take me into the beginnings of a dream, and his voice blurs as the grungy boarding room 212 of Wraith's Fate Tavern drifts away.

A stream of egg yolk drips down my thumb and lands on my ancient plate. I soak it up with a slice of burnt toast, which was surprisingly satisfying for being half charcoal.

Normally, I would've suggested we take off immediately, but it dawned on me this might be our only chance to eat today. Since our overnight stay included breakfast in the lodge dining room, it made sense not to let it go to waste. We are the only ones here this early, and the spirit waiters have been idly standing by the buffet since. They seemed eager to seat us when we arrived, and I guess they've been waiting to entertain for a while now. It begs me to question the freshness of our meal, given they are all technically dead and running a semi-functioning tavern, but I can't plan on an empty stomach. Preparation starts now. We've got a LOT of work to do and even more ground to cover today.

I finish my last slice of toast and take a bite of elk meat off a wooden skewer. All that remains on my plate now is a stale brambleberry pastry. Across the table, Euphoria sips apple cider. Dash hunches over a full plate of untouched food.

He pushes potatoes around with his fork. Then opts for a gulp of water.

Strange. "Dash, you're not hungry? That isn't like you."

He shakes his head without looking up. I wipe my mouth, alternating my gaze between them both. Slumped shoulders. A deeper bluish tint to their lips. Sunken cheeks. Their veins are extra prominent in this light, and their eyes seem opaque. This is bad.

Euphoria sighs. "You don't have to say it. We know we look terrible."

I wipe pastry crumbs off my mouth. "Oh, well, I—"

"I don't think I can eat." Dash clutches his gut.

Euphoria forces down another sip of cider. "I don't know if it's soul sucker related, but I lost my sense of smell on the first day, and my appetite went soon after."

Interesting. "Dash, can you still smell?"

He nods. Maybe the worms affect their hosts differently. It explains why rushing for the viscera lake didn't affect Euphoria yesterday. She couldn't smell the putrid acid eating away at the rotting flesh. Or taste it in the back of her throat.

"I suppose we'll know death is near when we lose functionality in our limbs," she continues. "Or black blood oozes out of us beyond our control."

"Like Roger," Dash mutters.

"OK. That's enough. Both of you." I toss my utensils in the center of my plate, and they clatter. "Nobody is dying. You'll both make it until tomorrow. We're getting the cure."

Dash frowns. "You don't know that."

"I know sitting here and talking about it is wasting time." I gather the toast from the table and wrap it in a holey cloth napkin. "I'm packing this up in case you're hungry later."

He lifts his head and gets up, pushing away from the table. "Mhm. Maybe just the toast or a few crackers? Nothing too heavy. I'm going to the bathroom before we leave."

After he's gone, I get out my journal and check its damage. Mostly dry, save for the crinkles and crud stuck to the pages. Next, I survey the troll Gallivant. I press my finger into the reset button, but the device won't power up. *Great.* I don't think anything can save it now.

"Did your journal end up drying all the—"

"Look, I need you to be completely honest—"

Euphoria and I stare at one another.

"You say what you want to say first," she says.

I clear my throat. "I need you to be completely honest about how much longer my brother has left."

"I honestly, from the bottom of my heart, don't know, Shea. I don't even know how he's still alive. My magic is holding mine off, but he should be dead by now."

Magic is holding her sucker at bay. Maybe she wasn't in my head at the dam. Maybe she used magic to save me, and somehow her thoughts became mine? Still, if magic prolongs her death, she wouldn't want to waste any of it. She'd be speeding up her own fate. But why is Dash different? *How* is he still alive?

"Your journal ended up making it, then?" Euphoria asks.

Small talk. She's making small talk. Kill me now. "Uh, yeah."

"I hope it's not an invasion of privacy, but I woke up before you, and a few of the pages by the fire had fallen. I quickly re-hung them. They were interesting."

My lips press into a line. "You... you read my travel journal?"

"I apologize. I didn't mean to." She fiddles with the ends of her hair. "You've got some interesting bits in there. You have a keen eye for detail."

I can't believe she read my journal. *Who does that?* "Um. Thank you... I guess?"

She smiles. "I do still owe you more information about Ominous. I'd be willing to write a few pages of history to save time if there's a topic in particular you'd like to know more about."

"No way." I wipe berry juice off my palm. "If I ever wrote an essay on this planet or got published, I'd have to credit you. And the Board fellowship wouldn't accept it either."

"A Board fellowship?" She leans in closer, and my heart rate picks up. "You *should* write about Ominous. I think you'd do us some good."

"I—I don't—"

"And you wouldn't have to credit me." She does that thing where she searches my face, my soul, my everything—that thing I hate. "Knowing someone would be writing the truth about us is more than enough for me. Do you have a deadline?"

"No—" I grind my teeth. "It's not *like* that. It's a post-graduation program for students interested in exploratory careers." I can't believe I'm telling her this. Her of all people. But I'll admit, it feels good to tell someone. It feels good to be listened to for once. "They're very selective. Past fellows have joined out-of-realm voyages. Others travel with the Board of Galactic Studies all over the galaxies. It's a major honor and a once-in-a-lifetime opportunity."

"And you're applying? That's so exciting."

Heat rushes in my cheeks. *Reel it back in.* Telling her about the fellowship is one thing, but confiding in her my hopes or desires in any way, shape, or form is where I draw the line. She could still be leading us into something tricky. She cannot be trusted with personal information.

"I don't know what I'm doing yet." I push away from the table. "I should go check on Dash. He's been in there a long—"

"I could draw you a map of Ominous to get you started, at least? I was going to anyway, so you could see where we're headed."

A map of planet Ominous? My gaze alternates between her and the crooked 'Loo' sign nailed to the bathroom door. *A map of a planet nobody else has cartographed or documented in the Universal Database.* Oh, she's good.

"For the sake of safety, maybe you should." I pick up my journal. "I can see where you're taking us and learn about threats like viscera lakes before we swim in them."

"Of course. Though I would never purposely lead you into danger."

Sure she wouldn't. Maybe this is a bad idea. She'll probably draw me a fake map. "You know what, I just realized Dash never thrifted an ink stick, and I lost mine in the lake, so I'm not sure what you'd use anyway to—"

"I've got something to write with."

Euphoria abandons her seat and plops herself in the one next to me. I lower myself to her level, and our shoulders accidentally brush. As they do, an unsettling wave of energy washes over me. Something about her being near to me in this way.

I realize my hand is shaking, and I quickly turn my chair while she retrieves a silver tube of black lipstick out of a small, knitted, cross-body purse—one I'm assuming Dash stole for her last night.

This is a bad idea, Shea. This is a bad idea.

Euphoria motions to my journal. "May I?"

At my nod, she finds a blank page and begins her line work.

"Ominous is a quadrant planet," she explains, her eyes fixed on the page. "To the South is the Bone Wood, from which we came. Toward the West is the Viral Wild. I lived there in my last life. Nobody wants to go there. The entire land and population are plagued with contagion."

Her knowledge feeds me, the way it floats off her tongue and into the journal like a song. *What is wrong with me?*

"And to the East?" I press a palm on my leg to quiet its tapping beneath the table.

Euphoria looks up. A note of rosemary catches my nose. "Ruins of Ore. It was once a dreamy countryside. You would have loved it, I think. I know you would've loved it. At the start of the Great War, the villages, the ocean, the people, everything turned to stone." She pauses and admires her work. "Finally, we have the North. Our intended destination."

Right. The North.

"Hexes Pass is where Crowley Corner is located."

"Where you lived with Valerian and the other spellcasters, right?"

"We resided in the old Tower ride."

I look into her golden eyes once more. *Gods, I know them. I swear I know them.*

"You've been telling my brother a lot of things since you met him," I say, pushing the unsettled feeling aside, " and I don't know how much of it is fact, but for the sake of his life and us getting home, I want to know the truth about Valerian."

"Everything I've told you is the truth, Shea." Effs busies herself with shading in the rest of the map, a chunky black smear on the parchment. "That you can't bring yourself to believe it doesn't mean it isn't the case. Valerian isn't a malicious person. He isn't a villain."

"Don't make excuses for him. He created a creature capable of devouring souls. And I'm sorry, but he made a deal with my father, and my father only makes deals with villains."

"An assumption you're making without knowing the facts." Euphoria closes my journal. Her eyes find mine once more, her face softening in the tint of the lamp above our table. "Tell me, Shea, what memories did you see in your mind when you were drowning? Before I saved you? Were they malicious in any way, or were they pleasant?"

She holds my stare, and the familiarity in her eyes bores into me.

I grit my teeth and rise from my chair. "What the *hell* did you do to me down there—"

"I'm gonna need a chewable tummy tablet." We both turn our attention to Dash, now standing pale and hunched at the end of the table. "Preferably sooner than later, if possible."

Euphoria purses her lips. "I don't think we have those here on this planet."

Heat rises inside me, spreading in my skin. *She knows I saw something down there.* So, she is playing mind games. Who IS this girl? We need to ditch her ass.

"I had some in my old pack." I grab my journal and stow it away in the new backpack Dash stole for me. "We'll find you something along the way. Let's go. Now."

As we exit Wraith's Fate Tavern, my brother groans. I sneak a glare at Euphoria. She bumps shoulders with him, a smile on her face. As if she didn't just draw me a fake map and practically threaten me with her cryptic memory talk. She might have Dash fooled, but I'm not buying it anymore.

The town square is alive with an overwhelming number of spirits in old-fashioned police tunics. A cluster of apparitions gather around a shamble of a convenience store, which is also where two headless skeletons sulk on a wooden bench.

The new backpack on Dash's back lurches.

He knocks it straight. "Dang skulls."

I glare at him. "What happened to thrifting clean?"

"Oh, come on. They love it." He motions to the disarray. "It's the most exciting thing that's happened in this town since the Great War wiped them off the map."

"He's not wrong," Euphoria comments, which somehow irritates me more.

"See, Shea?" Dash side-steps to avoid a flock of curious detective ghosts in checkered hats carrying oversized magnifying glasses. "I did them a favor by ransacking that store."

I roll my eyes. Euphoria guides us from the courtyard toward a post: Carriage House. "We can catch a carriage to take us halfway to Hexes Pass, and then we'll have to walk the rest."

Dash glances up the hill. "Walk? I'm too tired to walk anymore."

"It won't be that far."

I allow Euphoria a head-start. As much as I'd love an endless supply of knowledge, her hint of subtle secrecy weighs on me. I lower my voice and turn to Dash. "I really don't trust Euphoria. She said some things that aren't settling well with me. She drew me a map. I can get us the rest of the way. I say we ditch her here and go on without her."

My brother groans. "*Gods.* I thought we were giving her a chance!"

I am. But I won't let chances outweigh my training. Or the sensation fluttering in my gut like a horde of moths scattered by a puff of pesticide. "Letting her tag along is a risk."

Dash scoffs. "Stop. Please stop. I can't deal with my stomach issues *and* your irrational paranoia right now. You wanted a plan. We stick together. *That's* the plan."

"That is not the plan."

He tries to sneak around me, but I grab a fistful of his jacket. "I know you have a crush on her, but you need to look past it and think logically. She may be 'one of the good ones,' but there's something she's not telling us. About this place. About Valerian. About her. I can feel it. We can't trust her."

"I'm asking you to trust *me.*" He wriggles out of my grip and walks on. "Were you half-asleep during our talk last night, or did I just imagine you coming to your senses for once?"

Uh, excuse me?

We clamber up the trail, shoulder to shoulder, toward the structure atop the hill where doleful apparition horses graze. Euphoria leans over the fence and runs a hand through a mare's translucent mane. The spirit horse lets out a neigh and nestles its head against her palm.

Good grief.

"Again. We need to think logically about this. That's all I'm asking. I'm begging you to look past your obsession with her so we can evaluate—"

"STOP. I don't feel well enough to argue right now. You're panicking, Shea-Lynn. Self-sabotage. That's what this is. That's all this is. You gotta reel in the panic tangent. Please."

I clench my fists. "Don't you dare raise your voice at me. You should be grateful that I have the common sense to scope out anyone within a mile of us." My next words come out meaner than I intend them to, but I can't help it. They spill out too fast. "Euphoria doesn't even like you, you know. She's using you, Dash. Just like Zena, Chip, and everyone else from the Academy that you desperately wish to return to. You forget that this business is *all* we have. All we have is each other."

His lips quiver. "Take that back, Shea."

"No. I'm not taking it back because it's true."

"It isn't true!" he shouts, and the mare enjoying Euphoria's gentle touch startles and gallops off across the enclosure.

She's watching us now, but I don't care. "It *is* true!"

Dash's cheeks flush. As I wait for him to compose himself, I think of how many other ways I could've approached this. How I didn't have to pull at his insecurities. But it's ingrained in me to win.

If I don't take the lead here—it's over.

I clasp my hands. "Here's how this is going to go, okay? I'm the Enforcer and the older sister. I'm making the executive decision that as soon as we get to Hexes Pass, we ditch the spellcaster and go our own way. We will find the cure and my key on our own."

"Sometimes I think you forget to separate the two roles," Dash mutters as he brushes past me. "And you know, Shea, I know Effs doesn't like me." He runs a hand through his hair, his voice dulling. "She likes you, but you'd never have the guts to open yourself up and let someone else in because you're too afraid to FUCKING feel anything."

My fists curl involuntarily. *Resist the urge to knock him out, Shea-Lynn. Remember, he's got a leech sucking out his soul.*

"You can't hurt me," I bark. "And swearing at me doesn't make you more intimidating."

He offers a half-hearted laugh. “Right, because Dad trained you to be an emotionless robot and commandeering hard-ass. How could I forget?”

I stare at the rusted water trough in the pasture, so I won’t strangle him. My brother leaves and meets Euphoria at the stables, where a drab carriage awaits, pulled by two spirit horses. As Dash steps up into the passenger cab, he glances back and shakes his head at me like Dad does every time I fail to do anything to his standards. A tightness envelops my chest.

So much for us making progress.

13

DASH

Soul suckers are all fun and games until they seriously damage your soul.

A drop of black blood drips from my nose. I quickly wipe it on my sleeve before anyone sees it. *Heinous Hades.* I *am* getting worse. My stomach churns. Hard to tell if it's because a worm is turning my insides into black sludge or because my anxiety is acting up.

I believe my official diagnosis was 'acute anxiety with specific triggers,' but it took a whole argument with Dad to let Mom book me an appointment. Forget helping them pinpoint the exact circumstances that set me off. It wasn't like I could say, hey, I steal for a living, and my family deals in illegal underground trades. I endure multiple near-death experiences on a weekly basis, my dad's a jerk, my mom's dying, and my sister is a grudge queen.

Still, this kind of flare-up hasn't happened since I was thirteen.

I look at the grudge queen now. She stares aimlessly out the carriage window at the occasional snow flurries and barren trees with knife-shaped leaves that roll by, an almost permanent curl stuck on her lips. Fall is my favorite season back on Spinners Pier. The trees change a trippy spectrum of red, yellow, purple, and blue. Everything on planet Ominous is brown and cold. All that's pulling us is a couple of wisps of light with tapping hooves. That, and our zombie coachman keeps whistling the same eerie tune.

Let's just say it's been pure, torturous silence since we left the Carriage House.

When she isn't staring out the window, Shea hunches over her journal, scrawling Gods knows what with a stick of chunky black lipstick. Effs tried making conversation a few times, but Shea nor I was up to it, so she resorted to staring out the window too. I haven't mustered up the strength to speak up, and I can't look at my sister without experiencing this immense surge of anger that boils my blood. Seems I'm the one with the grudge here.

All those things Shea said back in Specters Village about Zena, Chip, and the Holoblocks team at the Academy. About *me.* She was acting out of fear, but her words still hurt.

Because part of me knows she meant them.

Part of me knows she was right too.

I think I meant everything I said. My delivery was sub-par, but Shea needed to hear it. She'll never stop if I don't tell her like it is. She'll keep using me as an emotional punching bag.

I release the longest sigh. "What's the plan, Shea?"

"Oh, I don't know. I thought I'd let you take the lead since it's your last run and all." She makes eye contact with me for a split second, then continues her forced means of distraction.

Stellar. "Well, heck. I don't have a plan."

My sister shrugs. "Guess we're doomed then. You and your soul."

"You did not just say that." I strike the lipstick out of Shea's hand. It falls to the floor of the carriage and rolls in the dirt. "If I lost my soul, it would ruin you, and you know it."

A flush overtakes her. "I couldn't care less."

She says she's the more mature one, but when it comes to bickering, she acts like a First Year. "You're a piece of work. You know that?"

"Thank you. I take that as a compliment."

"You wouldn't know a compliment if it slapped you in the face."

Shea slow claps. "Great comeback, Dashiel. You're a real comedian."

"Thank you. I take *that* as a compliment."

"I must admit, I am very uncomfortable right now." Both Shea and I glance at Euphoria. She offers us a little wave. "Tensions seem high. Perhaps we could... compromise?"

"That's a great idea, Effs." Sweat soaks my back, and I lean against the seat, so my sweater will absorb it all. "When the carriage stops, Shea can go her way, and we'll go ours."

My sister's dagger eyes dart up. "You won't last the one day you have left without me."

Honestly, I was kidding. "You *wish* that were true."

An impish grin takes over her face. "Wanna bet?"

With you? Gods, no. The pain in my temples intensifies. My sister doesn't lose bets. I know her. She'd rather be set on fire in the Underrealm or kidnapped in an abandoned Skyway station than back down. What have I done?

"Well? What's it going to be?"

Shea picks up the lipstick crayon and blows it clean. She sets it and her journal in her lap. I look at Effs, who seems genuinely concerned. Eyebrows tight. Lips pursed. Wanting to speak her mind but knowing darn well she shouldn't. Because this is between my sister and me.

It always will be.

I hold out a clammy hand, palm up. "Fine. Make it a bet sealed in blood."

As if she expected this, Shea digs into her bag and takes out a tiny retractable blade I stole for her back in Specters Village. We haven't made a blood bet since our Middle Years. Back then, it was petty wagers like Shea daring me to sneak into high-end stores or me daring her to knock some sense into bullies on the Academy playground just for kicks.

We'd spent so many nights listening in on Dad's deals that we wanted to play too. Joke's on us. Now we're playing. And the game isn't fun anymore.

My sister guides the blade against the thickest part of her palm without flinching. Droplets of blood leak in her hand. A shiver rides my spine. She hands me the blade. I follow suit, shakily applying pressure to draw enough to seal the deal.

Black, coagulated liquid pools from my wound—definitely not normal—but before either of us can comment, Shea slaps her hand into mine and squeezes so tight my temples throb again.

She pulls me closer. Her breath tickles my ear. "What's your wager, little brother?"

I focus on the drops of sludge dripping down my wrist. It's gotta be something good, that's for sure.

"If I make it on my own, you let me leave the business without holding it against me for the rest of eternity."

Shea's breath hitches. "And if *you* don't make it on your own, if I have to save you—you stay *in* the business. You don't finish your twelfth year at the Academy. You stick with me."

We glare at each other. It's clear to me now how serious this is. But there's no going back. Blood has already been drawn. I'm trying to prove a point, but I'm only screwing myself over.

"Fine," I say.

"*Fine*."

Shea releases my grip and sits back, a contentedness about her. I catch Effs watching me wipe my bloody palm on my jeans. She offers a half-hearted smile, but I don't return the favor.

Honestly, all I can think about is Roger. His body contorting on the floor. The massive puddle of black blood surrounding him. What did Shea say about my loss of motor functions being a sign my death was near? Or being a sign I was already dead? Am I still good?

I wipe sweat from my forehead and swallow a lump in my throat, but it won't go down.

"Now, Euphoria," my sister says. "Assuming you'll be going with my brother once this carriage stops, I think it's only right that you tell me anything else you know about Valerian that might help me get home."

I shudder. "Wait. I can't even go home with you now? That isn't part of the—"

"You said you could make it on your own. I thought it was implied."

"Wha—*No*. It was not implied!"

Effs tilts her head. "Why would you assume I'd want to go with your brother?"

Oh, this is getting better by the minute.

My sister chuckles. "Well, you aren't coming with me, that's for sure."

Effs chews her lip. "If you truly feel that way."

"I do."

I rub my temples. The searing pain deepens. "Just—let her go on her own if that's what she wants. I'm done arguing about it. I'm literally done."

"I told you most of what I know." Effs motions for my sister's journal and lipstick pen. I expect Shea to protest, but she doesn't. Effs draws a stone high-rise that looks like it belongs to some medieval castle—a haunted one. "You'll likely find Valerian in the Tower."

My sister purses her lips. "How many stories?"

"Twenty-seven."

"High security?"

"Spellcasters on every floor."

"Could I get up without a recant box?"

Effs smirks. "For someone ordinary, no, but you are not ordinary."

The two share a quick look, and a chilling silence fills the cabin. This is the first time I've ever seen my sister at a loss for words. I glance between them, at Effs's gentle composure as she draws out detailed blueprints of the Tower, though Shea doesn't deserve them, and at the way my sister's tapping foot runs wild.

Ah, I get it now.

Great Goddess.

Shea *likes* her.

The idea tugs at my heartstrings. Almost makes me want to forgive and forget these past couple of days and our vindictive blood bet. My sister liking someone is rare.

It's a leap of faith she'll never take. Speaking your feelings takes guts. My sister is a blunt—tell-it-like-it-is—kind of girl, but over the span of a few years, she's let a handful of cruel rejections tell her she's unlovable. They'd know she has so much to offer if they could only see beyond the walls she's built around herself.

Effs and I didn't work out, but that doesn't mean they shouldn't have a chance. Whether my sister knows it or not, it's happening. And heck, all I've ever wanted was that novel-worthy romance, that quirky rom-com in space. But if it can't be me, then I want it to be Shea. Even if she is being a complete jerk. Even if she might be the reason I die today.

I know an experience like this would soften my sister. Prove her wrong. Prove every single idea she has about attraction and love and relationships wrong. She can sit with that proof and realize she *is* wrong about it all, about herself, about everything.

Yep. That's what she needs.

I lean back in my seat, and a tighter ripple of pain explodes in my chest. *Are these muscle spasms?*

"You know, maybe you should go with Shea, Effs. I'm feeling independent today. I'd like to prove that I can make it on my own."

"No. I'm going alone," my sister says, and *oh my Godddds.*

A sudden jerk rocks our carriage. The phantom horses let out staggered brays. They slow, and moments later, the tattered cabin door swings open to reveal our corpse of a coachman.

"Can't go any further," he tells us. "You'll have to walk from here."

Gah. The dude's eyeballs hang by a single thread of muscle. I wrinkle my nose. Shea forces her way out, past Effs and me. I'm last out, and as soon as my boots smack into the dirt, the drab coachman hops into the driver's seat and tightens his reins.

The carriage's rickety wooden wheels spin a sharp corner. They kick up a cloud of red dust. All of us cough. Raw sand coats my throat. I spit a mouthful of phlegm on the ground.

As the dust thins, Shea comes into view further up the path. Now standing at the mouth of a vine arch, twisted with oversized sage leaves. A labyrinth of vegetation soaks in the haze on either side of the entrance. Abnormally large toadstools with blackened caps and white-speckled stems glisten in the sunlight. Enormous coal-colored roses with satiny petals drape over one another, an array of white moths with fangs and red spots nestled in their grooves.

Shea sneezes, and the cluster of odd, winged creatures flee, stirring up an earthy aroma that smells cloyingly sweet. Settling back onto our feet in a fine red layer is the grime cloud that nearly choked us.

"It's called brick dust." Effs feels for the array of charms hanging around her neck, reminding me of Shea and her portal key. "The dead can't cross here. It's embedded in the mulch, along with salt. A ring around the entire garden."

"This is Tempters Garden, isn't it?" Shea asks. "You included it on your map."

Effs nods. "It's very important that you don't touch or take anything, no matter how tempting it may be."

The girls fix their gazes on me. Honestly, I'm a little offended.

Shea raises a brow. "Did you hear that, Dash? A bit of wisdom for you before you set off on your own. Good luck out there. And good luck getting home."

I roll my eyes. She's so full of it. She doesn't want this bet any more than I do. It's a game for her. I've opened a wound inside her, forced her to face it, and she's punishing me for it. I could say the same thing about her, but I won't.

The two skulls in my pack roll about, and I knock my backpack so they'll stop. Then, I take off ahead of the girls, ducking beneath a low-hanging canopy of bizarre metallic berries that ooze on their boughs. Shea and Effs walk in the same direction because there's only one way to go inside this sadistic place, but I attempt to speed up so it doesn't seem like I'm being clingy or tricky or that I'm weaseling out of our blood bet.

Shea isn't the only one eager to prove a point.

"Have fun, you two. See ya at home, Sh—" I turn around, expecting the girls to be paces behind me. They aren't. Which makes no sense because two seconds ago we were together.

Now they're gone.

The path itself has shifted. Before, I was standing in a canopy of metallic berries. Now, I stand in an overgrown patch of wild flora, twisted and torn. Vines nurturing a strain of green mold swing overhead. Bugs chirp in the tall, prickly grass surrounding me.

I glance around, my heart hammering in my chest. "Sh—Shea?"

My soul sucker clings to my veins. It pulses beneath my skin, and I tremble. This is legit. The girls literally disappeared. Either that or Tempters Garden is playing some serious mind games with me. Going off alone sounded brave in the moment, but I take it all back.

"I'm—I'm calling off the bet." The rustle in the flora makes me flinch. I crane my neck, checking my peripherals. "Shea? Please. This isn't funny. You've made your point. I'm a useless wreck without you. Don't make me trek through this horror maze alone."

The last time I wandered around by myself, Fake Death claimed to be Death, and a soul sucker slithered inside me and made a permanent home in my nervous system.

I cup my hands around my mouth. "Shea-Lynn! Euphoria!" My voice booms across the labyrinth and gets sucked into a cluster of withered tendrils. "I take it all back! I'm not—"

You know what? No. This is fine. Everything is fine. *You don't need your sister. You don't need Effs.* This is exactly what my sister wants. She wants me to need her. She knows I need her, and she's testing me. That's what this is. That's *all* this is.

It was Effs that told me to stop acting helpless. She called me capable. But am I capable? I haven't got Shea's kind of nerd brain. I've got my own kind of nerd brain. One hard-wired for video games, spice zingers, and theater. What good does any of that do for me out here? Who cares what I scored on my survival exam. Shea's the capable one.

"I'm okay." I run a hand through my hair. "I can do this. I'm going to be okay."

The skulls chitter in my pack. I take a moment to unzip the bag and wrap them in a spare long-sleeve shirt. *That oughta keep em quiet.*

As I close the zipper, something flickers in my peripherals.

"Shea?"

I peek in all directions.

Crane my neck. Double take.

"Shea-Lynn? Is that—"

Is that a life-size Holoblocks capsule simulator?

It's true, I swear. Ahead, a grayish-metal pod big enough for one player, with an array of blinking buttons and the metallic Maker's Games logo spread across the top, sits nestled in the thick overgrowth of toadstools and monotonous shrubbery.

"This can't be real." *Can it?*

No. I can't do this. Effs told me not to touch or take anything, and that especially includes playing a Holoblocks game.

I glance up at the blazing sun. "This is a *temptation*! And I'm *not* falling for it!"

In response, the capsule pod's door pops open, and the familiar advertisement sings out, "Play Holoblocks: Holocity—the game of strategy and strength—from the comfort of your home. Now for a limited time only. Immerse yourself in the *experience*."

"It is an experience I'd very much like to immerse myself in—Nope. Nope," I say with a chuckle. "Nevermind. I won't do it. I'm strong."

The capsule rotates, revealing the interior of the pod. As the ring light at the base glows, a curved leather gaming chair, sleek and smooth, reveals itself.

"A full body experience," it says in a suave tone.

"A full... body experience?" I say back. "In... the Holoverse?"

A set of custom gameplay gear plops down on the seat out of nowhere. Including the highest level of gaming goggles for grid play available on the tech market and a pair of new edition biometric gloves with double the sensitivity that aren't even out yet.

"Those gloves let you feel everything," I stammer.

The pod chimes. *"Immerse yourself in the experience."*

Gods. No, Dashiel. DON'T DO THIS. DON'T DO THIS. DON'T—

My body slams down into curved leather. The 360 degree-digital screen grid lining the interior of the pod comes online. Neon-blue light reflects into my eyes. I slip on the biometric gloves, and they shift, molding to the EXACT shape of my hands.

My fingers tingle to life. My grid goggles lock into place behind my ears.

A button pops up on the screen. *"Press start to immerse yourself in the experience."*

I slap the screen. "Button pressed. Take me into the Holoverse."

14

SHEA

"Dashiel!"

Not this shit again.

"Dashiel!"

I'm going to kill him.

"This is what you wanted." Euphoria hacks at the thick bunches of wild vines blocking our path. "He's gone his own way. You've gone yours."

Yet you're still here. "I was *kidding*. Acting vindictively. It was a tactic. He won't survive out there by himself. This place'll eat him alive. Are you really that daft?"

She blinks at me. "I'm not daft at all. What a rude thing to say."

I swallow a lump in my throat. This is the first time I've really been alone with Euphoria. Actually alone. Our moments in Wraith's Fate Tavern didn't count. She's been a neutral presence thus far, kept her nose out of our business, her thoughts to herself. Now that Dash is gone or lost or wherever he's disappeared to, she wants to get snappy with me?

I don't think so. "Stop pretending like you didn't know this would happen."

Euphoria awards me a look I know all too well. "This is not my doing. You two made that ridiculous bet, and now he's carried out his promise. If that feels wrong or like you've made a mistake, then I say we find him."

"There is no *we* in this."

"I have never met a more imp"—her hair catches on a low hanging vine, and she untangles it—"impossible human to convince of one's loyalty and sincerity." Then she pauses. "Actually, I have. I take that back."

Dash's words about Euphoria possibly liking me cross my mind for a SPLIT second, but hell, that could have been a figment of my imagination too. Not that it would make a difference. Not that it would change anything about how I feel about her or us or anything of the sort.

"I don't have to prove anything to you." With a heave, I push through a wall of shrubbery adorned with bleeding berries. A few roll at my feet and squelch beneath my boots. Like my brother, like this planet, this garden is wounded too. "To be blunt, I'm surprised you haven't pitched a fit yet about us trekking around like animals through this *sacred* space."

She keeps her head down, careful not to squish any berries. "Your words, not mine."

"And I know my brother. He didn't run off on the terms of a bet. He disappeared. Something happened to him, and I will figure it out on my own. Whether you knew about it or whether you led us here on purpose, your services are no longer needed."

I'll admit I reveled in learning more about Ominous history from her, but this is where I draw the line. My bet with my brother was foolish, a mistake, and I'll fix it. I'll make it better.

But *she* can't help with that.

"You'd like to rid yourself of me. You've made it painstakingly clear," Euphoria mutters, and my cheeks warm enough to put me on edge. "At least let me help you find Dash before I go. I know this garden better than the pair of you, whether you'd like to admit it or not."

"I won't travel with a liar."

She stops and throws her hands out. "What have I lied about? Please tell me, Shea. I've been honest with you. I've told you what I know. I'm not sure what else I can do to convince you."

"You've weaseled your way inside my mind. You've brainwashed my brother." I toss another clump of squashed berries over my shoulder to further clear our path.

Euphoria dodges it elegantly. "I have done nothing of the sort."

"Back at Wraith's Fate Tavern, you brought up the memories you intentionally placed in my head when I was drowning in Lake Ichor. And I'm not convinced you even know Valerian."

This time Euphoria laughs. "I can assure you, I know him. Possibly more than I'd like to admit."

She steps up and helps me hoist a cumbersome branch out of the way. We toss it into the underbrush. I glance up, now nose-to-nose with her.

"And I didn't intentionally place anything in your mind. What you experienced in Lake Ichor was a memory jolt. On the brink of death, our third eyes are more susceptible to seeing the unseen. Whether that be remembering the past or experiencing a glimpse into the future. Either way, it was all you down there."

I quickly distance myself. "Convincing story. How did you know about it then?"

A lock of hair falls across her face. She blows it away. "When I grabbed hold of you and pulled you to the surface, our physical connection also prompted the visions in my mind."

"That doesn't even make sense."

A stream of black blood trickles from Euphoria's nose. As she wipes it, the collar of her dress pulls back. "Are you even open to trying to understand it? My guess is you aren't."

My eyes draw to the charred skin covering her neck, glistening with sweat. *We're running out of time.* I yank another vine out of our way. "What the hell is that supposed to mean?"

"Deep down, a part of you knows I'm harmless. Otherwise, you wouldn't have agreed to let me tag along. It's why you let me live back at the Bone Bridge. Why you've put up with me thus far. Why all your threats are empty intentions and a defense mechanism you use when you're uncomfortable."

All this *talk* is another tactic. Euphoria thinks she can press deep into my wounds. That she can pull at my soft points and use them to her advantage. Maybe I should let her think she can. That's a strategy too. An illusion that I'm breakable when there's nothing left to break.

I brush my palms together and wipe them on my pants. "We needed you to help track down Valerian—*that's* why I agreed to let you tag along. And I've been using you for facts and research—*that's* why I've put up with you."

"That's all, is it?" She steps through the opening we've cleared. "It has nothing to do with the uncomfortableness you feel when I try to get to know you better?"

I scoff. Is that really what she thinks this is? *Please.*

"For your information, I'm not uncomfortable." I follow her through the opening, toward a meadow basking in a giant shadow. "I'm being logical. Realistic. You get screwed over as often as I have, and you realize that nobody cares about anyone but themselves."

Euphoria purses her lips. "Ah, I understand now. How could I forget?"

She continues on. I jerk her back without thinking. "Do *not* pretend like you know me."

My eyes wander to my own hand, gripped tight around her upper arm. My palm goes numb. The pounding in my chest returns. I release her, but she doesn't flinch. We've stopped at the edge of the meadow. I focus my attention on the flowers instead, realizing they weren't bathing in a shadow at all. They *are* the shadow, a thick sea of gray and black flora.

"You don't trust me. Fair enough." Euphoria bends down and brushes a moss-covered stone. A centipede with pinchers and horns crawls into her hand. She keeps it safe in her palm and admires it with grace. Glancing up at me, she adds, "Who do you trust then?"

I gaze into her gold eyes, deepening my scowl. Maybe I trust Mom, but I don't confide in her as I should. Dash is irresponsible most of the time. Though he does have his moments. Friends, I can't name one. I don't have time for friends.

And Dad—I *used* to think I could put my faith in him. But the error of his ways, his actions, they've proven he's about as dishonest as they come.

Other than that... nobody.

I push away the thoughts and turn a shoulder so Euphoria won't pry at me anymore. Even if she's telling the truth, I'm sick of it, and we still need to find Dash. A quick scan of the overgrown labyrinth concludes he is nowhere to be found.

My focus falls instead on the meadow, at the black flower buds. They drip a clear mucus film. I'm unsure of the species, and it makes me wish, yet again, that I'd been properly prepped for this pick-up-turned-rescue-mission.

I scooch, careful not to touch. "What kind of flowers are these?"

"They are mourner flowers."

I inspect their stems, the way their roots sit at the surface of the brick dust soil. "Is that their scientific name? They don't look like they belong to any of the typical plant families."

She watches me for a moment. Her gaze settles inside me. The moths living permanently in my gut flutter. They twist and gnaw at my insides. The further she sees, the deeper she looks.

I swallow the burn rising in my chest. "Quit trying to read me."

"You remind me of someone I know. They, too, thought they had to prove themselves to everyone they met. They, too, treated everyone like they'd already been wronged, and it wasn't fair to anyone involved."

"Maybe *they* didn't want your pity."

"Maybe if *they* had accepted that nobody is perfect and that sometimes we can't control certain outcomes or situations, maybe they wouldn't have succumbed to a life of—"

"What." I laugh. Tears burn my eyes, but I'm allergic to the slimy pollen in the air. *Probably.* "A miserable life alone? I happen to love being alone."

"I was going to say a life of pain and suffering." She takes a step toward me, and my entire body tenses.

"One of missed experiences and fear. One that seems redundant and wrong, where lashing out at others comes easier than accepting love." We're inches apart now, my heart ready to burst. I grit my teeth. If I don't, tears risk being shed.

"And I didn't get the chance to tell them this, but I'll tell you—I like that you are brave and resilient. I have been trying to understand the other parts of you too. The parts of you that care so fiercely for your brother, though you misunderstand each other's flaws."

"I—"

"I am *not* done." She further closes the gap between us. Now there's nowhere for me to go. I'm cornered and stuck. "The part of you that doesn't give up no matter how tough it gets. The passion you have for research and knowledge, how it sets a fire in you I will never know."

Another inch and her nose would brush mine, I swear to the fucking Goddess.

"I don't care if we're strangers, I'm going to say it all—I find you intriguing. You have yet to learn how to harness your own strength or use it for the better, but you have magnificently beautiful energy. And it is not a lie, trick, or misleading diversion."

My breath catches.

Flattery is a dangerous game.

I have nothing to say in response. I can't . . . formulate words at all. Nobody's ever spoken to me like this. My lips won't move. My tongue is raw. My jaw locks into place.

"My mother taught me that there will always be hurt in life, Shea, but we cannot be afraid of that hurt."

Euphoria slowly puts space between us again. "For every human or being meaning us harm, there are three times as many who'd have nothing but love for us."

I watch her stroke the curve of the centipede with her thumb. She allows it to uncurl. Then she lets it go on a crooked branch, higher off the ground, out of harm's way.

A tear trickles down my cheek. I don't wipe or hide it. I don't know why. Maybe it's because I don't care. Maybe because it's only one tear. There won't be any more.

Euphoria gives me privacy anyway. She doesn't think I notice, but I do. How she kneels and busies herself with a section of mourner flowers that have begun to bloom. Her delicate hand brushes a dark, tangled tress behind her ear. And for the first time, I notice small things about her. A birthmark on her earlobe, a little brown speck like a mini chocolate chip. The curve of her jaw and fullness of her slightly chapped lips. A recognized energy and warmth surrounds her. I felt it as I was drowning, I realize. I'd tried to convince myself it was wicked.

You always think the worst, Dash tells me.

In an ideal world, yes, *maybe* I'd indulge the idea of getting to know her or might even try letting her in. She has a familiar energy. That I can't deny. Her eyes are unlike anything I've seen before. When she smiles, I feel it deep in my soul.

So, why don't I trust her? Why *can't* I trust her? And are my potential reasons not reasons at all? Gods, I really am the queen of overthinking and over-analyzing.

I join her where she hovers over the blooms. "You never told me the scientific name."

A slippery petal breaks off into her palm. "Mortem Anthropophagous."

Mortem Anthropophagous. Mortem is Latin for death. Anthropophagous is Greek for... for... Gods, why can't I remember? I've been out here too long.

"I'm concerned because they aren't set to bloom until the spring equinox." Euphoria checks another few, which have also begun to open and stretch their sticky petals. "I took us through Tempters Garden because most of the garden hibernates in the cold season."

"Something woke them up too soon," I say.

We both give each other the same hollow stare.

Dash.

Eerie shrieks fill the air. Faint at first, the horrific sounds build around us like a wave, an undertow you wouldn't want to be caught in. The rippling screeches of the mourner flowers wake the others, and they all uncurl with shaking petals and oozing pistils.

Together they rise in volume.

Euphoria and I slap our hands to our ears.

"You have to make them stop!" I scream.

She shouts back, "They *can't* be stopped!"

Another octave sends the mourner flowers into overdrive. They rise from their roots and glide across the brick dust-coated dirt, revealing tiny mouths at their sepals. Razor-sharp teeth glint as they lurch, eager for a meal. Euphoria and I take off when it dawns on me... the Greek word for anthropophagous.

Cannibal.

"Man-eating flowers? Screw it all." I keep at Euphoria's side. We race among the sea of wakening flora. "I'm beginning to wonder if there's *anything* pleasant on planet Ominous!"

The mourners rise in masses behind us. Ready to devour us whole, they band together with intertwined petals and roots that smell of char and metal. *This isn't happening.* My heart pounds. I feel them, their warm breath laced with bitter floral notes at my heels, the tiny prick of their teeth, craving flesh as they sink into my right calf and devour a chunk.

I hit the ground, my stomach cushioned by a bed of velvet. Dirt fills my mouth. The acidic texture clings to the back of my throat. I hack it out. Gag on my own spit. And the sting, the sting is the worst. A sharp prick of agony floods my muscles. Blood gushes from my wound, leaking down my leg, and in my disorientation, Euphoria is there to drag me away.

The reality is I'm twice her size. She isn't going to be able to do this alone. I have to fight for these moments. Or my life will be the next thing in this garden to mourn. Together we move up from all fours onto a teetering two feet. Mourners or not, chunk of my calf missing or not, a hoard of palm-sized flowers will not take me.

Darkness closes in. A heaviness in my eyes.

There's something in me, in the sting of my wound.

A venom, maybe. A poison.

It leaks into my bloodstream. Pins and needles. My fingers go numb. My knees buckle. Euphoria keeps me up, conscious long enough to catch a glimpse of a great bird, the tutelary from the Hallway of Doors.

Those vast sparkling plumes. The mourners and their savage shrieks. Their rows of gnashing teeth. Their fusty decaying roots. The spellcaster who thinks my energy is magnificently beautiful. Who I might think has a magnificently beautiful energy too.

All I see now is the bird.

A stillness settles in the evergreen wood.

Soft specks of snow float in the air. My hot breath clouds. I trudge the deep snow, my knee-high boots sticking with each step. I'm me, but I'm not me. Not Shea. Someone else.

Inside a wandering mind. No control over my legs. She knows where she's going.

The edge of my navy cloak catches on a bough. I shake the dusting of snow, pull up my velvet hood, and cling to it for warmth. As I round the bend, laughter echoes in the trees.

Another girl, ahead. Dressed in a white cloak lined with fur. Knitted mittens on her hands. Knee-high leather boots like mine. Heat rushes in my cheeks. This body recognizes her.

Her eyes, tawny laced with gold.

She whistles, and the source of her amusement comes barreling through the brush. A grunt escapes the little beast. Piercing blue eyes. Paws to grow into.

"Come, Ace."

The girl bends over and scoops up the bear cub. In her arms, he squirms and rolls onto his back, begging for a belly rub. As the girl heeds his wants, she looks at me. No. Behind me.

"Mother Ominous," she says.

As I turn, a woman in a flowing, black cloak emerges from the thicket. She draws her hood, revealing long, dark hair and silver eyes. I notice the triple spiral sigil on her wrist.

An Enchantress, this version of me thinks.

She pursues her blood-red lips. "I'm here to make the deal."

The girl holding the bear cub steps forward and lowers her hood too. She moves aside her thick, orange curls, revealing her bare neck. Mother Ominous reaches forward and places her palm at the base of her hairline. A soft glow envelopes Mother Ominous's palm, and the girl winces. When Mother Ominous drops her hand, a triple spiral sigil now sits on the girl's neck.

My legs take me closer, and my hand lowers my hood. I sweep aside my locks of black. The chill tickles my exposed skin. Mother Ominous leans in, her palm warm on the nape of my neck.

"In return for agreeing to experience these lifetimes ahead, I promise you ascension into the Higher Realm. With each lifetime, your progress will ripple into the collective. My mark will fade when you've learned the lesson. When you've mastered duality."

Without warning, a searing pain finds my neck.

It radiates down my spine and into my nerves. Into my soul.

My screams carry far out into the evergreens.

An angelic white light pulls me back.

Oxygen floods my lungs. My eyes spring open. I gasp.

Euphoria comes into focus. Her fingers produce the spark.

She's straddling me. Back to me, her petite form leans in the dimming dark. Her hair falls aside as she hovers over my injured calf, revealing the back of her neck and a triple spiral marked on her skin. *What the*—I thrash. She squeezes her knees, keeping me down.

I reach for my own neck, frantically pulling at my collar.

"Relax, Shea. You haven't made any deals yet. You won't for several lifetimes."

"How did you—" I dig into the dirt, my fingers groping around the cavern we're situated in. Somehow, we've made it here. "Where have you taken me?"

My brain races, trying to process everything I've just seen. Heard. Felt.

"Shhhh." Euphoria's warm palm grazes my blood-soaked skin.

The sparks in her fingers shift from bright silver to gold.

What is she doing? She's using—

"Magic," I slur, trying to buck her off. "You'll make it... worse."

"My goodness, you have a vivid imagination." Euphoria glances back at me, her golden eyes settling a shade darker. Familiar. *Dash.* Those are Dash's eyes. I'm sure of it.

She chuckles. "You must relax. This won't take much longer."

The visions at the dam. Whatever I experienced just now in-between consciousness. Euphoria called it a memory jolt. Could she and I really be connected in this way? Could her stories be true? Those glimpses I've been getting. Is it possible they aren't visions at all? They may be. . . memories... of the past. Or, in this case, the future.

I can barely keep awake. I crave the truth like mourner flowers crave flesh. *It isn't possible.* Logically, it would mean—I can't even think it aloud.

"Don't deny the truth you so desperately sought out." Euphoria's voice prods the dark. Her weight keeps me pinned. Another string of light curves the shallow roof overhead, illuminating the tunnel and revealing how tight it really is. I attempt to sit up once more. She shoves me back.

My tongue swells in my mouth. "Stop using... magic... "

"You mustn't fight it," Euphoria says softly.

If she's—then I'm—No. I can't come to these conclusions in my condition. It wouldn't be wise. One would have to be wildly suggestive to assume this truth.

I won't say it.

I won't think it.

Euphoria glances over her shoulder at me once more, offering me another look in her eyes. They become gold again. Alternating between the two variations, windows into her soul.

"Stop. Stop it." I stumble over my thoughts, struggling to think of a logical explanation.

I truly don't have one.

"I'll tell you everything you want to know once we're in the clear." Euphoria climbs off my stomach and settles beside me, allowing one last wisp of gold to caress my cheek.

"You're... you're my..." I reach up and feel where the wisp soaked in. Her spark lingers, a sweet taste in my mouth. "You used your magic to heal me."

"As much as I could give. It was either that or watch you die."

Though the golden light fades in her fingers, it's clear the soul sucker's infection has gotten worse in minutes. Still visible. Still calloused. Still spreading. Only deeper. "We both know it isn't your time yet."

Blood drips from her nose. A bit from her ears. She's quick to wipe it.

"Why would... you waste your magic on me?"

"Accept the gesture, and let's not speak of it again."

The mourner venom in my blood is ruthless. I've barely any control of what comes out of my mouth. "Tell me... everything."

"You won't remember if I tell you now." Her wisps of light disappear, returning us to dark. My stomach twists. She reaches out and places her arm on mine. "I will tell you this. We're in an underground tunnel beneath the garden. An old smuggler's hatch leftover from the Great War. I tore away a layer of the vine and found one before the mourners caught up to us."

I sink into her. "You... you did something to me."

"Mourner flower venom," she whispers in my ear. "Another minute, and you'd have been paralyzed from the waist down. A healing spell mixed with a mending spell revived you, but you will need time to recover. But not here. We can't stay here."

Moments later, I'm up off the ground. Hunched over Euphoria's shoulder. Somehow, she bears my weight. *It was her in that vision. And me. Only, she didn't look like her. I wasn't me either. We were completely different people.* The numbness reaches the back of my throat.

My head droops.

Euphoria tilts it against her shoulder. "I don't suppose you've ever dealt with devious dirt gnomes?"

"We need... to find... Dash. If they could help us... "

"They aren't much help, I'm afraid. They are, however, fascinated with organs of any kind. Especially hearts, stomachs, and livers. Alright, let's get you through the hole."

There's a hole? I open my eyes, which are useless in the inky abyss. I can tell it's gotten narrower as I reach out to touch the wall. Barely tall enough to stand. Euphoria helps me up and over a hump. A crinkling noise sounds above. Dirt trickles over my face and into my hair.

She grunts and drags me the rest of the way through.

We tumble into the next cavern. My knees give out. I careen over. Our bodies intertwine.

Euphoria brushes the hair out of my face.

I swat her away involuntarily. "Don't... touch me you."

I am outside of my body now. The words I speak aren't mine.

Her laughter echoes in the dark. "My, you are a fun one, Shea. Alright. This next stretch is increasingly difficult to navigate." Her hand finds mine. She squeezes, and the dizziness takes over. "I don't have enough magic left to ward off anything that might come our way. You have my word. I'll get us through in one piece, but you'll have to trust me."

I tense my body and mumble on like a fool. My heels dig into the dirt.

"You can't fight me on this," I hear her say. "Eventually, the garden will fall asleep again, but Dash might not make it that long. You might not either if a herd of gnomes crosses this way on a hunt. I won't force you to come with me, but I recommend it."

I teeter. "I could... use... *you* as bait for the gnomes."

She helps me back up. "You won't."

"I... might."

"I trust you won't."

"You don't know me."

"I think we both know that isn't true. Our energy is a match."

She says something else, but the enveloping black absorbs her words.

I allow myself... rather, my body allows me, to be with her long enough to feel the energy she speaks of, that power that radiates from deep within her.

It's the same power that radiates inside me too. We *are* a match.

Duality, I think she called it. *Twin souls.* Only, she's one version of it. I'm the other. But we're both whole on our own. And my brother is another version of her. *Which means...*

Euphoria's magic is a lukewarm energy that slips into my aura and sidles its way out when it knows it doesn't belong. But her magic is nearly spent. What's left of her is her energy and hers alone. I can't describe what it feels like. If it's good. Or if it's bad.

All I know is that it isn't like any other.

15

Dash

I release the trigger on my glowbeam. The neon green curse crone in front of me explodes into holographic dust. From the corner of my eye, I spot another, this time a neon pink, floating in the air.

"Another curse crone up ahead in grid-space three," I say into my mouthpiece. "Where is my defense? Alex, Taylor—Cover me to clear another path for Nic. He's gotta make the run NOW if we're gonna make it up the north stairwell into the epicenter... "

Keeping my back against the brick wall, I lean around the corner and peer into the holographic expanse that makes up this level in Holocity. Like a replica of the city grid the Skyway train follows on planet Sarasing. Only here, in the Holoverse, curse crones lurk around every street corner, seeking the holoblocks we store in our holo-banks—the metal-plated chest piece we all wear—and they want *allll* the lives we've got.

Our team healer, Dakota, appears at my side, out of breath. "Nic lost a life. His health is down 5%. If he loses another, he'll respawn back to our meeting point. Should I send him to collect the last block in Zone 8?"

I switch out the cartridge on my glowbeam. "Send Liam too."

Dakota pulls out his holo-chart, detailing the remaining floors on this level, Level 16. "If they go now, they'll have thirty seconds to reach the landing, transfer all the blocks to you, and unlock the mechanism for us to move onto Level 17."

"Copy. Do you have the code?"

I glance at Dakota, eager for the numbers, but he's gone. The other guys are too.

Where did my freaking team go? Can't make it to Level 17 without my team.

All around me, Holocity glitches out. I hear a grunt, then a shout. I check my team stats on my goggle screen. My entire team is offline. All of them. *What in the—*

Shrieking sounds around me. A rush of curse crones? Couldn't be. The ground beneath me quakes. Static prickles my biometric gloves.

Something slimy wraps my ankle. *Too real.*

I tear off my Holoblocks goggles and my eyes re-adjust to the 3D world around me. As the shrieking grows louder, the simulator pod I'm sitting in begins to disintegrate. I tumble to the ground, whacking my butt on a rock.

Gahhhh. I force myself into a seated position, my eyes drawn to the wave of motion shuddering the foliage ahead.

I've touched something I shouldn't have.

But, like, what the heck are those?

Ahead of me, in the garden, a wave of black flora surges. I spring up and stumble back, my heart hammering in my chest. My grip tightens on my pack strap. As they near, the little heads of the black flora snarl, revealing razor-sharp teeth. *Are... those...*

"KILLER FLOWERS!" I spin on my heels and sprint along the path. The shrieking pierces my insides. I cup my ears, stumble forward, and trip over a root. As I fall, I tuck and forward roll into the motion. The wind knocks out of me as I tumble onto my back, clutching my throbbing head.

As I brace myself for the feeling of being eaten alive, a creature hops onto my stomach. I've seen a lot of creatures in my day as a Thief, but this one takes the grand prize. A pudgy little gnome wearing nothing but a long, burlap hat and scraps to cover its private bits ogles at me. It notices the soul sucker bulging in my arm and jabs it.

"AHHHH. STOP," I wail, and its eyebrows furrow. It slaps me across the face, back and forth, back and forth. "Please STOP slapping me across the face! GAH."

It motions to the other gnomes—wait, other gnomes—oh my *Gods*. There's gotta be fifty of them. They pour out of holes in the ground. They burst out of prickly bushes. An ambush of them, a mini army wielding tiny, rusted sickles. Together, they hack at the wicked flowers—choppity chop here and choppity chop there—with impish grins and grunts.

I sit up in awe, and a cluster of gnomes jumps back on top of me to pin me down. Their tiny toenails dig into my skin. They surround me. Tug at my clothes. Working hard together to haul me away. I can't tell if I should wrangle myself free or let them take me away at this point. They fought off killer flowers for me. Maybe they're bringing me to safer ground?

My head slams into the opening of a tunnel. "AH—"

I rub my head and avoid another hit. Between all of them, they pull me through the hole and into an underground cavern lit by miniature torches. I bite back the burn in my arm. My stomach scrapes the dirt. The gnomes carry me into a second cavern, larger than the first, toward a slab of stone that looks suspiciously like an altar.

A cold sweat breaks out on my forehead. This is vaguely reminding me of the time I almost joined a cult in Eighth Year.

That uneasy feeling in my gut grows when they hoist me onto the alter and tie rope around my wrists, stomach, and ankles.

I struggle. "Wait. WHOA. You can't tie me up! Stop! What are you—"

A gnome I'm deeming Leader Gnome, wearing a crown of black roses, hops onto my belly. She shoves her palm against my lips. I wish I had my Universal Comms earpiece because I can't understand anything she's saying. Three more gnomes convene nearby, preparing a clay bowl of chalky, beige paste. They chitter and speak in muted tones, and one of them guides the others in washing their hands in a rock trough of dirty cave water.

"I'm so thankful you saved me." I squirm and pull at my bonds. Man, are they tight. "But I do believe I've overstayed my welcome. I really should be going. My sister and friend are—"

Leader Gnome whips out a blade from a fold in her burlap skirt. She runs the blade through layers in my clothes and undresses me from the waist up. Another gnome plops down on my stomach with his bowl of chalk plaster. Humming, he works with Leader Gnome, and they scoop up the mix in their hands, warming it in their palms. Nice of them... I guess...

They slather three x's on my chest. One over my heart. Another over my stomach. One where I think my liver is? I dunno. Shea knows more about anatomy than I do.

Gods, I wish she were here. I find myself thinking that a lot now. Even though we're fighting, finding me would mean losing our blood bet. It would mean I'd have to stay in the business another year. Could I do that? Could I give up another 425 days of prime Holoblocks time and countless hours of playwriting beneath the moonlight to admit I was wrong, that I depend on my sister much more than I'd realized? That I take her for granted?

Maybe I could free myself without her. Shea would rather die than be taken. She'd choose ruthless tactics over impulsive choices. She'd show these dirt gnomes whose boss and get herself out of the situation no matter what it took.

I remember what Effs told me. *You're capable, Dash*.

I clench my fists. "OK. Listen, you half-naked gnomes—*Ah*, that's cold!" A stream of liquid gushes over my shoulders and neck. The water chokes me, catches in the back of my throat, and I close my eyes before the next bowl is tossed. "Uh, I appreciate the—stop that—gesture, but I took a shower last night, and now I'm good for the entire week."

Leader Gnome adjusts her lopsided crown. Using her thumb, she prods every inch of my abdomen, carefully examining the spider veins that have now spread across my chest. At her touch, I flinch, straining against my bindings. There *has* to be a way out of this, right?

I search my surroundings. Leader Gnome slaps her foot against my cheek, keeping my gaze in place. Another gnome jerks my arm upward, giving Leader Gnome a clear view of the soul sucker writing beneath my skin. The wound around it is charred and crusted over. As she pushes the bulge, it pusses, and I ride out a throbbing wave of pain.

"Please, don't touch that."

Leader Gnome squeezes the sucker again, this time harder. I scream as black blood pools into her tiny hands. My insides go cold. Sweat and tears stream down my face. The sucker inside me coils. Another otherworldly scream explodes in the back of my throat.

Who am I kidding? I need my sister.

I cry out, "Sheaaaa!"

My entire body shakes. Every time I move, my bindings tug. The rope gnaws at the skin around my wrists. The gnomes ignore my pleas. They don't care about me. With her dirt-caked fingernails and stubby fingers covered in green-tinted blisters, Leader Gnome pinches the soul sucker some more.

Black and pink pus squirts out of my wound and splatters their plump cheeks, but they only cheer. Another spasm of pain, this time sharp and twisty, hits in my insides.

I am going to die today.

The gnomes continue to cheer. I scream myself hoarse. They whip out their sickles. Leader Gnome shouts and slices my gut. Nothing too deep. Yet. Enough to make me wince. Enough to draw blood. My lungs constrict. I keep thinking I'll predict my own death. I thought I'd end up like Roger. I thought I'd end up at the bottom of a canyon. Heck, I thought I'd get pummeled by the Academy AI for forging our semester grades or be thrown off a moving Skyway train for thieving traveler pockets, but no—*this* is how it ends.

A bunch of dirt gnomes on a horror planet.

"I never got to play on the Holoblocks team." I sob. "The virtual spring musical will go on without me... Oh, *Gods*, my love life will never be fairytale-esque."

Leader Gnome laps up a dribble of my black, coagulated blood.

She licks her lips. Sucks her fingers clean.

Then her body goes rigid.

She clutches her throat, gasping for air. A very pretty shade of purplish-blue rises in her cheeks. The other gnomes stand by, watching and speaking in panicked whispers as their leader wavers back and forth, does a little deadweight spin, and falls on the ground. Her body twitches, and then her mouth opens, and her gray tongue splats out.

Huh. I rest my head back on my rock slab. *Didn't see that one coming.*

The remaining gnomes hover over their fallen leader. One pokes her limp form with a sickle. Another kicks her in the foot. They exchange a series of wide-eyed glances. In one sudden rush, they flee. Arms flailing in the air, the petite pitter patter of their feet and their screams fade away. I pull at my bindings. Strain my neck to look around. Nothing.

They left me here. They really left me here. As I clench my body, I feel the curve of a tiny sickle at my waist. My eager fingertips spring into action. *Freedom. Resting inches away.* It only takes me a second. Lots of floundering around. But I manage to fetch the sickle and maneuver it against the rope tying me down.

Eventually, the rope gives way with a snap and I let out a deep breath, carefully contorting my body to undo my other bindings. I sit up slowly and get a better look at the tunnel. Above me, a ceiling crawling with iridescent centipedes and spider webs drips sweet, luring nectar.

I hack through my ankle bindings and step off the altar. "I hate this place."

Human-sized footfall echoes in the passageway. I tighten my hold on my tiny sickle, which is about as useful as a spork, and steady myself on the curve of the cavern wall.

You can do this, Dash. Whoever is coming around that bend doesn't stand a chance. Just wait until Shea hears about this. I fought off an entire horde of dirt gnomes by myself, AND I'm about to fight off some rando *all* in the same day. I've never been more proud of myself.

Planting my feet, I hoist my miniature weapon. "I've got a tiny sickle, and I'm pumping toxic blood, so I *will* fight you to the death. Or at least until one of us passes out."

The footfall grows near. I raise my sickle higher. Effs, of all people in the galaxy, rounds the corner with Shea all but slumped over her shoulder.

Effs gasps. "Put that down!"

My big sister lifts her head. "Da—Dash?"

I drop my sickle, rush to Shea's side, and wrap her free arm around my neck. "What happened? Your leg is bleeding! Did the gnomes bring you here to cut out your organs and sacrifice you to their gnome Gods and Goddesses too?"

Both Effs and Shea award me an identical glare.

"I wanna strangle him." My sister huffs against Effs's neck. "Lemme at—"

Her head slumps again.

Effs strokes her cheek. "You must stay awake until we leave the garden. Only a little further now. Then you may rest."

"Is she okay?" I ask as Shea careens into me. My pulse skyrockets. I don't like this. I've never seen my sister like this. "What happened, Euphoria. Tell me. Right now."

"We must all stay calm." Effs grunts as Shea's weight shifts back toward her. "She was bitten by a mourner flower. I healed her as much as possible, but it will take time for the venom to subside and for my magic to wear off. Right now, she's what we spellcasters call... befuddled."

Ohhhkay. If Effs thinks I'm going to remain calm right now, then she doesn't know me as well as I thought. Sibling feud, blood bet or not, this is my sister.

I unhook a torch from the cavern wall and shine it in Shea's face. Her eyes are bloodshot like mine usually are after I've pulled an all-nighter playing Holoblocks at the Bay's Baubles arcade. She groans, pushing the brightness away, and curses at me under her breath.

"She's going to be okay, right? You promise?"

Effs forces a smile. "I healed her. She will recover."

"I feel like I'm floating... in the Pendragon Sea... on Planet Press... " Shea's warbling prods the silence. "Don't... make me... I... don't wanna leave... "

My sister's never been wasted. Or befuddled? As the spell-casters call it. Anyway, she's never had a drink other than one shot of Dad's malt whiskey last year on All Hallows Eve, but this is what I imagine it would be like. I tend to be a gushy drunk when I've had one too many. From what I'm witnessing, Shea's a mix of elated and irritated. If I wasn't so worried about her, I'd probably have some fun.

I let the torch hang at my side. It grazes my wound, and I grimace more than I'd like to admit. "Wait, Effs. You used magic? But that means that the soul sucker will—"

"Start to feed on my soul. Yes, I'm aware."

I shine the light on her face. "How much of your magic did you use?"

"Enough of that fire—" She knocks it out of my hand. It sizzles in the dirt beneath our feet, delivering us into the darkness. All the others have burned out too. "I'd rather not say."

Effs doesn't have to say. I feel like I already know.

"You used the rest of it, huh," I say softly, thankful the dark hides my smile and the tears watering in my eyes. "I knew you'd learn to love her once you got to know her."

"Love is a strong word for someone I've just met." Effs chuckles and adjusts her hold around Shea's waist. Then we walk. "I am, however, in the process of trying to get to know her."

"I can hear you both, and I'll kill you both," Shea grouses between us. "It isn't like that."

Effs lets out a sigh.

I. Love. This. "Okay. I feel like a third wheel. Should I go or nah? I mean, technically, we've still got that blood bet going, and we're fighting and—"

Shea tries to grab a fistful of my shirt, but I'm not wearing one, so it ends up being a painful fist of skin and fingernail scratches. "You're not going... anywhere. The bet is... off."

Truth is, I wouldn't have left her even if it wasn't.

I pat her head. "I was kidding, dear sister—" My foot hits an uneven path of dirt, and I stumble forward, dragging us all down. We topple over one another. A mouthful of dirt for me. My elbow in someone's side. Shea accidentally slaps Effs in the face.

"That torch would have come in handy," I say.

"What have we stumbled over?" Effs asks.

Shea winces. "The whole damn place is... spinning."

"I'm coming to help you." I feel around in the dark for a bloodied leg, finding Shea immediately. Her hand falls into mine. "You good? Did you hit your head?"

"No," she snaps. "Don't ask me stupid questions like that."

I chuckle. "Oh, Shea. We're all going to laugh about this someday."

A rustling sound. It's Effs's voice that follows, "I found something. I think it's clothes or supplies or—"

"My stuff!" I let go of Shea and lean forward to forage. My body brushes Effs'. She hands me what she's found. I grope, feeling the grooves of a zipper. "It's my pack! I think I have a glow stick or some kind of light in here. Let me see... "

I flip the pack upside down and let its contents spill out. The faintest neon flicker catches my eye. Sitting beside a crumpled pork crisp bag is my glow stick, a cylindrical tube I'd nicked back in Specters Village at that rinky-dink convenience store.

"Can be charged by magic or by breaking the seal," I read from the iridescent label.

Effs reaches over my shoulder for the tube. "Better go with option number two."

She cracks the stick in half, allowing it to radiate into her face, into the white of her eyes, where tiny black spider veins have begun making themselves known. She looks horrible, honestly, and all I can think is that she'll decline faster now. That, and—*I'm next.*

And all around us, the remaining contents of my pack lay askew. It's as if the dirt gnomes treated my bag like their personal supply piñata. I shove my extra shirt over my head. Tiny, dusty footprints have been left across the pack itself. Popped bags of snack crisps. Crunched candies. Flattened toast. Geeze. They snapped my sunspecs in half too.

"I think they took my skulls," I say. "That is *such* a disappointment."

"One of two things will happen now." Effs picks through the mess. I lean Shea against the wall so I can gather everything back up. "Either they'll roll home, or the gnomes will bury them somewhere in ritual—These appear to be bandages. I'll need to dress both your wounds."

"That's reassuring. Let's hope they stay buried. You don't seem that worried." I put on my jacket, dusting off the grime and muck stuck to the sleeves. "I'm also sure you're wondering how I got out alive. My blood killed a gnome. I'm essentially untouchable."

Effs raises a brow. "While I'm proud, I'm inclined to warn you not to be so cocky. You never know what lurks around here."

"I am not being cocky." I zip up my pack and put that on too. "I thought you'd be proud of my independence. I thought you'd be impressed that I made it."

She finds another roll of muslin and tucks it into her dress pocket. "It doesn't matter what I think." I hand her a squished canister of antibiotic cream. She stows that too. "Relying on others to affirm your accomplishments isn't nearly as satisfying as realizing it on your own."

"Did... your... mom teach you that?" Shea asks groggily.

"Yes, she was a very wise woman. She persevered through the darkest days of the Great War." Effs helps my sister to her feet. "I learned everything I know from her."

As she motions me forward, I hold up a half-dried alcohol wipe that one of the gnomes must've ripped from its wrapping. "I thought we were going to clean our wounds."

Effs brushes past me. "Not until we're out of the garden."

I fall back in line on Shea's other side, and together we guide her through the narrow, winding maze of tunnels. At the end of the next curve, a streak of faint moonlight shines in, revealing a hole that leads to the surface.

On Effs's signal, I pull myself up first into the chilling nighttime air. An eerie wind shakes the trees, brushing my hair. A full moon hangs crooked in the sky, overlaid with a thin fog. I've surfaced in a wooded area. The garden basks in the nightlight about a mile from where I sit. Relief spreads through me. *There it is.* In all its tangled and twisted glory.

A place rotting from the inside out.

Shea's inebriated mutterings bring me back to focus. She waits at the base of the hole, and I reach down to grab her upper body, waiting on Effs to give her a boost from below. With one go, we've got her up, and then my sister is with me, laying in the hay-like grass. Bellies up to the sky, our heads brush. Shea's staggered breaths even out.

"Thought I was going to lose you for a second," I whisper.

"I'm... sorry about what I said... back at the... village." She could be speaking to me or the celestial beings above. I wouldn't know the difference. "I didn't... mean it. Any of it. Not the... bet...

or the... any of it." Her hand rests gently on my arm, where my soul sucker burns. "And you were right about... everything..."

"I'm sorry too, Shea." I place my hand over hers. "You were also right about me. I'm a useless heap of a teenage boy without you. I'm not as smooth as I think, but I'm trying." A smile finds me. "When we get home, I'll steal anything you want and wrap it up as if I bought it."

She lets out a small cry that seems happy and sad. The sound makes her laugh. She rubs her eyes like a tired child. "My tongue feels so... numb."

"It's still there," I assure her. "Gods, I can't wait to party with you on Spinners Pier when this is all over."

"This isn't over yet." Effs plops down next to me and motions for me to lift my shirt so she can access my stomach. "We will find a place to camp for the night so you and Shea can rest. Gather your bearings. You will need it." She opens a bandage with her teeth and begins to wrap my wounds. "Tomorrow morning, we head to Crowley Corner."

"Hear that, Shea? We're going to an old-fashioned amusement park tomorrow. It's going to be so fun. Fake Death will be there. I'll be there. Effs will be there. You'll love it."

"Dashiel," Shea murmurs, drifting off.

"Yes, you beautiful soul."

"Shut... the hell... up."

And that's exactly what I do.

16

Shea

Streaks of morning light filter through the trees. The crimson rays illuminate the dust particles in the air. I cling to the sweater that covers me, then roll onto my side and place a hand on the damp ground. Fog floats in and coats the forest floor where dark purple bell flowers grow wild in the soil. Their stems are shorter than those growing in the greenhouses on Sarasing. They sway in the breeze, offering a graceful chime.

A branch snaps. I look up.

At the woods edge, a bird with coral plumes takes off into the sky. *Pastel coral bursts mixed with gold. A soft flutter of wings.*

It's all coming back to me now.

Tempters Garden. Mourners. Devious dirt gnomes.

I run my thumb along my calf, the stretch of skin where a wound should be. I swallow. The familiar taste in my mouth intensifies. My head spins.

Our energy is a match.

Across a fire pit that looks like it was thrown together last minute the night before, Dash and Euphoria lay asleep. I examine them both. Glancing from her to him and him to her.

Could they really be the same soul? In two different bodies?

The Universal Database speculates the existence of past lives, of an immortal soul that lives on after physical death. Nothing is impossible given the mysteries we've uncovered in the last century. Each planet we mark on our galaxy maps, the research compiled after exploration—someone is always stumbling upon something we never thought existed.

This truth is yet another bout of knowledge worthy of studying or even submitting, so why am I still having such a hard time wrapping my head around it all?

Reincarnation. Non-linear timelines. An energy existing in many coherent forms.

How much of my brother is Euphoria? How much of him is her? Or is the only thing that ties them together a concept of energy that resonates deep within their inner being?

I know better than to challenge the metaphysical, but Euphoria is not my brother biologically. We aren't related in any 3D-physical way. I wouldn't be so reluctant to accept this truth if it didn't mean I'm the other half of that split soul essence. Dash's soul existing as someone like Euphoria isn't half bad. Why did my soul have to become something so potentially wicked?

Does that mean, at the core of my essence, a part of me is potentially wicked too?

Euphoria stirs in her sleep. As she stretches, her golden eyes flutter open. We stare at one another for a moment in silence. Then she gets up and takes off into the woods.

The urge to follow her to thank her hits me so hard I can't contain it anymore. I'm tired of trying to ignore it. I'm tired of being someone who acts fine when I am not. Of taking on everyone's responsibility when I can barely keep myself together.

And I'm so *over* going through everything alone.

Delicate specks of snow stick to the loose strands of hair that have fallen from one of my braids. I tug at the other elastic and let my long, wavy locks fall free around my face. Then I pull myself up off the ground and cross the fire pit to where Dash sleeps curled in a ball. I adjust his jacket-blanket to keep him warm, then I take off into the woods after Euphoria.

As I walk, I think of how my brother wants out of this business. I think of how I've never given much thought to a life beyond thieving and enforcing. If Dash wants to leave, he should be allowed to go on his own terms. If I shame him and bully him, I am no better than our father.

Dad and I aren't so different. We're both strong, stubborn, and resilient. We don't trust or ask for help. We neglect vulnerability because we think it's a sign of weakness. From the day Dad handed me a busted glowbeam and my first assignment, that was how I thought I had to be.

I thought I had to figure things out on my own. I thought I had to be resourceful. I was taught happiness, success, and love in life is earned or taken, not given. I was taught there's not enough to go around, so I might as well avoid it altogether or try to control it.

Why did I ever think this was the only way to be?

A tight pressure in my chest deepens. My father raised me to be this version of me in this lifetime, and I don't know if it's who I want to be. I was so sure before. I thought I knew. I thought I'd take over the business after graduation. Forget past lives. The truth is, I don't know who I am if I'm not Shea-Lynn James the leader, the compliant eldest child, the Enforcer...

My boots crunch the roots and sunken leaves along the trail. Euphoria becomes a speck in the haze until I find her again, trailing down a winding slope that leads to a thicket of frost-taken trees. She stops at a clearing at the end of the trail. Her back turned, admiring the view.

As I near, the tangle of wooden tracks, tattered flags, and machinery in the far valley comes into focus. Above it all is a stone structure, moss-covered and falling apart, wrapped in the haze of a stark orangey-pink horizon.

I step into a half-frozen puddle. The crack is subtle but enough to alert her to my presence.

Back still turned, Euphoria says, "I wanted to clear my head."

"I'm sorry. I can go back if you—"

"Stay."

I chew the inside of my cheek. *Breathe, Shea.*

She glances over her shoulder, motions me to her side, and I obey, leaving enough space for a horde of dirt gnomes to run between us. At first, I stare at one tattered flag in particular, but soon, I find myself staring at Euphoria. At her profile, the curve of her pursed lips. At her pale, spider-veined cheeks. At the crumpled rag in her hand, its edges soaked in blood.

Should I even be having these kinds of feelings if she's... I stop myself. She *isn't* Dash, though. She's not my brother. She's a whole other person, in a whole other lifetime, on a whole other planet.

From a scientific standpoint, this is only weird if I make it weird.

Euphoria points somewhere between the coaster and a giant rusted wheel. "Right over there is where Valerian and I first met. We were thirteen, and we quickly became best friends."

"How long has the park been out of service?" I ask.

"Since the Great War. Now a small group of spellcasters live there full-time, and the rest of them gather there every year for Festival. They wield all the harmless spells they've learned over the years and re-enact the last battle as an homage to the war."

I keep thinking I'll remember what she's saying as if knowingly being tied to Valerian's soul makes me more aware, but nothing resonates in that way.

She beckons me to follow her closer to the edge, to a flattened rock where she sits, facing the horizon. At first, I don't join her. Because I haven't shown her a lick of gratitude yet for saving my life. But then she gives me that look, and I know I have to join her.

As I settle down, Euphoria brings her knees to her chest. "Valerian and I were best friends for a long time. Until I developed feelings for him. When I told him, he panicked and ran. He couldn't handle that, despite his best efforts, he'd fallen in love with me too. It was around that time I started experiencing memories of our past lives. All divinely timed, of course. The deeper I sank into my subconscious Truth, the more I could pull to the surface. Eventually, Valerian started experiencing the synchronicities too, but instead of embracing them or trying to understand them, he denied them and claimed I'd put some kind of spell on him."

My entire body warms again. *Maybe Valerian and I really are the same variation of our soul.*

"He couldn't handle the concept of us being twin souls split into two whole parts. He even tried summoning Mother Ominous from the Realm of Souls and begged her to remove her mark." Euphoria grabs my hand, turns it over, and begins tracing the lines of my palm. Her touch gives me goosebumps. "He fought his realizations with logic instead of trusting the Divine."

"Nothing about this is logical."

"To admit the Truth, we'd have to admit that logic and reasoning only get us so far. Instead of trusting his intuition and embracing his role in this collective consciousness, Valerian resisted it. This, of course, delayed his progress and his awakening to the process itself."

I watch how she traces a wrinkle in my palm that Dash once told me is supposed to represent the lifeline, and another chill envelops me. "You said he knows you shared past lives."

"He knows we're connected on a soul level, but he doesn't know the extent. He thinks we simply made an agreement to help one another get into the Higher Realm. He thinks I owe him that."

I try to focus on what she's saying, but the warmth of her hand against mine makes it difficult. *It's only weird if you make it weird.* "Is that what I saw in those visions?"

Euphoria tucks a lock of hair behind her ear. "You were witnessing a moment in your soul's existence that won't consciously happen for you until many lifetimes from now."

I raise a brow. "You realize this is extremely confusing, right?"

She laughs. "Time and space are confusing concepts."

This time, I laugh. I think of how the Board of Galactic Studies would be so eager to get their hands on an explanation of this concept. It deserves to be known in as much truth as we can give it. "Do you really remember everything about the lives you've lived?"

"I remember vaguely *who* I've been, but I don't remember much more than that."

Fair enough. "But you knew who Dash was when you met him?"

She glances out at the view for a moment. I watch the contemplation wash over her, and then she smiles again. "Dash is a much younger version of my soul. I recognized my energetic frequency in him when we met, but other than a dream I'd had a week ago about the Door that delivered him here, I don't remember much else about that lifetime. That's why I was in the Bone Wood that day. I thought I could leave Ominous through the Door. When I refused to help Valerian get into the Higher Realm, he told me he was going to take my soul. It was my last attempt at trying to stop him."

"Why does he want to get into the Higher Realm?" I ask.

Her eyes start to water. "Imagine having unlimited access to all the knowledge in the Universe. From a human perspective, it is the ultimate treasure. His ego wants to obtain the higher knowledge and mysteries of the Universe without doing the deep work required to understand it all.

"What he doesn't realize is that the calling comes from his Higher Self. I believe his soul *wants* to ascend. Deep down, he wants to be his Higher Self, and whether he's conscious of it or not, he wants to go to the Higher Realm because he *wants* to fulfill his soul mission."

She drops my hand to wipe under her eyes. Should I comfort her? What can I tell her so she won't be upset?

"Maybe he can remember who he is. You don't know he won't be ready in time."

"That's oddly optimistic of you, Shea," she says through another laugh half-sob.

I let my fingers intertwine with hers. "I'm—I'm trying to be. And I'm trying my hardest to be better at not assuming the worst of someone before I get to know them."

She prods me gently, but with a playfulness that seems so natural I have to stop myself from jabbing her back. "Giving people a chance. Wonder where you learned that? Perhaps some of that knowledge will transmute into Valerian."

She sniffs in. "All joking aside, I've come to terms with us not being ready at the same time to cross into the Higher Realm in this lifetime. I cannot force someone else to change, heal, or realize a Truth they aren't ready for. All I *can* do is make sure you and Dash make it home safe. I can't help but blame myself for dragging you both into this."

"Euphoria, this isn't your fault," I find myself saying. "You didn't know what Valerian would do to Dash. You can't blame yourself for that. If anything, *I'm* ashamed."

She gives my hand another squeeze. "You have nothing to be ashamed about either. You and Valerian share a Divine frequency, but you aren't him. And he isn't you. His wayward ways don't reflect who you are in your lifetime as Shea-Lynn James."

"I don't even know who Shea-Lynn James is... " This time, it's me wiping under my eyes. *Gods.* I was hoping I wouldn't do this. "Also, I never thanked you for saving me. Both at the dam and last night in the garden. You did not have to waste the rest of your magic on me."

"You don't have to thank me. I did it because I wanted to."

"But why, though?" I ignore the lingering heat circulating my palms and how close we are. "I know Valerian and I share the same soul, but I'm not him. You don't love me like that. Or know me. You don't have those... feelings for me... so, why?"

Euphoria tilts her head, admiring me. "You don't understand. Of course, I love you. I love the soul that resonates inside you. I love the soul that resonates inside Dash, too.

"I have love and compassion for everyone I meet, even if I don't agree with them or understand them. It's a different kind of love we're talking about here. It's a love that accepts people for who they are without judgment. To understand that people are complex, beautifully flawed, and we can't expect anything more of them than what their limits allow them to offer."

I hear what she's saying, I do, but I don't know if I'm ready to have unconditional love for people like that. How can I choose to accept people when they've hurt me or let me down? How can I forgive Dad for everything he's ever said to me or for the uncertainty he's instilled in me?

"It seems more complex than love. It seems like giving people a free pass to be wicked."

She turns her body to face me, her other hand finding mine. "This conversation will be something you'll carry with you. You'll spend the rest of this lifetime and many others trying to understand this concept: You can love someone and still maintain healthy boundaries with them. You can have compassion and forgiveness for someone without allowing them a permanent place in your life.

"Others can only meet us to the extent of their own awareness. I don't blame Valerian. He's stubborn, and I won't hold anything against him. Not in this life. Or our next. I acknowledge the disappointment our situation fuels inside me. I'm not saying love diminishes or replaces the expression of hurt, confusion, pain, or the other emotions we feel. It just means I don't take anyone else's actions personally. I ultimately choose to love myself in those harder moments. So that I might align with those that *can* reach me in my level of awareness."

A breath of wind skitters through the barren trees as I consider her words. Sounds like *she* might be ready for the Higher Realm. All on her own. My mind races, trying to take it all in. Mom always said to love yourself first and to know your own worth, but it isn't always easy. And here Euphoria is, talking with me, trusting me, and being honest. We're having an actual conversation. One that I'm enjoying.

"You're crying, Shea," Euphoria whispers.

I exhale. "I can't help it. I'm sorry."

"You have nothing to be sorry for." She reaches forward and catches the tear rolling down my warm cheek. Her thumb wipes it away, and a shudder courses through me.

I wipe another. "I . . . I'm not..."

"Would it be alright if I hugged you?"

I let out another laugh, mid nod, and she leans forward. As she wraps her arms around me, I lean into her embrace. Her head nestles against my shoulder. My heart beats so fast, this time it'll surely burst.

"Oddly enough, it feels like hugging Dash," I mutter.

She mutters back, "It's the familiar energy you're sensing. I feel like home to you."

"You do." I chuckle. "You do feel like... home."

I don't know what that means, but it feels like the right thing to say.

"This is... weird, " I mutter through another laugh.

She releases me. "Your brother tried to hit on me earlier. *That* was weird."

"Of course he did." This time, we both laugh. Then my smile fades. "Don't—don't tell him about any of this deeper stuff. In his condition right now and just in general, I don't think he—"

"Dash doesn't need to know the details."

I chew my lip through a nod, reaching for the tangle of cords hanging around her neck to quiet my racing mind. It soothes me somehow. She lets me pick through the charms one by one. Brass coins with symbols. Raw crystals. Bits of carved bone.

If they could speak, they'd tell me stories about how they came to be a part of her. And I know she's accepted her life for what it is, but I want to help her. We'll find the cure for Dash, and we'll get my portal key, but I don't know if I can leave here without at least trying to help Euphoria.

"Aside from getting you the cure too, what can Dash and I do to help you and Valerian?" I ask.

"I don't think you can help me any more than you already have. You've both made good points. I can't sacrifice myself for Valerian or prolong my own progress to protect him. When Kellie's Comet arrives and the portal appears to the Higher Realm, I must make a choice. Regardless of Valerian, I must decide whether or not I'm going to go this time around."

"You'll figure it out. I know you will," I say as I separate a knot of charms around her neck. I find a wooden one that resembles a brown bear. I'm instantly taken back to my vision of the two girls in the snow with Mother Ominous. Then I see the single spiral etched on the bottom of the bear's foot. I look up at her. "This charm looks like a tutelary."

"It is. An homage to my tutelary—" Her eyes widen. "*Goddess.* Shea, I know why Dash's soul sucker has been delayed." She pulls away, stands, and starts to pace. "Why didn't I think of this before? It all makes sense. Even now, I've used up my magic, and I'm still here. It's why *neither* of us has died yet. Though, it's working double time right now. *Euphoria, how could you forget this? Could you really be this daft?*"

I get up as well. "Um. Can you possibly tell me what's going on?"

Euphoria grabs me by the shoulders. "The bear cub from your vision. It was an early lifetime. We were Nordic witches and lovers in the mountains. I had a pet cub that I'd raised and cared for deeply. He became my physical tutelary in that life, and when he died, his spirit went to the other side. Tutelaries reincarnate too. Sometimes they come back in physical form, or they exist as spiritual entities which can be summoned by Start Spirits and bound to us energetically. They remain bound until they decide to incarnate again in the physical."

Okay. Now she's speaking nonsense. "Neither Dash nor I have tutelaries. Maybe you mean we'll get them later on? I've seen a coral bird, but I thought it was random."

"Valerian's tutelary is a coral bird," Euphoria says. "It isn't random. You cannot see a tutelary unless it is yours. Ace was bound to me in my lifetime as Dash. He's been with me in spirit ever since."

She can't actually be suggesting I have a tutelary. "I think I would know if a spiritual protector was bound to my soul. Or at least someone would tell me."

"Sometimes I have dreams about Ace being bound to me in that life. Age two or three?"

I stare at her blankly. What is she talking about? *Neither of us has a tutelary.*

"Heinous Hades, I thought you two left me here."

Euphoria and I look up at Dash, now standing at the wood's edge. He glances between us both. "Did I… interrupt anything?"

"We were having a heart-to-heart," Euphoria says plainly.

Dash smirks. "Well, yeah. Obviously."

"I need to think," I say as I get up and walk back toward the tree line. I press my brain for any inkling of information regarding tutelaries from my research or our past that would help me remember. "Dash, I need my journal. It's in the back pocket of your pack."

He gets it out and hands it over. I flip through my history, through the knowledge I've spent forever jotting down to archive at a later date.

"Perhaps Dad got hold of some and bound them to us." I'm thinking aloud again, thumbing away at a crinkle of pages with smudges and leftover crud from Lake Ichor.

Dad would have said something, right? Maybe Aunt Merik acquired tutelaries, but she would have told us. Mom rarely gets out of bed. Otherwise, I'd say it was her.

There's got to be something else going on here. I can't focus until I figure it out.

I crouch. Euphoria drops down at my side. She sorts the loose pages that have fallen from the binding during my frantic search.

Dash hovers over our shoulders. "What are we talking about?"

"Do you remember anything else about when your tutelary was bound to you?" I ask Euphoria, careful of my phrasing. I meant what I said about keeping her identity between us.

"It was a Star Spirit. They're the only ones that can do it."

"Somebody *tell* me what's going on!" my brother exclaims.

"Hold on, Dashiel." I turn to Euphoria. "You're saying tutelaries are useless unless a Star Spirit is present? Like, if we gave someone one, they can't use it unless they go to Lark?"

Euphoria picks up another handful of pages. "From my understanding, yes, but I can see if there's anything else we might have missed in your research?"

I let her take my entire journal while I process. Meanwhile, my stomach sinks as low as it'll possibly go. "Dash, I... I think we gave that space vamp, Mathias Burgess, a dud."

My brother sighs. "That's low of us."

"That's low of *Dad.*" I tell myself this over and over to justify that I took the vamp's thumbs on top of everything else. "*He's* the one running fraud deals. Dad's the one that lied to us. He used us like he does everyone else."

Dash throws his hands out. "You're *just* figuring this out now?"

I clench my fists. "I turned down a fellowship interview for the Board of Galactic Studies for Dad. And he sent you here, Dash, even though he knew it was dangerous."

My brother gasps. "*No.*"

"*Yes.*" I meant to tell him earlier about the fellowship, but it never seemed like the right time to bring it up. "I'm sorry, Dash. I'm sorry for everything."

"You turned down a fellowship interview? Oh, Shea." And out of all he's heard, my little brother still finds it in his heart to ask something entirely unimportant right now.

"She can still apply." Euphoria inserts herself between us, two of my journal pages in hand. "We'll make sure she doesn't miss her deadlines, but for now, we must focus. I've found a few pages on tutelaries I think might be useful." She flips over the entry and reads, "There are rare occurrences of certain Star Spirits, those born of fallen stars that aren't caught. They take on human form and can venture away from Lark, but their existence is short-lived and—"

"They will eventually have to return home or their light will die out," I say, remembering the day I wrote that log. It was after an afternoon spent lounging in bed with Mom. She told me stories, and I jotted them all down without thinking twice.

Dash gives me a look. "Does that mean—"

"If soul suckers can transfer souls, maybe Dad wanted one because he thought Mom needed a soul in order to live," I say.

"No. Our mother has a soul." Dash runs his hands through his hair more than once. "Because Star Spirits don't have souls. Mom's human. Right?"

"There's no other explanation as to how we would have tutelaries." I place a hand on his shoulder. "I don't remember any Star Spirit's paying us a visit over the years, do you?"

"Well, maybe we were too young to remember."

"I would have remembered something like that."

Dash shrugs away from me. "Even as a baby? You wouldn't remember that."

I know he doesn't want to face this. I don't either, but it would explain a lot. The tutelary I've been seeing. Why Dash's soul sucker was taking its sweet ole time. Why nothing ever cured Mom, or why not even the Enchantresses could help us *fully* cure her. Mom didn't need magic or an herbal concoction to heal her. All this time, she needed the stars. That's where she belongs.

"Mom is a Star Spirit," I say to Dash.

I reach out, and he blocks my touch. "You're wrong. Mom is not a Star Spirit." He takes off between two trees. "If this is the case, what are we then? Huh! Half-human half-Star? That doesn't make any sense!"

"Because they take on human form, that would make you human," Euphoria says.

"Whatever. Doesn't matter. Still isn't true!" he shouts and disappears into the thicket.

There's no way we're doing this again. "Dash! Come back!"

I leave Euphoria's side and take off after him.

There will be a time to mourn and process this. There will be a time when we'll need to unpack this and lean on one another to get through this together, but I don't know how many more days or hours my brother has left with that soul sucker in his arm.

"Dashiel!" I call out, weaving my way through a cluster of twisted trees that all look the same. Beneath low-hanging boughs. Around stump-trunks. Eventually, I emerge from the thicket.

Another clearing enveloped by the dark-morning fog. An array of bent trees form nearly a perfect circle around the frozen ground. Almost ritualistic. Ringing fills my ears, and I look all around for any sign of him, anything that'll tell me which way he's gone.

Everything will be fine.

I'll hold him. Hug him tight.

Tell him it'll all be okay.

We'll get through this too.

Snow litters the ground. Specks float in the gray sky. Another gust of wind sends goosebumps up my arms. They prickle my skin, and I cling to myself.

It's too silent here. Until a branch snaps.

I spin around. "Dash?"

At first, there's nothing. No sign of anyone. Not my brother. Not Euphoria. I've met the edge of the circle, where the beyond is an endless pit of darkness. A flicker of pink light catches my eye, and I pivot on my heels, accounting for all sides.

I will my feet to move, but they won't budge. I'm stuck to the circle like a bug on glue. Weaponless. Vulnerable. Alone.

And then a whoosh of pink silk swallows me whole.

17

Dash

Shea's call has long faded in the distance. I don't even know where I'm going.

I'm two left feet floundering in the woods. Deadweight arms whipping through branches and low-hanging boughs. Sharp points, they cling to me. They scuff me up.

And the air is too thick here. Dense like smoke.

A sharp pain stabs me in the chest. It rides me like a high-speed coaster.

Gag reflex triggered. *Hardcore.*

Retching black sludge ranks high on the list of foul acts my body has put me through. I choke on a sob. Leaning against a tree, I wait for another surge and purge again. It's pure hellfire. Acid status. It seeps into a thin layer of snow that blankets the ground. Steams it into slush.

I tug at my clothes, drenched in sweat. Dripping down my forehead, at the base of my neck. Something like a moan escapes me. Then faster breaths. A rising pulse.

Crap. Crap. Crap.

Breathe. *Freaking breathe.*

I sink to my knees. Onto my side. Curled up like the worm sucking me dry. I grab a handful of dirt and let it sift through my fingers. Then again. Anything to distract me. Anything to calm me down. I haven't had a panic attack since I was thirteen. It was right after a major growth spurt. My voice had finally changed. It was triggered by something silly, one of those freak incidents that never make sense. But Shea was there at my side. All day.

All night. All morning. She held me. She brought me back. We slept in Mom's bed for two days straight.

I wish I didn't know the truth.

Breathe.

I wish it weren't real.

Breathe.

I wish she were here.

Breathe.

A wet tongue laps my neck. I flinch.

My vision focuses on a brown bear sitting at my side, nestled in the curve of my body. Out of nowhere.

Am I hallucinating? I must be. The blue-eyed creature nudges my face with his nose. I ruffle his soft fur, which slips through my fingers like translucent water.

On my next exhale, it rolls onto its belly and begs for another pet. A hoarse laugh escapes me and stings the back of my throat. "Are you some kind of man-eating beast or—" I wipe the snot running down my face on my sleeve and swallow through the burn. "Or are you just a friendly lone bear lost out here too?"

It nudges my arm with its paw. When I lift my sleeve, the soul sucker burrowed deep within me awakens. It squirms. The bear offers a deep gutted growl and proceeds to lick my wound until the throbbing disperses, the pain less than before. I notice the spiral mark on its ear.

"I think you're my tutelary." I pull myself off the ground. The bear leaps onto a rock, then lumbers down beyond the trees. Picking up speed, it curves the next trail. I stumble.

"You're the reason I'm still kicking. Come back!"

At the edge of a clearing, I catch up to the bear. My dutiful protector waits for me to reach his side, then slowly fades away in the next gust of wind.

Well, what the heck. I didn't even get its name.

I use the collar of my shirt to wipe away any leftover sweat on my face. It's speckled with stains—a little puke, spoiled blood, dirt, some spirit bear spit—you know, everything one could wish for after a near nervous breakdown in the middle of nowhere on a horror planet.

It'll happen again if I don't push myself. Force myself to forget what I know. At least until all this is over. Then I will succumb to my misery.

I see many restless nights ahead. Lots of days spent lounging in bed with Mom eating takeout until our stomachs burst. Lots of cuddles, hair braiding, and live readings of every play and poem I've ever written. She's always the first to hear them. Then Shea. Never Dad. I'll take as much as I can. For as long as I can have it.

A low hum sounds across the clearing. A glow nears.

Peering around a tree, I watch as a parade of hooded beings in a rainbow of colored cloaks emerge. Wisps of matching light rise from their fingertips.

Spellcasters. A group of them. Five. Maybe Eight. Casting their spells in the sky, a real heathen beacon. Effs said we were in their territory now, and she wasn't kidding.

I've personally crisis-wandered right into their path.

As long as I stay hidden, I think I'll be fine.

I won't ruin this. I won't get caught. Shea, Effs, and I have come too far for me to blow it all on a simple mistake like stepping with heavy feet or breathing too loud. As soon as they pass, I'll find my way back to my sister and beg for her forgiveness yet again.

I'm sorry I ran off, I'll tell her. *I don't know what came over me.*

The last spellcaster, a hoodless woman with blond hair so long it kisses the hem of her rose-pink cloak, storms the clearing. The wooden stretcher accompanying her hovers above the ground in motion with the silver beams of light discharging from her fingertips.

I squint my eyes at the lump of sorts lying in a crumpled heap atop the stretcher. It's wearing a cross-body bag and a familiar, purple-patterned sweater.

Wait a second. That's Shea.

They've taken my freaking sister.

No. That can't be her.

"Hey! Is this another trick of—"

A right hand covers my mouth from behind, yanking me away from the clearing and further out of sight. Adrenaline surges through me. Parchment pages float around us. The owner of the hand gasps as I clamp a hand on their wrist, pull them closer, and notice the now-mangled journal pressed against my chest with their left hand.

"Great Goddess. Euphoria?"

"You're *hurting* me," she snaps.

"I'm sorry. You shouldn't sneak up on people like that!"

"They'll hear you." She shakes me loose and steps back, careful not to crush any journal entries. "Keep your voice down. Please."

"What happened?" I kneel to help Effs gather pages.

"Shea went looking for you. Wandered right into Devils Halo." She points behind us, into the circle of twisted trees. "It's hexed. She must have triggered the energy snare."

Effs motions me around and shoves Shea's mangled journal into my pack. "The long-haired blonde is Lorelei. She and Valerian have been on and off since he and I parted ways. She despises me because she thinks I'm the reason he refuses to commit to her. More than likely, she and the others are helping him look for me... for *us* before Festival tonight. We can't be seen."

"Are they taking Shea to Crowley Corner?"

Effs rolls up her sleeves. "I believe so, yes."

I follow her beneath the brush, back onto a down-sloping trail, where sunlight finds us again. "We have to go after her. We can't just let them take her."

"I agree, but we cannot just waltz in there." She quickens her strides and combs the land with a hardened gaze as if searching for the way by the memory of a home she once knew.

A flight of stone stairs, overgrown with moss, basks in the dull rays ahead. Without a word, Effs descends the slope toward it. My heart races. I skip steps to keep up.

She's a girl on a mission. "We must think strategically."

No, we need more than that. "We need... like a solid plan."

"Yes. That might do the trick." Effs stops short. I bump into her from behind and nearly teeter over the edge of the stairs. "A plan is exactly what we need. What did you have in mind?"

Wait. She's asking me? "Well, I—"

"Right. You don't have one," Effs mutters. "How silly of me to think you would actually have a plan."

What in the galaxies is going on with her?

I slow my pace. "Uh, Euphoria?"

She reaches the bottom step but doesn't look back. "Yes?"

"You... good?"

Her lack of response moves me. I approach her. Putting a hand on her uninjured shoulder, I slowly guide her toward me. As she glances up, black sludge gushes from her nose.

My mouth goes dry. She lets me touch the decayed skin webbing from her sucker wound. Spread beyond repair. Risen her neck, it flecks against her jaw and veins across her left cheek. A sullenness has taken over her. My diabolical cellmate who feels like so much more now. A potential best friend. The girl who was patient enough to gain my sister's trust.

The beginning of an end.

This is what that soul sucker can do. Without any magic to feed on. Without a celestial protector to fight on her behalf. A soul as bare as the heart that beats inside Effs's freaking chest.

"Euphoria," I whisper. "Are you—"

"I don't know if I'm ready to die again," she whispers.

A chilling gust of wind overtakes her. She trembles. I tear off my outer jacket and wrap it around her, pulling her close. Her head against my chest. My chin atop her head. I shouldn't promise everything is going to be okay. Because I really have no idea.

I wipe the blood off her ear with my sleeve. "We're going to be okay. *All* of us."

She tightens her hold on me, taking more of my warmth. "What if he devours my soul before I convince him to cure you and let you and Shea go home?"

I tuck a bit of matted hair behind her ear. "Don't think like that, Effs. You're not going to die. I'm not going to die." She pulls away, but I hold her even closer to me. "Don't forget you've gotten us this far. Without you, Shea and I would've either been killed by this planet or killed one another by now."

She forces a laugh. "You are not wrong. You two are something else."

"Yes. Yes, we are." I chuckle. "We are complete and utter messes of humans. We know it's true. We aren't pretending to have it together. And yeah, we fight and bicker, but at the end of the day, we still love each other."

Effs focuses elsewhere, and I place a hand on her shoulder. She needs to hear this. "You're not going to die. Don't you worry."

"Well, alright. I suppose you're right." Effs secures the buttons on the jacket I gave her to wear. "It was just a moment of doubt. Fear, I suppose. This sucker is really getting to me."

"It's okay. It happens. Mine's getting to me too."

I watch her retreat from the stone stairs and assess the trail patterns ahead. She stops at a fork and waits for me to join her, but I remain where I am. I think of what she said about plans and complications and blah blah blah—

It doesn't have to be this hard. We'll figure this out. Heck, *I'll* figure it out if I have to.

That's what Shea would do. She'd figure it out. She'd save my butt in a heartbeat.

I should have returned the favor a long time ago.

"A weakened Thief and a Spellcaster void of magic," I say, to which Effs raises a brow. I jump off the last step and join her at the fork in the trail. "That's what we've got to work with."

"You're self-narrating again."

"Noooo. *Listen*. I have a point, I promise." I spot a stick on the ground and pick it up. Then I get down on my hands and knees. "I'm not a planner"—I flick my wrist and add lines and squares in the dirt—"or someone who knows how to do much else but put on a show and steal things, but there is one thing I'm *really* good at that I think might help us right now."

"I'm not sure how this is—"

"Holoblocks Volume 3: Gold Standard. X2VR Gameplay Mode. Holocity Classic." I glance up at Effs, the flush in my cheeks burning bright. "Level 17 is Asteria's Redemption."

She blinks at me. "You're not making any—"

"I know. I didn't exactly explain it right. I scored highest on my survival course because I thought of it like a game of Holoblocks. The object of Holoblocks is to collect a certain number of blocks by completing a series of brain teasers designed to test ingenuity. Those blocks are then brought to the stronghold, located in the epicenter of Holocity. That's how you rank and place all over the galaxy. I've beat it thousands of times. I'm a leader. Yes, in a game world, but a leader none-the-less."

I pull her down next to me so we're both kneeling, gazing over the elaborate grid replica I've drawn in the dirt. "Level 17's layout is an industrial city, a particular building populated by curse crones. The key to winning the level is hiding in plain sight, utilizing the landmarks and structures, and above all, avoiding hex bubbles."

"This isn't a game, though. This is very real," she says. "Not only are we going up against Valerian and his crew, it's Festival. There will be a very real battle reenactment going on. Spellcasters everywhere. Tossing spells at one another. It'll be madness."

"I realize this. Just listen please." I point my stick at the little x I've drawn at the edge. "On my team, I always play First Point and Captain. My job is to go in, organize the troops, dismantle any traps, set diversions to trick the crones, scour the grid for advantage points, and play the opponent to figure out where the blocks are. Kind of what I do as a Thief but also kind of different in the way that I'm the one everyone relies on."

I direct my stick across the other forms I've drawn. "If you can tell me more about the layout of Crowley Corner, I can get us into the Tower, get my sister, and get us back out without being seen."

"That was a very long-winded way of saying you have the skills to get us in to save Shea."

Effs takes the stick from me and wipes blood from her nose. "I'll tell you everything, but it's not going to be as easy. Valerian knows we're coming. He'll be waiting for us. He'll be waiting for *me*."

"Let him." I cross my arms. "I'm confident in this. This is what I'm good at."

"Again, this isn't a game. Spellcasters aren't holographic blobs." She wipes away my drawing to clear the dirt. She winces as she goes to work detailing the structures and rides and areas of impending doom. "But it's the only plan we've got, I suppose."

"It's truly the only plan we've got."

I observe the oblong forms being drawn, a Ferris wheel-like ride with curved carts called the Razor that Effs tells me used to torture humans, a House of Glass, Demon's Descent, the Haunted Teacups, Bumper Coffins, the entire midway, and more.

"There." I point between the Tower ride and the stretch of game booths and concession stand markers. "We can set a diversion somewhere around here to distract any spellcasters that might be patrolling the area. Then we can sneak into the Tower. What's the best access point?"

"Probably around the back. We could travel between the floors. There are gaps in the structure that used to be for the track mechanisms. It'll be tight, but I think we'll fit."

I smile. "Perfect. This is going to work. I promise you."

She stands and meets my gaze. "I don't know. Valerian is smart."

"Yeah, but my sister is smarter." I reach up and wipe the blood oozing from her ears, ignoring the darkness now seeping into the corners of her gold eyes. "Shea can handle herself."

"I hope you're right."

"I am right."

Before a Holoblocks tournament, Coach always tells us to utilize our strengths. This is my strength. I know that now. And the roles might be reversed here, and we may be running out of time, but my sister can handle herself too.

We're going to win this.

Metaphorically, Level 17 is ours.

18

Shea

The effects of magic are either intoxicating or vile.

Euphoria's spellwork was laced with dopamine. It tasted sweet. When it wore off, heat coursed through my body. I craved more of her. The hex surging through my veins now is poison. A detrimental kind of magic, reeking of rot.

As I fully wake, my palms clam up. Thick phlegm coats the back of my throat. I've broken what I'm assuming was a nasty fever, and am now drenched in my own sweat. My lymph nodes pulse. I'd chop off twenty vampire thumbs if it meant the luxury of tossing back a glass of ice water.

If this is one spellcaster's doing, I can only imagine what an entire coven can do.

Or what Valerian Bale is capable of.

Black velvet curtains come into focus around me. An ornate, four-poster canopy bed with a feathered mattress hugs my curves. I lift my head, neck stiff, then force my body into a sitting position.

I've been taken from the woods. The last thing I remember was running after Dash. My feet wouldn't move. I vaguely remember being carried here, but those moments are fading too.

Did they bring me to Crowley Corner?

I'm on a bed in a circular stone chamber, surrounded by bookshelves stuffed to the brim, apothecary supplies, and a desk that reminds me of Dad's. A bottle of ink lay open among a heap of parchment scrolls, its quill still wet. Someone's been here recently. This chamber is well-lived in.

As I scooch forward, the mahogany frame beneath me creaks. I pause. Listen. *It's too quiet.* I can't be at the amusement park. But where else would I be? *Think, Shea. Think.*

Too bad my brain is still on fire, purging the let-down of whatever hex trapped me.

I flex my bare toes. As I rub my calloused heels, I scan the chamber and access any exit points—a door that is more than likely locked, though I'll give it a go anyway, and a set of blue, stained-glass windows on the far side of the chamber.

I shove my feet into my boots, which have been left on the wool rug by the bed, and then proceed toward the windows. As I tug the moth-eaten drapes aside, my stomach hardens. *Not what I was expecting at all.* I'm about 400 feet up and then some. Across a midway scattered with old game booths and concession stands, the rusted tracks of the roller coaster glisten in the dewy haze.

This *is* Crowley Corner. *They must be holding me in the old Tower ride.*

My instincts kick in. I double back and try the door next, finding it locked and missing a handle altogether. *Ugh.* Without a recant box, there's no way the window is a viable escape. Without a lock, there's nothing to pick. Not that I'm good at picking locks. But if Dash were here—I force away the thought. *He's fine, Shea. You can't think about him right now.*

An unseen bang shakes the cobweb-draped chandelier above me. I stop and reel in my staggered breaths. Where did that come from? And how long do I have before Valerian's coven returns for me? Or Valerian himself?

With quick feet, I circle the chamber, pulling at books and supplies shoved into every nook and cranny of the space. Dust kicks up in the air, making me cough. I wave it away, taking quick but thorough peeks at everything my fingers touch. Book titles like *History of Ominous*, *Everyday Herbalism*, *A Study of Quantum Physics,* and... the last binding is blank.

My throat goes dry. I swallow, take the unnamed book, and thumb through its thin parchment pages. Okay. Not a book. *A journal.* Full of endless ink scribbles and sketches. All familiar in the way they're documented, organized, even written.

I make my Q's like that too. I flip the journal over, see the tiny VB engraved in the lower back corner, and it becomes clear—this journal belongs to Valerian. *Makes sense.* Different lives, same soul. Parts of me are bound to evolve, blend, and mesh with one another as time and space finds a way to make sense of it all.

I open the journal again. Valerian's drawn a diagram of the Tower ride on a page in the middle. Kellie's Comet blazes overhead. Both the comet's dust and plasma trails extend directly over the Tower, forming some kind of gateway labeled '*quantum portal*.' All around the diagram, he's written notes about consciousness and the different states of being.

He knows Kellie's Comet is the portal to the Higher Realm.

What else does he know? Maybe he knows more than Euphoria thinks he does.

I slap the book shut, set it back where I found it, and I move on to Valerian's desk, which is set beneath a massive tapestry of the constellation Orion. I accidentally knock a few items off Valerian's desk and onto the floor. *Impeccable timing.* I quickly drop down on my hands and knees, crawl forward, and gather the spare ink bottle that got away.

My knees creak on the floor. I freeze. Was that... a hollow creak? I lean forward, feeling the floor beneath me sag. *There's something under the floor.* I forget the ink bottle and pull at the carpet, huffing, revealing the hardwood beneath. That, and the outline of a trapdoor.

My breathing deepens. I grope for any grooves. Again, like the main entry door, there's no handle or release. If there's a way out of here, this must be it. *It has to be.* Chewing the inside of my cheek, I try again, but it's useless. Maybe I will take the window after all.

I spring up and grab for the old-fashioned bronze telescope set in front of the glass. I need to know how much time I have, how many members of Valerian's coven might be patrolling the grounds, though they'd be indistinguishable, and I need to know if there are any grooves in the stone.

I'll scale the damn Tower if I must, but I'm getting out of here.

As I peer through the eyepiece, which is pointed between the Tunnel of Heartbreak and House of Glass, a deep but smooth voice says behind me, "That telescope belonged to my father. It's a family heirloom, and I'd appreciate it if you didn't toy with it like that."

I stiffen, my grip tight around the scope. I don't even need to see his face. I know it's him. The guy responsible for my little brother's deteriorating soul. The guy Euphoria's stuck in an endless cycle of soul lessons with. The guy that is... me... in another form.

Euphoria might have unconditional love and understanding for her counterpart in this life, but in my humble opinion, Valerian deserves a punch in the face for what he's done.

I shove up my sleeves, fully intending to make it happen. As I turn to face him, an unexpected wave of calm washes over me. It lightens the vile taste in the back of my mouth. Settles the moths in my belly. My jaw unclenches, and I release the tension in my shoulders. Is this what it feels like to recognize your own soul in another body? Is this how Euphoria feels around Dash? Because if it is, I suddenly understand their ease for each other.

I'd heard it might be disorientating or might warrant the effects of motion sickness, but this isn't any of that. And the one question gnawing at me most is if he recognizes me too.

Does Valerian *know* who I am?

I release my hold on the telescope, keeping my shoulders squared and my stance steady. I may recognize how I feel, but he doesn't need to know it. "Do you hex all your guests before inviting them over, or am I just lucky?"

Expressionless, he says, "That was an unfortunate mistake."

I take in the depth of his gaze, two silver pools ready to suck me in. Dark brown hair styled perfectly on his head. Taller than I thought he'd be. Though, I'm not sure what I expected from an encounter like this. It is the oddest experience I will ever endure in this lifetime. Still, judging by his research, Valerian's mind is the most attractive thing about him.

And how did he get in here? The trap door remains shut, as does the main door. My gaze narrows in on my portal key hanging around his neck. Ah, I see. *Screw him and his smarts.*

"Overthinking every detail?" He removes a hand from his pocket and picks at the ornate detailing on one of the bedposts. "I hate to spoil it for you, but that part of us never fades."

I take a step forward. "So, you do know who I am."

He shoves his hand back in his pocket, leans against the bedpost, tilts his head, and gives me a good look over. "I recognize you are a former form of the particles and atoms that make up me now, a state they took on long ago, yes."

I arch an eyebrow. "Even I don't understand what you just said."

Valerian chuckles to himself, walking past me toward his desk to straighten the row of ink bottles I tipped over earlier. "I believe Euphoria calls it past lives, souls, and reincarnation. Does that help clear it up a bit?"

"Wait. You *know* about Euphoria's theory?" I ask.

He smirks. "I do. I suppose you're not going to tell me where she is."

Euphoria said Valerian knew who she was but didn't understand the greater mission they shared. Maybe it was never that he didn't understand, more so that he couldn't wrap his head around it. Kind of like how I still can't quite wrap my head around us sharing a soul.

"You would be correct," I say. "And *I* suppose you don't believe a word of it."

"Oh, I believe in the concept."

He waves his hand over a part of the desk I didn't see before. The outline of a drawer appears. It pops open, and he retrieves a rectangular, glass box holding two dual-vials. The moths in my gut stir again. *Those must be the cure.*

"But I'm not sure I believe in the concept of souls or past lives in the way she does. Euphoria's a fantasist, a romantic."

I gaze between the door and the glass case containing the dual-vials. Valerian observes me, perhaps basking in the awkward pause between us. The corners of his mouth turn up. I know the power inside him is itching to be summoned. Everything I want lays a foot away. The cure. My key. His magic might make us an uneven match, but maybe I can beat him at his own game. Maybe I can outsmart him. Because that part of us is the same.

"You like that she's a fantasist and a romantic. It's what draws you in. It challenges you."

I'm stalling for time, trying to formulate some semblance of a plan to grab what I need and get out. *Being a Thief would be handy about right now.* "But if you don't believe in past lives, how else would you explain all of this? I'm as logical as you are, but Euphoria has a good point."

The smile plastered on his face hasn't budged. Neither has his grip on the glass box in his hands. "Think of it this way. All the matter in the Universe has always been here. It just changes the form it takes. For a brief moment, the atoms are in the form of you. In the next moment, they are in the form of me. See? Same concept. Less fantastical."

I round the bed, letting my finger run the length of the footboard, finding a deeper collectedness. *He's confident. I need to be too.*

"I saw some of your notes earlier on quantum physics. If we're to assume that atoms can be in two states at the same time as quantum physics implies, is that how you explain us both being here now—together—in the same space physically? Because I would argue that if multiple variations of our atoms exist at the same time," I shrug, "you know, because time isn't linear—then it isn't just atoms at play here. There's something metaphysical here. It's a soul existing in multiple lifetimes.

I spread my hands out at my side. "It's, well, it's magic."

"Magic *is* science, Shea. Magic is just science we have yet to understand."

I dare to inch closer, now putting less than a foot between us. I'm so close I can make out the details of the dual-vials, secured safely in their clear box.

If I shatter the box, will I destroy the cure? If I lunge at Valerian to grab my key, will he summon his power and toss me across the room like it's nothing?

Keep pushing him.

"But you're a spellcaster. You wield magic for Goddess' sake. How can you not distinguish the two concepts from one another?"

Valerian raises a brow. "Spellcasters are native to Ominous. Much like humans were native to Old Earth. We've adapted to keep up with our ecosystem. Our ability to wield energy in the form of what you call magic is simply evolution."

"*I* believe her," I say. "I think what Euphoria says makes more sense."

He taps his fingers against the glass box. "I'm sure you do. Right now, you're a younger version of me. You'll still entertain her perspective because your mind has yet to expand. That, and you may even have a bit of a... crush on her. Therefore, you're bound to agree with her theories. You're only human, after all."

A bit of the tranquility inside me fades. *What a conceited asshole.* Is this what he thinks it means to be further 'aware.' He thinks he *knows* me just because we share an inner being? I don't think so.

"You just said a younger version of *me*. A younger version of your soul, Bale. You're proving my point about this concept being past lives and souls."

He shakes his head. "Atoms. Particles."

"It's the SAME thing. What you're saying is the SAME thing." I cross my arms and let out a laugh at the thought I'm essentially arguing with myself. Euphoria was right. He *is* stubborn. "And I don't have a crush on her. I believe her because her reasoning makes sense."

Valerian lets out a long sigh. He crosses his chamber to flip on a metal tea kettle. I keep focused on the glass box, but he tucks it away in his cloak.

Now my window of opportunity lessens.

"Unfortunately, unless we are biologically related or fated platonic, it doesn't matter what form our pair of atoms takes or which lifetime they manifest in. The pair of us will always develop some sort of feelings for each other," he says.

"Then you agree. You and Euphoria share a soul."

"I agree with quantum physics that our identical atoms have developed the capacity to exist in two separate states at the same time."

I blink at him. *This is why Dash hates when I talk so much, isn't it?*

As he unhooks two teacups from the cabinet over his makeshift tea station, I notice the triple spiral marked on his neck. *He thinks this is just a deal with an Enchantress.* It brings me back to my vision in the smuggler's hatch and the other flashes I had at Lake Ichor. Whatever they may have been, their existence isn't backed up by his theories. *Does he have them too?*

"Why are you overcomplicating it?" I ask. "Why can't you just say we're souls, eternal, and we live many lifetimes as different people?"

Valerian's kettle beeps. He plucks it off the heat, divides its contents out, and dips a tea bag in each cup. "Why are *you* overcomplicating it? Why can't you just say that we're atoms, particles, and that we are neither here nor there and exist in many forms?"

He smirks. I scowl.

Now I also know why nobody ever wanted to go up against me in the Academy's debate club. Valerian really thinks he's right. Does that mean he thinks Euphoria is wrong? Or is he not willing to see both sides? Not everything has an explanation or can be seen through his objective lens. That mindset alone is a block, a wall he's putting up.

It's what's holding him back from the Higher Realm.

Also, there's no way in hell I'm drinking his tea.

Push him, Shea. Find his weakness. Gain the upper hand. "What about intuition? Prophetic dreamers? Seers? Visions? Prophecies? How do you explain all of that?"

He carries what I assume is supposed to be my tea cup over and sets it on the bedside table closest to me, then retreats to his desk and takes a sip of his with elegance.

Now I really want to punch him in the face.

"I don't believe in anything prophetic, Shea," he says as he messes with the bone rings around his fingers. "The brain is, in a way, a giant computer. It essentially calculates outcomes and scenarios given all the information around any situation. If Euphoria were to tell me she had a vision or a dream that then came true, I'd say her brain came up with a possible outcome, given what she already knows. An outcome that *happened* to come true."

"You're impossible."

"Wouldn't it be that *you're* impossible, too, then?"

I clench my fists. "Okay. Whatever. I'm not going to argue with myself. Despite whether we are atoms or particles or souls that reincarnate, if you know all this, do you really think devouring Euphoria's soul is going to give you the answers you seek? Do you really think it's going to help you get into the Higher Realm? Because she doesn't think so. She says you aren't ready."

Valerian sets down his cup, his eyes brightening a shade of silver. "First of all, in no way, shape, or form do I think 'devouring Euphoria's soul' is going to give me answers. That is yet another one of her skewed, fantastical assumptions that paint me in this narrative that I am somehow this broken half-man, half-soul dredging through an endless void searching for himself."

Well, if he's insisting that he's healed, I'm not sure I'm convinced.

He continues, "Second, *she* doesn't get to decide whether I am ready for anything. We both signed the contract. It is time for *her* to do her part. *She* agreed to go first. *She* agreed to step into awareness and anchor this level of consciousness for us both."

That word. *Consciousness.* "You wrote about this in your journal."

He glances off for a moment, then right into my eyes. "As per the quantum system, atoms and particles can shift states. We can shift from lower to higher states of being or, in this case, consciousness. Kellie's Comet is the quantum portal to the Higher Realm."

Goosebumps prickle my skin. "Right. But if you want to put this in a quantum perspective, wouldn't you both have to be in your higher states to make the jump? You both must be in alignment with the frequencies of energy that the portal emulates. I think that's what Euphoria means."

"Please. I've mastered more in this lifetime than she knows. I'm ready, and I'm going whether she likes it or not." Valerian crosses to the window and peeks out as if he's looking for someone or something, and the Enforcer in me awakens yet again. *Nerves?* No. *Is he stalling?* Yes. "Besides, it doesn't matter about me. She's the anchor. If she goes first, I'll be able to follow her."

He joins me at the foot of the bed now. I straighten as he reaches into his pocket and pulls out the glass case containing the two dual-vials. If he weren't a spellcaster, I'd kick him between the legs, grab it, yank my portal key from his neck, and vacate this chamber altogether.

"Suddenly lost for words?" he asks, and I focus again.

"No, I'm thinking. You and Euphoria both have opposing, yet complementary perspectives. It's hard to decipher which one of you is right or wrong."

He glances out the window again. Now I know there's something important out there. I watch him, the furrow in his brows. *No*. Not something out there. Something in here he doesn't want to face. He doesn't want to look at me. Why is that? Avoidance? He's avoiding my gaze because my words trigger some truth in him he refuses to admit... or does he know something else...

"You know something Euphoria doesn't know." I watch the way he avoids watching me, the sudden shift in his expression. Yes. *That's it.* "Otherwise, you wouldn't have gone to such lengths to try and get her to go to lead you into the Higher Realm."

He scowls. "You think you've figured me out."

I smirk. "Am I wrong? I don't think I am."

"We only have twenty lifetimes to make the jump."

"And what number lifetime is this?" I ask.

"Twenty," he replies, giving me his attention but not direct eye contact. "It is our last chance to cross into the Higher Realm if we want to fulfill our contract."

No pressure or anything. "And if you don't?"

He taps his fingers against the glass box again, and the unsettling tension in my body returns. "If we don't succeed, we're stuck in this loop forever. We won't ever get the chance again."

Valerian motions for my hand. I'm reluctant, but I give in and let him take it. He places his palm against mine, and a glow envelopes my entire hand. As he releases his grip, I see the pattern he's left behind. It's the triple spiral marked on his neck. The one marked on Euphoria's neck, too.

"Until Euphoria lets go of the fantasy that we are lovers trying to find each other again for the sake of some greater Love that will ripple into the collective consciousness, we won't ascend," he says, and the triple spiral in my palm fades. "Each lifetime, she puts all her worth in my external validation of her. She lets my perception of her shape her. She sacrifices herself for me."

"Why do you keep hurting her?" I ask. "If you know that's what you're doing, why do you do it consciously? Why don't you sit her down and tell her the truth?"

"Don't think I revel in hurting her." He glances at me, a solemn expression having replaced his stoicism. "I can't be what she wants me to be right now because I signed that contract too. I promised to fulfill my role, and I've worked tirelessly to do so."

"Yeah? What is your role? Conceited asshole?"

Valerian scoffs. "Every action has a reaction. Euphoria is the anchor. I am the trigger. I promised to force her to face her fears and insecurities so that she may evolve into her Higher Self and learn to love herself so fiercely that nobody can make her question her worth. I even attempted to steal her soul."

Part of me agrees with Valerian. In the time I've known Euphoria, it's clear to me she *is* a walking example of untapped potential. She is everything one could ever be. She's beautiful, strong, nurturing, talented, and resilient, and she genuinely cares about life in general.

Without her, Dash and I would've never made it. I would've never been able to have this conversation right now had I not spent time with her. Her presence triggers *me*. She makes *me* want to understand myself. Purely by the way she makes me feel when I'm around her. She doesn't see the flaws that I see. She sees my less-than-desirable qualities as strengths in themselves. She just sees me for me.

Euphoria is the light. I think she always has been.

At the same time, I can't accept that people like Valerian are given free passes for the hurt they thrust upon others because of promises they might have made to help others grow. It would mean that every hardship, struggle, and shitty situation is planned or pre-ordained for some greater good. It would mean my relationship with Dad serves a bigger purpose. It would mean Mom's death does too. *And* my ongoing struggle with Dash.

That's a lot to take in. Even more to process in this short moment we have here on this planet today.

I peel away from the footboard. "You want me to believe you're doing all this *for* her?"

"It's for both of us," he says. "We both signed that contract. I value and respect it. I am... protective of her. That is where the sentiment... ends."

Another waver in his voice. I was wrong. He *does* care for her. *Interesting.*

"And you swear it isn't love? Maybe even a deep, Divine love you don't understand?"

Valerian rolls his eyes. "Goddess. Now you sound like her. As I said before, it would be impossible to assume I wouldn't develop feelings or attraction given our agreement."

"You know what I think?" I say with a smirk. "I don't think you want to get to the Higher Realm as a means to just fulfill some soul contract. I think maybe you do love her, and you do see glimpses of her so-called gushy, fantasist story. I think you care about her so much it scares the living shit out of you. You *want* to ascend. You *want* to be with her. Act tough all you want, but you know she's right. You're just too damn stubborn to admit it."

My gaze shifts to Valerian's palms, where a spark of light now hovers. A subtle red creeps up his neck. There. Now *I've* triggered the so-called villain. He said I still entertain Euphoria's perspective because I'm young and my mind has yet to expand. That the age of my soul, the younger version of his soul, gives me that disadvantage.

I disagree. I tell Dash all the time how life isn't a movie, how romance isn't like the books he reads, and that people aren't the fantasy he thinks them to be, and while I stand by those statements, I don't think leaning too far one way or the other is the answer either. I think it's both. Being expanded enough to see the bigger picture. But in touch enough with your inner child that you dare to keep seeing the magic in this world.

Euphoria sees both sides. She sees my logic, and she sees Dash's fantasy. She sees the magic in this world and the science supporting it. I don't think Euphoria is just an energetic leader. She isn't just an anchor. Euphoria *is* the bridge to the Higher Realm.

She doesn't even know it. I need to get to her. We need to talk.

But I still need the cure for my brother's soul. And I'm not leaving without my portal key.

Teatime is over. "Let's get on with it, Bale."

He opens his mouth to say something just as the chamber door opens and a skeleton enters. I don't waste another breath. My focus is on the glass box in his hands. I aim for his neck. Portal key. Cure. Portal key. Cure. *Escape*. But Valerian is quicker than I give him credit for.

A hot spark of magic hits me square in the chest.

19

Dash

Man, is it silent out here in these woods.

Effs and I crouch at the edge of a clearing. Fog wraps the mangle of trees behind us tighter than a Tee Tee's grilled burrito. The sickly smell of decaying trash festers in the air. I spot Crowley Corner's faded LED sign hanging crookedly from half a chain, just ahead and to the right. A gust of wind jams the stench up my nose, and I scowl. Effs doesn't seem bothered by it.

Then again, Effs's nose is gushing blood.

I offer her the spare long sleeve I have in my pack to mop up the mess, but black streaks still smear across her chin and down the front of her dress. Flashes of Roger bleeding out on the mausoleum floor plague my rattling brain, and I push them away.

She's going to make it. We both are.

A wrought-iron fence stands between us and the fairgrounds. A wasteland of warped metal and structures adorned in frayed canvas beckons. The plan is as follows: we distract Fake Death's spellcasters, sneak into the Tower, and save Shea-Lynn.

Then we kick Fake Death's crusty butt and steal the cure.

Effs sneezes, and another gush of blood pours out of her like the thickest brand of Mr. Moos chocolate-chocolate milk at the Skyway stop snack cart. "It's—it's getting worse."

"You're okay. You're okay." I take the shirt from her and wipe bits of blood she missed off her cheek. A glob sticks to my palm, and I grimace. It's not even warm. It's freezing cold.

Heinous Hades.

My voice softens. "I promise we'll be okay. I've never lost a teammate."

"I don't doubt it," she says, reaching up to touch my right ear. As her damp finger prods my lobe, I shiver. She pulls back, revealing more blood.

"Now you're bleeding too. I can accept this circumstance is my karma for being such a foolish girl, but you and Shea shouldn't be involved in this mess. I'll never forgive myself if we don't make it to the Tower."

"We're going to make it. Besides, I've got Ace. Don't worry about me."

Effs frowns. "Ace?"

"My tutelary. He's a bear. I thought about what I should name him. Ace came to mind first."

I cup her chin in my palm, ignoring the streaks of dried blood across her pale complexion. "And you gotta stop putting yourself down when times get tough. You're human—well, spellcaster—but the point is, you saw something in Fake Death, fell for him, and he ended up being what he is. That doesn't make you foolish. It makes you brave to be vulnerable enough to open up your heart to someone. *My* mom taught me that."

She forces a smile. "I know. I just shouldn't have let him treat me that way."

"Yeah, you're right. But don't hate yourself for it."

We walk along the fence, shoulder to shoulder.

Effs chews her lip. "I just—I thought I was right about our connection and the work we have to do together. I don't think I imagined that. A part of me, my gut, still tells me I am right."

"You probably are!" I chuckle, keeping my eyes peeled for any wider gaps in the fence so we can slip into the park unseen. "Just because it's not happening exactly as you want it to doesn't mean you're wrong. Maybe this is the beginning. Maybe it happens differently, or better, than you thought. You don't know how this story ends. Nobody does."

I pause, considering, before adding, "And did you ever think that maybe he doesn't deserve you right now?"

She glances up at me. "Now you sound like Shea."

"It's true! He's literally trying to suck out your soul, Effs. Doesn't sound like a loving relationship to me."

"He doesn't remember who he is. He's not himself."

"And it's your job to make him? Nahh. You can't wait around for him to figure out his life. Maybe you're trying too hard to make him something he isn't, or maybe he isn't willing or ready to wake up to the idea of loving someone like you."

"Oh, Dashiel." She chuckles. "You always know what to say."

Does she mean that? I guess I am good at this. When the people I date are hung up on their exes, I always listen to them. They've never given me that compliment before. It hits differently inside me. It means something.

"You deserve someone who knows how amazing you are."

She smiles at me. "I hope you listen to your own advice."

My stomach churns. I never thought about that. I keep hanging out with people who don't always appreciate me. Whether that's needing someone to vent to or help with a school project. Once, I was even a plus one at a birthday party spa day so they could get the couple's discount. Maybe I relate more to Effs than I thought. It's kinda like we're the same person.

I spot a weakened gap in the fence and slow us to a halt. "You know, my Aunt Merik is going to hook me up with her therapist. You should come with me. We'll go together."

She tries to laugh but ends up coughing up more blood. I look away, and she hacks a clot into the brush. When I'm sure she's ready to move, I wave us onward. We can't stay here.

I'd like to think we have an entire weekend to play this level like my team does in the tournament arena, but the truth is we don't.

Effs hand falls into mine. I squeeze and gently tug her by my side. We peer through the other side of the fence, through the cracks, at the outline of an old chair swing ride. The chipped chairs hanging from the carousel top shift and groan. Some cables are missing, leaving seats toppled over. A kind of prickly vine has since claimed them.

I pry a fence bar open wider. "Alrighty, Effs. In you go."

She uses me to steady herself as she wriggles through the gap. I slip in behind her, ready to move on to our next destination, but she's stopped. Too busy staring at the sky.

"Uh, everything okay? We should—"

She points at the greenish-blue hue that has taken over the sun. "Night is coming. It always comes early before Festival. They'll start the battle re-enactment an hour before Kellie's Comet crosses the sky. We must find Shea and convince Fake Death to give us the cure before that happens. Otherwise, I'll lose my soul and my magic, and you'll never make it home."

I crack my knuckles. "I'm not going to let Fake Death take your soul."

"Just like we aren't going to let anything happen to your sister?"

"I'm offended you doubt my capability." I give her a playful nudge.

She doesn't return the gesture. "I am doubting *our* capability to do everything in such a brief span of time."

A black drop forms in her left eye. She catches it quickly. Another dribbles out of her mouth. "If I must die, then I must die—I'll make peace with it—but you and Shea are what's important right now. Remember that. Even if we get there and things go awry."

"It's *all* going to work out," I assure her again.

Her blinking stare isn't comforting by any means, but she's going through a lot. I won't hold her lack of trust against her. And I know I'm the last person she should put her faith in, but I just feel like this is my time. I fought off dirt gnomes for Goddess' sake.

I'm a seasoned hero now.

Despite her reservations, she bites her tongue and follows me. I guide us to the nearest free-standing booth—a zombie-themed water game with busted squirt guns. Effs knocks away a cluster of hanging plushies fashioned to look like rotting limbs, and we hunker behind the counter side by side. I take out the Looky Specs I nabbed from the little Specters Village shop and give them a whirl, hoping they function as some sort of wide-range viewing device. They're nothing like my ten-thousand coin gaming goggles or my sister's high-tech interdimensional specs, but they get the job done. A full area POV.

"Tunnel of Heartbreak north-east of us looks like a good contender for the diversion. Or Bumper Coffins directly north-west." I spin the thumbwheel on my Looky Specs. "I'm thinking we go for a heavy hitter though—Demon's Descent—further north-west."

Effs pops up next to me. "You want to blow up the roller coaster? That was *not* the plan."

"The plan is to cause a diversion massive enough to preoccupy Fake Death's minions while we go after Shea-Lynn. Demon's Descent is the biggest mechanism in the park. Plus, it's the furthest attraction from the Tower."

She snatches the Looky Specs out of my hands, comments about how 'these binoculars are filthy,' and peers through. "What about the Razor? Or maybe the Thunderousbolt? It dispenses poisonous gas on the backward rotation *and* plays the screams of a thousand children over its loudspeakers."

"Poisonous gas, huh?" I raise a brow. She hands my Looky Specs back. "As good as those sound, we need something big. Something that's gonna take time to get under control."

I gaze through once more. "Any reason you're opposed to destroying the roller coaster?"

"It's where I first met Fake Death," Effs says.

"I get it. I've had a lot of first kisses at Tee Tee's Tentacle shack, and I would be devastated if Tee Tee ever went out of business." I take another look through the eyepiece. My gaze falls on the Haunted Teacups across the park. The exterior base of the structure is wooden. Maybe that'd be a wicked fire starter. "Any opposition to the Haunted Teacups?"

"That one is a well-loved ride too."

I pry the Looky Specs from my face and glance at her. "Effs, you're not giving me much to work with here. We need a ride with a wooden base so the spark ignites."

She chews her bloody lip. "Fine. Just do it."

"Got it. Phase one: choose a ride to obliterate. We're going in for the Haunted Teacups." I glance at my mission partner and she smiles for the first time since we set off together. It makes me feel all warm and fuzzy inside like I do when the A-Squad back at the Academy locks in a target hit on the Holoblocks board.

"I'll take that reaction as confirmation. Moving on to phase two." I direct my specs towards a gathering of concession stands and novelty booths a half mile from our hideout. "Gather fire-breathing rollie pollies."

Effs straightens. "I... copy that? Am I saying that right?"

A smirk takes over my chapped lips. "Heck yeah. That was good."

"Good. Because I've given up using actual logic to do this."

"Fair enough."

I check our surroundings again, noticing how desolate everything seems. Debris carries in the wind. Flapping canvas wracks against metal frames. For a place about to be the scene of a huge Festival or battle reenactment, the ghost-like presence is clear now more than ever. And I'm pretty sure I hear uncanny carnival music, but I can't pinpoint where it's coming from.

I clear my throat. "Looks like the coast is clear. Not a spell-caster in sight. I thought you said this place would be crawling with them."

"It will be soon enough. Though, don't be fooled. I'm sure there are plenty somewhere around her already."

She's right. In Holoblocks, the curse crones always hide. They're expert illusionists in disguise.

"Maybe they want us to think they're doing something else." I slip my Looky Specs into my pack and analyze the nearest rifle-style water gun bolted to the booth. Aside from those coming to gather for Festival, Fake Death's gotta have a minion squad on patrol. *Draw them out.*

"Any chance we can get this game started the old-fashioned way? I want to test something."

Effs places a palm on the counter. "Not unless we flip the park breaker. That's over by the Tower." She glances behind us at a hose nozzle on the control panel beneath the prize pegs. "We could get the water going. I think it runs off an underground grid system that spans all over Ominous. It pulls directly from Lake Ichor."

"Lake Ichor." I cross the booth and crouch next to the control panel. My finger hovers over the water switch. "As in liquified organs and gut juice, Lake Ichor?"

"Yes."

"Perfection."

If I'm right about the spellcasters hiding in the shadows like Holocity curse crones, they'll scurry once I set this game off. That gives us time to cross over into concessions, grab the rollie pollies, then move on to the main distraction.

Flip switched, soul suckas.

Nothing comes out at first. Then the water valve shakes. A gurgle erupts behind the panel. Slowly, the tubes connected to the water guns fill up with gut slop, and that memorable vision is all too fresh in my mind. Once the tubes reach capacity, the flow slows and stops.

"Now what," Effs asks.

"Now, we get ready to run." I suck my teeth and grab the handle of a water gun. *Please work.* With one twist at the base, slop leaks into my hands. *Gotcha.* "Once it blows, we bolt."

"Copy that."

I huff a breath, wiggling the gun so it'll give. I rear back and give it a good kick. Upon impact, the water gun snaps. The flow of gut juice erupts. It all happens too fast. Liquified organ rain pelts the surrounding area, and a smell I thought I'd never experience again catches in my throat.

Effs grabs my hand. We scramble over the counter and around the next booth, backs splayed against the pinstriped walls of a ring-toss game with coiled snake skins instead of rings. Hooting and hollering fills the air. Multi-colored cloaks billowing, spellcasters rush toward the water-gun booth.

They scuttle. Out of ride compartments. From in-between the shadows. More light wisps fly as they do what they can to stop the flow of slop water from continuing.

"We have seconds before one of those hocus-pocus goons figures out they can just flip off the water switch," I say in Effs's ear. "We have to go now. And we have to hurry."

She's lost in a trance, taking in the scene before her. "How did you know they were—"

I jerk her onward. "We don't have time!"

Heinous Hades, now I really do sound like my sister.

Is this what Shea feels like every time I take my sweet ole time doing anything on a mission? Geeze. I'm going to have to apologize again.

I race through the midway, fingers locked around Effs's wrist. She can barely keep up, but I'll get her there. Never leave a teammate behind on the Holo-grid. I don't look behind me. I can't, or it'll slow me down. My mind ticks off objectives: Curse crones preoccupied. Mission target ahead. My destination is a tiny concession stand marked by a tattered flag, embroidered with a rotting candy apple.

Effs told me about the rollie pollies on our way over here. This is where she said I'd find them. I pull her inside the stand and tug the curtain behind us. She crumples in a heap, out of breath, and coughs, trying to gather her bearings. I wipe a trickle of blood from my nose and survey the shelves. *Come on. Come on. Target item is here. It's gotta be.*

Tipping over jars and wrappers from years ago, I pop open a tin of sugary, brown sauce, swimming with maggots and black mold. My stomach lurches, and I move on before my mind takes me elsewhere.

"How are you doing down there?" I eye Effs, now curled into herself on the floor. She coughs, says something I can't hear, and I keep searching. "It's okay. You're okay."

Then her soft utterance repeats itself. "Leave me here, Dash."

"What? No way." I tear through a container coated in space spores. "We're sticking together. Teammate down doesn't mean leave them behind. We just have to—"

"*Dashiel.*" She grabs my pant leg. I stop shuffling.

"No, Euphoria. We're sticking together."

"You don't understand." She shakes her head. Black blood seeps from her mouth now, down her neck. "I am going to slow you down. You will move quicker on your own."

"It's not happening." I tear through boxes of deteriorating paper goods. If I were a jar of fire-breathing rollie pollies, where would I hide?

"Yes. It must."

I kick a box, and it hits the wall, exploding next to where Effs rests. She's so out of it she doesn't even flinch. "No, it doesn't! Okay? This morning I learned we have to give my mother back to the galaxies above. I'm not—*we're* not losing you too. This whole time you've gone back and forth between giving up and pushing through. I know you're tired. I'm tired too. But we're *pushing* through. Now, will you stop saying otherwise so I can find the bugs?"

She lifts her head and points toward a cabinet beneath the counter. As she does, the soul sucker bulging on her neck writhes. "Did you check over there yet?"

I shudder. "Nope. Let's check." I kneel and whip open the latch. Another empty box, two more moldy tins, and then an array of critter-filled jars. *Heck yeah*. "Effs, you're a genius."

It's hard to tell what's in the jars, given we're practically sitting in the dark. So, I bring them to my mission partner and hold them up for confirmation.

"That one," she utters breathlessly.

I unscrew the lid and pull out a stone, palm-sized egg. "How do I tell if it's still kicking or not? What's it been? Like a gazillion years since this place was actually open?"

"Rollie pollies are archaic... " Effs makes a smashing motion with her hand. "You crack the egg. They've been hibernating all these years. They're immortal."

"Ahh, so that's why they're the perfect fire-starters. Spellcaster magic is no match for them."

Using my fingers, I pry a hole in the speckled egg. Stone crumbs fall into my palm. From the mess awakens a flat, shiny, red beetle the size of my thumb. "And people used to eat these?"

"Nooo." Effs hacks a thick phlegm over her shoulder. "They'd use them for cooking with. Like flame-broiled, but less fragrant. If you make them angry enough, they combust."

The rollie pollie climbs up my arm, and I set it back in my palm. As I tickle its underside, the tiniest flame erupts between its antennae. A smile spreads across my face. Phase two is well underway.

Time to make these buggers *very* angry.

20

Shea

Valerian's hex squeezes my lungs.

Doesn't matter. You can't give up.

As the pressure in my chest deepens, I leap for the bed, to rush toward the door, and two silver wisps of light drag me back. They slam me on the mattress. I thrash and ruffle the bedding. A hot burn rises in my throat. My vision blurs. Another wisp expels from Valerian's hands, and he binds my arms and legs to each of the four posts.

I'm not going anywhere now.

Valerian snaps his fingers. The skeleton near the door comes forward.

"Take this to Lorelei," Valerian says, handing the skeleton the glass case containing the dual-vials. "Tell her to meet me on the Tower right before the comet passes. I'll be up after I open Festival and commence the battle reenactment."

The skeleton nods and clinks away. As the door clicks shut, I shudder.

There goes the cure. "Let me *go,* Bale! I swear to the—"

"Swear to whatever maker you want," Valerian barks. "It won't make a difference."

He sits at my side and adjusts the binding on my left wrist with another pulse of magic, so it won't burn my skin. I spit at him. Saliva speckles his cloak. He doesn't flinch.

"You just had to fight me, Shea. We could have worked through this together."

I let out a half-hearted laugh. "I don't care if we share a soul; I would never work with you. *You* just had to be another one of Dad's vile clients."

"That's a little rude, don't you think?"

I turn my head away from him. He forces it back straight, his fingers pinching my chin. "I'm doing you a favor by keeping you here out of harm's way. I'm doing this for us. For the greater good of *our* soul."

He pinches my chin tighter, and I grit my teeth. "I believed you were, but if you truly cared about Euphoria or *our* soul, you'd cure my brother and let us all go home."

"I'll admit bringing your brother into this was a mistake, but it's done now. Even if I wanted to cure him, the box containing the dual-vials has been charmed, and it can only be opened by Euphoria's Higher Self."

What. I blink at him.

"You didn't think it was a coincidence Dash ended up on this planet, did you?" he says, and the pounding in my head returns. "I thought if I could go back to the beginning, to our very first 'incarnation' as Euphoria calls them, following the division of our atomic particles, I'd successfully trigger her into her Higher Self this time."

Dash and I... are the first lifetime after our one soul split into two parts? *We're* the beginning of this mess? What does that make Euphoria and Valerian? The end? Of it all?

"I couldn't let this be the end," Valerian says as if reading my mind. "Euphoria told me she'd had a dream about your lifetime. She remembered the name of the family business—James Co.

"I did my research and contacted your father, and from there, it was easy. He was so desperate to find a cure for your mother. I knew he'd want one of my creations. Thus, I knew he'd send his Thief in the one contact request. You coming after your brother was a bonus."

A scream escapes me. I'd blamed Dad for all this. Part of me still does. Wanting to save your dying wife doesn't justify putting your children's lives at risk. But Valerian intentionally brought Dash here. He knew how to lie his way into the deal. He knew how to make it convincing enough for Dad to bite.

Is that part of him leftover from me? Did he carry that skill from one life to the next after being an Enforcer in this one? Is this really what I become? A conceited spellcaster so lost in his own logic that he can't see the bigger picture? Tears well in my eyes. This time, I welcome the burn in the back of my throat.

No. This isn't your fault, Shea. Valerian Bale is a—

"You're a coward," I say. He stands, ignoring me.

"Did you hear me? You're nothing but a coward. Euphoria *sees* you like nobody else does, and she still chooses to love you. She doesn't want you to be something you aren't. She wants you to be who you are."

"Very poetic, Shea-Lynn."

"Instead, you hide from who you are. Because it's easier to be surrounded by people in your life who don't challenge you to dig deeper and face your darkness head-on."

"Don't act like you aren't like me. Don't make me more wicked than I am."

I let my eyes focus on the black velvet material draped above the canopy bed. A tear streaks down my face.

I hear Valerian clear his throat as he crosses the room. But he says nothing. I close my eyes and blink past the burn. Dad says I'm like him too. *You're like me, Shea. Tough. Resourceful. You never give up. You'll figure it out.* My father doesn't know me any more than Valerian knows me. I am the version of me my father built me to be. And I am a younger version of Valerian he's forgotten to nurture.

He won't hurt me. He can't.

"You *are* my darkness, Bale," I mutter, and another tear streaks my cheek. The dampness coats my lips, making my tongue taste of salt. "And I'm the part of you that you refuse to face."

I stretch my neck and try to get a look at him. I'd expected a comeback. Instead, I've been met with silence. He shuffles about the room. I lay there, listening to him busy himself with something. I wish I could see. I wish I could see the contemplation on his face. I know what I said made him think. I know he knows I'm right about this.

A beep sounds from the bedside table. Valerian grumbles, crosses back into view, and tugs open the drawer. He pulls out a communication device with an antenna that looks like something Great-grandpa Alden would turn into a Gallivant, and presses a side button. It beeps again.

His dull, monotone voice returns. "What do you want? I'm... busy."

I lift my head as far as my bindings will allow. The device warbles. On the other end, the device paired with Valerian's, there's commotion. Shouting. Crackling. A crash.

As Valerian listens, his expression twists. I notice the flush in his cheeks and, dare I say, a glossiness in his eyes.

He speaks into his device again, "What in the hell is going on down there?"

Moments later, a spellcaster bursts through the door to the chamber. Steam rises from the burnt holes in his gray cloak. He wipes soot off his smooth, bald head.

"I'm terribly sorry to bother you amid"—the spellcaster glances at me, then alternates his gaze to Valerian—"whatever intimate act this is."

Bile rises in my throat. "*Ugh*, no. Gods no. *No*."

"Right. Right. Of course," the spellcaster says.

Valerian scoffs. "Oh, get on with it. Why are you here?"

"There was a bit of a mishap with one of the rides. We can't seem to get it under control, and they won't stop—"

"You'll have to be a bit more specific, I think." Valerian leaves the bedside, but his hex bindings remain. I grit my teeth and tug, wincing at the burn. *You have to get out of here.*

"The Haunted Teacups. They're on fire."

"And? They'll do worse to the place in the battle reenactment. Tell the others to use a dowsing spell or turn on a spigot and put it out manually."

"They are trying. But... " The spellcaster rubs a burn on his arm, looking at the floor. "It seems that fire-breathing rollie pollies have gotten in the framework."

Valerian lets out a yell. "Damn it all. Are you all incompetent?"

This has Dash written all over it. I let out a chuckle. Valerian jerks his head toward me. Any emotions he might've been processing are no longer evident. I raise a brow and stare at him.

His lips curl. "Watch her until I get back."

The spellcaster stammers. "Uh, alright."

Valerian wipes his hands on his cloak. As he waves his fingers, the door opens by itself and slams shut behind him. My bindings buzz. I tense. *How am I supposed to get out now?*

The spellcaster lingers by the door, picking his teeth.

I could talk my way out of this. Though, sweet talking isn't exactly my expertise. It's more Dash's style. At least he's the one I always send when I want the job done.

My tactics are a bit more brutish. "So... how long have you been one of Bale's hirelings? Are you two... friends or... "

"I'm not supposed to talk to the people he kidnaps, beds, or invites up for tea."

"Ah, so this is a regular occurrence then. Got it. I've been kidnapped, by the way. That's the category I fall into."

I purse my lips. *Smooth, Shea. Real smooth.*

A scratching sounds beneath the floor. The spellcaster's ears perk up.

"You hear that?" he asks. "Gee, I hope those rollie pollies aren't in here too."

I strain my neck and watch him pace the chamber, kicking around on the floor. The scratching stops then starts again when he nears the trap door.

"You should probably check," I say.

Because maybe he'll open the door, and I can find some way to get out of these bindings and out of here before Valerian gets back.

As the scratching intensifies, the spellcaster kneels next to the trap door. Before he can do anything else, it whips open and whacks him in the face. He flies back across the floor, knocked out like one of Dad's hirelings when they don't put the right orders in for Headquarters.

I let out a deep breath. I can't see anything more. My neck doesn't crane far enough.

Something... someone... crawls across the hardwood floor, knees heavy and dragging as dramatically as one could. Then my little brother's head pops up next to the bed.

"I think I killed that guy," he says.

I let out a half-hearted laugh. "Is that really you? Or am I hallucinating?"

"I'm offended you think I'm a hallucination."

"Oh, Dash. I'm more thankful for you than you know."

He throws himself over me in a hug. "Yep. I saved *you* for once."

"Yes, you did." I pull at my restraints. They spark. He examines the tethers with burnt fingers, and I notice the ash on his cheeks and his blood-soaked shirt now scorched with holes. "I'm guessing the Haunted Teacups was you?"

He wipes his bloody nose. "Yep. Effs and I are on a mission to win Level 17. Now I need to figure out how we're getting you out of these spell bindings."

"Something metal will break the current," Euphoria croaks from somewhere on the floor.

I clear my throat to get Dash's attention and bring my voice down to a dull whisper. "Is she okay? How is she doing? And you're okay? How's the sucker? How are you feeling—"

"Shea, I'm all about family reunions, but we've gotta move onto phase four of my master plan here. See, getting you was phase three. Saving our souls is next."

"That's what I was—"

"We don't have much time." He glances around, grabs a pewter vase from the bedside table, tosses out the dead black roses inside, and waves it across the first wisp of light binding my left arm. The current breaks, and he moves to the right, slowing near my ear. "She's bleeding a lot."

I thought her tutelary was protecting her soul on the other side. Unless it can only handle fighting for one of them, and it's favoring Dash. I wait for him to free my legs, and then I sit up. My first instinct is to run and check on Euphoria, but I need a second.

I stare at my brother long enough to catch my breath. I still can't believe it's him. With composure. With a plan. With such self-awareness.

"Who are you, and what have you done with my little brother?" I say, and Dash's cheeks fill up with a little color. "I'm so pro—"

"Not *now*, Shea. Time's a ticking! We have to move. We're running out of time."

I shake my head and pull him into the biggest hug I can manage. "We have enough time for me to tell you how glad I am that you're okay and how proud I am of you for stepping up."

He ruffles my hair. "Aw, you're making me blush."

"Good." I ruffle his blood-smeared hair back. "You smell very bad, by the way."

"Rough run-in with Lake Ichor fallout and everything else that's been going on." Dash motions toward the trapdoor. "Anyway, shall we? You good to go?"

"Do you even have to ask?"

He smirks, helps me off the bed, and steadies me so I can gather myself. As we head for the trap door, I find it's more of a crawl space between the floor, only big enough to travel on our hands and knees. As I step down, I see Euphoria slumped against the wall. Her tilted head grazes the low ceiling, and a continuous dribble of blood flows from her lips.

Oh, my Gods.

"Sh—Shea?" her dull voice manages.

My stomach flips. This is worse than I thought.

I lower my body inside, making room for Dash.

He closes the trapdoor behind us and maneuvers around me. "Careful of the gaps in the floorboards. It's the old ride structure."

I blink at my brother. It's like he's speaking another language, and I don't care about any of it. Instead, I focus on Euphoria. Checking her ears, getting a closer look at her eyes. Blood seeps from her ear canal, and the spider veins in the whites of her eyes have clouded, but her irises remain the dullest shade of gold. Using my sleeves, I try to wipe her up the best I can.

Soon, I'm covered in her blood, and she isn't any better off.

I glance at Dash, preoccupied with deciding if we'll go right or left next, then I lower my voice to speak to Euphoria. "What happened to your tutelary? You're progressing faster than—"

"*Shea. Shhhh.*" She lifts her hand onto my arm.

I wait for her touch, finding it cold.

My voice cracks. "Don't you dare shush me."

"I've told Ace to make Dash a priority. It'll give him more time."

My heart sinks. I was right then. She's sacrificing herself. "Look, I got to know Valerian a bit while I was with him, and we need to focus less on him and more on you right now."

Euphoria coughs. "You and Dash need to leave me behind."

"Nope. Not this again." My brother forces his way between us and waves a hand in her face. "Hey, what did I tell you? We're not giving up. We're *not* leaving you behind."

He turns to me. "She's been doing this. I had to practically drag her here. Wasn't easy. Lemme tell yah."

Euphoria wipes the blood under her eyes. "Shea. Dash. I know I'm going to die. Valerian and I are *not* going to complete our lesson this time around. It's okay. I've accepted it."

"Dash is right. You need to stop." I scooch in closer to her and let my hand fall on her slimy, cold cheek. "And what do you say we help you get to that portal so *you* can go to the Higher Realm?"

She shakes her head. "No... I'm not ready... "

"Yes, you are," Dash says. "We're going to help you."

"I'm sorry I... got you two... involved in all this."

"Our father got us involved in this. Valerian got us involved in this. Not you," I correct her, squeezing her hand. "Don't you ever apologize about that ever again."

I look into her eyes, taking in her sallow face. There isn't enough time to explain everything Valerian and I spoke about to her. And if her Higher Self is the only one that can open that dual-vial case, how will she find the strength to ascend when she can barely walk?

Get it together, Shea. You'll figure it out.

We'll figure it out together.

Dash hovers over my shoulder. "Again. Sentimental reunions are my favorite, but... "

I shoo him away. "I know. I know."

"*Phase four*. It's all about the phases," he says.

Euphoria sighs. "He thinks this is... a Holoblocks game."

"Of course." I help her forward, onto her hands and knees.

Dash slips in beside us and aids me in getting Euphoria along the passageway. He brushes cobwebs out of our path. Keeps checking his peripherals. The glow of the building illuminates through the wooden structure of the crawl space. I have no idea where we're going or any sense of direction. But for once, I let Dash deal with it. For once, I'm just too damn tired to take control. Eventually, we reach another trap door that leads down instead of up.

I wipe the sweat off my brow. "Lorelei is meeting Valerian on top of the Tower with the cure before Kellie's Comet passes in the sky."

My brother opens the trap door. It creaks. He peeks inside.

"We might not have to go to the top of the Tower," he mutters.

I leave Euphoria's side and join Dash at the opening.

As I cram myself next to him, we gaze at the scene below. Another chamber, this time decorated in shades of pink. A faded, rose-shag rug covers half the floor. Two blush-colored antique loveseats positioned across from one another are set directly below the trapdoor. And in the center of the coffee table between them—the glass box containing the dual-vials.

Dash leans forward, and I stop him. "Someone might see you." He nods. I glance back at Euphoria. "Frilly, pink room with matching loveseats. Lorelei's chamber?"

She whispers, "Yes."

I nudge my brother. "Check to see if she's in there."

He throws me a glare. "Why me? Why do I always—"

"Fine. Move." I lay flat on my belly. "I'll do it."

"You don't have to be so pushy," he says.

Using my palms to steady me, I tip myself forward bit by bit until I'm halfway through the trapdoor's opening. I look in all directions. A full-sized bed draped in pink satin. A brick fireplace burning coals. It's oddly cozy for an abandoned amusement park, but it's empty, all the same. *Thank the Goddess.* The only issue is that I'm too high up to reach the dual-vials.

I yank my body back up through the trapdoor.

"Did you get them?" Dash asks.

"Not even close. Do you think you can reach them if I hold your feet?"

Dash's eyes go wide. "What? *No*! Have we learned nothing about acting impulsively? I really think we should take a moment and think this through first. Safely."

This is the boy that eats tentacle tacos prepared by a giant space slug with no proper sanitary measures, and *now* he wants to play it safe? I don't think so.

"Euphoria is running out of time. You are too. We need those vials." I jab him, urging him closer to the edge. "Lorelei could come back any minute. Come on. Let's *go*."

He blocks another prod. "I've got a bad feeling about this."

I scoff. Now this is getting ridiculous. By now, Valerian knows I'm gone.

"Look, I'm proud of your newfound responsibility and care, but I need 'young and reckless' Dash right now. Now, shimmy down the trapdoor and grab the dual-vials before it's too late."

Dash scowls. "Okay. *Fine.*"

He pulls his body forward. We shift around one another. I grab his legs and guide him down over the edge. His stomach grazes the wood. His shirt rides up and dangles over his head as he slips further upside down over the hall below.

"That's it, Dash. You got this," I say.

He huffs. "A little lower. I can't reach!"

I brace my feet against the wooden beams on either side and lock in a good grip so I can support his weight. He doesn't weigh much, but the exhaustion of being mentally titillated by Valerian and everything else is starting to catch up with me.

"How about now?" I ask.

"I—I can't—" He swings forward and stretches his fingers. I grip him tighter, so he won't slip. "I can't reach it, Shea. Can you go any lower? I'm almost there."

Not without dropping you on your ass. Which we should have just done in the first place, but then we wouldn't have been able to get back up. And who knows what lurks in these halls.

But he's right. The gap's too far.

I dig my fingers into my brother's ankles. "Just—try harder."

"I *am* trying! Whatever blood I have left is rushing to my head."

"Not hard enough."

He flops in the air. "Don't you dare get sassy with me now."

"I'm *not.*" I lean back to anchor our weight. The more he moves, the harder it is to keep him steady. In fact, he's slipping. "There's a lot on the line here. We're running out of time."

"Yeah, you keep saying that. As if I don't already know."

Again, Dash stretches his arm as far as he can reach. He twists his torso to get a better angle, but no matter how much he strains to grasp, he's too far away.

We're too high up from the chamber below.

"It's not as easy as it looks!" he whines.

Mind over matter, Shea. I close my eyes. Lock my arms as tight as I can. "I know. One more time. You've got this, Dash. I know you do."

"Okay. Swing me forward," he says, and I do as I'm told.

As his weight fluctuates in my grip, there's a tug. My stomach leaps into my throat. I can't really see from where I am anymore. I'm trying too hard to keep him steady.

Then he's yanked out of my arms.

"SHEA!"

"—Dashiel!"

Sheer panic sets in. I scramble over the opening and peer down into the face of a spellcaster I'm assuming is Lorelei, with blonde hair that reaches her bare feet. She pulls back her pink hood. Purses her glossy lips. Her pink eyes glimmer—*Goddess,* is everything pink?—and I spot the two fellow coven members that have Dash pinned against the wall.

He squirms, but they've got him, and without the dual-vials in his hands.

A spell hits me like a punch in the teeth. *Not this again.* The power of the pulse shoves me back, and I yelp. This spell feels familiar, like the one from the woods. It was Lorelei's spellwork that caught me and brought me in.

With a wisp of light, I'm forced from the opening and lowered into the chamber below with surprising grace. Then, with another burst of light, Lorelei retrieves Euphoria from above like a bug from a hidden hole. A sinking feeling settles in my gut. They weren't supposed to find her. Valerian wasn't supposed to get what he wanted. And a part of me knows that it's *my* fault. Dash knew this wasn't a good idea. How come I didn't?

Why do I keep doing this?

"Eugene will take Euphoria to the roof. Valerian will meet us there," Lorelei tells her comrades, and when they ask her what they should do with us, all she says is, "Them? Lock them in the Razor."

21

Dash

I push against the cold iron bar currently squeezing the life out of my legs, but I might as well be straining against the ropes of those nasty gnomes. Frustration and anger churn in my chest. I don't let out the growl building up in my throat.

I was SO close to getting those dual-vials.

Another inch, another swing back and forth, and Effs and I could've reclaimed our souls. Then again, the whole 'dangle from the sketchy tower ceiling while curse crones are on the prowl' strategy was a bust. What was Shea thinking?

I mean, I know what she was thinking.

I've been there. I know the feeling all too well. When you care about someone so much, your logical reasoning shuts off, and you suddenly live by impulse and rash decisions.

Kind of like when Dad agreed to send me here because he thought Fake Death's soul suckers could save Mom somehow.

It's a side of Shea I've never seen. It's a feeling I'm sure she doesn't know what to do with. She must really care about Effs. Still, she's the reason we're packed side-by-side in a Razor ride cage barely large enough for two.

I think I remember Effs saying this ride used to be a torture device. Got a decent look at it on my way in, between screaming and thrashing in the spellcaster's arms that dragged us here. It's like a Ferris wheel but on steroids. Twelve cages identical to ours rotate freely on a massive oblong axis. Faded, red vinyl seats curve our backs. We're about a story up, which is high enough for me. And the lap bar is so tight, I can't flex my stomach or my butt, which is now numb, resulting from being suspended in the same teetering angled position for so long.

Maybe in its prime, the Razor was an exhilarating form of entertainment. Now it's all rusted framework, shattered LED displays, and jammed gears. I doubt it would pass a safety exam, let alone be desirable to anyone without a death wish.

I certainly don't have a death wish.

Someone, on the other hand...

I glance at Shea. Her lips are drawn tight.

"Stop staring at me," she says.

"You should have listened to me."

"I know, okay? I *know*."

"So, you *can* admit that it's your fault we've been captured." I grip the support rungs bolted to the latched door. There's nowhere else to put my hands. Besides, it steadies the free-swinging cage cart from tipping forward or nearly upside down. "And you can admit that we should have gone with my plan too, right, because—"

"Oh, please. Don't act like you're the king of plans now."

"I'm not saying that!" Shea jerks her head away from my shrill protest, and our cage cart dips. My stomach whirls along with it. "And watch the sudden jolts. This cart is finicky. I'm going to toss whatever stomach bile is left in my empty stomach if this sadistic vertigo ensues."

Shea sets her hard gaze forward. "I'm not doing anything."

"*Yes*. You're moving it on purpose."

"You want on purpose? I'll give you on purpose." I can practically feel the heat rolling off her as she uses her upper body to rock us back and forth.

"Shea-Lynn! I mean it."

With no visible emotion, she thrusts our cage cart in the opposite direction it was angled before. The force of her movement sends us upside down. One full rotation. I let out a sound I'm not particularly proud of. Then we topple back around, and she gears up for another go.

Heinous Hades. "Enough!"

She huffs, slams back, crosses her arms, and focuses on something else. This is what that *feeling* does to you. Whether it's like or love, you become someone else when you care so deeply about someone.

"I know you're angry at yourself. You don't want anything to happen to Effs because you care about her, but you gotta think with your head."

She still won't look at me. "I do think with my head."

"Yeah," I say with a chuckle. "Well, you've never been in 'like' with someone. Love, like, the feels—it clouds your judgment sometimes. Trust me, it happens to me all the time."

"I'm aware."

"Then you get what I'm saying." I force a smile and awkwardly set a gentle hand on her shoulder, willing her to look at me. Instead, she deflects the gesture.

"Come on. Don't be like that."

I try again, because sometimes it takes more than once to get through to her, and again she dodges my touch. Nostrils flared, she tries to cross her arms, but the cramped quarters make it impossible.

"*Hey.* Let's just start over—"

My sister screams as loud as she can. It's so random, it shakes me to the core. She slams her palms against the lap bar attached to the latched door directly in front of us. The scream continues until her face is beat red. Until her eyes water, not prematurely.

Our cage cart sways but maintains an upright position.

We've gone from the feeling of liking someone to potentially what she'd be like after a broken heart or something... perhaps an emotional breakdown of sorts... I really don't know what's going on. All I know is I want her to stop doing what she's doing.

"Okay. Okay." I run a hand through my hair and try to remember all the times she's pulled me through something tough. Because that's what this is. A moment. A moment she has to have, or we can't move on or find a way to save Effs or take the cure from Lorelei or find Fake Death so we can retrieve her portal key.

All before Kellie's Comet crosses over Ominous.

Wow. We have a LOT to do.

I try to remember what Shea always says to me. She sometimes finds wisdom when she isn't telling me to suck it up. Actually, Mom's better at it than both of us. *Gods.* Our mother is going to die too and leave us with our wicked father, and then we're all going to—

Dashiel. You gotta get it together.

I've never once been in a situation where *I* have to be the stable one. But it wouldn't be fair if I didn't try. Right? Effs just got done telling me I was good at giving advice. I can do this too. Shea's chest heaves forward, sending our cage cart facing down before it tips back up. I ride out the motion with white knuckles. Then the sound of my big sister's muffled sobs fills our claustrophobic, mechanical prison.

"Oh, Shea-Lynn," I whisper.

She finally lets me reach out for her, and we awkwardly adjust so she can rest her head somewhat on my chest. It'll do for now. This is about all I can do right now.

"I keep blaming you," she says, "but it's really my fault."

"Don't say that." I try to console her, though I can't hold her the way I'd like. I'd like anything more for her not to be sad. "We're equally at fault here."

"Who knows what they're doing to Euphoria. I let her down. I let you down."

"You didn't let anyone down. We'll fix this. *I* will if I must."

"I'm not sure how you're going to fix this." She wipes her face. "We're stuck in a ride cage. They took your pack. And Valerian has my key. Also, we've been crying way too much."

I smirk. "Crying isn't a bad thing. It's a release!"

She peers out the grate toward the fairgrounds. "Whatever it is, you've always been much better at talking about how you feel. I don't know how to do that."

"You're being way too hard on yourself." I position my head next to hers and glare at the shadowy array of broken-down rides and turned over concession carts resting in their muddy graves beneath us. "You're good at lots of things. You can be good at this too."

"Maybe. But it's not going to help you or Euphoria."

"Don't worry about me," I say. "I've got my tutelary delaying the sucker's effect."

She wipes under her eyes. "If I can't save you, I fail. And I can't save you. So, I failed."

"Who said you failed? You've saved our butts more on this job than I can count. You've saved *my* life more times than I can count. That doesn't mean you failed. My life is completely out of your control. Most things are. You gotta stop putting so much pressure on yourself. Didn't we *just* get done telling Effs this?"

She wipes her nose. "I know."

"If you're worried about Dad, screw Dad. Because he puts too much pressure on you too. He always has, and he always will. He's a miserable man who needs to face his own inner demons.

"We aren't responsible for those either," I add. "And, dearest sister, I don't care what you think, you are not perfect. You don't need to be perfect. You are as human as the rest of us disastrous mortals are. The phantom at the Hover Rink told me that one."

She's smirking at least, so I'll take it that my words made at least some impact. But she doesn't get a chance to respond fully because a burst of multi-colored light explodes in the sky overhead like a firework. The fallout reflects into our eyes and dissipates over the approaching crowd of cloaked spellcasters.

"I think Festival is going to start soon," I whisper.

Shea's fingers curl around the lap bar at her stomach. "Great."

They gather around a small, wooden amphitheater that I imagine was once used for spectacular themed shows in which the actors shoved uniformed dances and campy show tunes down the audience's throats. Any other day that'd be an absolute dream to think about.

As the crowd parts, the skull prince wannabee returns. Looking much better than when we met in the Bone Wood. *Geeze.* This guy must have one heck of a glam squad because the version of him I encountered in the mausoleum was enough to keep me up at night.

Fake Death passes through to the stage with Lorelei, a horde of skeleton henchmen behind them. When they reach the stage, the murmuring crowd falls silent.

Shea tenses. "Do you see Euphoria anywhere?"

"Uhhhh." I squint, scanning the throng for a bloodied heap of a girl, but fail to locate her. Instead, I spot a couple of headless skeletons that seem all too familiar. "Nope. I don't."

"She's probably being kept at the top of the Tower."

From the center of the stage, Fake Death raises a hand. The remaining clatter dies down. The soul sucker burrowed deep inside me writhes, making me shiver.

Something wicked is about to go down.

"We have to get out of here," Shea says.

I try, and fail, to shift in my seat. "I couldn't agree more."

Fake Death's voice carries, amplified somehow. "Every twenty years, we gather here at Crowley Corner to commemorate the many lives we lost in the Great War."

I sigh. "Annnd cue the diabolical speech. Maybe you should submit that to the Board of Galactic Studies, Shea. A collection of villainous speeches. We've heard enough of them."

Shae doesn't respond. She starts feeling around our cage cart, a fire lighting in her gaze. "Let him talk. The longer he goes on, the more time we have to figure out how to get out of here." Her fingers land on the bolts that connect the door to the rest of the cart. "Look for any weak points."

A smile takes over me. My wisdom was more influential than I expected it to be. Because this is my sister. *This* is the Shea I know and love and need so much.

"We participate in a reenactment of the last battle to remember the lives lost and to let off any residual feelings leftover from the war itself," Fake Death continues. "If you have never participated in this event—this is my first year leading, and what an honor it is—I must remind you of the rules. Kellie's Comet crosses over Ominous in exactly one hour. You have until then to fight to your heart's content. So long as the spells are not life-threatening."

"Can we use torture curses and other hexes?" someone in the audience calls out.

Fake Death raises a brow and glares at Lorelei. She considers the question and nods.

Another spellcaster shouts, "What about other weaponry!"

Lorelei puts her hands on her hips. "Come forward and show me."

The rainbow of cloaks parts for the brave spellcaster. He makes way for the stage and sets a sword, an old bow and arrow, and a glowbeam of all things at Lorelei's feet.

"That looks like a first model," Shea mutters, peering through the bars.

Lorelei inspects the spellcaster's offering and scrunches her nose. "Your request is denied. Our ancestors fought with magic only. Thus, we will stick to magic."

With one wave of her hand, she emits bubblegum-pink light and flings the weapons off the stage. They tumble into the carousel out of sight.

Ah, man, what a waste.

"This lifetime is Euphoria and Valerian's last chance to cross into the Higher Realm," Shea says, and she manages to untwist one of the rusted screws. It clatters at our feet.

I locate another loose screw. "How do you know?"

"He told me, and I believe him."

Below, Fake Death summons a spark of green in his hands. One by one, all the spellcasters in the crowd follow suit, a range of colors in their palms too.

"It is tradition," Fake Death says, "that we will open the ceremony with a silent reflection in honor of the spellcasters who lost their lives in the Great War. Let us all bow our heads in reverence."

As the crowd dips their hoods, Shea loosens another bolt. It plinks away to the ground as she starts on another. "He thought if he attempted to steal her inner being, she'd become so fed up with him she'd give into him or go on her own. Which would then trigger the ascension."

"Do you think he'll really let her die?" I ask.

"It's hard to say. I think he loves her. But he's stuck on the logic of this deal they made with the Enchantress. He doesn't want to fail. He knows he won't get another chance."

I put a hand on her shoulder. "We can do this, Shea."

"Together?" She pauses, a slight blush in her cheeks. "One last run for our lives?"

"A scrape by at the last-minute kind of gig," I add, because her words mean that she's okay with my decision to be done with James Co. after this.

"Yes. That's exactly what I mean."

"Then I'm in. One last run."

Shea smiles. "Let's make it count."

Another bolt falls at our feet. As the door shifts, it groans. Our lap bar loosens, but not nearly enough to give. I find one more bolt at the hinge on the latch. I twist, and it falls too.

"That was the last one over here," I say.

Shea leans forward, and our cage cart dips slightly. "I think we loosened enough to push our way out. Question is, how do we sustain the drop? We should be okay if we can do it without injury or drawing attention to ourselves."

I glance out at the spellcasters, still deep in their moment of reverence. "What are we doing once we get out of here? Do we have a legit plan or—"

As Shea puts pressure on the cage door, our cart tips further forward. My stomach churns. It's a free-spinning cart. Any amount of pressure will do it. I follow her and push.

She says, "Wait. Back again. Let's use our weight to move with the motion of the cart. Hopefully, that'll collapse the door."

We arch our backs and lean forward, pressing all our weight against the latched door. It nearly pops open but needs another go.

Shea huffs. "One more time. This time with more force!"

My arm muscles tighten. We get our cart back into position for another spin. We jet forward in motion, and our stomachs slam against the lap bar attached to the door so hard I feel it structurally give a bit more.

Ugh. "My body's gonna bruise!"

"You'll be fine. *Again.*"

Below us, a round of applause ensues.

Shea slams the latch on the door.

Valerian crosses the stage to the left wing, where an electrical box sits mounted on a wooden pole. Every spellcaster in the audience summons their power. As Valerian flips open the box, I spot the switches and levers. An uneasiness settles in my gut.

Oh, Gods. "Uh, Shea, I think... I think he's going to power up the park."

My sister's eyes go wide, her arm halfway out the cart door.

Valerian flips a switch. "Happy Festival!"

A flash of white light explodes overhead.

Brisk wind tousles our hair. All at once, a symphony of rolling wheels, rubber tires, and steel gears sound. The ground quakes. The thrum of old generators and systems, the blinding LED lights and displays, the racket of whirls, and menacing carnival music—Crowley Corner park comes alive around us.

Including the Razor.

22

Shea

Fuck. I grab for the lever holding us in place. "Secure the door! Secure the door!"

"Secure the door?" Dash clings to the rungs. "Yeah. Lemme just gather all the busted screws we removed and tossed over the edge real quick."

"Now is *not* the time, Chaos Comedian."

Think, Shea, think. But there's no time to think. Our massive oblong prison jerks into motion. Spinning slowly at first until its axis shifts into high gear. My breath quickens. Both Dash and I cling to the latched door, keeping it as steady as possible. A nearly impossible task when you can't tell if you're right side up, upside down, or in between. Either way, the chances of this now compromised door holding for the entire duration of this hell ride are slim to none.

"We're going to dieeeee." Dash hollers as we rotate forward rapidly four times in a row. Dash's head bobs into me with each rotation. "Please. Please, Gods. Goddesses. Shea-Lynn, we're going to dieeee."

"Shut up! You're not helping!"

My brother's face collides with the latched door, popping it ajar. Black blood spurts from his nose, and warm, sticky droplets streak my cheeks. We slip forward in our seats. I snap the hinge shut as soon as we tilt back again, and we ride out the next rotation.

At the next jolt, the ride pauses briefly and switches from a clockwise motion to a counterclockwise. *Come onnn. Think, Shea.*

It pauses again, gearing up to switch back to a clockwise motion.

"That's it!" My eyes spring open with the next menacing lurch. Our not so latched door swings ajar again. Dash and I both gasp and slam it shut, wedging our feet and knees into the corners of our cart to keep it in place. "If we open the door and release ourselves when the ride pauses to switch directions, we should be able to tuck and roll out... I think."

Dash does a double take, wide-eyed. "You *think*?"

"It's all we've got!" I yelp as our bodies rise to the lap bar.

We slam down against the curve of our seats. We flip right-side up again. This time Dash slips too far. His leg dangles out of the cage cart. We have no other choice now. I grab under his arms and try pulling him back up.

He scrabbles as much as he can. "I'm too young to dieeee."

Clinging to my brother, I shout, "On the next revolution, before it switches back to counterclockwise motion—I'm releasing us—GET READY!"

Dash screams. He burrows his face into my belly.

Energy drones. Our cage cart completes its rotation. It reaches the bottom of the ride's loading dock, pausing briefly. Groaning and churning, it picks up again, ready to thrust us in the opposite direction. I release our door and both Dash and I tumble out across the dirt.

He lands flat on his face. I land flat on my ass.

A stinging surges in my semi-healed leg. I flex away the muscle cramp, wincing through the pain. Dash writhes nearby in the bushes, clutching his bloody nose.

Rogue spells whiz by on either side of us.

No time to dilly-dally. Reenactment or not, this is still a war zone.

I crawl toward my brother. "Are you okay? Look at me."

He groans. "I'm *okay*... Mentally, I'm still going to need therapy for the rest of my life."

A volley of hexes and colored light blazes overhead. I slam to the ground next to Dash and keep low, barely missing a spurt of silver. The three spellcasters battling it out race right by us and continue their duel, one spellcaster easily taking down the other two with what looks like some kind of curse that temporarily knocks its victims out.

"Valerian has my key. Lorelei has the dual-vials," I tell Dash, keeping my nose low in the dirt. "We need to find them and make it to the Tower before Kellie's Comet crosses the sky."

Dash sighs. "Not a big task or anything."

The question is, where did Valerian and Lorelei go? Did they already head over to the Tower, or are they lurking in the fight around us?

It's hard to see anything from our shrubbery hideout.

"If we split up, we can cover more ground," I say.

Another battery of spellwork shoots over our heads.

Dash grimaces. "Even if we spot them in the chaos, they'll know we're coming. We stick out like a couple of rotten vamp thumbs. They'll always have the upper hand."

Point taken, little brother.

I scan our surroundings, inching forward to see further. My gaze lands on the two spellcasters lying unconscious nearby.

Dash wriggles up next to me. "You thinking what I'm thinking?"

"That we put on their cloaks to somewhat blend in? *Yes*."

He swipes a bloody lock of hair out of his face. "Like that time on planet Melancy when we fooled the Sirens by dressing up as guards and then snuck into lockup. I like where this is going."

"It's not foolproof," I say. "Sooner or later, they'll figure us out, but it'll buy us time."

I check my peripherals, and then we jet out from hiding to grab the cloaks.

Dash helps me tear them from the unconscious spellcasters, and we put them on, mine purple and his red. Then we duck behind a tipped-over Kiss of Death booth and survey the messy stretch ahead.

I pull up my hood. "Do you think you can find Lorelei and get the dual-vials?"

He pulls up his too. "Of course. What about your key?"

"Valerian has it. I'll find him. I'm not scared of him."

"You sure?" Dash asks.

"Oh, I'm sure. He's mine."

My brother smiles. "Phase five is officially on. I'll meet you at the Tower." As he readies to rush off, he glances back and adds, "One heck of a last gig, huh?"

"You literally have no idea."

Dash tips his head at me and disappears in the rush. I don't like the idea of us being apart after everything we've been through, but we both have separate tasks to complete here. And I trust him. He's the best at what he does. He'll come through for me.

This time, I know he will.

I suck in a breath of stale air and release it to ground myself. The speaker overhead blares some sadistic carnival tune with eerie accordion fanfare. It goes static for a moment, starts up again, and that's when I move.

Adrenaline keeps my strides long and strong. My lungs constrict the faster I go, slinking behind booths and ride control stands for cover. I don't know where Valerian is, but I'll find him. And he'll be sorry he ever messed with me, Euphoria, my brother's soul, or my portal key.

But I'm not senseless.

I know his magic will give him the upper hand.

The carousel comes into view ahead. A bewitched merry-go-round gone wrong. Most of the skeleton horses and winged dragon-like sea creatures have fallen off their tracks, further falling apart as the circular platform spins.

My heart races in my chest. I know what I'm looking for. The glowbeam one of the spellcasters brought to the fight landed somewhere over here. If I stand a chance against Valerian, I will need it and one setting included in the original models.

Please be here. I drop to my hands and knees, feeling around under the exterior of the ride. The cranking rods groan above me. The canvas covering the top of the ride flaps and catches zings of cerulean-colored light. A spellcaster wielding some kind of elemental spell sends a bluster of wind and rain throughout the carousel, and it knocks the breath out of me.

The spell's blow spatters hail, and I duck for cover in the control booth. Chunks of ice explode around my head. The panel board sizzles and sparks. My hood tips back. One massive glob of ice grazes my cheek. It burns, and I bite back the urge to scream. Then I see the familiar neon flare of a glowbeam barrel tucked beneath the carousel's lever system.

Maybe Euphoria was right about the higher powers after all.

I fumble for the weapon, praying it has the cartridges I need. On the mechanism screen, I thumb through the charged settings: *stun, equilibrium, shock, obliterate.*

Yes. All settings I can work with here.

I switch to stun, climb onto the control board, and aim my barrel out the display window at the spellcaster wreaking havoc on the carousel. She sees me and my weapon, gearing up another sphere of cerulean that reeks of fire and ash.

Thumb on trigger. Aim like I was taught. Direct hits only.

I release. The glowbeam sends an invisible energy surge at the spellcaster. Perfect shot. She flies backward into a skeleton horse with a golden, spike horn. The spellcaster stays down, stunned. I blow the smoke off my barrel and flee the control booth, keeping my weapon up.

Eyes in my sight, I comb every inch of my surroundings.

I'll find you, Valerian. You can't hide from me anymore.

It doesn't take long to spot him. In a sea of bright-colored cloaks and the prism of spellwork that follows them, only one spellcaster dons the deep, satiny black.

Over by the funhouse, House of Glass, he slinks in the shadows.

The attraction's flickering LED sign hangs sideways on a single bolt. Full panels of shattered glass catch the reflection of a greenish sky. He stares up at the glittering stars.

Is he looking for the comet? I focus my range of vision, hovering my aim over him in the sight. Suddenly, he jerks his head, and his gaze locks on mine with a jolt that strikes me in the pit of my stomach.

Valerian's smile widens as if to draw me in.

He darts inside the House of Glass, and I take off after him.

23

Dash

Playing a spellcaster is easy.

Save for the cloak that occasionally catches my heels, it's the best role I've been cast in so far. Better than playing the obsidian dagger in *Romeo and Ghouliet.*

I zig-zag through the fairgrounds at high speed. Vault over an upturned finger-fries booth. Shimmy around the frenzy of spellcasters paying homage to their Great War. A wisp of golden light grazes my back, missing me by an inch. I duck into another game booth, fixed with a blood-spattered throwing wheel and knives. Keeping my back pressed against the back of the tent, I wait until the coast is clear before I dare move again.

Heart pounding. Sweat soaking my back. Black blood seeping into my front.

A glimpse of bubblegum-pink to my left. *No.* Dead ahead.

"There you are," I mutter, spotting Lorelei by the Tunnel of Heartbreak.

She toys with another spellcaster, knocks him between the legs, and as she turns and drop-kicks him, her long, blonde hair strikes the air like a whip.

The spellcaster crawls, fumbling for a turnstile to steady himself. Lorelei comes up behind him, jolts him again, and he falls in a heap.

A laugh escapes her. My stomach twists. *She enjoys the torture.*

Lorelei runs a hand through her hair and glances up at another spellcaster nearby. He races into the Tunnel of Heartbreak, and she tails him, palms blazing bright magenta.

"Look like we're heading into the tunnel too, Ace," I say to my tutelary, now crouched beside me. I double-take. "Wait. Ace? What are you doing here!" A warmth fills my being. I reach out and ruffle his fur. "You came back. I'm so happy to see you."

The bear nestles his snout in the curve of my hand.

"Can you help me get the dual-vials back safely?" I ask.

He lets out a soft noise, neither a roar nor a huff. I take that as a *yes* and let him go ahead of me. Inching my way out from the cover of the booth, I let my hood fall. Ace crawls toward the massive, broken heart making up the entrance of the Tunnel of Heartbreak.

We reach the loading bay, where a concrete track runs pure murk water. At least it isn't gut juice. I'd rather breathe in mud than stomach acid any day. Ace pulls himself onto one of the small, wooden boats bobbing at the dock. It floats in line with the others along the water channel.

I step in behind him and sit on the middle bench, peering over the side to gauge how deep the water is. *You could probably stand. Might be faster than this.* Ahead, a neon pink glow illuminates the mouth of the tunnel. Close but out of sight. Lorelei and the other spellcaster are far enough ahead, but we'll catch up soon.

Our boat passes through the broken heart crack. Then, the track releases us into the natural flow of the channel. We're delivered into the pitch-black darkness, and my shoulders tense.

Be brave, Dash. I fought off dirt gnomes. I saved my sister.

I can do this.

I stand, and my boat lurches. I step off the edge, landing in the channel. Murk water rises to my knees. My cloak soaks it up, weighing me down, but I push on with Ace.

Lorelei's spellwork guides me, a pink beacon. That, and the ear-shattering screams of whoever she's tormenting. As I follow the curve of the tunnel, she comes into view. A burst of pink shoots from her palm and sends the other spellcaster sailing into one of the boats.

My soul sucker pulses beneath my skin. I wince.

Lorelei looks up and scowls. "*You.*"

"*Me*," I say. "I want the dual-vials."

"Aw, really?" She hops up onto the next boat floating along the channel with a splash, crosses it, and jumps down, landing before me. Her fists glow. "Well, you can't have them."

"I have a tutelary. You can't hurt me."

She raises a brow. "Watch me."

Lorelei calls forth her power, a wicked ball of light. Next to me, Ace lets out a roar. I stand my ground, knees locked into place, ready for whatever she thinks she'll do. I'm not scared anymore. I'm done letting other people get the best of me.

As Lorelei releases her hex, Ace cuts between us and takes the blow. His transparent form distorts, becoming thinner, and he takes another shot of magic in his underbelly.

I climb up onto the approaching boat, keeping my heels at the stern. Lorelei forces herself beyond Ace. She hops up to the bow. I look to my spiritual protector, but he fades away, and suddenly I'm on my own. *Doesn't matter.* I crack my knuckles. Keep my eyebrows furrowed. If she's got the dual-vials in her cloak, I only need her close enough to me once.

Our boat floats along the channel, into a portion of the ride that narrows and takes us through a passageway decorated with human hearts. Above us, the ceiling shifts. Compartments slide open and release arrows that pierce each pulsing organ. They squelch. Neon-pink blood pours out of them, and another bout of arrows release in sync with Lorelei's hex.

I duck. Her spell explodes behind me. Glitter residue floats in the air. She lunges for me, grips my cloak, and our bodies slam down into one another at the prow of the boat. It rocks with our clatter. I slick neon-pink blood through my hair, shielding my eyes. As Lorelei straddles me and summons another spark, something box-shaped grazes my hand beneath her cloak.

"Wipe that smirk off your face." Lorelei deepens the pink electricity between her fingers. "You remind me of her, you know. It's your energy. The look in your dying, soulless eyes. I bet you're itching to take me out, aren't you?"

"On a date? Nah, you aren't my type."

She scowls. "No. *Ugh.* What is wrong with you?"

"So many things," I say, allowing my hands to curl around the box containing the dual-vials. She doesn't even notice. "Did you think I was going to hurt you? That wouldn't be very effective. I'm more of a lover than a fighter, that's for sure."

Lorelei scoffs. "Oh, shut up."

As she readies to suffocate me with whatever pink curse cocktail she's got strung between her fingers, a streak of light guides us toward the end of the tunnel. The last stretch of the channel. A dip beneath a raging waterfall, spurting from a giant pair of rubber lips.

We drop down a hill. Murk water drenches us, jolting us aside.

In one motion, I grip Lorelei's arms, roll over her so I'm on top of her now, and gently keep her down so she can't hex me. Our boat floats out of the tunnel and knocks into the others gathered at the end of the line. Lorelei squirms beneath me, avoiding my gaze.

I release her and back away, off the boat and toward the gate exit. "Just so you know, Euphoria never hated you. She respects you. It was never a competition, and she genuinely would've been happy seeing you two together if that's what he wanted."

Lorelei sits up slowly. Her long hair falls across her shoulder, splattered in neon-pink sludge like mine. She glares at me. Doesn't say a word. And she doesn't have to. The fact that she's letting me leave this fight without blazing a trail of wrath magic is enough.

She scrambles from the boat. Her cloak billows behind her as she jets off toward the midway. I reach into my own cloak and pull out the glass box containing the dual-vials.

I can't believe I did it all on my own. Is it weird that I'm proud of myself?

The box pops open immediately. With a shaking hand, I pluck up one of the dual-vials, close the box, and tuck it away for safekeeping. I uncork the purple end of the dual-vial I'm holding in my hand and toss back the extracting essence. A mix of century-old cough syrup and a cherry heart slushie that's been sitting out in the sun too long coats my throat.

Sure enough, the slimy soul sucker in my arm retreats from my body. Pus oozes around the opening. A sour smell wafts from my pores. The sucker hisses, and my expression twists. *It's utterly repulsive.*

For the soulless moment in-between, the wooziness sets in. I use my teeth to uncork the red side of the vial. Another bitter flavor, like perfume, slicks my tongue. I pluck up the sucker, take a deep breath, and place it on my opposite wrist.

Immediately, the spider veins covering my body recede. The black blood coating my skin dries up. My eyes close involuntarily. As I reclaim my inner being, a refreshing sensation similar to waking up from a long sleep, or the rush after winning a Holoblocks tournament even though the other team reaped all the blocks, takes over.

It's like kissing someone you really like for the first time. It's the wave of warmth that washes over you and tickles your gut as you remember their lips long after they go home and tell all their friends about it.

I steady my wavering self, high on my own supply, and eventually, the soul sucker shrivels up and makes me wonder how it would taste on a Tee Tee's tentacle taco at the shack.

Man. I didn't realize how *hungry* I was either. As my soul settles, my stomach growls. I stretch my neck. Re-crack my knuckles. Shake the dead weight from my arms and legs.

There will be time to feast, Dash.
After Shea and I help Effs.

24

Shea

If Valerian is fire, I am rain.

The torrent he knows is coming.

His laughter taunts me like a siren. At the mouth of a giant, revolving cylinder with a rainbow of peeling stripe decals, it draws me further into the House of Glass.

I keep my hands tight around the grip of my glowbeam. The flickering strobe lights overhead confuses the night vision mechanism. I keep my focus ahead and on my peripherals. He could be anywhere. Despite Dad being a jerk, he taught me how to stalk my prey.

The revolving cylinder takes me into another dark room. Compressed air jets up from the cracks in the uneven floor, which shifts beneath my weight. Trick floors. All of them. Gliding back and forth. Sinking. Popping. A sure way to break an ankle if you aren't paying attention.

I step over a rotating metal plate, knocking a set of hanging strobes aside with the barrel of my glowbeam. A metallic smell lingers in the air. It sits on my tongue, burning with each swallow.

Everything is still. Too still.

Silver light zings by my ear. I drop to the floor. A fog machine spits out a hazy cloud, covering me. Another burst of light rattles the bolts on the wall.

Directly behind you, Shea.

Rolling over, I slam my thumb on the trigger. Power surges from my weapon. It misses the target, stunning a strobe box instead. Halogen light streaks across my face. The box shatters, sending slivers of plastic and metal splaying through the air.

I shield my eyes.

A glimpse of black silk whizzes by on my left.

I'm up off the floor in seconds. Aiming. Scoping him out.

"Don't play games, Valerian. I'm not leaving without my portal key." I feel around in the dark while my vision adjusts, keeping my barrel focused.

Another eerie round of laughter sounds. Only this time, it's closer. A slight bluish hue overlays the darkness. My boots crunch over something, but I don't look down. *Never look down.* A crooked archway paves the way for the mirror maze, and that's telling enough. Valerian's lured me into the belly of the funhouse beast, a complex passageway fixed with panels of glass, upside-down mirrors, and other reflective surfaces.

I slip behind a contorted mirror and scan the near distance.

The pitter-patter of his boots. His black cloak flowing in the stuffy space. It billows behind him as he darts between panels, creating the illusion of more than one of him.

I don't know which one of him is real. It's all an illusion.

"Don't waste a shot, Shea," his voice echoes.

"*You* don't waste a shot," I say back, my voice echoing with his. "If I know anything about spellcasters, you have to see your target to aim a spell."

I chew the inside of my cheek. It's at a 45% charge now. I'm out of stun rounds. And I don't have the power to shock or obliterate according to the mechanism screen.

Think Shea, think.

Valerian emits a blast of magic. It hits hot and heavy directly to my left, splintering a mirror with my reflection to smithereens. A glass shard grazes my cheek, another my lip, and I taste blood. He sends a second silver bolt to my right, into an oval-shaped mirror with another version of me that isn't real.

His expression twists. He thought he had me.

I thought he had me. I give a smirk.

Valerian doesn't know which one is the real me either.

"Trying to scare me, huh?" I watch him move in the reflection of the warped surfaces that cover the ceiling. He keeps his back to the wall, while hot, white sparks linger between his fingers. "And you thought this place would give you the advantage."

He growls and tosses a beam in a direction that isn't even close to where I stand. With my sight, I evaluate every reflection of him. Careful of my movements. Strategic with my footing. How quickly I step. How deeply I breathe.

I spin the setting dial on my weapon to equilibrium—mainly used in situations like this. It's no stun setting, but if I can hit him square in the chest, it should temporarily disarm his spellcaster abilities. Balance us out a bit. He won't be able to manipulate me hex-wise should he get the chance. We'd be on a level playing field.

Then I wouldn't need a weapon.

I stare at the reflection of the back of his head. Is that really him? Or is that other one, the closer version, really him? My eyes focus. His neck catches a strobe, and faintly, I make out the triple spiral mark on the back of his neck.

"I've been thinking a lot about that deal you made with the Enchantress." I keep my gaze pinned on his many reflections. "I think you *do* know it's more than a soul contract. I think you know what's in the Higher Realm. And I think you believe in Euphoria more than you lead on."

He turns slightly, offering me a glimpse of his defined jaw and his lips. They don't quiver. They remain steady. "Why don't you come out, and I'll tell you if you're right or wrong."

Highly unlikely. The back of my heels crunch a scatter of glass shards. Valerian jerks his head my way, and I gasp.

We fire at the same time. I hit him first, diverting his aim.

He's thrown back against a reflective panel, his streak of magic fizzing away midair before it can reach me. I scramble into view, but he's quick, even in a disoriented haze.

Valerian tries to summon his power to no avail.

He flinches. Tries again. His lips curl. Blood rushes to his cheeks, and even in the dim light, I can make out the rage spurning in his eyes. It spreads like a virus deep inside him.

I sheathe my glowbeam. I yank up my sleeves.

I grit my teeth. "Give me back my portal key. Now."

Valerian balls his fists. I widen my stance. *Are we going to spar, or are we going to stand around?* His choice. Either way, I'm ready. His cloak falls open, revealing a black tunic, a leather belt, and pants. His eyes dart toward the corridor that leads out of the mirror maze and into the next chamber.

Shit. We're not going to spar. He's going to run.

"Valerian!" I snap.

He chuckles and races deeper into the maze, me at his heels. Our many reflections become a blur. Guiding us is a glimmer of light. The end of the maze offers a metal ladder with rungs that shift like the trick floors. Valerian makes it to the bottom and climbs.

I jerk him back. He throws a punch. I block it.

I yank him to the floor, straddle him, and pin him down. "Not so tough without your magic, are you? You hide behind it like you do everything else."

"Get *off* me," he snarls.

"Give *me* my key."

He attempts to headbutt me. Again, I block him with my arm, and the impact sends a shot of pain through my nerves. I flex. I wince. He bucks me off and twists my arm. Now he's on top of me, tugging at my hair, keeping me down. *Damn.* This guy doesn't give up. *Neither do I.*

Together, we roll over one another. As we come back around, he slips from my grasp. My knee rams the floor. He gets in a punch, and I yell out. My cheek throbs. Heat finds the mark.

Pinpricks of pain web in the wound Euphoria once healed. I bite back the sting and force myself up, ready for another go. But, again, Valerian's quick on his feet. He's up the ladder now, nearly to the top.

I climb after him. Rung by rung. My fingers jam in the moving parts. I swallow the burn in my throat and make it to the platform above. I just need my key. That's all I need. I don't care about him. As Euphoria would say, karma will take care of him. For what he's done to her and Dash. For what he's doing to himself and to me.

Reasoning didn't work. I thought I could get through to him. I felt sorry for him at one point, but he's running from himself now. *Literally.*

I can't help someone that doesn't want to change. Euphoria couldn't either. I see why she tried for so long, but it's clear now—he wants to stay stuck. He wants to stay wounded. For all I know, he *wants* to fail.

Sometimes staying in old cycles feels safer than breaking them. All I know is I'd rather admit defeat than stay the same. Instead of forcing my brother into another year of this life for my own comfort, I'd rather let go. I'd rather die today, in this fight with myself, then let Dad control my life.

I barrel into the adjoining chamber. A weighted bag swings at me, and I duck, dodging another two that rotate in the opposite direction. The laughter in the air isn't Valerian's but that of a clown. *Naturally.* It blares from the speaker overhead, becoming louder. The wall narrows and expands, closing in around me as I travel through the maze.

As I squeeze my body through the bulging walls, I spot Valerian at the top of a giant slide. He clutches his ripped and bloodied sleeve at the shoulder. His hair falls a mess in his face.

"Just *give* me the key, Bale. This can all be over!"

He grits his teeth. "It'll be over when Kellie's Comet crosses the sky."

A heaviness sinks into my gut. Before I can catch him, Valerian jumps off the ledge into the slime ball pit below. I race to the edge, my stomach grazing the railing. I peer down into a pit filled with brown and green balls, and the pungent smell of rotting slime hits my nose.

Valerian brushes a clump out of his hair. I ready to jump too, but again, he's faster. He crawls over the lip of the pit and flees the House of Glass.

I slam my butt down at the top of the slide and take it into the pit. He thinks he's won. But I'm not giving up. I know where Valerian is going.

This close to Kellie's Comet, I'll just follow him to the Tower.

I will myself to move, pulling myself from the pit onto the dirt. As I get up, I search for the exit and find the gate immediately. The weight of my slime-encrusted cloak sinks around me. I'll have to ditch that now. I make sure I'm out of harm's way before untwisting the clasp to let the cloak fall.

A hooded spellcaster nears. *I've had enough.*

Fumbling for my glowbeam, I power up.

Dash lowers his hood.

An actual laugh escapes me. "Thank the Gods."

"Were you really going to shoot me?" he asks.

I shake my head and grab him into a sticky hug.

Dash grimaces. "*Ugh.* Shea. What are you covered—"

"Did you get the dual-vials?"

"Yup." He pats his cloak, which is now splattered with neon-pink paint. "And I got my soul back."

"You—you did?" I ask, remembering what Valerian said about Euphoria's Higher Self being the only one that could open the box.

Dash raises a brow. "Uh, yeah, ya weirdo. Wasn't that the whole point?"

"I know. Nevermind." I'm still not sure I understand, but I don't have time to question. If anything, it means Euphoria can also open the box.

"Did you get your key?" he asks.

"Valerian got away."

"Then let's go!"

As he grabs my hand and pulls me along, a massive bolt of green lightning lights up the sky. We both halt and glare up at the stars. Mom comes to mind briefly, only because they're so bright.

Dash yells, "Kellie's Comet is coming!"

I nod, and together we sprint toward the Tower.

25

Dash

Shea leads us to the backside of the Tower toward the rusted, metal rungs embedded in the stone. They start from the bottom and run the length of the Tower, all the way to the top. My fingers grip the first rung. As I climb behind her, my cloak tugs heavily at my neck, still wet from the Tunnel of Heartbreak.

I quickly untie it and let it fall. Halfway up, Shea shouts, "Don't look down!"

Well, now I have to.

I do, and I immediately regret it.

My entire body shakes, rattling my bones. I stop climbing and cling to the rungs, resting my forehead against the one in front of me.

Shea stops too. "I told you not to look!"

"I know. I'm—I'm coming. Keep going."

My sister waits a moment. When I look up at her again, the sky shines another streak of greenish-blue. A burst of lightning crackles. Thunder booms, hollow and heavy, in the distance.

Move, Dash. You're almost there.

Soon, I'm moving again. The higher we climb, the more the reenactment chaos from below us and around us blurs. Shea reaches the top, turns and holds out a hand, locking her grip on mine and pulling me up. As I grace the top of the Tower, a gust of wind whips us in the face and wreaks havoc on the tattered Crowley Corner flag strapped to a metal pole in the center of the circular rooftop. Next to it, one of the spellcaster's, Eugene, hovers over Effs, who lays a heap on the ground.

Eugene's eyes go wide the moment he spots us. He springs up and summons a yellow bit of magic in his hands. Shea rushes forward, powers up her glowbeam, and hits him before he even casts.

As the spellcaster's body falls unconscious on the ground, my sister secures the rest of the rooftop. I take out the glass box containing the final dual-vial and kneel at Effs's side.

Another bang echoes in the sky. It's been a while since I've thought of Roger and his morbid death in the mausoleum, but as I get a good look at Effs, those thoughts return.

No matter how hard I try, I can't make them go away.

Effs is awake but barely. Matted hair covers her face. Her blood-soaked dress hangs three sizes too big, draped over her frail frame. Spider-veined body nearly translucent, I spot the soul sucker on her neck, which has grown larger too.

The inflamed skin around its initial entry point gushes blood.

I'm lost for words. I look to Shea, searching for her usual wisdom, a plan or anything that'll tell me what we can do to help our friend. We didn't think this far ahead.

She shakily takes the glass box from me. "We made it here before Valerian. No idea how long we have before he shows up, but he won't have magic when he does. I used the equilibrium setting on the glowbeam while we were in the House of Glass."

She tries to open the box, but it won't budge. "I thought you said you opened it. Why isn't it—"

I reach over and undo the latch. It pops open.

She furrows her brows. "How did you do that?"

I pluck up the dual-vial. "Does it matter? Help me tilt her head!"

It takes a moment for my sister to stop staring at me with that odd expression on her face, but eventually, she snaps out of it and sits Effs up a bit. I uncork the purple side of the vial.

As I go to tip the potion into her mouth, Shea grabs my hand. "What if Euphoria doesn't want this? Valerian will use her to get into the Higher Realm if she lives. She said he isn't ready to go there, that he can't. If he tries before he's ready or tries for the wrong reasons, he'll suffer. What if curing her does more harm than good?"

"Are you kidding me, Shea?" I exclaim. "*Look* at her. We can't let her die. If she dies, Fake Death still wins. He either uses her to cross into the Higher Realm, or he literally takes her soul. Either way, he gets what he wants. Either way, he wins. What about her?"

"A third... option... " Effs croaks, and both Shea and I lean in closer. "I go... without him, and he... learns the hard way... on his own... he heals on his own."

Shea cups her cheek with her palm. "Even if he suffers? You said you didn't want that for him. You said you loved him too much to let him suffer."

A black tear streaks Effs's face. "I love him too much to... do this work *for* him."

My sister and I exchange the same look. The sky glows a brighter shade of greenish-blue behind her, giving her a temporary crown of stars. It flashes, and then it's gone. A moment later, she nods, and I tip the purple liquid into Effs's mouth.

The soul sucker inside her neck retreats, a bulging black worm covered in sludge. I pluck it up between my thumb and forefinger. It hisses at me. *I'm never going near these things again.* Then I pop off the red side of the vial. Shea takes it and tips it inside Effs's mouth too.

After a moment, I let the sucker rest against Effs's wrist.

It settles into her skin. The surrounding area glows. Tears well in my eyes as her veins begin to glitter. Her cheeks fill out. Tiny threads in her clothes tighten, and her outfit falls crisp and clean against her frame. The sparkle in her golden eyes returns, switching between a multitude of colors before landing on a vibrant violet. Her glow encompasses her entire form, becoming a white satin cloak, and as it settles, she sits up and lowers her hood.

At the same time, a wooden Door appears on the rooftop. Fake Death stumbles through, Shae's portal key dangling in his left hand. Effs puts herself between us as the wind continues to press against us. The length of Fake Death's black satin cloak flaps behind him, the tail of it covered in the same sticky mess Shea's covered in. I still don't know what it is.

Something tells me I don't want to know.

He tucks away Shea's key. "You look well, Euphoria."

"Thank you," Effs replies. But there's no warmth in her tone.

Fake Death approaches her, his expression shifting into one that reminds me of Chip when he tries to lie and sweet-talk the girls at the Academy. "I hope you don't think I'm just using you to get into the Higher Realm. We made a promise to an Enchantress, if you remember."

Effs nods reverently. "I remember."

There's something different about Effs now, I realize. Maybe it's because she's wearing a white cloak that she didn't come here with, or maybe it's because she has her soul and all her magic back for the first time in a while, but she feels... bigger, taller, brighter... than she did before. And Fake Death seems... so much smaller than he did before.

I glance at my sister and watch how she watches them.

"If you remember, then you also recall how important the portal Kellie's Comet is bringing us is," Fake Death says. "You know we must open it, or we'll miss our chance."

Again, Effs nods. "I know."

Fake Death runs a hand through his hair. "Good. I'm glad you've come to your—"

"Unfortunately, though, you won't be joining me in the Higher Realm," Effs cuts him off. "Not yet."

"Excuse me?" Fake Death says with a half-hearted chuckle. "We are bound to one another. Do tell me how you'll stop me from following you, Euphoria... *enlighten* me."

"I do not need to enlighten you. You will do that all by yourself."

He scoffs, loosens the collar of his cloak, and wipes sweat from his brow. As he opens his mouth to say something more, another crackle overtakes the sky. A bright flash of green light nears. Shea shields her eyes. I do too, but then I sneak a peek at the swirl.

The whipping wind carries a metallic smell in the air, mixed with the smoke off whatever rides are burning below us. I fall in line beside my sister. Our shoulder brush.

"Kellie's Comet," she whispers.

A ringing echoes out around us, followed by a high vibrational hum. Wind picks up, tousling both Euphoria and Valerian's cloaks. Satiny black and soft white flow together.

The Tower quakes. Its tremor throws Fake Death to the ground. Euphoria remains unaffected, hood now up and hands behind her back. I grab onto Shea, and she grabs onto the railing next to us to steady us. The enormous ball of greenish-blue light known as Kellie's Comet streaks across the sky. Its vibrant blaze trails behind it. It's light falls like rain, showering us in a glittering glow. Time lags. I reach out to touch the glimmer, noticing the numbness tingling in my fingers.

Behind us, below us, and around us, Crowley Corner slows down too. The motion of the rides. The flicker of the LED lights. A rainbow of rogue spells and hexes volleying back and forth all trickle to a stop, frozen in this moment.

"Whoa. This is trippy," I say to Shea, but she isn't paying attention to me.

I follow her gaze to where a giant swirl of sea-foam green hovers at the edge of the Tower, right at the ledge. *Is that the quantum portal thingy?* Its mesmerizing swirl lures me in. I inch closer and closer, startled at the slightest touch on my shoulder.

Effs smiles at me. "I never thanked you for curing me."

I glance from her to the portal, to Shea, still in awe, to Fake Death picking himself up off the ground, back to Effs.

"Of course," I say. "I wasn't going to let you die. I made a promise to you."

"You are wonderfully rare, Dashiel James. I hope you never forget that." She lowers her hood again and leans over to plant a kiss on my cheek.

Her lips spark against my skin. A silly smile overtakes me.

Then she approaches Shea and whispers something in her ear. Her words make my sister blush and tear up. Effs motions for Shea to open her palm. When my sister does, Effs places her portal key in her hand. *When did Effs get that from Fake Death?* I furrow my brows and look at the skull prince wannabee himself.

He's up, waiting by the swirling portal. After Effs is finished talking with Shea, she approaches him. I move closer, so I can hear them. Shea does the same. Together, we watch Effs take Fake Death's hand.

"I'll show you why you aren't coming with me right now," she tells him.

Effs waves her hand at the portal, and the portal offers her greenish-blue streaks of light. They flow into her through her fingers, her forehead, and her heart. Her eyes light up the same color green. As she puts her palm over Fake Death's heart, a chill washes over me. The metallic smell in the air grows stronger. My arm hair shoots straight up.

Fake Death's eyes glow green too. He buries his face in his hands. "I'm—I'm sorry—"

"Enough of that," Effs says, drawing him closer to her. She takes him into her arms and embraces him tight. The green light envelops them both briefly. As it fades, I hear Effs say to him, "I promise to keep loving myself if you promise to find your way back to me."

Instead of answering, Fake Death kisses her gently on the lips.

Effs closes her eyes and takes in the kiss before resting her forehead against his. They smile at one another. She steals one last kiss, and then her hand falls into his. He walks her to the edge of the swirling portal, extends his hand, and guides her through.

As he does, the green light connecting them remains like a thread. Fake Death backs away from the portal. He puts his hands in his pockets and watches it swirl smaller until there's nothing left but the hint of a floating, green glimmer in the air.

26

Shea

A soft, pink sun has risen at Crowley Corner.

It all looks different now.

More alive, maybe. More colorful.

I walk along the midway, past the spellcasters putting their home back together again after the traditional battle reenactment. They use manipulation spells to contort the metal frames and gears, stand them upright, and mend the holes in faded flags.

Morning fog rolls in heavily, blanketing the dirt. I spot Dash's backpack at the edge of the amphitheater, sitting untouched on a bench.

I unzip the side pocket and take out my travel journal. It's seen better days. Crinkles and pages soaked with gut juice and Goddess knows what else. A binding that will need to be re-woven. But the story is there. All the research and knowledge I've collected is there.

As I thumb through, Dash appears between two game booths. "Looking glum for someone who just cured their brother and helped two spellcasters make peace with one another."

I force a smile. "I'm just tired, is all. And uh, my brother cured himself."

Dash smiles back. "Yeah, I'd say it was an even contribution." He watches me run my thumb along the faded Board of Galactic Studies sticker on my journal. "Seriously, Shea. You seem sad. You wanna to talk about it? I'm here for you if you do."

"I'm fine. I just think I'm going to take a break from the business for a while." I brush a lock of hair behind my ear. "I've never really thought about a life that isn't about stealing and strong-arming people, and I didn't think I could have things like the fellowship or a normal life before. That was always kind of your thing. I don't even know who I am without the business or Dad giving me orders. Like... maybe I'll enjoy having fun and dating..."

"I'm proud of you, Shea," my brother says. "I celebrate that for you."

"Don't, like, say anything to Dad, though. I'm not ready yet. Not right now. Not for a while. I think I need time to process everything that's happened first."

He nods. "Fair enough. Same here."

"You know, if I turn in this journal to Mr. Beachum as part of my submission, ISR will be at our door tomorrow."

"Yeah," Dash says. "But I think it'll be a good thing."

I force another smile. Even though I'm not ready to have a conversation with our father, I don't dread it. Because I know now that I need to figure out who I am outside my father's influence. It feels like starting over, finding myself again, or embarking on a journey. Dad's turned everyone against him. Mom needs to go back to planet Lark. We'll need time to spend with her before she goes.

Wait until she hears what Dad's been up to. However, I'll try not to hold a grudge. If I learned anything from Euphoria in the time I knew her, you *can* forgive someone and release the space they take up in your life.

Even if it takes time. Even if it's not easy. Even if it's an ongoing practice.

Dash pats his stomach. "Welp. I don't know about you, but I've eaten so many things in the last hour from the concessions here that my stomach might burst, and not in a good way."

I furrow my brows. "You know some of this stuff is centuries old, right?"

"Uh, you know. We're just not going to talk about that."

A chuckle escapes me. My gaze lands on Valerian coming up the walk.

Dash nudges me. "That guy got a rude awakening back there, huh?"

I make eye contact with Valerian for a moment. Another spell-caster approaches, and he helps them turn a concession stand upright.

Dash continues, "I stand by what I said, though. He really should model."

I take my portal key off and hand it to him. "Alright. Can you, uh, go call a Door back to Sarasing? I'll catch up with you in a few minutes. I want to talk to someone first."

He smirks. "You want to talk to Valerian? Yeah, I figured."

I pat him on the shoulder. After he walks off, I approach the spellcasters. Valerian wipes his hands on his cloak and leaves the others.

We awkwardly linger in one another's presence before he clears his throat and asks, "Did you get your portal key back?"

"Yeah, I did."

"Good. I'm glad."

He keeps his head down and his hands in his pockets. I watch him kick some broken glass from the path. Euphoria's final words to me, the words she whispered in my ear before she disappeared through the portal to the Higher Realm, have been on my mind ever since. *Tell the stubborn guy you forgive him and hug him for me, will you?*

"This might be weird, but can I hug you?" I ask.

Valerian looks up. "Hug... me?"

"Yeah."

"Uh, okay? I guess that'd be... alright."

He removes his hands from his pockets and clumsily maneuvers his arms around me to take in my embrace. I hold him for a moment. Much like when I hugged Euphoria in the clearing, the surprising feeling of home finds me as I hug Valerian too. Does he feel it? Does it soften him like it softens me? Eventually, his shoulders relax. He embraces me back.

Maybe it does soften him.

As he releases me, I smile. "I forgive you."

"You forgive me? Ah, well... " He runs a hand through his hair. "I don't know if I deserve that right now, but I appreciate the sentiment."

"Don't be too hard on yourself. Everyone makes mistakes."

"I'm sorry for the things I did to you and your brother," he says.

"I know you are. Euphoria knew it too." I tuck my journal into the backpack and sling it over my shoulder. "She loved you, you know. She didn't want you to suffer."

"Despite what you may think, I love her too. I can humbly admit to being wrong. I thought once she anchored the frequency in the Higher Realm, I'd be able to cross over with her no problem, but I know now we both must be a vibrational match separately. Her anchor gives me time and a chance to work on myself, to heal, and it gives me time to find a way back to her."

"You seem more at peace than before."

"I feel it. I do. She... woke me up in a way. I can't explain it. I was hiding before. And now that I know what I know, I couldn't hide even if I wanted to."

He raises his hands and lets them fall back at his side. "Euphoria was trying to protect me from the pain that comes from realizing I haven't been living in my authentic Truth, but this is inner work that I need to do myself. She can't do it for me. Nobody can but me."

"I think you'll do it," I say. "And I think you'll find her again in this lifetime."

Valerian smirks. "I hope you're right, Shea. I really do. In the meantime, Euphoria will be met and surrounded by more love, abundance, and happiness than she'll know what to do with."

I nod. As much as it hurts me, I'm glad for her. I clear my throat, and with it the awkward emotional moment. "I do have to ask, what do *you* think your mission is really about?"

His expression softens. As he thinks about it, his smile widens.

"Honestly? It's about Love. A kind of love that ripples out into the galaxies and resonates with every being it touches. Romantic love. Self-love. Unconditional love. Just... Love. That's why it's so Divine. That's why the connection is so sacred. Our job is to integrate that love in the collective whether we are in physical union with one another or not."

"I'm glad you're in a good place, Valerian."

He laughs this time. "Me too, Shea."

"Sheaaa-Lynnn!" My little brother calls up the path. "Are you coming or what? The Door I called to Sarasing keeps disappearing, and I have to keep calling it. It's almost dinnertime."

Valerian shrugs. I grip my pack strap, ready to meet my brother, just as a coral bird crosses the sky. It caws and lands on Valerian's shoulder. He ruffles the bird's feathers then looks at me.

And we exchange one last smile.

One Year Later
Shea

Beams of Sarasing sun illuminate Mom's mobile.

It hangs above the window seat in my room at Aunt Merik's house. As I pull my sweater on and brush through my long hair, I stare at the coral bird and bear figures hanging among the crystals and charms. They glint in the soft morning rays. One catches a streak, projecting a rainbow prism of color on the opposite wall. I dip my fingers into the jewelry box that also belonged to my mother and dig through for my nametag and a pair of earrings to wear for the workday.

I've been given the evening shift at the local Archives Center. One of the oldest libraries in Sarasing, it's home to some of our planet's last remaining physical books. They're worn and well-loved, and though nobody may check them out, we get hundreds of readers per week who sit in the many reading alcoves.

The pin on my nametag pricks my finger. I wince. As I suck the blood off my finger, I stare at myself in the mirror above my dresser. *You're happy, Shea. Your life is... normal now.*

It's been a year since Dash and I quit the business. Seven months since Dad got arrested and sent to *Ophelia*, and five months since Mom returned to planet Lark.

We soaked up every bit of time with her we could. Her departing ceremony was symbolic because it meant our lives as Thieves and Enforcers were over. Yet, I still get up every morning at dawn, scour the Universal Database, and pace my room as if my next assignment is going to pop up.

I pluck up a pair of simple, silver drop earrings to wear. Straighten my collar. Push a strand of hair behind my ear. Not much prepping to be done for a shift at the library, that's for sure. As I shut the jewelry box, I spot my portal key tucked beneath a bracelet.

A part of me wants to pick it up, call a Door, and go somewhere far away for the day, but much like I have to resist unsheathing the glowbeam tucked away in my undergarment drawer, my portal key is off limits too. Dash and I are off the hook, but ISR is watching us. After I submitted my research to Mr. Beachum, they immediately came for Dad and James Co. In the chaos that followed, I never heard back about the fellowship.

Aunt Merik, Dash, and I packed up enough inventory to fill every inch of empty space in her storage unit at Pippa's Storage before Commander Derry showed up to shut us down for good. She confiscated what was left, put Dad in cuffs, and escorted him to ISR's holding center on *Ophelia*. With satisfaction, it seemed.

I let my thumb brush my portal key a moment more, and then I close the jewelry box, grab my shoulder bag, and leave my room. When I didn't hear from Mr. Beachum, I had no choice but to figure out what to do with my life. I still don't know what I want or who I am, but I'm discovering myself more every day.

In layers, Aunt Merik says.

According to Dash's therapist, healing takes time. It doesn't happen overnight. Neither does processing all the shitty things that happened to you. My first session is next week, and I don't even know where to begin. Dash says she listens to him ramble on with vigor. That she's an energy healer among other things. But how does one explain everything we've been through? How do I look this woman in the eye and tell her about the struggles

I've endured, the dangerous situations I've been in... or about Euphoria and Valerian?

Lately, I find myself thinking of them a lot.

Familiar laughter carries in the hall. It mixes with the sound of Aunt Merik's giggling children frolicking in the playroom and the clanks of pots and pans as she prepares breakfast in the kitchen. Fresh bacon sizzles on the hotplate. Her pancakes smell of cinnamon and clove.

I head for the stairs, stopping at Dash's bedroom door, which is ajar. I spot him through the gap. He sits on the bed in his Holoblocks uniform, embossed with the Academy colors red and gold. They're the Phoenix. Which I found symbolic after everything.

His girlfriend, Juliet, whom he calls Juju for short, is with him.

They met three months ago at an audition for the spring theater production. She's everything I could've hoped for. She shares his love of romance and quirky sayings. She laughs at his jokes. Every single one. And they go on cutesy dates together to the cinema and to Tee Tee's tentacle shack. She genuinely cares about him.

I watch the two of them for a moment. Juju sitting in front of him, a book of poems splayed open in her lap. As she reads to him, he curls her long, red hair with a curling device he bought. Emphasis on the bought. He takes a bobby pin out of his mouth and tucks it behind her ear.

He hugs her from behind and steals a quick kiss.

Sometimes I wonder if I should've told my brother what I know about our past lives and souls, about Euphoria and Valerian—about everything that happened in those final moments on the Tower at Crowley Corner a year ago. But when I see him happy like this, in some semblance of peace, I know not telling him was the right choice.

As I walk away, Dash says, "You still coming tonight, Shea?"

I smile, double back, and poke my head into his room. Juliet offers me a little wave, and I return it. "To your Holoblocks tournament? Of course."

"It starts at seven-thirty," my brother says.

I roll my eyes. "I know what time it starts."

"Ohhkay. Good." He crawls around Juliet, does a forward roll off his bed, then joins me at the doorway. "Then I'll hug you goodbye and tell you that I love you before you go."

He throws his arms around me. I give him a squeeze and let out a laugh.

"Love you," I mutter.

"You too," he mutters back.

Dash releases me and returns to his bed. I wave them off, shut the door behind me, and head down the stairs. Aunt Merik meets me in the foyer with a plate of pancakes wrapped to-go, and I hug her too, taking in the notes of rosemary on her clothes.

She ruffles my hair. "Have a good shift, Love."

"It's pretty mundane work. Especially on weekdays. Not much going on other than a senior citizen read along at noon."

I fetch my vest off the hook near the front door and notice a hand-knitted bag filled with odds and ends, including a digireader and an art pad, on the floor.

"It's for your father," Aunt Merik says. "I'm going to send it to *Ophelia*. He's bored in his cell and has resorted to passing the time making amends. I've gathered some things for him. Hopefully, we can one day sit down and talk about everything."

I open the front door. "I'm happy you two are working it out."

Aunt Merik's morph cat greets me on the front porch. It leaps off the swing and rubs its head at my ankles. I reach down to pat it before heading out. I tuck my wrapped pancakes in my bag and take in the morning sun some more as I head down the sidewalk and toward the walking path behind the residential block.

The Archive Center is a short walk away, one I look forward to each morning. A soft breeze washes over me, rippling into the vibrant, green leaves of the trees overhead. I take in the neighborhood bliss. Children hoverboarding in the path. Some drawing with paint orbs on the freshly laid tar. A Mee mows his lawn two houses down. And two Slogs walk side-by-side, enjoying the weather and the promise of another beautiful day.

I am now ordinary. The thought makes me half-smile.

So much free time now that I'm not dashing from Door to Door to Realm to Realm, and I'm spending my days behind a circulation desk at the Archive Center.

As if summoned by my thoughts, the familiar concrete building comes into view ahead. I shove my hands in my pockets and cross the street. As I locate my scanner card, I spot a Door, a random Door, sitting beneath the one willow tree on the Archive's grounds. The Door is square and made of mahogany wood, alive with thick, green vines and wild flora.

You must be imagining things. I blink, but the Door is still there.

I glance around. A Door means someone is either coming or going. A Door means someone has access to the Hallway of Doors. One would need a Master Door or a... portal key. Mine's back at home, in Mom's jewelry box. What does it mean?

My grip around my scanner card tightens. Another gust of wind blows through the trees, shaking the willow's long, draping boughs. Before I take another step, a hand stops me.

I glance behind me. A flutter courses through my gut. It's Mr. Beachum, a hot and sweaty mess. Behind him, his hover vehicle looks like it was thrown into park on the side of the street.

"My apologies." He dabs his forehead with a handkerchief. "I've had the hardest time tracking you down."

"Excuse me?" I say.

"I went to your... home on Spinners Pier, but you'd moved." Mr. Beachum takes off his glasses, wipes them on his sweater vest, puts them on, and blinks at me. "Then I tried contacting the Academy, but you'd graduated. They told me you were living with your aunt."

"I am. I uh—" I eye the Archive Center, where a little girl in a yellow sundress with shoulder-length, brown hair waits patiently with her face pressed against the window, peeking inside "My shift starts in a few moments. I don't have a lot of time. Is everything alright?"

"Ah, yes. This will only take a minute." Mr. Beachum digs into his pocket and pulls out a crinkled parchment scroll. "On behalf of the, oh—" He struggles to undo the wax seal. "On behalf of the Board of Galactic Studies, we'd like to offer you, Shea-Lynn Marie James, a position on the Board in our Exploration Division."

He tries handing me the scroll, but I'm frozen.

All I do is laugh, and the little girl at the Archive's window looks over at me, offering me a wide smile that seems vaguely familiar. "You're kidding. But the fellowship—"

"The fellowship was for hopefuls, an education-based program." Mr. Beachum places the scroll in my hands. "We'd like to hire you officially. Our next expedition leaves this week to the Realm of Time. A spellcaster, captain of the *Starlit*, is searching for an uncharted planet. He claims it leads to a hidden realm. You were the first person he inquired about, oddly enough. He said your keen eye and attention to detail would be an asset to our team."

My heart flutters in my chest.

"Tha—thank you."

He offers out a hand to shake, but I hug him. I don't care. Thanks to Dash and his therapist, I'm a hugger now. "I can't believe this. Thank you so much."

Mr. Beachum smiles and pats my back. "Of course, Shea. It is well deserved. We'll chat soon."

As Mr. Beachum heads back to his hover vehicle, I stare at the parchment scroll. Looks like my life won't be so ordinary after all. However, there's nothing wrong with ordinary. As Aunt Merik says, who gets to decide what's ordinary anyway?

I can't wait to tell Dash. He's going to freak out.

I lift my gaze to the Archive Center, where I expect to find the little girl still waiting for me. She isn't there anymore. I spin, facing the willow tree again. The Door is gone too.

How bizarre. Maybe I imagined it.

But a... spellcaster captain? It couldn't be...

I unroll the parchment scroll in my hands.

As Mr. Beachum described, the call is indeed for a crew to assist the captain of a ship across the Realm of Time in search of a planet called Amavetra—signed *Captain V. Bale.*

A smile spreads on my face. Valerian did it. He found Euphoria. And now he's going after her.

Now *we're* going after her.

KAYLA MAURAIS

Turn the page to read the first chapter of Kayla's sophomore novel . . .

Now available on all platforms.

1: VAIDA

Planet Nevarnost: Year 3051

Today, the chancellor dies.

I wipe sweat from my brow and tighten my grip on my brother's old hunting knife, its worn hilt heavy against my palm. A gift from our father on his eleventh birthday, it's one of the only pieces of him left. It was once intended for cracking open desert melons and spearing the sand lizards that invade our sleeping quarters, but now, it craves blood.

A drop of cool liquid splashes my cheek, and the nectar bats roosting in the stalactites hanging overhead chitter in my presence. One flaps its greasy wings at me before fleeing into a hollow groove coated in red lichen. If they weren't so sacred to the Nost, I'd scare the lot of them off. But they play their role in the underground ecosystem like everything else. Perched in tangles of plump saccharine roots until they molt and spurn sharper teeth. They tear away the tap points so the roots will leak sugar water, which the Nost then collect for remedial use.

Nia, who walks beside me on her four tentacle-like legs, is used to them. Having worked in these caves for years, she doesn't think twice before taking me through their nesting tunnels. I, on the other hand, can't stand the smell. Cloyingly sweet, it carries in the cool air current, and nausea rolls through me with each breath.

I consider putting on the carbon filtration mask I stole for today's quest but leave it hanging loose around my neck. Even if I have to stop and ralph up the questionable porridge I ate this morning in the Hub, it's still better than using anything manufactured by the enemy.

That would be a shame, though. Cook's porridge is the only thing I've eaten in days.

Nia picks up her pace as we approach a fork in the tunnel we've been following for the last hour. My two human legs don't stand a chance against her lofty four, but I push myself harder, reclaiming the lead. Humans are rarely welcome in the labyrinth of underground passageways connecting the Outskirts to our rival's dome-like fortress, but there's no way in hell I'm letting a little thing like this mess up my opportunity to face the chancellor.

We slow beneath a curve of mossy stalactites at the fork. Nia guides the oozing orb of light clutched in her right tentacle along the serrated rock walls.

I immediately head left. "This way is faster."

"I have to disagree," she says, remaining where she stands.

But I'm already in the dark, swallowed by the shadows.

"You don't have to come," I call back with a shrug.

Moments later, her light follows, its shine hitting the back of my neck. "Why is it you insist you know Nost Territory better than a Nost? I will never understand."

I sweep a low-hanging stone spider's web out of my face with the tip of my brother's blade and clean it on my khaki green cargo pants. "Look, I appreciate you getting me past the guard, but I don't need a babysitter. I do this all the time. I don't need help—"

Nia's free tentacle shoots out, stopping me short. A horde of nectar bats scatter, wafting the sickening odor of hardened sap up my nose. She lifts her glowing orb, revealing the edge of a gaping half-crystallized pit overlayed in a shimmering mist.

She raises a crooked brow. "You were saying . . ."

I roll my eyes, swallow the dry heave threatening to climb my throat, and spin on my heels, knocking gravel into the pit as I turn back the way we came. "If we'd taken the southeast path like I originally wanted to, we wouldn't be here."

"A simple thank you would have sufficed," she says flatly.

Of course, she wants me to thank her. And maybe she did just save me from falling to my own death, but who's to say I would have died? I would've found a way out like I always do.

Plunging into a bottomless pit of discarded sugar wouldn't have been *that* big of a deal.

When Nia moves back in step beside me, her orb illuminates the intricate patterns and decorative swirls covering her body from the shoulders down. Dark brown ink blends seamlessly into her slippery skin, my favorite being a set of ornate wildflowers that twine around her left tentacle and weave in between the eight suckers at the end.

It's how I tell Nia apart from the others. Nost markings are unique to each of them. Otherwise, they all look similar, towering a foot above the rest of us with hairless, oblong heads and two wide eyes that radiate an ethereal gray-blue hue.

We reach the fork once more and veer right this time against my own free will.

About halfway down the passage, Nia whispers, "We are getting close."

Before I can ask how she knows, bits of stone and dirt rattle around us. A resounding shriek whizzes by as the solar train passes above ground overhead.

Dammit. She was right. This *was* the correct tunnel.

Nia hands me her glow orb, and I cradle the bright, sticky blob, savoring its raw heat in my palm. A gust of air ruffles the tattered drapes of brown cloth swaddling her slim frame. In one motion, she reaches upward. Her tentacle stretches twice its length, snapping as she yanks down a rope ladder with wooden rungs.

A ripple courses through my gut. *Soon, Chancellor. Soon.*

She swings the ladder toward me. I catch it, then hand her back the orb.

She affixes it to the cavern wall, where it settles into a groove.

"What is your plan if the chancellor refuses to give you what you want?" Nia asks, holding the ladder steady so I can climb. "The likelihood is high he won't concede, and you are not a killer, Vaida. Whether your urgency for revenge makes you believe you are or not."

I ignore the possible truth in her words. The Nost aren't always right, despite what they think. Anyone is capable of anything if the timing is right. I've learned that the hard way.

My fingers curl around a rung. "You don't know what I'm capable of. I can be whatever I want to be. Just—let *me* worry about it. You're always up in my business."

"It is not that I am 'up in your business' . . . whatever that means." Her voice follows me as I climb. "Humans are creatures of habit. You are no exception. You get impulsive ideas."

"You don't know everything about us, okay? Or me. So stop."

"Fair enough. But what about the last ridiculous infiltration you attempted? You told me you were going to Nucleus to get close to the chancellor's son, gain his trust, and convince him to help you attack the chancellor in his sleep with a paperweight if he refused to back down and hand over the Hemisphere. Which, if I recall, was another unsuccessful endeavor."

"It was unsuccessful because talking to the chancellor's son made me want to rip my hair out." I grit my teeth and continue climbing. "Obviously, I'm not going to move forward with a serious plan if a guy has zero personality or capability. Soren couldn't handle it."

I reach for the thick, metal-plated hatch above my head and lock a steady hold around the wheel handle. "I could have sworn I told you all that."

"All I know is you were gone for almost a week."

I ignore her comment because I don't owe her anything, and I twist the wheel. It pops, releasing the seal with a deflated hiss. Stale air catches in my lungs, but at least it isn't laced with the sickly-sweet stench of nectar and ground water.

"I do not believe we ever had a *real* conversation about it all," Nia adds.

I peer down at her. I know she knows I'm lying. The downfall of having a Nost best friend. Their species reads minds and emotions with a single touch of their tentacle, but everything is so black-and-white with them. *Normal human tendencies included.*

Probably not the greatest foundation for friendship, or whatever it is we have, but Nia's been in my life since the day the Unity Arch fell. She was there in the medic tents, bandaging the injured. She comforted me when they found my mother's and brother's bodies in the rubble. And every day, whether I like it or not, she sticks by my side.

She's the only friend who's ever stuck around. Which is why I've learned to put up with her nagging, steer clear of her suckers, and get really good at lying. Or at least try to.

Nia wouldn't understand what really happened with Soren Bay. I've done a lot of shitty things in my short nineteen years, but even after two months, I still wake up haunted by those four days. Maybe someday I'll tell Nia, but for now, it's my secret.

And I won't let her close enough to read it off my psyche, either.

"If you must know, my plan is to break into the chancellor's office, find something worthy of blackmail, and force him to back down." I slip on the carbon filtration mask still hanging around my neck. "And if he doesn't, then he dies. It's really that simple."

Nia reaches up and pushes open the hatch, leaving enough space for me to climb through. "I think you'll make it halfway and turn around before anything comes of it."

Oof. I might be a liar, but she never fails to give it to me straight.

I tuck my knife into the sewn-in loop in my sleeve. "Then I hope I prove you wrong."

"Me too," she says with a grin. "May Goddess Cassia be with you."

The hatch delivers me to an empty alleyway across the street from the solar train station, at the outer edge of Zone 6: Agriculture, a border zone to the forgotten Zone 7.

My vision adjusts to the haze, taking in the thick dust hanging in the air.

We didn't always wear masks. But we learned fast: our bodies can't filter the Nevarnost dust that catches in our lungs. Not like the Nost, with their throat slits that flutter open and shut like petals—a natural filtration system. Their slime-coated, rust-tinted skin also protects them from the harsh ultraviolet rays of Nevarnost's two scalding suns.

The Nost were born on this planet. They belong here. We humans just burn.

I climb a flight of bowed stairs with broken rails. Ahead of me, littered streets and skeletal buildings cut stark silhouettes against a backdrop of gray. I dodge a few sweepers, the flying bots programmed to spot-clean the air. Nothing more than nuisances if you ask me.

The everlasting hue in the sky space won't fade, no matter how much dust they filter and suck up. Surprisingly, it's still an upgrade compared to living in the Outskirts.

I merge into a sea of olive-green uniforms and carbon masks on the walkway. A myriad of wandering eyes in every shade pass me. You can tell a lot about someone from their eyes. The nebulous silvers meeting mine before darting away? *He wants to be left alone.* The glittering blues sneaking a peek at me over the bridge of her nose? *She thinks she's better than me.*

Any other day, I'd indulge in the rush of sizing people up. But today, I need to go unseen. Today, I'm the heavier-set girl with downcast eyes nobody bothers to notice. I like my size and own it proudly, but sometimes blending in is easier when you're me.

You can't stop what you don't see coming.

I approach the far end of the street, stepping into Unity Commons, the public courtyard where the remnants of the Unity Arch still stand. Each zone is separated by 30-foot metallic pillars, linked by a hexagonal grid-like energy field that can be turned on or off as needed. The solar train and patrol officers who regulate the connecting walkways hold special pass keys, making them the only ones able to cross with ease. This central courtyard, once meant to be a communal gathering place, now fades into patches of dirty artificial grass, decaying ironwood trees, and crumbling stone ruins. The entrance to Zone 7: Industrial is so tightly boarded up with panels and scrap metal that even the solar train doesn't pass through it anymore.

I pull up my hood, avoiding the attention of a small gathering of people and Nost clustered in the fallout's remains. For years, this place was a dead zone. But with the 10-year anniversary of the tragedy approaching, Unity is just itching to make its comeback.

Old members hand out flyers. Others chat with bystanders. A Nost perches on a rotting crate, waving a brightly colored banner stamped with the image of a budding oak tree.

The Unity symbol—the artistic brainchild of my mother and her best friend, Billy Hale—was meant to represent peace and harmony. But for me, and the many others who lost loved ones the day the Arch fell, the tree is a painful reminder.

Everyone claimed I was lying when I said it was Billy Hale who blew up our arch. Nobody could fathom how our former chancellor, someone so devoted to humanity and his so-called peace project, could commit a crime that wiped out an entire zone. I was only nine, but I remember seeing him standing amid the smoke and wreckage, a weapon in his hand.

These reconcilers plant themselves on the graves of our loved ones, pretending it's in their honor rather than heaping on insult to injustice. They parade around their symbols and ideals of the past, preaching forgiveness, as if that will bring back jamborees, unification, and our families.

But I know better. I know the truth.

Nothing will bring back my mother and Ethan. Nothing can undo what happened here. Some say we should be over it, let the past be the past, but even if we could go back in time and stop Billy Hale from doing what I *know* he did, it wouldn't change anything.

The Arch falling wasn't even the worst thing that happened to us. It was Chancellor Bay taking over as leader of the Hemisphere. Still, I can't imagine why anyone would want to revive a forbidden organization that divided us and sparked a greater struggle for power.

A whistle blows. I slip between two old Arch posts, out of sight, before patrol officers storm in and break up the fallout assembly. The few remaining are hauled off in electric cuffs.

Thankful for the chaos, I jog toward the high rises in the distance, drawn to the towering building where our current chancellor sits on his inherited throne.

Zone 5: Nucleus.

My fingers curl around the weighted identification card in my pocket. I take the front steps with ease, scanning in at the double doors as if I do this every day. Acting like I belong. Downcast eyes are useless here. Self-assurance is the key. I keep my focus forward, locked on the mirrored lift ahead, passing through the vast lobby.

Around the sandstone columns are a scattering of plush, misshapen love seats and artificial desert plants in clay pots begging to be dusted. In the corner, a blender bot whirls as a barista prepares beverages at a small refreshment cart.

The barista holds up a steaming tin mug. "For . . . Annie?"

At the front desk, the receptionist stands, and I pause to let her pass. In response, she flashes me her pearly-white veneers. For a moment I let myself imagine the luxury of working a day job with not just fancy drinks but proper indoor air filtration too. We can get away without wearing a mask inside the Hub or in our dwellings on a good day, but too many nights, I've fallen asleep with the blankets up to my nose and a heaviness in my lungs. And some Outskirters don't even know what real boxed milk tastes like, let alone a cup of herbal tea that hasn't been brewed using the same tea bag as the person before them. A casual smile like *Annie's* isn't a comfort I know, and it unsettles me more than it should.

I press the call button on the lift, catching my reflection in the glossy doors. My carbon mask silences me, but my brown waves with violet-tipped ends frame my round face boldly.

My lurid hazel eyes, however, give me away.

You're not a killer, Vaida.

But I'll be anything if I have to be.

I clench my fists at my side, ready to board, finding comfort in the cool touch of my brother's knife against my wrist beneath my sleeve. I imagine the look on the chancellor's face when I waltz into his quarters like the scorch beast of his nightmares. So many have suffered because of this man and his commands. What will it feel like to watch him suffer?

The lift arrives. A ding fills the silence. The doors glide open.

"Vaida Marie Wardell," Dad says, and the blood surging through my veins freezes over. "What in Nevarnost are you doing here?"

My heart thunders as I realize he isn't alone. Behind him, Matron Nost Far steps forward, clutching the woven cords dangling with crystals and bones around her slim neck. And then, emerging like a haunt, the heinous ruler himself—Chancellor Ezra Bay.

I force my hands to stay relaxed at my side, though they long to curl around his neck. This man exploited our greatest tragedy, dismantled Billy Hale's remediation plans, and exiled *my* people from the Hemisphere. All to conserve air for his precious few. And Dad stands next to him like they've just been playing a friendly game of virtual disc golf.

"Steven, you didn't tell me your daughter would be joining us today," Chancellor Bay says, raising a neatly trimmed brow.

This has to be a mistake. I checked Dad's calendar before I left the Outskirts. This wasn't scheduled. He's supposed to be laying boundary markers at the quicksand pits right now.

Dad's expression twists. "I am terribly sorry about this, Ezra. I had no idea she was here in the Hemisphere. Especially when she isn't supposed to be . . ."

"Surely she must have a good reason," Matron Nost Far says, clutching the bone talisman with a spiral sun carved in its center. "An emergency, perhaps?"

Her gaze is light but knowing. *She's helping me.*

"Yes," I say quickly. "There was a fire in the Hub. We put it out."

From behind his mask, Dad crow's feet crinkle. *He doesn't buy a word I'm saying.* Like with Nia, I've never been able to lie to him either. At least not to his face.

"I think if everyone is safe, this could have waited until I got back," he says.

"Don't stress, Commander." Chancellor Bay straightens the collar of his plum-colored suit, not a lock of quaffed, ashy gray hair falling out of place. "It's no big deal. It happens."

It happens, I mimic in my head. He probably thinks dooming young children to a life of lung sickness just happens, too. Or sentencing adults to poverty and weekly ration tokens. I fix my gaze on a candelabra on the nearby wall. Forget the blackmail. Forget demanding surrender and knives. One good swing to the back of his head, and the chancellor would be out like a light.

Oh, you know, it happens, I'd say, if there were any repercussions left to face.

Dad clenches his jaw, the straps of his mask going taut. "Again, I apologize."

"Much obliged," Chancellor Bay says, returning to the lift. "It was nice seeing you again, Miss Wardell. I look forward to working with the Outskirts. A brighter future is ahead."

That's it. I let out a growl and lunge forward just as the lift snaps shut.

Dad jerks me back, and he and Far drag me away like they do to the Hub thieves who steal rations while the night watch take their piss breaks. Soon we're out of the building and down the front steps, back onto the streets of Zone 5: Nucleus, and I've never felt more on edge.

I was *so* close this time.

Dad's voice cuts into me. "What has gotten into you?"

"You acted like a rabid animal," Far adds, not bothering to look at me.

I shake off their arms and storm ahead, pushing past surprised pedestrians who quickly give me space to pass through. I don't care what Dad or Far think. They weren't even supposed to be here. I tear off my carbon mask because the privileged act is over and dig into my pocket for my normal face covering, a worn galaxy-speckled rag with stars.

Infiltrating the chancellor's high castle was a bust. No need to play Hemisphere girl any longer than I have to. Even if their masks are 99.9% more effective, I'd rather get lung sickness than admit anyone beneath this stupid dome did something right.

Far's tentacle loops around my arm from behind, stopping me in my tracks.

"If only you knew the cost of carrying that much rage in your heart, child." She reads me and whips me around to face Dad. "Your father was talking to you."

I roll my eyes. Curse the Nost and their cat-like reflexes. And I don't care what she feels or hears coming from my body. I don't need a lecture. Not from her. Not from him.

Dad's face, what little I can see around his mask, is beet red. More from hauling ass to catch up with me than anything else.

"I will not have you jeopardize the progress we've made with the Hemisphere, young lady. We've worked too hard convincing Chancellor Bay to join our merger."

"Your father is right," Far says. "Calm yourself if you can."

Calm myself? They don't get it. They've fallen for a monster's wit and charm.

"Didn't you see the look on his face?" I look straight into Dad's eyes. "Chancellor Bay doesn't want to help us. He's manipulating you. He's manipulating us all. That's what he does."

"I've heard enough." Dad adjusts his mask. His eyes quickly scan left and right, as if looking for eavesdroppers. "Our people have been without clean water for months. I'm done justifying myself because you can't let go of the past."

Naïve. He's so naïve.

I cross my arms over my chest. "It's not about letting go of the past. It's about trust. Having a meeting with the chancellor means nothing. He's never agreed to anything before."

"He's had a change of heart," Far says evenly, taking the lead to guide us toward the solar train pulling up to the platform.

I scoff. "He doesn't have a heart."

"The damage in Zone 7 has gotten worse. Air quality in the Hemisphere is dropping," Dad says. "It needs to be mended. In return for sending us the mechanism specialists we need to repair our irrigation grids, we'll send him laborers to reinforce the crack."

I let out a bitter laugh. "You can't be serious. At least they have air quality inside the Hemisphere. We can't let these people into our home. They won't respect us."

"My word is final." Dad ushers me into the nearest solar train compartment. "And do you have any idea how humiliating it was for me to be escorted into the Hemisphere because I didn't have my scanner card this afternoon? Hand it over. Now."

Ugh. I dig into my pocket.

Dad swipes his Nucleus-issued identification card from my hand and scans us into a double seat. Far sits across from us, expressionless. Our compartment could be on fire and it wouldn't faze her. Nothing ever fazes the Nost. I slam into the seat and press my head against the window, letting the lurch of the train's motion roll through me.

"Trusting him is a mistake," I say. "He'll just use us. And if you won't help our people or stand up for the change we deserve, then I will. Even if I have to do it alone."

"No, you won't." Dad straightens his glasses and sighs. "I know this is hard for you, Vaida, but need I remind you, this isn't a war. Violence isn't the answer. Sometimes, a calculated approach alongside those who share our goals is a better long-term solution. That's what Far and I are doing here. We can't force others to change. We have to work together."

I let out a sniff of disgust. Before Mom died, he wanted nothing to do with community meetings and unification strategies. He claims violence isn't the answer, but peace isn't either. Peace didn't help Mom or Ethan, or anyone forced to leave when Zone 7 was boarded up to preserve air quality. And working with other like-minded individuals? That wouldn't work either.

Nobody hates the chancellor as much as I do.

I won't give up. I'll try again. Billy Hale may have caused this mess ten years ago, but instead of fixing his mistake, Chancellor Bay took Hale's place and sentenced us all to a life of suffering. He uses people. He pretends to build them up, only to discard them when he gets what he wants.

I would know.

His son did the same thing to me.

Acknowledgments

I'd been told it takes a collective of people to publish a book, and they weren't kidding. My gratitude extends beyond my own comprehension. I'll do my best to go in order and to thank everyone involved in *Soul Sucker's* journey while still keeping it short. First and foremost, I want to thank my parents, Phil and Stacie. It's not easy raising such a free-spirited child, much less one with wild dreams and a fierce sense of imagination. I partially blame that on the fact that I grew up watching movies like *Jurassic Park*, *Tremors*, and *Back to the Future*.

To my four younger siblings—Morgan, Connor, Hannah, and Faith—I wouldn't have been able to write such candid sibling banter without you. I'm honored to have grown up with you all. My grandparents—Memere, Nana, and Grampa—who took me in on various weekends and fed me delicious meals when I needed a change of scenery to fight writer's block. Pepere, I know you were there in spirit. To the aunts and uncles, cousins, and childhood friends that let me be my authentic self without judgment throughout my formative years, thank you.

To two of my teachers, Colleen and Susan, you graciously edited books for me in my teens, and that version of me never forgot that. The teacher in middle school who told me I was writing too cinematically for English class—I don't think you meant your words to be so discouraging at the time, but I ended up carrying them with me, went on to get a master's degree in screenwriting, and wrote a book anyway.

Speaking of screenwriting, to my professors in my master's program—Nunzio, Christina, Matt, Justin, Doc, John—you saw a potential in me that I wasn't able to see in myself at the time. I see it now. You all taught me valuable lessons in craft, and I'm going to keep writing no matter what.

Mariah and Bri, you've seen all versions of me in this lifetime so far. Thank you for cherishing each and every version. I don't know how many times you both listened to me go on and on about imaginary worlds, characters, and scenes, but you did it with vigor. I love you both more than you know. You are part of the village of people that helped shape me as a person.

I almost gave up on becoming a writer. One of my film school professors enthusiastically told us that it takes on average five years for a writer to establish themselves. I went so far as to keep a tally in my journal, and as the years went by following my completion of the program in 2017, I felt defeated. I didn't know what I know now—which is, spoiler, there's no right or wrong time to do anything in life, nor does timing depict your worth or success. But after being rejected endlessly in the query trenches with multiple manuscripts, I began thinking I wouldn't be a writer after all. Then, in late 2019, while I was dog sitting by a lake in Maine, an adventure surrounding two disaster siblings came to mind. The idea of starting yet another project that could 'potentially fail' scared me, but I started outlining the first draft regardless.

2020 happened. I set *Soul Sucker* aside, and then a few months into 2021, I felt called to submit *Soul Sucker* to Author Mentor Match, a Twitter-promoted program that paired unagented writers with mentors to help them prepare their manuscripts for industry eyes. I didn't get chosen as a mentee, but I won in another way. Thank you to one of the AMM mentors, Rosiee, for matching me with a group of writers I still hold near and dear today.

Caroline Fowler Davis, Nyssa Rae, and Leah Alexandra—you are *Soul Sucker's* rock. You read the early versions, fell in love with Shea and Dash as much as I did, and cheered me on through this publishing process. Thank you endlessly. I'd also like to thank Jessica Renwick for being my writer buddy and mentor over these last few years. You shower me in love and support on the regular, and I would be truly lost without you in this process.

Soul Sucker went from a blip of an idea in 2019 to publication in 2023. I can't deny that a very special group of middle school students helped push me into taking the leap to putting *Soul Sucker* into print. This group of students inspires me every day. I hope you know how wonderfully rare you all are, and I hope you never give up on following your own dreams!

When I announced my debut, so many people in my community stepped up to support me. This journey has been made better because of you all. To the work friends—Stacy, Bernadette, Jessica, Erica, Carey, and Catherine—that hold space for me always, even if it's just in passing. The night staff who saw me spend many evenings and weekends in my classroom, working tirelessly in front of my laptop. You were the smiling, encouraging faces that made those days better. Shawn, you entertained my many 'what-if' questions with humor and endearment.

Nic, thank you for answering my obscure science questions with curiosity and a smile, even when it didn't make sense. Kelly, you know I couldn't have done this without you. You have been my main confidant in the unfolding of this publication process. This journey has been magical with you by my side. From helping me work out story elements to answering my many texts and listening to my revelations—I thank you from the bottom of my heart for being there for me. I cherish you. I cherish all of you. Truly.

Jasmina Belarbi, I am so glad we connected. I am thankful for you. You created the cover of my dreams, and you have such a talent for creative design. Rachel with Luff Studios, your map added such a wonderful layer to this story. Pantonia over at PantoniaWorld, Isabel Phillips, Sel and Rey, Kat at Sanctum Flames

Candles, Aimee at magnolia_mountainsidefl, ConnyArtz with https://www.artstation.com/conny_artz, and Crystal at Magic Book Cover Design—thank you all for your art, finer details, merch, and contributions to *Soul Sucker*. You are all such talented humans and artists alike.

To my amazing second edition editor, Jennifer Lindsay. Thank you for helping me make *Soul Sucker* sparkle and shine. To my amazing team of past editors—Caroline Fowler Davis, Cassandra V, and Paige Lawson—we were on a time crunch toward the end with the first edition. You all put me at the top of your lists and truly helped me get through those last few weeks before I sent *Soul Sucker* off to the printing press. It is because of you I was able to push through and have faith that everything would get done in time.

To my lovely group of beta readers and street team members—Kayla, Martha, Tatiana, Blade, and Phoebe—thank you for cheering me on and supporting me behind the scenes. Jake, years ago you jokingly made me promise that I'd credit you in my first 'real book.' Well, I never forgot that promise. I did it! *Finally.* Thank you for watching over me all these years.

I'm almost done, I swear—I'd like to extend one additional and final thank you to my parents, Phil and Stacie. You two are the ultimate reason this book is where it is today. You let me move home (more than once) over the span of the last six years to give me the freedom to focus on these writer dreams. You've provided me an environment to prosper and grow in, authentically, and you've given me the time and space to see this accomplishment through.

This book very much encompasses who I am as a human being. I'm proud of *Soul Sucker*, and I can't wait to see what this author journey and my next book brings.

KAYLA MAURAIS is a young adult and new adult sci-fi/fantasy author from New England. She first started writing creatively when she was thirteen. Since then, she's gone on to get a master's degree in screenwriting. Her publishing imprint, Wraith's Fate Press, was established in April 2024. When she isn't writing, Kayla enjoys spending time by the ocean, visiting theme parks she wishes were haunted, and going on road trips to discover new places. She is also an educator, birth doula, developmental editor, and tarot reader. For more on Kayla and her offerings, visit kaylamaurais.com or connect with her on social media at @authorkaylamaurais.

www.ingramcontent.com/pod-product-compliance
Lightning Source LLC
Chambersburg PA
CBHW030808310726
48980CB00006B/418/J

* 9 7 9 8 9 9 2 9 6 6 5 4 1 *